THROUGH THREE CAMPAIGNS

A Story Of Chitral, Tirah And Ashanti

By

G. A. Henty

About G. A. Henty

George Alfred Hent was born in Trumpington, near Cambridge but spent some of his childhood in Canterbury. He was a sickly child who had to spend long periods in bed. During his frequent illnesses he became an avid reader and developed a wide range of interests which he carried into adulthood. He attended Westminster School, London, as a half-boarder when he was fourteen, :2 and later Gonville and Caius College, Cambridge, where he was a keen sportsman.

He left the university early without completing his degree to volunteer for the (Army) Hospital Commissariat of the Purveyors Department when the Crimean War began. He was sent to the Crimea and while there he witnessed the appalling conditions under which the British soldier had to fight. His letters home were filled with vivid descriptions of what he saw. His father was impressed by his letters and sent them to the Morning Advertiser newspaper which printed them. This initial writing success was a factor in Henty's later decision to accept the offer to become a special correspondent, the early name for journalists now better known as war correspondents.

Through Three Campaigns

Shortly before resigning from the army as a captain in 1859 he married Elizabeth Finucane. The couple had four children. Elizabeth died in 1865 after a long illness and shortly after her death Henty began writing articles for the Standard newspaper. In 1866 the newspaper sent him as their special correspondent to report on the Austro-Italian War where he met Giuseppe Garibaldi. He went on to cover the 1868 British punitive expedition to Abyssinia, the Franco-Prussian War, the Ashanti War, the Carlist Rebellion in Spain and the Turco-Serbian War. He also witnessed the opening of the Suez Canal and travelled to Palestine, Russia and India.

Henty was a strong supporter of the British Empire all his life; according to literary critic Kathryn Castle: "Henty ... exemplified the ethos of the [British Empire], and glorified in its successes". Henty's ideas about politics were influenced by writers such as Sir Charles Dilke and Thomas Carlyle.

Henty once related in an interview how his storytelling skills grew out of tales told after dinner to his children. He wrote his first children's book, Out on the Pampas in 1868, naming the book's main characters after his children. The book was published by Griffith and Farran in November 1870 with a title page date of 1871. While most of the 122 books he wrote were for children and published by Blackie and Son of London, he also wrote adult novels, non-fiction such as The March to Magdala and Those Other Animals, short stories for the likes of The Boy's Own Paper and edited the Union Jack, a weekly boy's magazine.

Henty was "the most popular Boy's author of his day." Blackie, who published his children's fiction in the UK, and W. G. Blackie estimated in February 1952 that they were producing about 150,000 Henty books a year at the height of his popularity, and stated that their records showed they had produced over three and a half million Henty books. He further estimated that considering the US and other overseas authorised and pirated editions, a total of 25 million was not impossible. Arnold notes this estimate and that there have been further editions since that estimate was made.

His children's novels typically revolved around a boy or young man living in troubled times. These ranged from the Punic War to more recent conflicts such as the Napoleonic Wars or the American Civil War. Henty's heroes – which occasionally included young ladies – are uniformly intelligent, courageous, honest and resourceful with plenty of 'pluck' yet are also modest. These themes have made Henty's novels popular today among many conservative Christians and homeschoolers.

Henty usually researched his novels by ordering several books on the subject he was writing on from libraries, and consulting them before beginning writing. Some of his books were written about events (such as the Crimean War) that he witnessed himself; hence, these books are written with greater detail as Henty drew upon his first-hand experiences of people, places, and events.

On 16 November 1902, Henty died aboard his yacht in Weymouth Harbour, Dorset, leaving unfinished his last novel, By Conduct and Courage, which was completed by his son Captain C.G. Henty.

Henty is buried in Brompton Cemetery, London.

Henty wrote 122 works of historical fiction and all first editions had the date printed at the foot of the title page.[15] Several short stories published in book form are included in this total, with the stories taken from previously published full-length novels. The dates given below are those printed at the foot of the title page of the very first editions in the United Kingdom. It is a common misconception that American Henty titles were published before those of the UK. All Henty titles bar one were published in the UK before those of America.

The simple explanation for this error of judgement is that Charles Scribner's Sons of New York dated their Henty first editions for the current year. The first UK editions published by Blackie were always dated for the coming year, to have them looking fresh for Christmas. The only Henty title published in book form in America before the UK book was In the Hands of the Cave-Dwellers dated 1900 and published by Harper of New York. This title was published in book form in the UK in 1903, although the story itself had already been published in England prior to the first American edition, in The Boy's Own Annual.

LITERARY CRITIQUES

George Alfred Henty (1832–1902) was a British novelist and writer known for his historical adventure stories for children and young adults. His works often combined fictional characters with real historical events, aiming to educate young readers about history while also providing entertaining narratives. Henty's writing style and themes have been the subject of various literary critiques over the years. Here are some common points made by critics:

Formulaic Structure: One common critique of Henty's works is that they tend to follow a formulaic structure. Many of his novels share similar plotlines, where a young British protagonist overcomes challenges, exhibits moral values, and plays a significant role in historical events. Critics argue that this predictable structure might make his stories less engaging for older or more experienced readers.

Simplistic Characterization: Some critics have noted that Henty's characters can be rather one-dimensional, often falling into stereotypical roles. The heroes are typically brave, resourceful, and morally upright, while the villains are often portrayed as scheming and unscrupulous. This lack of complexity in character development can limit the emotional depth of the stories.

Colonial and Imperialist Views: Henty's works are reflective of the time period in which he lived, which saw the height of the British Empire's power and influence. Some critics argue that his novels promote colonial and imperialist viewpoints, as they often depict British characters as heroic figures bringing civilization to "uncivilized" regions. This portrayal can be seen as ethnocentric and insensitive to the experiences and perspectives of other cultures.

Educational Value: Henty's novels have been praised for their educational value, as they introduce readers to historical events and periods that might not be covered in traditional history textbooks. However, critics have pointed out that his narratives sometimes prioritize historical accuracy at the expense of engaging storytelling, resulting in passages that read more like history lessons than compelling fiction.

Language and Style: Henty's writing style can be considered somewhat dated by modern standards. His prose tends to be formal and descriptive, which might not resonate with contemporary readers, especially younger ones. Some critics argue that the language could create a barrier for readers seeking fast-paced and accessible narratives.

Relevance to Modern Readers: Another point of critique is the relevance of Henty's works to modern readers. While his stories offer insights into historical contexts, some critics question whether his themes and values align with contemporary sensibilities and whether young readers today would find his narratives engaging.

Limited Diversity: Henty's works often lack diverse representation, both in terms of characters and perspectives. Critics have noted that his novels predominantly focus on white, male British protagonists, which can limit the inclusivity and relatability of his stories for a broader readership.

In summary, while George Alfred Henty's historical adventure novels have been cherished by many readers over the years for their educational content and engaging narratives, they have also faced criticism for their formulaic structure, simplistic characterization, colonial viewpoints, and limited relevance to modern audiences. It's important to approach his works with an understanding of the historical context in which they were written and to consider these critiques alongside their literary merits.

CONTENTS

Chapter 1: An Expedition................................. 9

Chapter 2: The Start..................................... 24

Chapter 3: The First Fight................................ 39

Chapter 4: In The Passes 55

Chapter 5: Promoted..................................... 78

Chapter 6: Unfair Play................................... 87

Chapter 7: Tales Of War................................. 101

Chapter 8: The Dargai Pass............................. 114

Chapter 9: Captured.................................... 129

Chapter 10: Through The Mohmund Country.............. 143

Chapter 11: An Arduous March.......................... 153

Chapter 12: A Tribal Fight.............................. 163

Chapter 13: The V.C. 180

Chapter 14: Forest Fighting............................. 196

Chapter 15: A Narrow Escape........................... 211

Chapter 16: The Relief Of Coomassie................... 225

Chapter 17: Stockades And War Camps.................. 240

Chapter 18: A Night Surprise........................... 254

Chapter 19: Lost In The Forest......................... 267

Chapter 20: At Home................................... 284

PREFACE.

Our little wars attract far less attention among the people of this country than they deserve. They are frequently carried out in circumstances of the most adverse kind. Our enemies, although ignorant of military discipline are, as a rule, extremely brave; and are thoroughly capable of using the natural advantages of their country. Our men are called upon to bear enormous fatigue, and endure extremes in climate. The fighting is incessant, the peril constant. Nevertheless, they show a magnificent contempt for danger and difficulty; and fight with a valour and determination worthy of the highest praise.

I have chosen, as an illustration of this, three campaigns; namely, the relief of Chitral, the Tirah campaign, and the relief of Coomassie. The first two were conducted in a mountainous country, affording every advantage to the enemy; where passes had to be scaled, torrents to be forded, and deep snow to be crossed. In the other, the country was a combination of morass and thick forest, frequently intersected by wide and deep rivers. The work, moreover, had to be done in a tropical climate, during the rainy season. The conditions, therefore, were much more trying than in the case of former expeditions which had crossed the same ground and, in addition, the enemy were vastly more numerous and more determined; and had, in recent years, mastered the art of building extremely formidable stockades.

The country has a right to be proud, indeed, of the prowess both of our own troops and of our native regiments. Boys who wish to obtain fuller details of these campaigns I would refer to Sir George Robertson's Chitral; H. C. Thomson's Chitral Campaign; Lieutenant Beynon's With Kelly to Chitral; Colonel Hutchison's Campaign in Tirah; Viscount Fincastle and P. C. Eliott Lockhart's A Frontier Campaign; and Captain Harold C. J. Biss's The Relief of Kumasi, from which I have principally drawn the historical portion of my story.

G. A. Henty.

CHAPTER 1: AN EXPEDITION.

"Well, Lisle, my boy, the time is drawing very near when you will have to go home. My brother John will look after you, and choose some good crammer to push you on. You are nearly sixteen, now, and it is high time you buckled to."

"But you have always taught me, father!"

"Yes, that is all very well, but I could not devote three hours a day to you. I think I may say that you are thoroughly well grounded--I hope as well as most public-school boys of your own age--but I can go no further with you. You have no idea what cramming is necessary, now, for a young fellow to pass into the army. Still I think that, by hard work with some man who prepares students for the army, you may be able to rub through. I have always saved up money for this, for my brother is by no means a rich man, and crammers are very expensive; so the next time I see a chance of sending you down to Calcutta, down you go. My agents there will see you on board a ship, and do everything that is necessary."

"Of course, father, if I must go, I must; but it will be beastly, after the jolly time I have spent in the regiment, to set to and do nothing but grind, for the next three years."

"We all have to do a good many unpleasant things, Lisle; and as we have decided that you shall enter the army, you must make up your mind to do the necessary work, even though it be disagreeable."

"All right, father! I know what depends upon it, and I will set to."

"I have no doubt you will, Lisle, for you have plenty of common sense, though you are a little inclined to mischief--not that you are altogether to blame for that, for the officers encourage you in it."

This conversation took place between Captain Bullen, of the 32nd Pioneers, and his son. The regiment was in cantonments near the northern frontier of India. The captain had lost his wife some years before and, as their two youngest children had also died, he had not been able to bring himself to send the remaining boy home. The climate was excellent, and the boy enjoyed as good health as if he had been in England. Captain Bullen had taken a great deal of pains with his son's education but, as he said, he had now taught the boy all that he knew; and felt that he ought to go to England, and be regularly coached for the army.

Next day the captain entered his quarters, hurriedly.

"I am off," he said. "Those rascally Afridis have come down and looted several villages; and I am to go up, in command of a couple of companies, to give them a lesson."

"They are not very strong, are they, father?"

"No, I don't suppose they can put a couple of hundred men in the field. We shall take the two mountain guns with us, and batter holes in their fortresses, and then attack and carry them easily. There is no sign of movement among the other tribes, so we need not expect any serious opposition."

A week later, the little detachment entered the valley in which the Afridi villages lay. The work had been fatiguing, for the country was very rough; and the mules that carried the guns met with such difficulties that the infantry had to turn to, and improve the paths--if paths they could be called, for they were often little better than undefined tracks. As the expedition moved up the valley, the tribesmen opened on them a distant fire; but scattered after a few shells from the mountain guns were thrown among them. The fortified houses, however, were stubbornly held; and indeed, were only carried after the guns had broken in the doors, or made a breach in the walls.

During the attack on the last house, a shot struck Captain Bullen in the chest, and he instantly fell. When they saw this, the Pioneers dashed forward with a howl of rage, carried the fort, and bayoneted its defenders. The doctor of the party at once examined the wound, and saw that it would probably be fatal.

"Patch me up, Lloyd, so that I may get back to camp and see my boy again," the wounded man whispered.

"I will do my best," the doctor said, "but I doubt whether you will be able to stand the journey."

The Pioneers, after setting fire to all the houses in the valley, started at once for home. Captain Bullen was placed on a stretcher, and four men at a time carried him down, taking the utmost pains not to jolt or shake him. His face was covered with light boughs, to keep off the flies; and everything that was possible was done to conduce to his comfort.

Through Three Campaigns

The doctor watched him anxiously. His condition became more serious, every day. As they neared the camp, a messenger was sent down with a report from the native officer of what had happened; and the Pioneers all came out to see their favourite officer brought in; and stood, mournful and silent, as he was carried to his bungalow.

"Don't come in yet, lad," the surgeon said, to Lisle. "Your father, at present, is incapable of speaking; and he must have a little rest before you see him, for the slightest excitement would probably cause a gush of blood to the wound, which would be fatal."

Lisle's grief was unbounded. He could not listen to the kind words with which the officers tried to soothe him, but wandered away out of camp and, throwing himself down, wept unrestrainedly for an hour. Then he roused himself, and walked slowly back. By a mighty effort he had composed himself, for he knew that he must be calm when he saw his father.

Half an hour later, the doctor beckoned him in.

"He is conscious now," he said, "and has whispered that he wishes to see you. He has been very calm, all the way down, and has spoken of you often."

"I will do my best," Lisle muttered, keeping down his tears with a tremendous effort; and then went into his father's room.

He could not trust himself to speak a word but, walking up, took his father's hand and, kneeling down, pressed it to his lips, his whole form shaking with agitation.

"I am glad I have held out until I got back," his father said, in a low voice. "It is all up with me, my boy, and I have only a few hours to live, at most. I am sorry, now, that you did not start for England before this happened; but I have no doubt that it is all for the best. I shall die, as I should wish to die, doing my duty and, except for leaving you, I shall feel small regret."

"Must you leave me, father?" Lisle sobbed.

"Yes, my boy, I have known it from the first. It is only my intense desire to see you again that has kept me up. The doctor said he did not expect that I should last more than two or three days, at most.

"You will bear in mind what I said to you, the day before we started. I have no fear about you, Lisle; I am sure you will make an honest gentleman and a brave soldier, and will do credit to our name. I should stay here a few weeks longer, if I were you, until some others are going down. The officers are all fond of you, and it would be better for you to have company, than to make the long journey to the coast alone.

"My voice is failing me, lad, and I can say no more, now; but you can sit here with me, till the end comes. It will not be long. When you have completed your training, the fact that I have died in this way will give you a good claim to a commission."

Lisle sat with his father for some hours. Occasionally the dying man moved and, leaning over him, he could catch the words "God bless you!" Before midnight the brave spirit had passed away, and Lisle went out and cried like a child, till morning.

The funeral took place next day. After it was over, the colonel sent for Lisle; who had now, after a hard struggle, recovered his composure.

"Did your father give you any instructions, Lisle? You may be sure that whatever he said we will carry out."

"He said that he thought it would be best for me to stay here for a few weeks as, among so many kind friends, I should be able to bear it better than if I went down at once."

"Quite right, lad! We shall all be very glad to have you with us. You can remain in the bungalow as long as you like. It is not likely to be wanted, for some months. Your father's butler and one or two servants will be enough to look after you; and you will, of course, remain a member of the mess. In this way, I hope you will have recovered some of your cheerfulness before you start."

It was a hard time for Lisle for the next week or two, for everything reminded him of his father. The risaldar major and the other native officers, with all of whom he was familiar, grasped him by the hand when they met, in token of their sympathy; and the sepoys stood at attention, with mournful faces, when he passed them. He spent the heat of the day with his books, and only stirred out in the early morning and evening, meals being considerately sent down to him from the mess. At the end of a fortnight he made a great effort and joined the mess, and the kindness with which the officers spoke to him gradually cheered him.

Then there came an excitement which cheered him further. There were rumours of disaffection among the hill tribes, and the chances of a campaign were discussed with animation, both among officers and soldiers. The regiment was a very fine one, composed of sturdy Punjabis; and all agreed that, if there were an expedition, they would probably form part of it. Lisle entered fully into the general feeling, and his eyes glistened as he listened to the sepoys talking of the expeditions in which they had taken part.

"It would be splendid to go," he said to himself, "but I don't see how the colonel could take me. I shall certainly ask him, when the time comes; but I feel sure that he will refuse. Of course, I ought to be starting before long for Calcutta; but the expedition will probably not last many weeks and, if I were to go with it, the excitement would keep me from thinking, and do me a lot of good. Besides, a few weeks could make no difference in my working up for the examination."

The more he thought of it, the more he felt determined to go with the column. He felt sure that he could disguise himself so that no one would suspect who he was. He had been so long associated with the regiment that he talked Punjabi as well as English.

His father had now been dead two months and, as the rumours from across the frontier grew more and more serious, he was filled with fear lest an opportunity should occur to send him down country before the regiment marched; in which case all his plans would be upset. Day after day passed, however, without his hearing anything about it, till one day the colonel sent for him.

"The time has come, lad, when we must part. We shall all be very sorry to lose you, but it cannot be helped. I have received orders, this morning, to go up to Chitral; and am sending down some sick, at once. You must start with them. When you reach the railway, you will be able to get a through ticket to Calcutta.

"As long as it was likely that we should be going down ourselves, I was glad to keep you here; but now that we have got orders to go off and have a talk with these tribes in the north, it is clearly impossible for us to keep you any longer. I am very sorry, my boy, for you know we all like you, for your own sake and for your good father's."

"I am awfully obliged to you all, colonel. You have been very good to me, since my father was killed. I feel that I have had no right to stop here so long; but I quite understand that, now you are moving up into the hills, you cannot keep me.

"I suppose I could not go as a volunteer, colonel?" he asked, wistfully.

"Quite impossible," the colonel said, decidedly. "Even if you had been older, I could not have taken you. Every mouth will have to be fed, and the difficulties of transport will be great. There is no possibility, whatever, of our smuggling a lad of your age up with us.

"Besides, you know that you ought to go to England, without further delay. You want to gain a commission, and to do that you must pass a very stiff examination, indeed. So for your own sake, it is advisable that you should get to work without any unnecessary delay.

"A party of invalids will be going down tomorrow, and you can go with them as far as Peshawar. There, of course, you will take train either to Calcutta or Bombay. I know that you have plenty of funds for your journey to England. I think you said that it was an uncle to whom you were going. Mind you impress upon him the fact that it is absolutely necessary that you should go to a first-rate school or, better still, to a private crammer, if you are to have a chance of getting into the service by a competitive examination."

"Very well, colonel. I am sure that I am very grateful to you, and all the officers of the regiment, for the kindness you have shown me, especially since my father's death. I shall always remember it."

"That is all right, Lisle. It has been a pleasure to have you with us. I am sure we shall all be sorry to lose you, but I hope that some day we shall meet again, when you are an officer in one of our regiments."

Lisle returned to the bungalow and called the butler, the only servant he had retained.

"Look here, Robah, the colonel says that I must go down with a sick party, tomorrow. As I have told you, I am determined to go up country with the troops. Of course, I must be in disguise. How do you think that I had better go?"

The man shook his head.

"The young sahib had better join his friends in England."

"It is useless to talk about that," Lisle said. "I have told you I mean to go up, and go up I will. There ought to be no difficulty about it. I speak three or four of these frontier languages, as well as I speak English. I have at least learnt that. I have picked them up by talking to the natives, and partly from the moonshee I have had, for four years. My dear father always impressed upon me the utility of these to an officer; and said that, if I could take up native languages in my examinations, it would go a long way towards making up for other deficiencies. So I am all right, so far as language is concerned.

"It seems to me that my best plan will be to go up as a mule driver."

"It is as the sahib wills," the old man said. "His servant will do all he can to help him."

"Well, Robah, I want you in the first place to get me a disguise. You may as well get two suits. I am sure to get wet, sometimes, and shall require a change. I shall take a couple of my own vests and drawers, to wear under them; for we shall probably experience very cold weather in the mountains."

"They are serving out clothes to the carriers, sahib."

"Yes, I forgot that. Well, I want you to go into their camp, and arrange with one of the headmen to let me take the place of one of the drivers. Some of the men will be willing enough to get off the job, and a tip of forty rupees would completely settle the matter with him. Of course, I shall start with the sick escort but, as there will be several waggons going down with them, they will not travel far; and at the first halting place I can slip away, and come back here. You will be waiting for me on the road outside the camp, early in the morning, and take me to the headman.

"By the way, I shall want you to make up a bottle of stain for my hands and feet; for of course I shall go in the native sandals."

"I will do these things, sahib. How about your luggage?"

"Before I leave the camp tonight I shall put fresh labels on them, directing them to be taken to the store of Messieurs Parfit, who were my father's agents; and to be left there until I send for them. I shall give the sergeant, who goes down with the sick, money to pay for their carriage to Calcutta.

"And about yourself, Robah?"

"I shall stay here at the bungalow till another regiment comes up to take your place. Perhaps you will give me a chit, saying that I have been in your father's service fourteen years, and that you have found me faithful and useful. If I cannot find employment, I shall go home. I have saved enough money."

An hour later, Robah again entered the room.

"I have been thinking, sahib, of a better plan. You wish to see fighting, do you not?"

"Certainly I do."

"Well, sahib, if you go in the baggage train you might be miles away, and see nothing of it. Now, it seems to me that it would be almost as easy for you to go as a soldier in the regiment, as in the transport train."

"Do you think so, Robah?" Lisle exclaimed excitedly.

"I think so, sahib. You see, you know all the native officers, and your father was a great favourite among them. If you were dressed in uniform, and took your place in the ranks, it is very unlikely that any of the English officers would notice you. These matters are left in the hands of the native officers.

"Yesterday a young private died, who had but just passed the recruit stage, and had been only once or twice on parade. You might take his name. It is most unlikely that any of the white officers will notice that your face is a fresh one and, if they did ask the question, the native officer would give that name. The English officer would not be at all likely to notice that this was the name of a man who had died. Deaths are not uncommon and, as the regiment is just moving, the matter would receive no attention. The book of this man would be handed to you, and it would all seem regular."

"That is a splendid idea, Robah. Which officer do you think I had better speak to?"

"I should speak to Risaldar Gholam Singh. He was the chief native officer in your father's wing of the regiment. If he consents, he would order all the native officers under him to hold their tongues and, as you are a favourite with them all, your secret would be kept."

"It is a grand idea, and I certainly don't see why it should not work out properly."

"I have no doubt that the risaldar major will do all he can for you."

"Do you think so, Robah?"

"I am sure he will. He was very much attached to your father, and felt his loss as much as anyone. Indeed, I think that every one of the native officers will do all he can for you."

"That would make it very easy for me," Lisle said. "Till you suggested it, the idea of going as a soldier never occurred to me but, with their assistance, it will not be difficult."

"Shall I go and fetch the risaldar here, sahib?"

"Do so. I shall be on thorns until I see him."

In a few minutes the officer, a tall and stately Punjabi, entered.

"Risaldar," Lisle said, "I know you were very much attached to my father."

"I was, sahib."

"Well, I want you to do something for me."

"It would be a pleasure for me to do so, and you have only to ask for me to grant it, if it is in my power."

"I think it is in your power," Lisle said. "I will tell you what I want. I have made up my mind to go with this expedition. I thought of disguising myself, and going as a baggage coolie; but in that case I should be always in the rear and see none of the fighting, and I have made up my mind to go as a private in the ranks."

"As a private, sahib?" the officer exclaimed, in astonishment. "Surely that would be impossible. You would be detected at the first halt. Besides, how could the son of our dear captain go as a private?"

"I do not object to go as a private, risaldar. Of course I should stain myself and, in uniform, it is not likely that any of the white officers would notice a strange face."

"But you would have to eat with the others, to mix with them as one of themselves, to suffer all sorts of hardships."

"All that is nothing," Lisle said. "I have been with the regiment so long that I know all the ways of the men, and I don't think that I should be likely to make any mistake that would attract their attention. As to the language, I know it perfectly."

"I hardly dare do such a thing, sahib. If you were discovered on the march, the colonel and officers would be very angry with me."

"Even if I were discovered, it need not be known that you had assisted me, risaldar. You may be sure that I should never tell. If you were questioned, you could declare that you had taken me for an ordinary recruit. If I deceived everyone else, I might very well deceive you."

The risaldar stood thoughtful for some time.

"It might possibly be managed," he said at last. "I would do much for Captain Bullen's son, even risk the anger of the colonel."

"I understand that a sepoy died yesterday. He was quite a young recruit, and the white officers had not come to know his face. I might say that I am a relation of his, and am very anxious to take his place."

"You could take his place in the ranks under his name."

"That would certainly be a good plan, if it could be carried out. I should only be asked a few questions by the sepoys of my company. It would seem to them natural that I should take my cousin's place; and that, as the regiment was moving, and there was no time to teach me drill, I should be expected to pick up what I could on the way. But indeed, I have watched the regiment so often that I think I know all the commands and movements, and could go through them without hesitation. Besides, there won't be much drilling on the march. There will probably be a good deal of skirmishing, and perhaps some rough fighting."

"But if you were to be killed, sahib, what then?"

"I don't mean to be killed if I can help it," Lisle said; "but if I am, I shall be buried as one of the sepoys. The officers will all believe that I have gone home and, though they may wonder a little that I never write to them, they will think it is because I am too busy. It will be a long time, indeed, before any of my friends write to ask about me; and then it will be supposed that I have been accidentally killed or drowned.

"At any rate, I should have the satisfaction of being killed in the Queen's service. All the men are delighted at going, and they will run the same risk as I do."

"Well, sahib," the risaldar said, "I will do it. I would very much prefer that you had never asked me, but I cannot say 'no' to you. I will think it over; and tell you, tomorrow morning, what seems to me the best plan. I don't see, at present, how you are to disappear and join the regiment."

"That is easy enough," Lisle said. "I am going to start tomorrow with the sick convoy; but shall slip away from them, after I have gone a short distance. Robah will meet me with my uniform and rifle; and I shall come into the camp again, in uniform, after it is dark."

"You appear to have thought it all out," the officer said, "and if your scheme can be carried out, there should be no difficulty, after the first day or two. You are more likely to pass unnoticed, on a march, than you would be if you were staying here. The men will have other things to think about, and you will only have three men marching with you in the column to ask questions. Indeed, there is very little talking on the line of march.

"Well, I will think it over, and see you in the morning."

This was as good as consent, and Lisle was highly delighted. In the morning, the risaldar called again.

"I have spoken," the risaldar said, "to the three officers of the company to which the soldier Mutteh Ghar belonged; and they all agreed, willingly, to help you to carry out your scheme, and think that there is very little probability of the fact that you are a new recruit being noticed. The general discipline of the regiment is in our hands. The British officers direct, but we carry out their orders. As the man was only on parade twice and, on neither of these occasions, came under general inspection of the white officers, it is probable that they do not know his face. It is certainly best that you should take Mutteh Ghar's name, as the soldiers will see nothing strange in our placing a young recruit in the ranks, after his cousin had died in the regiment. We are all of opinion, therefore, that you can take your place without difficulty; and that the chance of the change being detected by the British officers is extremely slight. We think, however, that it will be next to impossible for you always to keep up your character, and believe that you will find it so hard to live under the same conditions as the others that you yourself will tire of it."

"I can assure you that there is no fear of that," Lisle said earnestly. "I want to take part in the expedition, and am quite prepared to share in the habits and hardships of the men, whatever they may be. You know, if I were discovered I should be sent off at once, even if a fight were imminent. I think I can say that, when I undertake a thing, I will carry it through.

"I cannot tell you how grateful I feel to you all, for aiding me to carry out my wish. Will you kindly convey my thanks to the officers of the company, and particularly urge upon them that they must show me no favour, and pay no more attention to me than to the other men? Anything of that sort would certainly give rise to comment and suspicion."

"I have already told them that," the officer said, "and I think they thoroughly understand how they must act.

"The sick party are to start tomorrow morning. How do you wish the uniform of your supposed cousin to be sent to you?"

"If you hand it over to Robah, he will bring it out to me. The rifle, of course, should be handed quietly to me when I return to camp. I cannot march in with it. I shall not come in till after dark. Then the havildar must take me to one of the sepoy tents, and mention to the men there that I am Mutteh Ghar's cousin; and that, as a great favour, I am to be allowed to accompany the regiment."

"Of course, you will take with you the usual underclothes to put on, when you lay aside your uniform; and especially the loincloth, and light linen jacket, which the men use in undress."

"I will see to all that, risaldar. I can assure you that, so far from finding it a trouble to act as a native, I shall really enjoy it; and shall make very light of any hardships that I may have to undergo. When it comes to fighting I am, as you know, a very good shot; and should certainly be able to do my part, with credit."

"I will tell the havildar to be on the lookout for you, when you come into camp, and to bring you straight to me. I will then see that your uniforms and belts are properly put on, before I send you off under his charge. I hope the matter may turn out well. If it does not, you must remember that I have done my part because you urged it upon me, and prayed me to assist you for your father's sake."

"I shall never forget that, Gholam Singh, and shall always feel deeply indebted to you."

When the risaldar had left, Lisle called Robah in.

"All is arranged, Robah; and now it remains only to carry out the details. In the first place, you must get me the stain; in the second, you must go into the bazaar and buy me a loincloth and light jacket, such as the soldiers wear when they lay aside their uniforms. As to the uniform, that is already arranged for; and I shall, of course, have one of the sheepskin greatcoats that have just been served out, and which I expect I shall find indispensable. Put in my kit bag one pair of my thickest woollen vests and drawers. I cannot carry more, for I mean to take one suit of my own clothes to put on in case, by any accident, I should be discovered and sent back. I can get that carried on the baggage waggon.

"Tomorrow we shall start at five o'clock in the morning and, at the first halt, I shall leave the party quietly. I have no doubt that Gholam Singh will give orders, to the native officer in charge, that I am to be permitted to do so without remark. As soon as I leave the convoy you must join me with my uniform and, above all, with the stain. You can bring out a bag with some provisions for the day, for I shall not return to camp until after dark."

When Robah went away to make the necessary purchases, Lisle packed up his baggage and labelled it. His father's effects had all been sold, a few days after his death; as it would not have paid to send them home. They had fetched good prices, and had been gladly bought up by the other officers; some as mementoes of their late comrade, and some because they were useful.

Several of the officers came in and chatted with him while he was packing, all expressing regret that he was leaving. At mess that evening they drank his health, and a pleasant journey; and he gravely returned thanks. When the mess broke up he returned to the bungalow, and packed a small canvas bag with the suit he was going to take with him.

Then he examined and tried on the uniform of the dead sepoy; which Robah had, that evening, received from the risaldar. It fitted him fairly well. In addition to the regular uniform there was a posteen, or sheepskin coat; loose boots made of soft skin, so that the feet could be wrapped up in cloth before they were put on; and putties, or leggings, consisting of a very long strip of cloth terminating with a shorter strip of leather. These things had been served out that day to the troops, and were to be put on over the usual leg wrappings when they came to snow-covered country. They were to be carried with the men's kits till required. For ordinary wear there were the regular boots, which were strapped on like sandals.

"Well, I think I ought to be able to stand anything in the way of cold, with this sheepskin coat and the leggings, together with my own warm underclothing."

"You are sure," Robah said, "that you understand the proper folding of your turban?"

"I think so, Robah. I have seen them done up hundreds of times but, nevertheless, you shall give me a lesson when you join me tomorrow. We shall have plenty of time for it.

"Now, can you think of anything else that would be useful? If so, you can buy it tomorrow before you come out to meet me."

"No, sahib. There are the warm mittens that have been served out for mountain work; and you might take a pair of your own gloves to wear under them for, from all I hear, you will want them when you are standing out all night on picket work, among the hills."

"No, I won't take the gloves, Robah. With two pairs on, my fingers would be so muffled that I should not be able to do good shooting."

"Well, it will be cold work, for it is very late in the season and, you know, goggles have been served out to all the men to save them from snow blindness, from which they would otherwise suffer severely. I have been on expeditions in which a third of the men were quite blind, when they returned to camp."

"It must look very rum to see a whole regiment marching in goggles," Lisle laughed; "still, anything is better than being blinded."

"I shall see you sometimes, sahib; for the major engaged me, this morning, to go with him as his personal servant, as his own man is in feeble health and, though I am now getting on in years, I am still strong enough to travel with the regiment."

"I am delighted, indeed, to hear that, Robah. I shall be very glad to steal away sometimes, and have a chat with you. It will be a great pleasure to have someone I can talk to, who knows me. Of course, the native officer in command of my company will not be able to show me any favour, nor should I wish him to do so. It seems like keeping one friend, while I am cut off from all others; though I dare say I shall make some new ones among the sepoys. I have no doubt you will be very comfortable with the major."

"Yes, sahib, I am sure that he is a kind master. I shall be able, I hope, sometimes to give you a small quantity of whisky, to mix with the water in your bottle."

"No, no, Robah, when the baggage is cut down there will be very little of that taken and, however much there might be, I could not accept any that you had taken from the major's store. I must fare just the same as the others."

"Well, sahib, I hope that, at any rate, you will carry a small flask of it under your uniform. You may not want it but, if you were wounded and lying in the snow, it would be very valuable to you for, mixed with the water in your bottle, and taken from time to time, it would sustain you until you could be carried down to camp."

"That is a very good idea, Robah, and I will certainly adopt it. I will carry half a pint about with me, for emergencies such as you describe. If I do not want it, myself, it may turn out useful to keep up some wounded comrade. It will not add much to the load that I shall have to carry, and which I expect I shall feel, when we first march. As I am now, I think I could keep up with the best marcher in the regiment but, with the weight of the clothes and pouches, a hundred and twenty rounds of ammunition, and my rifle, it will be a very different thing; and I shall be desperately tired, by the time we get to the end of the day's march.

"Now it is twelve o'clock, and time to turn in, for we march at five."

The next morning, when the sick convoy started, the white officers came up to say goodbye to Lisle; and all expressed their regret that he could not accompany the regiment. The butler had gone on ahead and, as soon as Lisle slipped away, he came up to him and assisted him to make his toilet. He stained him from head to foot, dyed his hair, and fastened in it some long bunches of black horse hair, which he would wear in the Punjabi fashion on the top of his head. With the same dye he darkened his eyelashes and, when he had put on his uniform, he said:

"As far as looks go, sahib, it is certain that no one would suspect that you were not a native. There is a large bottle of stain. You will only have to do yourself over, afresh, about once in ten days. A little of this mixed with three times the amount of water will be sufficient for, if you were to put it on by itself, it would make you a great deal too dark."

They spent the day in a grove and, when evening approached, returned to camp.

"And now, goodbye, sahib! The regiment will march tomorrow morning, at daybreak. I may not have an opportunity of seeing you again, before we start. I hope I have done right, in aiding you in your desire to accompany the expedition; but I have done it for the best, and you must not blame me if harm comes of it."

"That you may be sure I will not, and I am greatly obliged to you. Now, for the present, goodbye!"

CHAPTER 2: THE START.

The havildar was on the lookout for Lisle when he entered the camp; but he did not know him, in his changed attire and stained face, until the lad spoke to him.

"You are well disguised, indeed, sahib," he said. "I had no idea that it was you. Now, my instructions are to take you to Gholam Singh's tent."

Here Lisle found the risaldar and the other two native officers. He saluted as he entered. The risaldar examined him carefully, before speaking.

"Good!" he said; "I did not think that a white sahib could ever disguise himself to pass as a native, though I know that it has been done before now. Certainly I have no fear of any of the white officers finding that you are not what you seem to be. I am more afraid, however, of the men. Still, even if they guessed who you are, they would not, I am sure, betray you.

"Here are your rifle and bayonet. These complete your outfit. I see that you have brought your kit with you. It is rather more bulky than usual, but will pass with the rest.

"The subadar will take you down to the men's lines. I have arranged that you shall be on the baggage guard, at first, so that you will gradually begin to know a few men of your company. They will report to the rest the story you tell them, and you will soon be received as one of themselves.

"I will see that that sack of yours goes with the rest of the kits in the baggage waggon. These officers of your company all understand that you are to be treated like the rest of the men, and not to be shown any favour. At the same time, when in camp, if there is anything that you desire, or any complaint you have to make, you can talk quietly to one of them; and he will report it to me, in which case you may be sure that I shall set the matter right, if possible."

"I don't think there is any fear of that, risaldar. I am pretty well able to take care of myself. My father gave me many lessons in boxing; and I fancy that, although most of the men are a great deal bigger and stronger than I am, I shall be able to hold my own."

"I hope so, Bullen," the havildar said gravely, "but I trust that there will be no occasion to show your skill. We Punjabis are a quiet race of men; and though, of course, quarrels occasionally occur among us, they generally end in abuse, and very seldom come to blows. The greater portion of the regiment has been with us for some years. They know each other well, and are not given to quarrelling. They will scarcely even permit their juniors to go to extremes, and I need not say that the officers of the company would interfere, at once, if they saw any signs of a disturbance.

"I have had a meal cooked, which I hope you will eat with us. It is the last you are likely to be able to enjoy, for some time. We shall feel honoured if you will sit down with us."

An excellent repast was served, and Lisle did it full justice. Then the officers all shook him by the hand, and he started with the subadar for the men's lines, with hearty thanks to the others. When they arrived at the huts, the subadar led the way in.

"Here is a new comrade," he said, as some of the men roused themselves from the ground on his entrance. "He is a cousin of Mutteh Ghar, and bears the same name. It seems that he has served in another regiment, for a short time; but was discharged, owing to sickness. He has now perfectly recovered health, and has come to join his cousin; who, on his arrival, he finds to be dead. He is very anxious to accompany the regiment and, as he understands his work, the risaldar has consented to let him go, instead of remaining behind at the depot.

"He is, of course, much affected by the loss of his cousin; and hopes that he will not be worried by questions. He will be on baggage guard tomorrow, and so will be left alone, until he recovers somewhat from his disappointment and grief."

"I will see to it, subadar," one of the sergeants said. "Mutteh Ghar was a nice young fellow, and we shall all welcome his cousin among us, if he is at all like him."

"Thank you, sergeant! I am sure you will all like him, when you come to know him; for he is a well-spoken young fellow, and I hope that he will make as good a soldier. Good night!"

So saying, he turned and left the tent.

Half an hour later, Lisle was on parade. There were but eight British officers; including the colonel, major, and adjutant, and one company officer to each two companies. The inspection was a brief one. The company officer walked along the line, paying but little attention to the men; but carefully scrutinizing their arms, to see that they were in perfect order. The regiment was put through a few simple manoeuvres; and then dismissed, as work in earnest would begin on the following morning.

Four men in each company were then told off to pack the baggage in the carts. Lisle was one of those furnished by his company. There was little talk while they were at work. In two hours the carts were packed. Then, as they returned to the lines, his three comrades entered into conversation with him.

"You are lucky to be taken," one said, "being only a recruit. I suppose it was done so that you might fill the place of your cousin?"

"Yes, that was it. They said that I had a claim; so that, if I chose, I could send money home to his family."

"They are good men, the white officers," another said. "They are like fathers to us, and we will follow them anywhere. We lately lost one of them, and miss him sorely. However, they are all good."

"We are all glad to be going on service. It is dull work in cantonments."

On arriving at the lines of the company, one of them said:

"The risaldar said that you will take your cousin's place. He slept in the same hut as I. You will soon find yourself at home with us."

He introduced Lisle to the other occupants of the hut, eighteen in number. Lisle then proceeded to follow the example of the others, by taking off his uniform and stripping to the loincloth, and a little calico jacket. He felt very strange at first, accustomed though he was to see the soldiers return to their native costume.

"Your rations are there, and those of our new comrade," one of the party said.

Several fires were burning, and Lisle followed the example of his comrade, and took the lota which formed part of his equipment, filled it with water, and put it in the ashes; adding, as soon as it boiled, the handful of rice, some ghee, and a tiny portion of meat. In an hour the meal was cooked and, taking it from the fire, he sat down in a place apart; as is usual among the native troops, who generally have an objection to eat before others.

"Those who have money," his comrade said, "can buy herbs and condiments of the little traders, and greatly improve their mess."

This Lisle knew well.

"I have a few pice," he said, "but must be careful till I get my pay."

As soon as night fell all turned in, as they were to start at daylight.

"Here is room for you at my side, comrade," the sergeant said. "You had better get to sleep, as soon as you can. Of course, you have your blanket with you?"

"Yes, sergeant."

Lisle rolled himself in his blanket and lay down, covering his face, as is the habit of all natives of India. It was some time before he went to sleep. The events of the day had been exciting, and he was overjoyed at finding that his plan had so far succeeded. He was now one of the regiment and, unless something altogether unexpected happened, he was certain to take part in a stirring campaign.

While it was still dark, he was aroused by the sound of a bugle.

"The men told off to the baggage guard will at once proceed to pack the waggons," the sergeant said.

Lisle at once got up and put on his uniform, as did three other men in the tent. The kits and baggage had already been packed, the night before; and the men of the guard, consisting of a half company, proceeded to the waggons. Half an hour afterwards, another bugle roused the remainder of the regiment, and they soon fell in.

It was broad daylight when they started, the baggage followed a little later. The havildar who was in charge of them was, fortunately, one of those of Lisle's company. There was but little talk at the hurried start. Two men accompanied each of the twelve company waggons. Half the remainder marched in front, and the others behind. Lisle had been told off to the first waggon.

It was a long march, two ordinary stages being done in one. As the animals were fresh, the transport arrived at the camping ground within an hour of the main column. Accustomed though he was to exercise, Lisle found the weight of his rifle, pouches, and ammunition tell terribly upon him. He was not used to the boots and, before half the journey was completed, began to limp. The havildar, noticing this, ordered him to take his place on the top of the baggage on his waggon.

"It is natural that you should feel it, at first, Mutteh Ghar," he said. "You will find it easy enough to keep up with them, after a few days' rest."

Lisle was thankful, indeed, for he had begun to feel that he should never be able to hold on to the end of the march. He remained on the baggage for a couple of hours, and then again took his place by the side of the waggon; receiving an approving nod from the havildar, as he did so.

When the halt was called, the men at once crowded round the waggons. The kits were distributed and, in a few minutes, the regiment had the appearance of a concourse of peaceable peasants. No tents had been taken with them. Waterproof sheets had been provided and, with these, little shelters had been erected, each accommodating three men. The sergeant told Lisle off to share one of these shelters with two other men. A party meanwhile had gone to collect firewood and, in half an hour, the men were cooking their rice.

"Well, how did you like the march?" one of them said to Lisle.

"I found it very hard work," Lisle said, "but the havildar let me ride on the top of one of the waggons for a couple of hours and, after that, I was able to march in with the rest."

"It was a rough march for a recruit," the other said, "but you will soon get used to that. Grease your feet well before you put on your bandages. You will find that that will ease them very much, and that you will not get sore feet, as you would if you marched without preparation."

Lisle took the advice, and devoted a portion of his rations for the purpose, the last thing at night; and found that it abated the heat in his feet, and he was able to get about in comfort.

Each soldier carried a little cooking pot. Although the regiment was composed principally of Punjabis, many of the men were of different nationalities and, although the Punjabis are much less particular about caste than the people of Southern India, every man prepared his meal separately. The rations consisted of rice, ghee, a little curry powder, and a portion of mutton. From these Lisle managed to concoct a savoury mess, as he had often watched the men cooking their meals.

The sergeant had evidently chosen two good men to share the tent with Lisle. They were both old soldiers, not given to much talking; and were kind to their young comrade, giving him hints about cooking and making himself comfortable, and abstaining from asking many questions. They were easily satisfied with his answers and, after the meal was eaten, sat down with him and talked of the coming campaign. Neither of them had ever been to Chitral, but they knew by hearsay the nature of the road, and discussed the probability of the point at which serious opposition would begin; both agreeing that the difficulties of crossing the passes, now that these would be covered with snow, would be far greater than any stand the tribesmen might make.

"They are tough fighters, no doubt," one of them said; "and we shall have more difficulty, with them, than we have ever had before; for they say that a great many of them are armed with good rifles, and will therefore be able to annoy us at a distance, when their old matchlocks would have been useless."

"And they are good shots, too."

"There is no doubt about that; quite as good as we are, I should say. There will be a tremendous lot of flanking work to keep them at a distance but, when it comes to anything like regular fighting, we shall sweep them before us.

"From what I hear, however, we shall only have three or four guns with us. That is a pity for, though the tribesmen can stand against a heavy rifle fire, they have a profound respect for guns. I expect, therefore, that we shall have some stiff fighting.

"How do you like the prospect, Mutteh Ghar?"

"I don't suppose I shall mind it when I get accustomed to it," Lisle said. "It was because I heard that the regiment was about to advance that I hurried up to join. I don't think I should have enlisted, had it been going to stay in the cantonment."

"That is the right spirit," the other said approvingly. "It is the same with all of us. There is no difficulty in getting recruits, when there is fighting to be done. It is the dull life in camp that prevents men from joining. We have enlisted twice as many men, in the past three months, as in three years before."

So they talked till night fell and then turned in; putting Lisle between them, that being the warmest position.

In the morning the march was resumed in the same order, Lisle again taking his place with the baggage guard. The march this time was only a single one; but it was long, nevertheless. Lisle was able to keep his place till the end, feeling great benefit from the ghee which he had rubbed on his feet. The havildar, at starting, said a few cheering words to him; and told him that, when he felt tired, he could put his rifle and pouch in the waggon, as there was no possibility of their being wanted.

His two comrades, when they heard that he had accomplished the march without falling out, praised him highly.

"You have showed good courage in holding on," one of them said. "The march was nothing to us seasoned men, but it must have been trying to you, especially as your feet cannot have recovered from yesterday. I see that you will make a good soldier, and one who will not shirk his work. Another week, and you will march as well as the best of us."

"I hope so," Lisle said. "I have always been considered a good walker. As soon as I get accustomed to the weight of the rifle and pouch, I have no doubt that I shall get on well enough."

"I am sure you will," the other said cordially, "and I think we are as good marchers as any in India. We certainly have that reputation and, no doubt, it was for that reason we were chosen for the expedition, although there are several other regiments nearer to the spot.

"From what I hear, Colonel Kelly will be the commanding officer of the column, and we could not wish for a better. I hear that there is another column, and a much stronger one, going from Peshawar. That will put us all on our mettle, and I will warrant that we shall be the first to arrive there; not only because we are good marchers, but because the larger the column, the more trouble it has with its baggage.

"Baggage is the curse of these expeditions. What has to be considered is not how far the troops can go, but how far the baggage animals can keep up with them. Some of the animals are no doubt good, but many of them are altogether unfitted for the work. When these break down they block a whole line; and often, even if the march is a short one, it is very late at night before the last of the baggage comes in; which means that we get neither kit, blankets, nor food, and think ourselves lucky if we get them the next morning.

"The government is, we all think, much to blame in these matters. Instead of procuring strong animals, and paying a fair price for them; they buy animals that are not fit to do one good day's march. Of course, in the end this stinginess costs them more in money, and lives, than if they had provided suitable animals at the outset."

Lisle had had a great deal of practice with the rifle, and had carried away several prizes shot for by the officers; but he was unaccustomed to carry one for so many hours, and he felt grateful, indeed, when a halt was sounded. Fires were lighted, and food cooked; and then all lay down, or sat in groups in the shade of a grove. The sense of the strangeness of his condition had begun to wear off, and he laughed and talked with the others, without restraint.

Through Three Campaigns

Up to the time when he joined the regiment, Lisle had heard a good deal of the state of affairs at Chitral; and his impression of the natives was that they were as savage and treacherous a race as was to be found in Afghanistan and Kashmir. Beyond that, he had not interested himself in the matter; but now, from the talk of his companions, he gained a pretty clear idea of the situation.

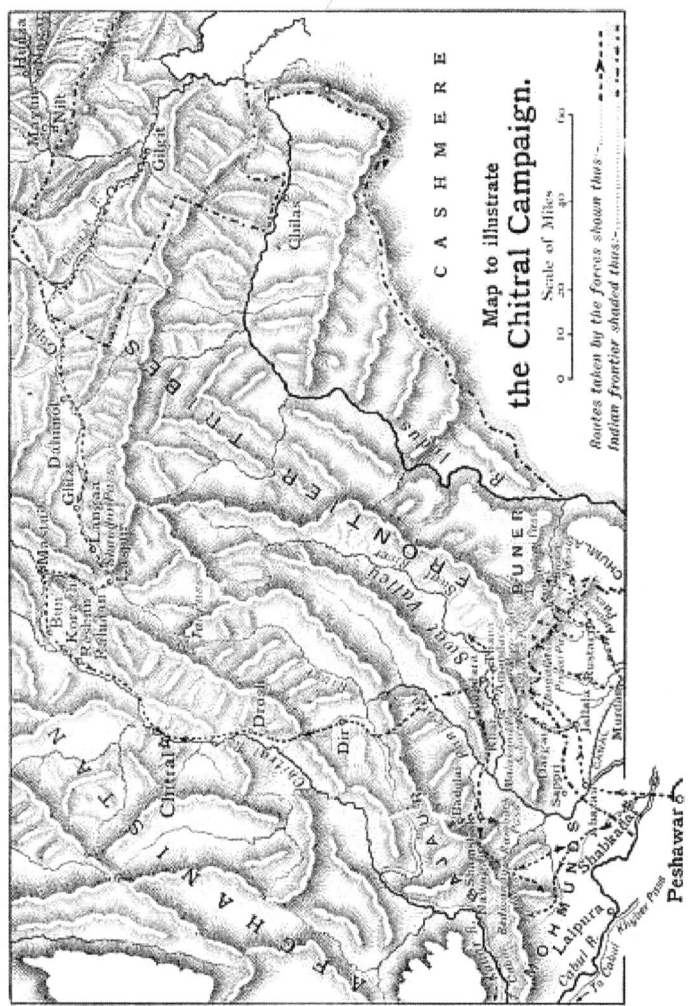

Map to illustrate the Chitral Campaign.

Old Aman-ul-mulk had died in August, 1892. He had reigned long; and had, by various conquests and judicious marriages, raised Chitral to a position of importance. The Chitralis are an Aryan race, and not Pathans; and have a deep-rooted hatred of the Afghans.

Through Three Campaigns

In 1878 Aman placed Chitral under the nominal suzerainty of the Maharajah of Kashmir and, Kashmir being one of the tributary states of the Indian Empire, this brought them into direct communication with the government of India; and Aman received with great cordiality two missions sent to him. When he died, his eldest son Nizam was away from Chitral; and the government was seized by his second son, Afzul; who, however, was murdered by his uncle, Sher Afzul. Nizam at once hurried to Chitral; and Sher Afzul fled to Cabul, Nizam becoming the head of the state or, as it was called, Mehtar. Being weak, he asked for a political officer to reside in his territory; and Captain Younghusband, with an escort of Sikhs, was accordingly sent to Mastuj, a fort in Upper Chitral.

However, in November Nizam was also murdered, by a younger brother, Amir. Amir hurried to Chitral, and demanded recognition from Lieutenant Gurdon; who was, at the time, acting as assistant British agent. He replied that he had no power to grant recognition, until he was instructed by the government in India. Amir thereupon stopped his letters, and for a long time he was in imminent danger, as he had only an escort of eight Sikhs.

On the 8th of January, fifty men of the 14th Sikhs marched down from Mastuj and, on the 1st of February, Mr. Robertson, the British agent, arrived from Gilgit. He had with him an escort of two hundred and eighty men of the 4th Kashmir Rifles, and thirty-three Sikhs; and was accompanied by three European officers. When he arrived he heard that Umra Khan had, at the invitation of Amir, marched into Chitral; but that his progress had been barred by the strong fort of Drosh. As the Chitralis hate the Pathans, they were not inclined to yield to the orders of Amir to surrender the fort, and were consequently attacked. The place, however, was surrendered by the treachery of the governor. Amir then advanced, and was joined by Sher Afzul.

Mr. Robertson wrote to Amir Khan, saying that he must leave the Chitral territory. Amir paid no attention to the order, and Mr. Robertson reported this to the government of India. They issued, in March, 1895, a proclamation warning the Chitralis to abstain from giving assistance to Amir Khan, and intimating that a force sufficient to overcome all resistance was being assembled; but that as soon as it had attained its object, it would be withdrawn.

The Chitralis, who now preferred Sher Afzul to Amir, made common cause with the former. Mr. Robertson learned that men were already at work, breaking up the road between Chitral and Mastuj; and accordingly moved from the house he had occupied to the fort, which was large enough to receive the force with him.

Through Three Campaigns

On the 1st of March, all communications between Mr. Robertson and Mastuj had ceased; and troops were at once ordered to assemble, to march to his relief. It was clearly impossible for our agent to retire as, in order to do so, he would have to negotiate several terrible passes, where a mere handful of men could destroy a regiment. Thus it was that the Pioneers had been ordered to break up their cantonment, and advance with all speed to Gilgit.

Hostilities had already begun. A native officer had started, with forty men and sixty boxes of ammunition, for Chitral; and had reached Buni, when he received information that his advance was likely to be opposed. He accordingly halted and wrote to Lieutenant Moberley, special duty officer with the Kashmir troops in Mastuj. The local men reported to Moberley that no hostile attack upon the troops was at all likely but, as there was a spirit of unrest in the air, he wrote to Captain Ross, who was with Lieutenant Jones, and requested him to make a double march into Mastuj. This Captain Ross did and, on the evening of the 4th of March, started to reinforce the little body of men that was blocked at Buni.

On the same day a party of sappers and miners, under Lieutenants Fowler and Edwards, also marched forward to Mastuj. When Captain Ross arrived at Buni he found that all was quiet, and he therefore returned to Mastuj, with news to that effect. The party of sappers were to march, the next morning, with the ammunition escort.

On the evening of that day a note was received from Lieutenant Edwards, dated from a small village two miles beyond Buni, saying that he heard that he was to be attacked in a defile, a short distance away. He started with a force of ninety-six men, in all. They carried with them nine days' rations, and one hundred and forty rounds of ammunition.

Captain Ross at once marched for Buni, and arrived there the same evening. Here he left a young native officer and thirty-three rank and file while, with Lieutenant Jones and the rest of his little force, he marched for Reshun, where Lieutenant Edwards' party were detained. They halted in the middle of the day; and arrived, at one o'clock, at a hamlet halfway to Reshun.

Shortly after starting, they were attacked. Lieutenant Jones, one of the few survivors of the party, handed in the following report of this bad business.

"Half a mile after leaving Koragh the road enters a narrow defile. The hills on the left bank consist of a succession of large stone shoots, with precipitous spurs in between. The road at the entrance to the defile, for about one hundred yards, runs quite close to the river; after that it lies along a narrow maidan, some thirty or forty yards in width, and is on the top of the river bank, which is here a cliff. This continues for about half a mile, then it ascends a steep spur.

"When the advanced party reached about halfway up this spur, it was fired on from a sangar which had been built across the road and, at the same time, men appeared on all the mountain tops and ridges, and stones were rolled down all the shoots. Captain Ross, who was with the advanced guard, fell back on the main body. All the coolies dropped their loads and bolted, as soon as the first shot was fired. Captain Ross, after looking at the enemy's position, decided to fall back upon Koragh; as it would have been useless to go on to Reshun, leaving an enemy in such a position behind us."

Captain Ross ordered Lieutenant Jones to fall back with ten men, seize the lower end of the defile, and cover the retreat. No fewer than eight of his men were wounded, as he fell back. Captain Ross, on hearing this, ordered him to return, and the whole party took refuge in two caves, it being the intention of their commander to wait there until the moon rose, and then try to force his way out.

But when they started, they were assailed from above with such a torrent of rocks that they again retired to the caves. They then made an attempt to get to the top of the mountain, but their way was barred by a precipice; and they once more went back to the cave, where they remained all the next day.

It was then decided to make an attempt to cut their way out. They started at two in the morning. The enemy at once opened fire, and many were killed, among them Captain Ross himself. Lieutenant Jones with seventeen men reached the little maidan, and there remained for some minutes, keeping up a heavy fire on the enemy on both banks of the river, in order to help more men to get through.

Twice the enemy attempted to charge, but each time retired with heavy loss. Lieutenant Jones then again fell back, two of his party having been killed and one mortally wounded, and the lieutenant and nine sepoys wounded. When they reached Buni they prepared a house for defence, and remained there for seven days until reinforcements came up.

In the meantime the 20th Bengal Sappers and Miners, and the 42nd Kashmir Infantry had gone on, beyond the point where Captain Ross's detachment had been all but annihilated, and reached Reshun; and Lieutenants Edwards and Fowler, with the Bengal Sappers and ten Kashmir Infantry, went on to repair a break in the road, a few miles beyond that place. They took every precaution to guard against surprise. Lieutenant Fowler was sent to scale the heights on the left bank, so as to be able to look down into some sangars on the opposite side. With some difficulty, he found a way up the hillside. When he was examining the opposite cliff a shot was fired, and about two hundred men rushed out from the village and entered the sangars.

As Fowler was well above them, he kept up a heavy fire, and did great execution. The enemy, however, began to ascend the hills, and some appeared above him and began rolling down stones and firing into his party. Fowler himself was wounded in the back, a corporal was killed, and two other men wounded. He managed, however, to effect his retreat, and joined the main body.

As the enemy were now swarming on the hills, the party began to fall back to Reshun, which was two miles distant. They had an open plain to cross and a spur, a thousand feet high, to climb. During this part of the retreat an officer and several men were wounded but, on reaching the crest, the party halted and opened a steady fire upon the enemy; whom they thus managed to keep at a distance till they reached Reshun, which they did without further loss.

The force here were occupying a sangar they had formed, but so heavy a fire was opened, from the surrounding hills, that it was found impossible to hold the position. They therefore retired to some houses, where firewood and other supplies were found. The only drawback to this place was that it was more than a hundred yards from the river, and there was consequently great danger of their being cut off from the water.

As soon as they reached the houses they began to fortify them. The roofs were flat and, by piling stones along the edges, they converted them into sangars. The walls were loopholed, the entrances blocked up, and passages of communication opened between the houses. A party of Kashmir volunteers then went down to the other sangar and brought the wounded in, under a heavy fire.

At sunset the enemy's fire ceased, as it was the month of Ramzam, during which Mahomedans have to fast all day between sunrise and sunset. As night came on the little party took their places on the roofs, and remained there till daylight. By this time all were greatly exhausted for, during their terrible experiences of the previous day, they had had no food and little water.

When day dawned half the men were withdrawn from their posts, and a meal was cooked from the flour that had been found in the houses. A small ration of meat was also served out. During the day the enemy kept up a continuous fire but, as they showed no intention of attacking, the men were allowed to sleep by turns.

After dark Lieutenant Fowler and some volunteers started for the river, to bring in water. They made two trips, and filled up all the storage vessels at the disposal of the garrison. The night passed quietly but, just before dawn, the enemy charged down through the surrounding houses. Lieutenant Edwards and his party at once opened fire, at about twenty yards' range. Tom-toms were beaten furiously, to encourage the assailants; but the tribesmen could not pluck up courage to make a charge and, at nine o'clock, they all retired. During the attack four of the sepoys were killed, and six wounded.

Next night another effort was made to obtain water. Two sangars were stormed, and most of their occupants killed. The way to the water was now opened but, at this moment, heavy firing broke out at the fort; and Lieutenant Fowler, who was in command, recalled his men and returned to assist the garrison.

On the following day a white flag was hoisted, and an emissary from Sher Afzul said that all fighting had ceased. An armistice was accordingly arranged. All this, however, was but a snare for, a few days later, when the two British officers went out to witness a polo match, they were seized, bound with ropes, and carried off. At the same moment a fierce attack was made on a party of sepoys who had also come out. These fought stoutly, but were overpowered, most of them being killed.

The garrison of the post, however, under the command of Lieutenant Gurdon, continued to hold the little fort; and refused all invitation to come out to parley, after the treachery that had been shown to their comrades. The two officers were taken to Chitral, where they were received with kindness by Amir Khan.

The news of this disaster was carried to Peshawar by a native Mussulman officer, who had been liberated, where it created great excitement. As all communication with Chitral had ceased, the assistant British agent at Gilgit called up the Pioneers; who marched into Gilgit, four hundred strong, on the 20th of March. On the 21st news was received of the cutting up of Ross's party, and it was naturally supposed that that of Edwards was also destroyed.

Colonel Kelly of the Pioneers now commanded the troops, and all civil powers; and Major Borradale commanded the Pioneers. The available force consisted of the four hundred Pioneers, and the Guides. Lieutenant Stewart joined them with two guns of the Kashmir battery.

Two hundred Pioneers and the Guides started on the 23rd. The gazetteer states that it never rains in Gilgit, but it rained when the detachment started, and continued to pour for two days. The men had marched without tents. Colonel Kelly, the doctor, Leward, and a staff officer followed in the afternoon, and overtook the main body that evening.

The troops had made up little tents with their waterproof sheets. Colonel Kelly had a small tent, and the other officers turned in to a cow shed. The force was so small that the Pioneers asked the others to mess with them, each man providing himself with his own knife, fork, and spoon, and the pots being all collected for the cooking.

The next march was long and, in some places, severe. They were well received by the natives, whose chiefs always came out to greet them and, on the third day, reached Gupis, where a fort had been built by the Kashmir troops. At this point the horses and mules were all left behind, as the passes were said to be impassable for animals; and native coolies were hired to carry the baggage.

Lisle had enjoyed the march, and the strange life that he was leading. He was now quite at home with his company and, by the time they reached Gupis, had become a general favourite. At the end of the day, when a meal had been cooked and eaten, he would join in their songs round the fire and, as he had picked up several he had heard them sing, and had a fair voice, he was often called upon for a contribution. His vivacity and good spirits surprised the sepoys who, as a whole, were grave men, though they bore their hardships uncomplainingly. He had soon got over the feeling of discomfort of going about with naked legs, and was as glad as the soldiers, themselves, to lay aside his uniform and get into native attire.

The sepoys had now regular rations of meat. It was always mutton, as beef was unobtainable; but it was much relished by the men, who cut it up into slices and broiled it over a fire.

Not for one moment did Lisle regret the step he had taken. Young and active, he thoroughly enjoyed the life; and looked forward eagerly to the time when they should meet the enemy, for no doubt whatever was now felt that they would meet with a desperate resistance on their march to Chitral. Fears were entertained, however, that when they got there, they would find that the garrison had been overpowered; for it was certain that against this force the chief attack of the enemy would be directed. The overthrow of Ross and his party showed that the enemy were sturdy fighters; and they were known to be armed with breech-loading rifles, of as good a quality as those carried by the troops.

In the open field all felt that, however numerous the tribesmen might be, they would stand no chance whatever; but the passes afforded them immense advantage, and rendered drill and discipline of little avail.

CHAPTER 3: THE FIRST FIGHT.

And yet, though he kept up a cheerful appearance, Lisle's heart was often very heavy. The sight of the British officers continually recalled his father to his memory. But a short time back he had been with him, and now he was gone for ever. At times it seemed almost impossible that it could be so. He had been his constant companion when off duty; had devoted much time to helping him forward in his studies; had never, so far as he could remember, spoken a harsh word to him.

It seemed like a dream, those last hours he had passed by his father's bedside. Many times he lay awake in the night, his face wet with tears. But with reveille he would be up, laughing and joking with the soldiers, and raising a smile even on the face of the gravest.

It had taken him but a very short time to make himself at home in the regiment. The men sometimes looked at him with surprise, he was so different from themselves. They bore their hardships well, but it was with stern faces and grim determination; while this young soldier made a joke of them.

Sometimes he was questioned closely, but he always turned the questions off with a laugh. He had learned the place where his supposed cousin came from and, while sticking to this, he said that a good fairy must have presided over his birth; information that was much more gravely received than given, for the natives have their superstitions, and believe, as firmly as the inhabitants of these British islands did, two or three hundred years ago, in the existence of supernatural beings, good and bad.

"If you have been blessed by a fairy," one of the elder men suggested, "doubtless you will go through this campaign without harm. They are very powerful, some of these good people, and can bestow long life as well as other gifts."

"I don't know whether she will do that. She certainly gave me high spirits. I used to believe that what my mother said happened to her, the night after I was born, was not true, but only a dream. She solemnly declared that it was not, but I have always been famous for good spirits; and she may have been right, after all."

There was nothing Lisle liked better than being on night picket duty. Other men shirked it, but to him there was something delightful to stand there almost alone, rifle in hand, watching the expanse of snow for a moving figure. There was a charm in the dead silence. He liked to think quietly of the past and, somehow, he could do so far better, while engaged on this duty, than when lying awake in his little tent. The expanse and stillness calmed him, and agreed far more with his mood than the camp.

His sight was keen, even when his thoughts were farthest away and, three times, he sent a bullet through a lurking Pathan who was crawling up towards him, astonishing his comrades by the accuracy of his aim.

"I suppose," he said, when congratulated upon the third occasion on which he had laid one of the enemy low, "that the good fairy must have given me a quick eye, as well as good spirits."

"It is indeed extraordinary that you, a young recruit, should not only make out a man whom none of us saw; but that you should, each time, fetch him down at a distance of three or four hundred yards."

"I used to practice with my father's rifle," he said. "He was very fond of shikari, and I often went out with him. It needs a keener sight to put a bullet between the eyes of a tiger, than to hit a lurking Pathan."

So noted did he become for the accuracy of his aim that one of the native officers asked him, privately, if he would like to be always put on night duty.

"I should like it every other night," he said. "By resting every alternate night, and by snatching a couple of hours' sleep before going on duty, when we arrive at the end of a day's march in good time, I can manage very well."

"I will arrange that for you," the officer said. "Certainly, no one would grudge you the duty."

One night, when there had been but little opposition during the day, Lisle was posted on a hill where the picket consisted of ten men; five of whom were on the crest, while the other five lay down in the snow. The day had been a hard one, and Lisle was less watchful than usual. It seemed to him that he had not closed his eyes for a minute, as he leant on his rifle; but it must have been much longer, for he suddenly started with a feeling that something was wrong, and saw a number of dark figures advancing along the crest towards him. He at once fired a shot, and fell back upon the next sentry. Dropping behind rocks, they answered the fire which the enemy had already opened upon them.

The whole picket quickly gathered and, for a time, checked the advance of the enemy; but these were too numerous to be kept at a distance, and parties of them pressed forward on each flank.

"We must retire till we can find better shelter," the sub-officer in command said. "We shall soon have reinforcements up from the camp, when it is seen that we are seriously engaged. Fall back, men, steadily. Take advantage of every bit of cover, but keep as well together as possible, without risk."

Firing steadily, they made their way down the hill, and finally took up a position among a clump of rocks. Two had been shot dead, and two others were wounded; and it was because these could not be left behind that the stand was made. The two wounded men, though partially disabled and unable to crawl, could still use their rifles; and the little party kept up so hot a fire that, though the enemy were massed from twenty to thirty yards away, they could not be brought to unite in a general attack; not even by the shouts and yells of their comrades behind, and a furious beating of tom-toms.

LISLE GIVES THE ALARM

The defenders were all lying down, each of them having chosen a position where he could see through a crevice between the rocks. Lisle was lying next to the sergeant. Presently the latter gave an exclamation, fired his rifle, and shifted his position behind the rock.

"Mutteh Ghar," he said, "I have seen you bring down three of the skulking ruffians. Do you see those two there close together, about forty yards away? There is a man behind them who has just carried off two of my fingers.

"Keep your eye on those rocks. Just above where they touch each other there is an opening, through which you can see the snow behind. That is where he fired from. Oblige me by putting a ball in his head, when he raises it."

A couple of minutes passed. Lisle was lying with his rifle on the spot. Presently the opening was obscured, and he fired at once.

"Thank you!" the sergeant said. "You got him, sure enough. The head did not disappear to one side or to the other, but went straight back. I fancy that you must have hit him between the eyes."

Presently the enemy's fire became still more furious and, several times, some of them rose and ran two paces forward, but only to fall prone under the defenders' fire.

"I expect they see help coming up," Lisle said, "and are making a last effort to wipe us out before they arrive.

"I think they will try a rush," he continued, in a louder voice; "see that your magazines are filled up, lads, and don't waste a shot if they come at us."

A minute later there was a shrill and prolonged cry and, at once, twenty dark figures burst from their shelter and rushed forward. The defenders also sprang to their feet, and their rifles flashed out with a stream of fire. But the vacancies thus caused in the enemy's ranks were immediately filled.

"Now with your bayonets," the sergeant shouted. "Keep in a close body, and do you two wounded men cover us with a constant fire."

Then, with a cheer, the six men and the sergeant rushed forward. Much as the Afridis feared the bayonet, confident in their strength they withstood the charge. They had, fortunately, emptied their rifles before rushing forward but, drawing their knives, they fought fiercely. These, however, were no match for the bayonets and, consequently, they suffered heavily.

Three of the Pioneers received severe gashes. The group were brought to a standstill, and they stood in a little circle while the attack continued. One sepoy was stabbed to the heart by a fanatic, who rushed at his bayonet and, pushing himself along, fell dead as he struck his fatal blow.

Things were looking very bad. Scarce one had escaped without a wound, and the sergeant had dropped, bleeding profusely; when, to their delight, a volley burst from within fifty yards of them and, in an instant, their assailants turned and bolted.

After the sergeant had dropped, Lisle had somehow taken his place, cheering the men on and lending his aid to those most severely pressed. Once or twice he managed, after despatching an assailant, to slip a couple of cartridges into his rifle, and so added to the execution. Indeed, it was in no small account due to his exertions, after the sergeant fell, that the resistance was maintained.

A minute later, the active little Ghoorkhas rushed forward; and those who first arrived passed the little knot of defenders with a cheer, and set off in pursuit of the enemy. Presently, however, one of their officers came up.

"You have had a stiff fight, lads," he said, "and by the look of the ground round about, you must have defended yourselves gallantly; for there are a dozen dead bodies lying near you, and I can see many more, a little way up the hill. What have been your losses?"

The sergeant raised himself on his elbow.

"We had two killed, as we came down," he said, "and two others wounded. I believe one has fallen here, and I think most of us are wounded with knife thrusts."

"Well, you have done splendidly, sergeant. I will detach men to help to carry you and the wounded men down to the camp. The others can accompany them. We shall take up the work, now; but I am afraid we sha'n't have any fighting, though we may shoot down a few as they make off. I fancy, however, that the lesson you have given the beggars has taken all fight out of them."

When half down the hill, they met a party of the Pioneers coming out. The Ghoorkhas at once handed the wounded over to them, and started up the hill again. The sergeant had fainted from loss of blood, and no questions were asked till the injured men were all placed in little hospital tents, and their wounds attended to. Two of them had bullet wounds, and three had received knife wounds on the shoulder or arm. Only Lisle and one other escaped unhurt. As soon as the wounds had been attended to all, except the sergeant, and two more seriously wounded than the others, were sent off to their tents.

One of these was Lisle's tent fellow. He said:

"Mutteh Ghar, I don't know what to say to you. You seem but a lad, and a light-hearted one; but you have proved yourself the best of us all. I was lying next to you, and I will swear that you brought down eight of them with your rifle, before they charged. Even while I was fighting I always heard your voice, like a trumpet; and after the sergeant had fallen you seemed to take command, as if it was your right. You saved my life when you bayoneted two of the three who were grappling with me, and you seemed to be everywhere."

"I did what little I could," Lisle said. "I certainly did not intend to take the command, when the sergeant fell; but somehow I could not help shouting and, as our circle had closed in so, I slipped out of my place and fought wherever the pressure was greatest."

"There is no doubt," the soldier said seriously, "that your mother's statement was a true one, and that a fairy did promise her to look after you. Out of the eleven of us, only one besides yourself has escaped without a wound; and yet none of us exposed himself more than you did. I shall not forget that I owe my life to you. We must find some other name for you. You can't be called 'the boy' any longer."

In the morning, one of the colonel's orderlies was told to fetch Lisle.

"The colonel wishes to see you, Mutteh Ghar."

Lisle put on his uniform with some uneasiness. He was conscious that, in the excitement of the fight of the night before, he had frequently shouted in English; and he feared that the sergeant had reported this. However, he marched to the spot where the colonel and a group of officers were standing, and then stood at attention.

"Mutteh Ghar," the colonel said, "the sergeant this morning made his report; and he states that, though all his men behaved admirably, you distinguished yourself in a singular manner. He says that before the final attack began you had killed eight or ten of the Pathans, that you were fighting beside him when he was wounded, and that you then seemed to take the command. Although lying on the ground, he was able to see what was going on; and he says that but for your cheers, and for the manner in which you went to the assistance of men hard pressed, he is convinced that the whole detachment would have been killed before the Ghoorkhas arrived."

"I had no idea of assuming the command, sir; but my tongue always runs fast, and I dare say I did shout, almost unconsciously. I think the sergeant has made more of my doings than I deserved."

"I don't think it likely. It is no small thing for so young a soldier to so distinguish himself. The sergeant will not be able to resume his duties for some time, and I therefore appoint you a corporal; and shall put your name in orders, today, for very distinguished service. How long is it since you joined the regiment?"

"A short time before we marched."

"Well, you have done honour to the corps and, in the name of myself and my officers, I thank you."

Lisle saluted, and returned to the lines.

"The colonel has made me a corporal," he answered, as the others gathered round and questioned him.

A cheer burst from them, for his tent companion, and the other men who had returned, had all spoken in the highest terms of his conduct. Lisle was quite confused by the heartiness of their reception.

"He is a wonderfully young fellow," the colonel said, as he left them. "The sergeant said that he was young, but really he looks little more than a boy. Curiously, his face reminds me of someone, though I cannot say whom; and yet, if he only joined a short time before we marched, it is not likely that I should have noticed him before."

"It was the same thing with me, colonel," the major said. "I have noticed him several times on the march and, while the rest of the regiment were plodding on in silence, he always seemed the centre of a merry group. I have often said, to myself, I wished we had a few more men in the regiment who could take the hardships they had to undergo as lightly and as merrily as he does. His face has also struck me as being somehow familiar.

"I was speaking to the sergeant about him, and he said that he was the most popular man in his company, and a general favourite. His temperament is altogether different from that of the majority of our soldiers, which is earnest and quiet."

Two or three of the other officers also spoke of noticing the cheerful influence he seemed to have on the men.

"I must have a talk with him," the colonel said, "after the campaign is over, and find out something about it. It is quite evident that his pluck is as great as his cheerfulness, and it is certainly very extraordinary that a young and recently-joined soldier should have such an influence with men many years older than himself. If I am not mistaken, we shall find him in the ranks of the native officers, before long. Considering his age, and what he has already done, he may well hope some day, if he escapes being killed, to be risaldar major of the regiment.

"I should almost fancy that he must be the son of some native of good family, but without influence to secure him a post as officer; and that he has run away to endeavour to fight his way up to a commission."

Henceforth Lisle stood in high regard among his comrades, and was known as the 'fighting boy' in the regiment. He himself was always ready to answer to any name by which he was addressed. He had no desire to push himself forward to any prominence among them, or of thinking himself any way above his comrades; but naturally he was pleased at finding himself generally liked. He had come to see the fighting, and take part in it, and had no thought of distinguishing himself especially; as he intended to leave the regiment as soon as the campaign was over, and carry out the plan which his father had formed for him. He feared to excite the jealousy of his comrades and, though there were no signs of this, he felt that his promotion caused some difference in the manner of other men towards him.

This was so marked, indeed, that he could not help thinking that the men by whose side he had fought had reported to their comrades that, in the heat of the fight, he had several times shouted in English; and that there were general suspicions as to his identity. As long as this was not communicated to the officers it did not matter; and indeed this was not likely for, if the feeling was noticed by the native officers, it would soon come to the ears of Gholam Singh, who would at once order the men to keep silence concerning it.

Gradually his nickname changed, and he became known among the sepoys of the regiment as the "young sahib." He protested against it, but in vain. It was not, however, without its advantages. At the end of a long march, the men who had brought in firewood always handed him some. Men would offer to clean his rifle, cook his dinner, and do other little offices for him. He would, however, never accept these kind offers.

"Why do they call you sahib?" one of the English officers asked him, when he heard him so addressed.

"I do not know," he answered. "It is a silly joke of the men. I have protested against it, without success. If they chose to call me 'colonel,' I could not help it. I suppose it is because they see that I am, like the white officers, always cheerful and good tempered. There is certainly no other reason that I know of."

"The regiment have taken to call Mutteh Ghar 'the young sahib,'" the officer reported, at mess that day. "I asked him about it, and he says no doubt it is because he is, like us, always good tempered and cheerful."

"He is certainly very unlike the others," the major said. "I have no doubt the men consider it a great compliment, to him, to call him so."

"Do you know, colonel," one of the subalterns said, "the idea has struck me that he may be young Bullen, who may have joined the regiment surreptitiously, instead of going down to Calcutta."

There was silence among the others.

"It can hardly be that, Macdonald," the colonel said, "though it is certainly curious that we seemed to feel that we knew his face, when he came up before us. The young scamp could never have played such an audacious trick upon us."

"I don't know, colonel," the major said, "he is just the sort of lad that would try such a scheme. I know I have twice seen him talking with my butler; who was, as you know, Captain Bullen's servant."

"Well, it may possibly be so," the colonel said, "but at any rate it is only suspicion, and we had better leave the matter as it stands. If it is young Bullen, I don't know that he has done a bad thing for himself. If he goes on as he has begun, his experience will go a long way towards getting him a commission; and he will be a great deal better off than if he were grinding up for two years in England. Such a strong recommendation as I could give him would be of great value to him and, moreover, he has a claim on the ground that his father was killed on service.

"At any rate, we must take no action, whatever, at present. It is no slight thing he has done; that is, if it be he. Few of us would care to go through this campaign as sepoys--their work is terribly hard, poor fellows--to say nothing of the unpleasantness of having to live among the natives. I certainly shall consider that he has well earned a commission, if he comes through the campaign."

"But he is too young for one," the major said.

"I should not think it necessary to mention his age, in recommending him," the colonel said. "We know that he is doing a man's work, manfully. He has earned, as you say, the general liking of the men; and is a deal better fitted for a commission than half the fellows they send out to us.

"Well, we may all be mistaken, and he may only be a brave young fellow of good ancestry; so we will think no more of it, at present, and we will wait to see how things turn out, before showing any signs of our suspicions."

Now, however, that the idea had been mooted, the officers, as they went up and down the line, looked closer at Lisle than they had hitherto done; and all agreed that, in spite of his uniform and his colour, he was Captain Bullen's son. Ignorant of their suspicions, Lisle carried out his work, as usual, as a sub-officer. He shared the shelter tents of the men, and performed his duties regularly. He still carried a rifle; and indeed, if this had not been the rule he would not have accepted his promotion, as he preferred fighting with a weapon to which he was accustomed.

His work during the day was but little changed. When the regiment was marching in a column, four abreast, he had his appointed place by the side of it and, when they arrived in camp, it was part of his duty to see that the little tents were all pitched, rations distributed, kits handed over, and the men made as comfortable as possible. No sub-officer was obeyed with greater alacrity and, when he returned from his picket in the early morning, he always found his ration ready cooked for him.

It was impossible for him to help feeling pleased at these signs of the liking of the men, and he redoubled his efforts to cheer them on the line of march; and to aid any men who seemed unable to climb up through the snow, by carrying their rifles and ammunition pouches for them. He had long since grown accustomed to carrying weights, and was able to keep up with the most seasoned marchers.

On two or three occasions Gholam Singh was able to report favourably of his conduct, in thus relieving men of their arms. The colonel always took these communications in the ordinary way.

"There is no doubt," he said, when the conversation turned on the subject, "that Gholam Singh must have been an accessory to young Bullen's plot. I have been looking up the list of the deceased sepoys, and I find that a recruit of the same name died, two days before we marched. In some way young Bullen, if it is really the boy, contrived to take the dead man's place and name. This could have been very well done, without any of us knowing. None of us were familiar with the dead man's appearance, and Gholam Singh, and some of the other native officers, must have arranged that he should take his place. If this has been the case I shall, of course, be obliged to speak sharply to the risaldar major; but in reality I shall not be very angry with him, for he will certainly have done young Bullen a good turn."

"I am sure it is Bullen," one of the officers said, "for when I came up suddenly behind him, today, I heard him whistling an English tune. Of course, it may have been played by the band when we were in camp, but whistling is not a common Punjabi accomplishment, and I don't know that I ever heard native boys whistle before. He stopped directly I came up, but I could make no mistake about the tune; for I hung behind a little, and was amused at seeing the men marching by him trying to keep step, while they were over their knees in snow. I caught a grin on their faces at their failure, though they looked as grave as usual when they saw me."

"Well, we must let things go on as they are," the colonel said, "until we get to Chitral. Then we will have him up, and get to the bottom of the affair. If it turns out to be Bullen, he must at once leave the ranks and join us again. I shall then have to ask for a commission for him, and give him temporary rank as junior lieutenant, until an answer to my recommendation arrives. Even if it is not Bullen, it may be--unlikely as it seems--some other Englishman; but in any case, we could not allow an Englishman to be in the ranks."

"I don't think there is any doubt about it, colonel," the major said. "I have had a good look at him, several times, and could almost swear to his identity, well as he is got up."

Lisle pursued the regular course of his work, in happy unconsciousness that any suspicion as to his identity entered the minds of his officers. His spirits were now not forced; the fatiguing marches, the night pickets, and the pressure of his duty so occupied his thoughts that he had little time to dwell upon his loss. It was now three months since his father had died, and yet it seemed to him in the far distance, so much had happened since. Occasionally he thought with disgust that, when this was all over, he must return to England to the uncle he had never seen, and become a schoolboy, spending his days in study; and perhaps, in the end, fail to pass his examination. He would be a stranger amongst strangers. He could not expect that his uncle should feel any particular interest in a lad he had never before seen, and he drew pictures to himself of the long, friendless interval before, even at the best, he could again don a uniform.

But upon such thoughts he did not allow himself to dwell. It had to be done, and he would, he supposed, get through it all right. He might find friends among the fellows at the same crammer's. At any rate, three years would soon pass, and he must make the best of it.

"I suppose the crammer will be in London," he said. "Everything there will be new to me and, no doubt, I shall find it very interesting. They say that it is an immense place, to which even the biggest Indian city is but a mere trifle. It will be curious to see everyone in dark clothes, with none of the gay colouring of India.

"Father often said that the pleasantest time of his life was the years he spent in England, while he was cramming for his exam. There were theatres, and all sorts of other places of amusement. He had the best of companions and, after they had finished their work, they were at liberty to do pretty nearly whatever they liked.

"I think I shall get my uncle to send me to the same crammer as father went to, if he is still alive. I put down his address once, in my pocketbook, and shall be able to find it again when I get down to Calcutta, and recover my traps.

"Well, I need not worry myself by thinking of it, now. It will all come some day, and I dare say I shall find it pleasant enough, when I once get accustomed to it."

Such thoughts often passed through his mind at night for, during the day, he had not a minute to himself. He was almost sure, now, that the men had discovered his identity, by the many little marks of kindness they had shown him, and by the manner in which his fellow sub-officers always spoke to him with a certain air of respect. This, however, did not worry him. He felt certain that they would keep the secret; and at the end of the campaign he must, of course, disclose himself and obtain his discharge. Until then, no one would have time to think much of the matter, still less find any opportunity of reporting it to Colonel Kelly.

He wondered how the colonel would take it, when he went up to say who he was. He did not think he would be very seriously angry, though probably he would wig him sharply. At any rate he had not done badly, and had brought no discredit to the regiment.

He had unconsciously adopted the regimental belief that he was a lucky man, and should get through the campaign unhurt. He was particularly anxious that he should do so as, were he confined in hospital for a few days, he would have no opportunity of renewing his stain; in which case he would undoubtedly be detected. They had advanced so far now, however, that even if he were discovered, they could hardly send him back before he got to Chitral. He might, of course, be detained at Reshun, which would be a horrible nuisance.

One night his camp mate said to him:

"You ought to be with the officers, Bullen sahib. It is not right for you to be working as we do."

"Why do you call me Bullen Sahib, Pertusal?"

"Everyone knows it, sahib. Little by little we nave found you out. We had some suspicions from the first, but now we are sure of it. Only your father's son would have fought as you did on the hill and, when we came to look very closely at you, we all recognized you, in spite of your dye."

"Then I wish I hadn't fought quite so hard, Pertusal, for I had hoped that I had altogether escaped recognition. I thought that I could have gone through the campaign without anyone suspecting who I was."

"We did not suspect at first, sahib. We quite took you for one of ourselves. No, the cheerfulness with which you bore your hardships, and your readiness to assist anyone, surprised us. You were so different from us all that we could not help wondering who you were; but I don't think any of us really suspected that you were Captain Bullen's son, till that fight. I know that when I was busy fighting, sorely pushed as we were, I wondered when I heard you shout in English; and I had heard you call out so often, when you were playing cricket with the officers, that I recognized your voice at once.

"Then the wonder that we felt about you ceased. It seemed for a moment impossible, for I had seen you go off with the sick convoy. Then it seemed to me that it was just the thing that Captain Bullen's son might be expected to do. You would naturally want to see fighting, but I did wonder how you managed to come back and get enlisted into the regiment. I remember, now, that I wondered a little the first night you joined. You were in uniform and, as a rule, recruits don't go into uniform for some time after they have joined. It was therefore remarkable that you should turn up in uniform, rifle and all."

"It was the uniform of the original Mutteh Ghar," Lisle said. "My servant had managed to get it; and the story that I was the man's cousin, and was therefore permitted to take his place, was natural enough to pass."

"But some of our officers must have helped you, sahib?"

"Well, I won't say anything about that. I did manage to join in the way I wanted, and you and your comrade were both very kind to me."

"That was natural enough, sahib. You were a young recruit, and we understood that you were put with us two old soldiers in order that we might teach you your duty. It was not long, however, before we found that there was very little teaching necessary for, at the end of a week, you knew your work as well as any man in the regiment. We thought you a wonder, but we kept our thoughts to ourselves.

"Now that we know who you are, all the regiment is proud that your father's son has come among us, and shared our lot down to the smallest detail. I noticed that you were rather clumsy with your cooking, but even in that respect you soon learned how things should be done.

"I suppose, sahib, we shall lose you at the end of the campaign?"

"Yes; I shall have to start for England, at once; for in order to gain a commission, I must study hard for two or three years. Of course, I shall then have to declare myself to the officers, in order to get my discharge. I am afraid that the colonel will be very angry, but I cannot help that. I am quite sure, however, that he will let me go, as soon as he knows who I am. It will be rather fun to see the surprise of the officers."

"I don't think the colonel will be angry, sahib. He might have been, if you had not done so well; but as it is, he cannot but be pleased that Captain Bullen's son should have so distinguished himself, even in the 32nd Pioneers, who have the reputation of being one of the best fighting regiments in all India."

"Well, I hope so, Pertusal. At any rate, I am extremely glad I came. I have seen what fighting is, and that under the most severe conditions. I have proved to myself that I can bear hardships without flinching; and I shall certainly be proud, all my life, that I have been one in the column for the relief of Chitral--that is to say, if we are the first."

"We shall be the first," the soldier said, positively. "It is hard work enough getting our baggage over the passes; but it will be harder still for the Peshawar force, encumbered with such a train as they will have to take with them."

"Ah! Sahib, if only our food were so condensed that we could carry a supply for twelve days about us, what would we not be able to do? We could rout the fiercest tribe on the frontier, without difficulty. We could march about fifteen or twenty miles a day, and more than that, if necessary. We could do wonders, indeed."

"I am afraid we shall never discover that," Lisle said. "The German soldiers do indeed carry condensed meat in sausages, and can take three or four days' supplies with them; but we have not yet discovered anything like food of which men could carry twelve days' supply. We may some day be able to do it but, even if it weighed but a pound a day, it would add heavily to the load to be carried."

"No one would mind that," Pertusal said. "Think what a comfort it would be, if we could make our breakfast before starting, eat a little in the middle of the day, and be sure of supper directly we got into camp; instead of having to wait hours and hours, and perhaps till the next morning, before the baggage train arrived. I would willingly carry double my present load, if I felt sure that I would gain that advantage. I know that the officers have tins of condensed milk, one of which can make more than a gallon; and that they carry cocoa, and other things, of which a little goes a long way. Now, if they could condense rice and ghee like that, we should be able to carry all that is

53

necessary with us for twelve days. Mutton we could always get on a campaign, for the enemy's flocks are at our disposal; and it must be a bare place, indeed, where we could not find enough meat to keep us going. It is against our religion to eat beef, but few of us would hesitate to do so, on a campaign; and oxen are even more common than sheep.

"It is very little baggage we should have to take with us, then. Twenty ponies would carry sufficient for the regiment; and if government did but buy us good mules, we could always rely upon getting them into camp before dark. See what an advantage that would be! Ten men would do for the escort; whereas, at present, a hundred is not sufficient."

"Well, I wish it could be so," Lisle said. "But although some articles of food might be compressed, I don't think we should ever be able to compress rice or ghee. A handful of rice, when it is boiled, makes enough for a meal; and I don't imagine that it could possibly be condensed more than that."

"Well, it is getting late, and we march at daylight. Fortunately we have not to undress, but have only to turn in as we are."

CHAPTER 4: IN THE PASSES

The march after leaving Dahimol was a short one. Here they were met by the governor of the upper parts of the valley, and he gave them very useful details of the state of parties in Chitral, and of the roads they would have to follow. He accompanied the force on the next day's march, and billeted all the troops in the villages; for which they were thankful enough, for they were now getting pretty high up in the hills, and the nights were decidedly cold.

They were now crossing a serious pass, and had reached the snow line; and the troops put on the goggles they had brought with them to protect their eyes from the dazzling glare of the snow. At two o'clock they reached the post at Ghizr, which was held by a body of Kashmir sappers and miners. The place had been fortified, and surrounded by a strong zereba. The troops were billeted in the neighbouring houses, and they halted for a day, in order to allow the second detachment of the Pioneers and the guns to come up. Here, also, they were joined by a hundred men of the native levies.

When they prepared for the start, the next morning, they found that a hundred of the coolies had bolted during the night. Two officers were despatched to find and fetch them back. Fifty were fortunately discovered, in a village not far off, and with these and some country ponies the force started. They passed up the valley and came upon a narrow plain. Here the snow was waist deep, and the men were forced to move in single file, the leaders changing places every hundred yards or so.

At last they came to a stop. The gun mules sank to their girths in the snow and, even then, were unable to obtain a footing. Men were sent out to try the depth of the snow on both sides of the valley, but they found no improvement. Obviously it was absolutely impossible for the mules and ponies to get farther over the snow, in its present state. It was already three o'clock in the afternoon, and only eight miles had been covered. The force therefore retired to the last village in the valley. Two hundred Pioneers under Borradaile, the sappers, and the Hunza levies were left here, with all the coolie transport.

Borradaile's orders were to force his way across the pass, next day; and entrench himself at Laspur, the first village on the other side. He was then to send back the coolies, in order that the remainder of the force might follow.

With immense trouble and difficulty, the kits of the party that were to proceed were sorted out from the rest, the ammunition was divided and, at seven o'clock, the troops who were to return to Ghizr started on their cold march. They reached their destination after having been on foot some fifteen hours.

Lisle was with the advance party. They were all told off to houses in the little village. Fires were lighted and the weary men cooked their food and, huddling close together, and keeping the fires alight, slept in some sort of comfort. Next morning at daybreak they turned out and found, to their disgust, that the snow was coming down heavily, and that the difficulties would be even greater than on the previous day. Borradaile therefore sent back one of the levies, with a letter saying that it was impossible to advance; but that if the sky cleared, he would start on the following morning.

The Kashmir troops at Ghizr volunteered to go forward, and make a rush through the snow; and Stewart and his lieutenant, Gough, set out with fifty of them, taking with them half a dozen sledges that had been made out of boxes. On arriving at Tern, Stewart found fodder enough for the mules, and begged that the guns might be sent up. Borradaile had started early; and Stewart with the fifty Kashmir troops followed, staggering along dragging the guns and ammunition. The snow had ceased, but there was a bitter wind, and the glare from the newly-fallen snow was terrible.

The guns, wheels, and ammunition had been told off to different squads, who were relieved every fifty yards. In spite of the cold, the men were pouring with perspiration. At one point in the march a stream had to be crossed. This was done only with great difficulty, and the rear guard did not reach the camping ground, at the mouth of the Shandur Pass, until eleven at night; and even then the guns had to be left a mile behind. Then the weary men had to cut fuel to light fires. Many of them were too exhausted to attempt to cook food, and at once went to sleep round the fires.

Early the next morning, the Pioneers and levies started to cross the pass. The Kashmir men brought up the guns into camp but, though the distance was short, the work took them the best part of the day. The march was not more than ten miles; but Borradaile's party, though they left Langar at daylight, did not reach Laspur till seven o'clock at night. The slope over the pass was a gradual one, and it was the depth of the snow, alone, that caused so much delay. The men suffered greatly from thirst, but refused to eat the snow, having a fixed belief that, if they did so, it would bring on violent illness.

On arriving at the top of the pass, the Hunza levies skirmished ahead. So unexpected was their arrival that the inhabitants of the village were all caught and, naturally, they expressed their extreme delight at this visit, and said that they would be glad to help us in any way. They were taken at their word, and sent back to bring up the guns. Their surprise was not feigned, for the Chitralis were convinced that it would be impossible to cross the pass, and letters were found stating that the British force was lying at Ghizr.

The feat, indeed, was a splendid one. Some two hundred and fifty men, Hindoos and Mussulmans had, at the worst time of the year, brought two mountain guns, with their carriages and ammunition, across a pass which was blocked for some twenty miles by deep, soft snow; at the same time carrying their own rifles, eighty rounds of ammunition, and heavy sheepskin coats. They had slept for two nights on the snow and, from dawn till dark, had been at work to the waist at every step, suffering acutely from the blinding glare and the bitter wind. Stewart and Gough had both taken their turns in carrying the guns, and both gave their snow glasses to sepoys who were without them.

Borradaile's first step was to put the place in a state of defence, and collect supplies and coolies. In the evening the guns were brought in by the Kashmir troops, who were loudly cheered by the Pioneers.

Lisle had borne his share in the hardships and had done so bravely, making light of the difficulties and cheering his comrades by his jokes. He had escaped the thirst which had been felt by so many, and was one of those who volunteered to assist in erecting defences, on the evening of their arrival at Laspur.

At two o'clock the next day, the rest of the force came into camp. A reconnoitring party went out and, three miles ahead, came upon the campfires of the enemy. They were seen, three miles farther down the valley, engaged in building sangars; but as the force consisted of only one hundred and fifty men, it was not thought advisable to attack, and the troops consequently returned to camp.

The next day was spent in making all the arrangements for the advance. Messengers were sent out to all the villages, calling on the men to come in and make their submission. This they did, at the same time bringing in supplies and, by night, a sufficient number of native coolies had been secured to carry all the baggage, including ammunition and guns.

A native chief came in with a levy of ninety native coolies. These were found most valuable, both in the work and in obtaining information. From their knowledge of the habits of the people, they were able to discover where the natives had hidden their supplies; which was generally in the most unlikely places.

The reconnoitring party had found that, some six miles on, the snow ceased; and all looked forward with delight to the change. A small garrison of about a hundred, principally levies, were left at Laspur; with instructions to come on when the second party arrived. The main force started at nine o'clock.

At Rahman the snow was left behind. Here they learned that the enemy would certainly fight, between the next village and Mastuj. Lieutenant Beynon went on with a party of levies and gained a hill, from which he could view the whole of the enemy's position. Here he could, with the aid of his glasses, count the men in each sangar, and make out the paths leading up the cliffs from the river. When he had concluded his observations, he returned and reported to Colonel Kelly; and orders were issued for the attack, the next day.

The levies were expected to join the next morning. They were to advance with a guide, and turn out the enemy from the top of a dangerous shoot; from which they would be enabled to hurl down rocks upon the main body, as it advanced. Beynon was to start, at six, to work through the hills to the right rear of the enemy's position. The main body were to move forward at nine o'clock.

Beynon encountered enormous difficulties and, in many places, he and his men had to go on all fours to get along. He succeeded, however, in driving off the enemy; who occupied a number of sangars on the hills, and who could have greatly harassed the main body by rolling down rocks upon them.

The enemy's principal position consisted of sangars blocking the roads to the river, up to a fan-shaped alluvial piece of ground. The road led across this ground to the foot of a steep shoot, within five hundred yards of sangars on the opposite side of the river and, as it was totally devoid of any sort of shelter, it could be swept by avalanches of stones, by a few men placed on the heights for the purpose.

When the troops arrived within eight hundred yards, volley firing was opened; and the guns threw shells on the sangar on the extreme right of the enemy's position. The enemy were soon seen leaving it, and the fire was then directed on the next place, with the same result. Meanwhile Beynon had driven down those of the enemy who were posted on the hill; and general panic set in, the guns pouring shrapnel into them until they were beyond range.

The action was over in an hour after the firing of the first shot. The losses on our side were only one man severely, and three slightly wounded. After a short rest, the force again proceeded, and halted at a small village a mile and a half in advance. A ford was found, and the column again started. Presently they met a portion of the garrison who, finding the besieging force moving away, came out to see the reason.

In the meantime, the baggage column was being fiercely attacked; and an officer rode up, with the order that the 4th company were to go back to their assistance. The company was standing in reserve, eager to go forward to join in the fight and, without delay, they now went off at the double.

They were badly wanted. The baggage was struggling up the last kotal that the troops had passed, and the rear guard were engaged in a fierce fight with a great number of the enemy; some of whom were posted on a rise, while others came down so boldly that the struggle was sometimes hand to hand. When the 4th company reached the scene, they were at once scattered along the line of baggage.

For a time the enemy fell back but, seeing that the reinforcement was not a strong one, they were emboldened to attack again. Their assaults were repulsed with loss, but the column suffered severely from the fire on the heights.

"We must stop here," the officer in command said, "or we shall not get the baggage through before nightfall; and then they would have us pretty well at their mercy. The Punjabis must go up and clear the enemy off the hill, till the baggage has got through."

The Punjabis were soon gathered and, led by an English officer, they advanced up the hill at a running pace, until they came to a point so precipitous that they were sheltered from the enemy's fire. Here they were halted for a couple of minutes to gain breath, and then the order was given to climb the precipitous hill, which was some seventy feet high.

It was desperate work, for there were points so steep that the men were obliged to help each other up. Happily they were in shelter until they got to within twenty feet of its summit, the intervening distance being a steep slope. At this point they waited until the whole party had come up; and then, with a cheer, dashed up the slope.

The effect was instantaneous. The enemy, though outnumbering them by five to one, could not for a moment withstand the line of glittering bayonets; and fled precipitately, receiving volley after volley from the Pioneers. As the situation was commanded by still higher slopes, the men were at once ordered to form a breastwork, from the stones that were lying about thickly. After a quarter of an hour's severe work, this was raised to a height of three feet, which was sufficient to enable the men to lie down in safety.

By the time the work was done, the enemy were again firing heavily, at a distance of four hundred yards, their bullets pattering against the stones. The Punjabis, however, did not return the fire but, turning round, directed their attention to the enemy on the other side of the valley, who were also in considerable force.

"HE CAREFULLY AIMED AND FIRED"

"Here!" the officer said to Lisle, "do you think you can pick off that fellow in the white burnoose? He is evidently an important leader, and it is through his efforts that the enemy continues to make such fierce attacks."

"I will try, sir," Lisle replied in Punjabi; "but I take it that the range must be from nine hundred to a thousand yards, which is a long distance for a shot at a single man."

Lying down at full length, he carefully aimed and fired. The officer was watching through his field glass.

"That was a good shot," he said. "You missed the man, but you killed a fellow closely following him. Lower your back sight a trifle, and try again."

The next shot also missed, but the third was correctly aimed, and the Pathan dropped to the ground. Some of his men at once carried off his body. His fall created much dismay; and as, at that moment, the whole of the Punjabis began to pepper his followers with volley firing, they lost heart and quickly retired up the hill.

"Put up your sights to twelve hundred yards," the officer said. "You must drive them higher up, if you can; for they do us as much harm, firing from there, as they would lower down. Fire independently. Don't hurry, but take good aim.

"That was a fine shot of yours, Mutteh Ghar," he said to Lisle, by whose side he was still standing; for they had gone so far down the slope that they were sheltered from the fire behind. "But for his fall, the baggage guard would have had to fight hard, for he was evidently inciting his men to make a combined rush. His fall, however, took the steam out of them altogether. How came you to be such a good shot?"

"My father was fond of shooting," Lisle said, "and I used often to go out with him."

"Well, you benefited by his teaching, anyhow," the officer said. "I doubt if there is any man in the regiment who could have picked off that fellow, at such a distance, in three shots. That has really been the turning point of the day.

"See, the baggage is moving on again. In another hour they will be all through.

"Now, lads, turn your attention to those fellows on the hill behind. As we have not been firing at them for some time, they will probably think we are short of ammunition. Let us show them that our pouches are still pretty full! We must drive them farther away for, if we do not, we shall get it hot when we go down to join the rear guard. Begin with a volley, and then continue with independent firing, at four hundred yards."

The tribesmen were standing up against the skyline.

"Now, be careful. At this distance, everyone ought to bring down his man."

Although that was not accomplished, a number of men were seen to fall, and the rest retired out of sight. Presently heads appeared, as the more resolute crawled back to the edge of the crest; and a regular duel now ensued. Four hundred yards is a short range with a Martini rifle, and it was not long before the Punjabis proved that they were at least as good shots as the tribesmen. They had the advantage, too, of the breastwork behind which to load, and had only to lift their heads to fire; whereas the Pathans were obliged to load as they lay.

Presently the firing ceased, but the many black heads dotting the edge of the crest testified to the accurate aim of the troops. The tribesmen, seeing that their friends on the other side of the valley had withdrawn, and finding that their own fire did not avail to drive their assailants back, had at last moved off.

For half an hour the Pioneers lay, watching the progress of the baggage and, when the last animal was seen to pass, they retired, taking up their position behind the rear guard. The column arrived in camp just as night fell.

"That young Bullen can shoot," the officer who commanded the company said, that evening, as the officers gathered round their fire. "When, as I told you, we had driven off the fellows on the right of the valley, things were looking bad on the left, where a chief in a white burnoose was working up a strong force to make a rush. I put young Bullen on to pick him off. The range was about nine hundred and fifty yards. His first shot went behind the chief. I did not see where the next shot struck, but I have no doubt it was close to him. Anyhow, the third rolled him over. I call that splendid shooting, especially as it was from a height, which makes it much more difficult to judge distance.

"The chief's fall took all the pluck out of the tribesmen and, as we opened upon them in volleys, they soon went to the right about. We peppered them all the way up the hill and, as I could see from my glasses, killed a good many of them. However, it took all the fight out of them, and they made no fresh attempt to harass the column."

"The young fellow was a first-rate shot," the colonel said. "If you remember he carried off several prizes, and certainly shot better than most of us; though there were one or two of the men who were his match. You did not speak to him in English, I hope, Villiers?"

"No, no, colonel. You said that he was to go on as if we did not know him, till we reached Chitral; and of course spoke to him in Punjabi.

"One thing is certain: if he had not brought down that chief, the enemy would have been among the baggage in a minute or two; so his shot was really the turning point of the fight."

"I will make him a present of twenty rupees, in the morning," the colonel said. "That is what I should have given to any sepoy who made so useful a shot, and it will be rather fun to see how he takes it."

"You will see he will take it without winking," the major said. "He will know very well that any hesitation would be noticed, and he will take it as calmly as if he were a native."

Accordingly the next morning, as the regiment fell in, the colonel called Lisle out from the ranks.

"Mutteh Ghar," he said, "Lieutenant Villiers reports that you did great service, yesterday, in picking off the leader of the Pathans who were attacking the column from the left. Here are twenty rupees, as a token of my satisfaction."

Lisle did not hesitate for a moment, but took off his turban, and held it out for the colonel to drop the money into it; murmuring his thanks as he did so. Then he put on his turban again, saluted, and retired.

"I told you he would not hesitate, colonel," the major laughed. "The young beggar was as cool as a cucumber, and I doubt if we should catch him napping, however much we tried."

"He is a fine young fellow, major, and will make a splendid officer. I shall be disappointed, indeed, if I fail to get him a commission."

"I don't think you are likely to fail, colonel. The young fellow has really distinguished himself greatly. Even without that, the fact that he enlisted to go through the campaign, and took his share with the troops both in their fighting and their hardships, would show that he really deserved a commission; even putting aside the fact of his father's death. It would be a thousand pities if such a promising young fellow should have to waste the next three years of his life, cramming up classics and mathematics. It would be like putting a young thoroughbred into a cart."

"That is so," the colonel said; "but there is no answering for the War Office, or saying what view they may take of any given subject. However, if we get first to Chitral, as I feel sure we shall do, I suppose I shall be in high favour; and they won't like to refuse so small a request, backed as it is by the facts of the case."

At half-past five the force marched into Mastuj, and found the garrison comfortably settled there, and well fed. The fort was a square building, with a tower at each corner and at the gateway. Late in the evening the baggage came in. The enemy had made no serious attack upon the place; and Moberley, who was in command, had even been able to send a force to Buni, whence they brought off Jones and the survivors of Ross's force.

The next day a fatigue party were sent out to destroy the enemy's sangars and, on the same day, the remaining half of the Pioneers came up. The day was spent by those in the fort in examining the state of supplies; and despatching messengers to all the villages round ordering them to send in supplies, and coolies to carry the baggage.

On the morning of the 1st of April, Beynon was sent on to reconnoitre the enemy's position; and returned with the report that it was a strong one. They had got very close to it, and had a fair view of the position. Next morning the force started, the levies being ahead. It was a fine, bright morning. They crossed the river on a bridge built by the sappers.

When they reached the maidan, they found that it was a gentle, grassy slope. The levies were in advance, with two companies in the firing line, two in support, and the Kashmir company in reserve. In this order they pushed on, until they came under the fire of the sangars. Stewart brought his guns into action. After a time, the fire of the levies drove the enemy from the nearest sangar; while three of the Pioneer companies paid attention to another sangar.

Beynon was sent on, to find some way down into the valley. He found no path leading to the nullah. The drop from the edge was sheer, for some seventy feet; then came a ledge from which he thought they could scramble down to the edge of the stream, and thence to the opposite side, where he noticed a track. With this information, he went back to report to Colonel Kelly.

The sappers were brought up and, also, a reserve company of Kashmir troops. When Beynon got back to the nullah, he found the Pioneers extended along the edge, and Oldham's sappers already at work. These, aided by ropes and scaling ladders, got down to the ledge; and from this point they and Oldham slung themselves down to the bed of the stream, by the same means. A few sappers had followed, when a box of dynamite exploded with a violent detonation, and the rest of the company were called back.

Lisle happened to be stationed at the point where the descent was made, and when the explosion took place he seized the rope and, sliding down, joined the two officers and the eleven sappers who had passed. They scrambled to the opposite side, and saw that the Pioneers were moving down the nullah towards the river, while the levies were nearing the sangars. The enemy were seen bolting, and the little party opened fire upon them. The sappers were armed only with carbines, which were uncertain at so long a range; but Lisle, with his rifle, brought down an enemy at every shot.

"That is a good one," he muttered, as a mounted officer at whom he had aimed fell from his horse.

He was startled when the man behind him said:

"Hillo, young fellow, who on earth are you?

"I will tell you after it is done, sir," Lisle said. "But I hope you will keep my secret."

Some of the levies and a few Pioneers now came up, and they learned what had been the cause of the explosion. The Kashmir company had not followed and, as the sappers were at work, they had laid down cakes of dynamite at the head of the pass. One of the enemy's bullets striking these had ignited them, and the troops there were called upon to retire. The enemy, seeing our men falling back, rushed out of their sangars and opened fire; but were speedily driven in again by volleys from the Pioneers. Just then the levies showed on the ridge, and the Pioneers moved down the nullah, by a goat track they had found.

The battle was now over, and a company of Pioneers were sent ahead to the next village, while the rest of the force encamped. When all were settled down, Lisle saw Lieutenant Moberley walking along the lines of the regiment, and evidently looking for someone. Lisle hesitated a minute. If he remained quiet he might not be recognized by the officer, but in that case the latter might report what he had heard, and an investigation might be made. He therefore went forward to the officer.

"Ah!" the latter said, "you are the man I heard speak in English."

"It was very foolish, sir, but I had no idea that I should be overheard."

"Well, who are you, and how in the world is it that you are a private in the Pioneers?"

"My father was Captain Bullen, who was killed in a native raid. I remained with the regiment for a time, because there was no opportunity of my being sent home. I wanted to see the campaign, so I took the place of a sepoy who had died and, as I speak the language perfectly, it has never been suspected that I was anything but what I seem."

"Well, lad, I will keep your secret for a time, but when we get to Chitral I think it will be my duty to tell the colonel; especially as I shall report that you were with me, and behaved with the greatest coolness, accounting for at least eight of the enemy. The campaign will be over, then, for we know that the Peshawar column are also near Chitral, so that there will be no chance of further fighting.

"I don't suppose you will be sent home. You have shown yourself a man, and I have no doubt that Colonel Kelly will make some mention in his report of your conduct, and strongly recommend you for a commission. In the circumstances, I should think it would be granted."

"Thank you indeed, sir! I am very comfortable as I am."

"How old are you?

"I am nearly sixteen, sir."

"Well, it won't be necessary to report that, for the people at home would consider you too young. I am sure you deserve a commission for the pluck you showed, in taking your place as a private among the natives. Your knowledge of the language, too, will be an argument in your favour.

"How was it that you joined our little party?"

"I acted on the impulse of the moment. I happened to be at the spot when your party were going down, and I saw that you would soon be in the thick of it, while we were only firing. I was just thinking about it, when there was a great burst of flame behind me. I did not know what it was, but that decided me. I caught hold of the rope and slipped down.

"Thank you very much for your promise, sir," and, saluting, Lisle drew back to his comrades.

"What was he saying to you?" one asked.

"He was asking how it was that I came to be among his party; and when I explained how it was that I left my place, he seemed perfectly satisfied; so I don't expect I shall hear anything more about it."

On the first day's march they came upon a deserted fort, where enough grain was discovered to last the force for months. Enough flour was also found to give a shovelful to each of the coolies; who were highly gratified, for most of them were altogether without food. The remainder of the flour was distributed among the sepoys, and as much grain was taken as carriage could be found for.

The next day's march was through a cultivated country. Six more marches took them to Chitral. They met with no opposition whatever, and their greatest trouble was in crossing rivers, the bridges having been destroyed.

When within a day's march from Chitral, they met a man bearing letters from the town. It was from Mr. Robertson, saying that Sher Afzul had fled on the night of the 18th of April; and that on that night the siege was raised. It also contained a list of the casualties, to be forwarded to England; the number being a hundred and four killed and wounded, out of one thousand and seventy combatants.

The force marched in at noon, the next day; and were received with great joy by the garrison. They bivouacked round the castle and, on the following day, the Kashmir garrison came out and camped with them; rejoicing much at the change from the poisoned atmosphere of the fort. They were mere walking skeletons.

Some days later the 3rd Brigade under General Gatacre arrived, followed by General Low and the headquarter staff.

The day after their arrival at Chitral, one of Kelly's orderlies came into the line and enquired for Mutteh Ghar. A short time before, Lisle had noticed Gholam Singh leave the colonel's tent; and guessed that he had been sharply questioned, by the colonel, as to the name he had gone under in the regiment. He at once followed the orderly to the tent.

"This is a nice trick you have played us, Lisle," the colonel said, as he entered. "To think that while we all thought you on your way down to Calcutta, you were acting as a private in the regiment! It was very wrong of Gholam Singh to consent to your doing so; but I was so pleased to know that you were here that I could not bring it in my heart to blow him up as he deserved. Unquestionably, he acted from the respect and affection that he felt for your father.

"What put the idea into your head?"

"I had quite made up my mind to go with the regiment, sir; and should have come as a mule driver or a coolie, if I had not got into the ranks."

"Well, it is done and cannot be undone. Lieutenant Moberley has reported most favourably of your conduct in the last fight, and Gholam Singh says that your conduct as a private has been excellent. You have become a great favourite with the men, by the cheerfulness with which you bore the hardships of the march; and kept up the spirits of the men by your jokes and example.

"But of course, this cannot go on. You must again become one of us and, on the march down, do officer's duty. I shall not fail to report the matter, and shall recommend you for a commission. I feel sure that, as the son of Captain Bullen, and for the services you have rendered during the campaign, together with your knowledge of the language, my recommendation will be effective.

"But I don't know what we can do about clothes. We are all practically in rags, and have only the things that we stand in."

"I have brought a suit with me in my kit, sir; and as we have had no inspection of kits, since we marched, they have not been noticed."

"Very well, lad. Put them on, and come back again in an hour. I will have the other officers of the regiment here. They will, I am sure, all be heartily glad to see you again.

"I suppose that stain won't get off you, for some time?"

"I don't think it will last over a week, sir; for I have had no chance of renewing it since our last fight. It is not so dark as it was, by a good bit; and I had intended to steal away, today, and renew it."

"We are all so sun burnt, or rather so snow burnt, that you are not much darker than the rest of us. Well, then, I shall expect you in an hour. You will, of course, hand over your uniform, rifle, and accoutrements to the quartermaster sergeant."

"Yes, sir."

Lisle went back to the lines and, taking his kit, went some little distance out of camp. Here he took off his uniform and put on the clothes he had worn before starting. He folded the uniform up and placed it, with his rifle and accoutrements, in a little heap.

Then he went to the tent where Robah's master lived. He had often spoken to Robah during the march and, waiting till he could catch his eye, he beckoned to him to come to him. Robah was immensely surprised at seeing him in his civilian dress, and hurried up to him.

"I have been found out, Robah, and am to join the officers on the march down. I am at present a young gentleman at large. You see that tree up there? At the foot you will find my uniform, rifle, and accoutrements. I want you to carry them to the quartermaster sergeant, and tell him to put them in store, as Mutteh Ghar has left the regiment. Of course, the story will soon be known, but I don't wish it to get about till I have seen the colonel again. I am glad to say that he is not angry with me; and has not reprimanded Gholam Singh, very severely, for aiding me in the matter."

Robah at once started on his mission, and Lisle then went into the camp, and strolled about until it was time to repair to the colonel's tent. He found the eight officers of the regiment gathered there.

"We were not mistaken, gentlemen," the colonel said. "This young scamp, instead of going down to Calcutta, left the convoy after it had marched a mile or two. Gholam Singh was in the secret, and had furnished him with the uniform and rifle of a man who had died, the day before. He put this on and marched boldly in. The other native officers of the company were in the secret, and gave out to the men that this was a new recruit, a cousin of the man we had just lost.

"Under that title he has passed through the campaign; living with the soldiers, sharing all their hardships; and being, for a time at least, altogether unsuspected of being aught but what he appeared. Gholam Singh said that his conduct was excellent; that he was a great favourite, with the men, for the good humour with which he bore the hardships. He was with Beynon and Moberley, and showed great pluck and steadiness in picking off several of the enemy, as they fled.

"Fortunately, Moberley overheard him mutter to himself in English, and so the matter came out. Moberley promised to keep silence till we got here and, this morning, he told the whole story. Of course, we could not have poor Bullen's son remaining a private in the Pioneers, and he has joined us under the old conditions. I have given him the rank of lieutenant, and shall recommend him for a commission; which I have no doubt he will get, not only as the son of an officer who had done excellent service, but for the pluck and enterprise he has shown. His perfect knowledge of Punjabi will also, of course, count in his favour."

The officers all shook hands cordially with him, and congratulated him on the manner in which he had carried out his disguise; and he was at once made a member of the mess. Afterwards, two or three of them walked with him down to the lines of his company. The men regarded them with interest, and then burst into a loud cheer.

"That is good," the officer said. "It shows that you like him. Henceforth he will rank as one of the officers; and I hope you will all like him, in that capacity, as well as you did when he was one of yourselves."

They then walked off, leaving the company in a state of excitement.

In the afternoon, at mess, Lisle learned the whole details of the siege, which had been gathered from the officers of the garrison. On March 2nd, Mr. Robertson received information that Sher Afzul had arrived in the valley and, the next day, news came that he was, with a large following, at a small house in a ravine, about a mile and a quarter from the fort. Captain Campbell, with two hundred of the Kashmir Rifles, was sent out to make a reconnaissance. He was accompanied by Captains Townshend and Baird, and by Surgeon Captain Whitchurch and Lieutenant Gurdon. The rest were left in the bazaar, to hold the road.

The enemy, one hundred and fifty strong, were seen on the bare spur which forms the right bank of the ravine. To test whether or not they were hostile, a single shot was fired over them. They at once opened a heavy fire on the party and, at the same time, Captain Townshend became engaged with some of the enemy who were in hiding among rocks--evidently in considerable strength. It was subsequently discovered that, very shortly after Captain Campbell's party left the fort, and before hostilities began, the enemy had opened fire on the fort, and had crossed the river.

Captain Baird now advanced across the mouth of the ravine, and charged up the spur; the enemy retreating before them, firing as they went. Captain Baird fell, mortally wounded; and Lieutenant Gurdon, who had carried a message to him, was left in command. The enemy descended into the ravine and, crossing to the left bank, took Gurdon in rear.

In the meantime, affairs had not been going well with Captain Townshend's party. He had advanced within two hundred yards of the hamlet, keeping his men as well as he could under shelter, and firing in volleys. The enemy, however, kept on advancing, and overlapping his force on both flanks. They were well armed and skilful marksmen, and took shelter in such a marvellous way that there was nothing for our men to fire at, except a few puffs of smoke.

Captain Campbell then ordered a charge with the bayonet, to clear the hamlet. It was gallantly led, by Captain Townshend and two native officers. The ground being perfectly open, and the fire of the enemy being steady and continuous, the two native officers and four sepoys were killed at once.

When they got within forty yards of the village, which was concealed in a grove of trees, they found that it was a large place; with a wall, three hundred feet in length, behind which the enemy were posted in perfect cover. There was nothing for it but to retreat. Captain Campbell was, at this moment, shot in the knee; and Captain Townshend assumed the command. Captain Campbell was carried to the rear, and the force retired in alternate parties.

The retreat, however, was conducted slowly and deliberately; though the enemy, who came running out, soon overlapped the little column--some even getting behind it, while groups of fanatic swordsmen, from time to time, charged furiously down upon it. From all the hamlets they passed through, a fire was opened upon them by the Chitralis, those who were supposed to be friendly having gone over to the other side. So heavy was the fire that, at last, Townshend ordered his men to double. This they did with great steadiness; and he was able to rally them, without difficulty, at a small hamlet, where he found Mr. Robertson encouraging the men he had brought out. A message was sent to the fort for reinforcements, and Lieutenant Harley led out fifty of the Sikhs, and covered the retreat to the fort.

In the meantime Gurdon, with his detachment and Captain Baird, were still far away on the steep side of the ravine. Dr. Whitchurch, who had dressed Baird's wound, was sent to take him to the rear; and it was then that Townshend's party began to retreat and, after fierce fighting, arrived at the fort, where they found that Whitchurch had not arrived.

The doctor had with him a handful of sepoys and Kashmir Rifles, and some stretcher bearers, under the command of a native officer. Matters had developed so rapidly that, in a very short time, they were behind Townshend's retreating parties, round which the enemy were swarming; and when the retirement became a rapid retreat, they dropped farther behind. Small detached parties soon became aware of their position, and attacked them. Three men, who were carrying the stretcher, were killed by successive shots and, when the fourth was hit, the stretcher could be no longer carried; so Captain Baird was partly carried, and partly dragged along the ground.

The enemy's fire became so hot that the party were compelled to make for the river bank. They had to charge, and carry, two or three stone walls. Once they were completely surrounded, but the gallant Kashmirs charged the enemy so furiously with rifle and bayonet that, at last, they made a way through them and reached the fort, where they had been given up for lost. Thirteen men, in all, came in; but only seven of these had fought their way through with Whitchurch; the other six being fugitives, who had joined him just before he had reached the fort. Half of Whitchurch's little party were killed, and Baird had been, again, twice wounded. Whitchurch, himself, marvellously escaped without a wound. No finer action was ever performed than that by this little body.

The total casualties of the day were very heavy. Of the hundred and fifty men actually engaged, twenty non-commissioned officers and men were killed, and twenty-eight wounded. Of the officers, Captain Campbell was badly wounded, and Captain Baird died on the following morning. The two native officers were killed.

The enemy's strength was computed to be from a thousand to twelve hundred men. Of these, five hundred were Umra Khan's men, who were armed with Martinis. Many of the others carried Sniders.

The whole of the Chitralis had now joined Sher Afzul, most of them doubtless being forced to do so, by fear of the consequences that would ensue should they refuse. The little fort thus stood isolated, in the midst of a powerful enemy and a hostile population. The villages stood on higher ground than the fort and, from all of them, a constant fusillade was kept up on the garrison, while they were engaged in the difficult work of putting the fort into a better condition of defence.

The first thing to be done was, of course, to take stock of the stores; and the next to estimate how many days it would last. Everyone was put upon half rations, and it was calculated that they could hold out two and a half months. It was found that they had two hundred and eighty rounds per man, besides Snider ammunition for the Kashmir Rifles, and three hundred rounds of Martini ammunition for the Sikhs.

When the fort was first occupied, it was found that there was an exposed approach to the river from the water tower, about thirty yards in width; and a covered way was at once built, going right down into the water. All through the siege this covered way was the main object of the enemy's attack; for they knew that, if they could cut off the water, they could easily reduce the garrison.

An abutment in the south wall of the fort, overlooking the garden, had been converted into a little bastion. The worst feature of the fort, however, was the large number of little buildings immediately outside the walls. These and the walls of the garden were demolished by moonlight. The stables, which were on the river face near the water tower, were loopholed; and efforts were made to loophole the basement walls of the tower, but these had to be abandoned, as there was a danger of disturbing the foundations.

Among the various ingenious plans hit upon by the besieged, one proved particularly useful. Loopholes were made in the gun tower; a wall was built up in the face of the water gate; and fireplaces were constructed by which the wood, being laid on a slab of stone, was pushed out some feet from the wall, and could be drawn into the fort when it was necessary to replenish the fire, without those attending it being exposed. These fires proved invaluable, when attacks were made upon dark nights. Projecting, as they did, seven feet from the wall, they threw it into shadow, so that the enemy could not see what to fire at; and, at the same time, they lit up the ground in front brilliantly, so that the defenders could make out their assailants, and fire with accuracy.

The fort was eighty yards in length. The walls were twenty-five feet in height, and the five towers fifty feet. It lay in a hollow in the lowest part of the valley, and was commanded on all sides by hills, on which the enemy erected numerous sangars. As, from these, the men moving about inside the fort were clearly visible to the enemy, barricades of stones had to be erected, along the sides of the yards, to afford cover to the men as they went to and from their posts.

On March 5th a letter was received from Umra Khan, stating that the British troops must leave Chitral at once, and that he would guarantee them a safe conduct. The offer was, naturally, refused. Next night the enemy, about two hundred strong, made a determined effort to fire the water tower. They brought faggots with them and, in spite of the heavy volleys poured upon them managed, under cover of the darkness, to creep into the tunnel leading to the water, and to light a large fire underneath the tower. They were, however, driven out; and three water carriers went into the tunnel, and put out the fire. They were just in time, for the flames had taken a firm hold of the wooden beams.

After this, twenty-five men were always stationed in the tower and, at night, another picket of twenty-five men were placed in the covered way leading to the water. The entrance to this, at the water side, was exposed to the enemy's fire; but a barricade of stones, with interstices to allow the water to go through, was built into the river, and formed an efficient screen to the water bearers.

On the night of the 14th, the enemy again made an attack on the water bearers, but were repulsed with loss. The water way was, indeed, a source of constant anxiety. Between it, and the trees at the northwest corner of the fort, there was a stretch of seventy yards of sandy beach; lying underneath an overhanging bank, which entirely covered it from the fire of the fort, so that the enemy were able to get right up to the water tunnel without exposing themselves.

On the 15th, Sher Afzul sent in a messenger, to say that a party of sepoys had been defeated at Reshun, and that an officer was captive in his camp. The next day a letter was received from Lieutenant Edwardes. A truce was made for three days and, afterwards, extended to six; but this came to an end on the 23rd of March, and hostilities again began.

The prospect was gloomy. The men were beginning to suffer in health from their long confinement, the paucity of their rations, and the terribly insanitary condition of the fort; and they had not heard of the approach of either Colonel Kelly's force or that under Sir Robert Low.

During the truce, a union jack had been made, and this was now hoisted on the flag tower, as a symbol of defiance. This cheered the spirits of the men and depressed those of the enemy, who began to see that the task before them was far more serious than they had hitherto supposed.

Gradually the attacks of the enemy became more feeble and, although the firing was almost continuous, it seemed as if the assailants trusted rather to famine, to reduce the fort, than to any exertion on their part. On April 6th they were very active, making two large sangars close to the main gate. Near these, and only fifty yards away from the gun tower, they were also hard at work, all day, in the summer house to the east of the fort.

The garrison, however, now received the news that a relief force had already arrived at Mastuj; in consequence of which they were saved from a further diminution of their scanty rations, which was already under discussion. The officers were comparatively well off, as they had plenty of horse flesh; but this the sepoys would not eat. The supply of ghee, which forms so prominent a part in the diet of the natives, had already given out; and the sepoys had nothing but a scanty allowance of flour to maintain life.

The news that the relief party had arrived at Mastuj greatly cheered the garrison. That relief would come, sooner or later, they had no doubt; but they had not even hoped that it could be so near. While, however, the news thus raised the spirits of the defenders, it at the same time showed their assailants that, unless they obtained a speedy success, the game would be altogether up.

Before daybreak on the morning of the 7th, a terrific fire was opened upon the walls. The enemy were evidently in great strength. In an instant everyone was at his post, and steady volleys were poured into the darkness, on the garden side of the fort, whence the chief attack seemed to be coming. Suddenly a strong light was seen near the gun tower, and it was found that the enemy had heaped faggots against the walls. These, being constructed partly of wood, gradually caught fire.

Mr. Robertson, with some of the levies, horse keepers, and servants, at once set to work to extinguish the flames; but the conflagration was too much for them. The troops in reserve were then sent to aid them. The work was dangerous and difficult, the flames raged fiercely, and the enemy kept up a tremendous fire from behind the walls of the summer house. Nevertheless the men worked their hardest, throwing down earth and water on the fire.

Many were wounded at the work. The fire was so fierce that large holes had to be knocked through the lower stories of the tower, through which to attack the flames; and it was not until ten o'clock that the efforts of the besieged were crowned with success, and all was again quiet. Nothing could have exceeded the bravery and devotion shown by the native levies, the non-combatants, officers' servants, water carriers, syces, and even the Chitralis.

Great precautions were taken to prevent similar attempts to fire any of the towers. Earth was brought up, and water stored. The water carriers slept with the great leathern bags which they carried, full; and a special fire picket was organized. When, on the evening of the 15th, the enemy again tried to fire the gun tower, they were repulsed without difficulty. On the following night a determined attack in force was made, on all sides of the fort; but was defeated with much loss.

The enemy now began to make a great noise, with drums and pipes, in the summer house. This lasted continuously for several days, and one of the natives, who was aware that the enemy had started tunnelling, guessed that this stir might possibly be made to drown the noise of the mining. Men were put on to listen and, at midnight, the sentry in the gun tower reported that he heard the noise and, next morning, the sound was distinctly audible within a few feet of the tower.

It was evident that there was no time to be lost and, at four o'clock in the afternoon, Lieutenant Harley and a hundred men issued from the fort, at the garden gate, and rushed at the summer house. It was held by forty of the enemy, who fired a volley, and fled after some sharp hand-to-hand fighting. The head of the mine was found to be in the summer house, and the tunnel was full of Chitralis.

Harley stationed his men in the summer house to repel any attack and, with five sepoys, jumped down into the mine. The Chitralis, about thirty in number, came swarming out but, after a fierce fight, they were bayoneted. The mine was then cleared, and gunpowder placed in position.

Two Chitralis, who had lain quiet at the other end of the tunnel, tried to make their escape in the turmoil. One of the sepoys fired, and must have hit a bag of gunpowder; for immediately there was a violent explosion, and the mine was blown up, from end to end. Harley was knocked over, and the Sikhs who were with him had their hair and clothes singed; but none of the party were otherwise hurt.

All this time, the sepoys in the summer house had been subject to a heavy fusillade from a breastwork, close by, and from the loopholed walls in the garden; while from all the distant sangars and hills a continuous fire was opened, the natives evidently believing that the garrison were making a last and desperate sortie.

The work done, Harley and his men hurried back to the fort, having been out of it an hour and ten minutes. Of the hundred that went out twenty-two were hit, nine mortally. In and around the summer house, thirty-five of the enemy were bayoneted, and a dozen more shot. That evening the garrison began to drive a couple of counter mines, to intercept any other mines that the enemy might attempt to make.

On the 18th the enemy were very quiet and, in the middle of the night, a man approached the fort and called out that Sher Afzul had fled, and that the relieving force was near at hand. Lieutenant Gurdon was sent out to reconnoitre, and he found that the whole place was deserted. The next afternoon, Colonel Kelly's force arrived.

CHAPTER 5: PROMOTED.

As he was not now in uniform, Lisle kept carefully out of sight when General Gatacre's force marched in, which it did very shortly after Colonel Kelly's arrival. This was probably unnecessary caution for, in addition to Mr. Robertson, there were two or three other civilians in the garrison; but he was desirous of escaping observation until General Low, who would arrive next day, should have heard of his escapade.

At mess, however, several officers of General Gatacre's force dined with the regiment; who had exerted themselves to the utmost to provide a banquet for their guests. Most of these had, at one time or other, been cantoned with the Pioneers. Two or three of the junior officers were introduced to the newcomers, among them Lisle.

"This gentleman," the colonel said, "is Mr. Lisle Bullen, son of the late Captain Bullen; who you have doubtless heard was killed, some little time ago, while storming a hill fort. He is at present acting as temporary lieutenant of my regiment."

The officers looked with some surprise at Lisle's still darkened face.

"I see you are surprised, gentlemen," the colonel said, "but there is a tale that hangs to that colour. I will relate it to you after dinner; but I may say that Bullen is not a half caste, as you might think, but of pure English blood."

At this moment dinner was announced. A temporary mess tent had been erected. It was open at the sides, and composed of many-coloured cloths. The party sat down under this. There was no cloth, and the dinner was served on a miscellaneous variety of dishes, for the most part of tin. Each guest brought his own knife, fork, and stool. It was a merry party and, after the table had been cleared, the colonel said:

"In the first place, Maneisty, you must give us the story of your doings; of which we have, at the present, heard only the barest outline."

"It is rather a long story, colonel."

"We have nothing else to talk about, here. We have seen no newspapers for a long time, and know nothing of what is going on outside; and therefore can't argue about it, or express opinions as to whether or not the government have, as usual, blundered. Therefore, the more detail you tell us, the better pleased we shall be."

"As you know, the first army corps, fourteen thousand strong, were ordered early in March to concentrate; so that when the news came that the garrison of Chitral were in serious danger, the manoeuvres were being carried out, but it was not until late in the day that the troops were able to move forward. The brigade marched to Jellala without tents, taking with them supplies sufficient for twenty days. The next morning the 2nd and 3rd Brigade went on to Dargai. The weather was cold and wet, and the roads soft.

"It had been given out that the 1st Brigade were to go by the Shakot Pass. This was only a ruse to deceive the enemy, and keep them from concentrating on the Malakand. Subsequently an officer rode up the Shakot Pass, and found it to be much more difficult than the Malakand, and more strongly fortified. Orders were sent, in the middle of the night, for the 1st Brigade to proceed at once to Dargai. Early in the morning a reconnaissance was made by General Blood, and a large body of the enemy were seen. It was evident that the passage of the pass was to be disputed.

"Starting from Dargai, the pass went through a gradually narrowing valley for about two miles; then bending to the northeast for a mile and a half, the hills on the west rising precipitously to a great height. On reaching the bend, the pass was strongly held on the west side.

"The 4th Sikhs went out on the flank. The Guides Infantry were directed to ascend the highest point of the western hill and, from this, to enfilade the enemy. It was a most arduous task, as they had to ascend the highest peak of the range, some fifteen hundred feet. Here several sangars had been erected by the enemy, who hurled down rocks and stones.

"In the meantime the main force advanced, and could make out the general position of the enemy. They occupied the whole of the crest of the western hill, having constructed numerous sangars down its side, each commanding the one below it. The greater part of their force was more than halfway down the hill, at the point where it descended precipitously into the valley. It was only at this point that the western side of the pass was held.

"Three batteries were sent up on this side. These attacked position after position on the eastern slope, and their fire was so accurate that it effectually prevented the enemy on the eastern side from concentrating.

"When the advance began, it was evident that little could be done until the Guides had secured the position they had been ordered to take. It was soon seen that they were very seriously outnumbered. The Gordon Highlanders had moved up the crest of the western hill, at the point where it touched the valley. The Scottish Borderers had hastened up the centre spur; the 60th Rifles were ordered up the slope, farther back in the line; while the Bedfordshire and 37th Dogras rounded the point on which the Gordon Highlanders began the ascent and, turning to the left, climbed the hill from the northern side. The 15th Sikhs were held in reserve.

"The brunt of the fighting fell upon the Gordon Highlanders and the Borderers. Making as they did a direct attack, they met with a sturdy resistance. Several of the sangars were carried by hand-to-hand fighting; indeed, had the advance not been so well covered by the fire of our guns, it is doubtful whether the position could have been captured.

"It was one of the finest scenes I ever saw. The hillside was literally covered with fire. We could see the two Scotch regiments pushing on, and attacking the sangars by rushes; while above them the shells from the guns and fire from the Maxims prevented the holders of the upper sangars from coming down to the assistance of those below. The moment the attacking troops reached the top, the enemy fled down the western slopes. The action began at 8:30 A.M., and concluded at 2 P.M. The enemy's loss was admitted, by themselves, to be about five hundred; ours was only eleven killed, and eight officers and thirty-nine men wounded.

"The 1st Brigade remained at the top of the pass, while its baggage mules moved up. The path was so bad that only a few mules reached the top that night. It was afterwards found that, if we had taken the path, we should have suffered most severely; as it was discovered that the walls of the sangars had been perforated with lateral slits, commanding every turn.

"On the following day the 1st Brigade descended into the Swat Valley. Its place on the pass was taken by the 2nd. As soon as the 1st Brigade got free of the pass, they were fired upon by the enemy, who had taken up a position on the Amandarra.

"The mountain battery was at once brought into action, and began shelling the sangars. Under its cover the Bedfordshires moved forward, and drove the enemy from their position. Here they fought with extreme obstinacy. The 37th Dogras carried a spur to the left, and sent back news that a great body of the enemy were advancing. A squadron of the Guides cavalry charged them, killing about thirty, and putting the rest to flight.

"The transport was now being gradually pushed up, and the brigade encamped at Khar, at half-past seven. As the enemy were in great force on the surrounding hills, a night attack was expected, and the troops lay down with fixed bayonets.

"The capture of these passes spread great consternation through the Swat valleys, as the tribes had always believed that they were impregnable, and boasted that an enemy had never entered their territory. They had fought with desperate bravery to defeat us; although we had no quarrel with them, and merely wished to get through their country to reach Chitral. Curiously enough, they had a strong belief in our magnanimity, and several of their wounded actually came into camp to be attended to by our surgeons.

"On the 5th of April the 1st Brigade remained all day in camp, the 2nd Brigade going on seven or eight miles farther. Early on the morning of the 7th, a party went down the river to make a bridge. A heavy fire was opened upon them, and the whole of the 2nd Brigade and the 15th Sikhs from the 1st Brigade went out in support.

"While the 11th Bengal Lancers were searching for a ford, they came under a heavy fire from a village at the foot of a knoll, 600 yards from the river. A mountain battery quickly silenced this fire, and two squadrons of Bengal Lancers and one of the Guides, crossing the ford, pursued the enemy five or six miles, and cut off about a hundred of them. Opposite the village they discovered another ford, where two could pass at once and, the next day, the rest of the brigade followed them. The people of the Swat Valley speedily accommodated themselves to the situation, and brought in sheep, fowls, and other things for sale.

"On the 9th, headquarters joined the 2nd Brigade at Chakdara, and the 3rd Brigade encamped on the south side of the river. On the 11th the headquarters and the 2nd Brigade arrived at the Panjkora River. A bridge had to be built across this but, on the 13th, just as it was finished, a flood came down and washed it away.

"A party were sent across at daybreak to burn the villages; which had, during the night, been firing on the advance guard of the 2nd Brigade. They accomplished their work but, while engaged upon it, were attacked by a very large force. The carrying away of the bridge rendered the position extremely dangerous, and the force was ordered, by signal, to fall back upon the river; while the Brigade covered their retreat from the opposite bank. The retreating column was sorely pressed, although the Maxim guns and the mountain battery opened fire upon the enemy. Colonel Battye was mortally wounded, and so hotly did the Afridis follow up their attack that a company of the Guides fixed bayonets, and charged them.

"As, however, the enemy still persisted in their attack, the force set to work to entrench themselves. This they managed to do, with the aid of a Maxim gun of the 11th; which had crossed one of the branches of the river, and got into a position flanking the entrenchments. All night the enemy kept up a heavy fire. In the morning the force were still unable to pass. However, during the day the 4th Sikhs came across on rafts, and passed the night with them. The force was much exhausted, for they had been more than forty-eight hours without a meal.

"Working day and night, in forty-eight hours another bridge was constructed, on the suspension system, with telegraph wires. Until it was finished, communication was maintained with the other bank by means of a skin raft, handled by two active boatmen.

"We had only one more fight, and that was a slight one. Then the news reached us that the position of Chitral was serious, and General Gatacre was hurried forward with our force."

"You had some tough fighting," the colonel said, "but the number of your casualties would seem to show that ours was the stiffer task. At the same time we must admit that, if you hadn't been detained for six or seven days at that river, you would have beaten us in the race."

"Yes, we were all mad, as you may well imagine, at being detained so long there. Our only hope was that your small force would not be able to fight its way through, until our advance took the spirit out of the natives. Certainly they fought very pluckily, in their attacks upon the force that had crossed; and that action came very close to being a serious disaster.

"The flood that washed away our bridge upset all our calculations. I almost wonder that the natives, when they found that we could not cross the river, did not hurry up to the assistance of the force that was opposing you. If they had done so, it would have been very awkward."

"It would have gone very hard with us, for they are splendid skirmishers and, if we had not had guns with us to effectually prevent them from concentrating anywhere, and had had to depend upon rifle fire alone, I have some doubts whether our little force would have been able to make its way through the defiles."

"Well, it has been a good undertaking, altogether; and I hope that the punishment that has been inflicted will keep the tribes quiet for some years."

"They will probably be quiet," the officer said, "till trouble breaks out in some other quarter, and then they will be swarming out like bees."

"It is their nature to be troublesome," the colonel said. "They are born fighters, and there is no doubt that the fact that most of them have got rifles has puffed them up with the idea that, while they could before hold their passes against all intruders, it would be now quite impossible for us to force our way in, when they could pick us off at twelve hundred paces.

"I wish we could get hold of some of the rascally traders who supply them with rifles of this kind. I would hang them without mercy. Of course, a few of the rifles have been stolen; but that would not account in any way for the numbers they have in their hands. A law ought to be passed, making it punishable by death for any trader to sell a musket to a native; not only on the frontier, but throughout India. The custom-house officers should be forced to search for them in every ship that arrives; the arms and ammunition should be confiscated; and the people to whom they are consigned should be fined ten pounds on every rifle, unless it could be proved that the consignment was made to some of the native princes, who had desired them for the troops raised as subsidiary forces to our own."

The colonel then related Lisle's story in the campaign, which created unbounded surprise among the guests.

"It was a marvellous undertaking for a young fellow to plan and carry out," one of them said. "There are few men who could have kept up the character; fewer still who would have attempted it, even to take part in a campaign. I am sure, colonel, that we all hope your application for a commission for him will be granted; for he certainly deserves it, if ever a fellow did."

There was a general murmur of assent and, shortly afterwards, the meeting broke up; for it was already a very late hour.

The rest of the campaign was uneventful. Lisle speedily fell back into the life he had led before the campaign began, except that he now acted as an officer. He already knew so much of the work that he had no difficulty, whatever, in picking up the rest of his duties. He was greatly pleased that the colonel said nothing more to Gholam Singh, and the native officers of his company and, by the time the regiment marched back to Peshawar, he was as efficient as other officers of his rank.

He had, after his father's death, written down to his agents at Calcutta; and had received a thousand rupees of the sum standing to his account, in their hands. He was therefore able to pay his share of the mess expenses; which were indeed very small for, with the exception of fowls and milk, it was impossible to buy anything to add to the rations given to them.

The march down was a pleasant one. There was no longer any occasion for speed. The snow had melted in the passes, the men were in high spirits at the success that had attended their advance, and the fact that they had been the first to arrive to the rescue of the garrison of Chitral.

A month after they reached Peshawar, Lisle was sent for by Colonel Kelly.

"I am pleased, indeed, to be able to inform you that my urgent recommendation of you has received attention, and that you have been gazetted as lieutenant, dating from the day of our arrival at Chitral. I congratulate you most heartily."

"I am indeed most delighted, sir. I certainly owe my promotion entirely to your kindness."

"Certainly not, Lisle; you well deserve it. I am sorry to say that you will have to leave us; for you are gazetted to the 103rd Punjabi Regiment, who are stationed at Rawalpindi."

"I am sorry indeed to hear that, sir; though of course, I could hardly have expected to remain with you. I shall be awfully sorry to leave. You have all been so kind to me, and I have known you all so long. Still, it is splendid that I have got my commission. I might have waited three or four years, in England; and then been spun at the examination."

Lisle marched down with the regiment to Peshawar. Here he had his uniforms made, laid in a stock of requisites, and then, after a hearty farewell from his friends, proceeded to join his regiment, which was lying at Rawalpindi. He took with him Robah, whom the major relinquished in his favour.

On his arrival at the station, he at once reported himself to the colonel.

"Ah! I saw your name in the gazette, a short time since. You must have lost no time in coming out from England."

"I was in India when I was gazetted, sir."

"Well, I am glad that you have joined so speedily; for I am short of officers, at present. There is a spare tent, which my orderly will show you. We shall have tiffin in half an hour, when I can introduce you to the other officers."

When Lisle entered the mess tent, he was introduced to the other officers, one of whom asked him when he had arrived from England.

"I have never been to England. I was born out here. My father was a captain in the 32nd Punjabis, and was killed in an attack on a hill fort. That was some months ago, and I remained with the regiment, whose quarters had always been my home, until there should be an opportunity for my being sent down to Calcutta."

"Well, it is very decent of the War Office to give you a commission; though, of course, it is the right thing to do--but it is not often that they do the right thing. Your regiment did some sharp fighting on their way up to Chitral, but of course you saw nothing of that."

"Yes; I accompanied the regiment."

"The deuce you did!" the colonel said. "I wonder you managed to get up with it, or that Colonel Kelly gave you leave. I certainly should not, myself, have dreamed of taking a civilian with me on such an expedition."

Lisle nodded.

"The colonel did not give me leave, sir. With the aid of one of the native officers, with whom my father was a favourite, I obtained a native uniform; and went through the campaign as a private."

The officers all looked upon him with astonishment.

"Do you mean to say that you cooked with them, fought with them, and lived with them, as one of themselves?"

"That was so, sir; and it was only at the last fight that the truth came out, for then one of the officers heard me make a remark to myself, in English. Fortunately, the native officers gave a very good account of my conduct. I was one of a small party that descended a cliff with ropes, and did a good deal towards driving the Chitralis out of their position."

"But how was it that you were not recognized by the soldiers?"

"I speak the language as well as I speak my own," Lisle said quietly. "Having lived with the regiment all my life, I learned to speak it like a native."

"Well," the colonel said, "it was a plucky thing for you to do. The idea of disguising yourself in that way was a very happy one; but not many officers would like to go through such a campaign as a private in the Pioneers, or any other Indian regiment.

"Well, I congratulate myself in having acquired an officer who must, at any rate, understand a great deal of his work, and who can talk to the men in their own language; instead of, as I expected, a raw lad.

"How old are you, Mr. Bullen? You look very young."

"I am only a little past sixteen," Lisle said, with a laugh; "but I don't suppose the War Office knew that. Colonel Kelly was kind enough to send in a strong recommendation on my behalf; stating, I believe, the fact, that I had disguised myself as a private in order to go to Chitral with the regiment, and that, as he was pleased to say, I distinguished myself. He at once appointed me, temporarily, as an officer; and as such I remained with the corps, until their return to Peshawar. He also, of course, mentioned the fact that I am the son of Captain Bullen, who lost his life in bravely attacking a hill fort. I don't think he thought it necessary to mention my age."

"Well, you have certainly managed very cleverly, Mr. Bullen. I am sure you will be an acquisition to the regiment. I think we can say safely that you are the youngest officer in the service.

"Gentlemen, will you drink to the health of our new comrade, who has already shown that he is of the right sort, and of whom we may be proud?"

The next day the colonel received a letter from Colonel Kelly. It ought to have arrived before Lisle himself, but had been delayed by the post. It spoke in very high terms of his conduct, and then said that he was a general favourite in the regiment, and that he was sure that he would do credit to the corps he had joined.

The next year and a half passed quietly. Lisle was soon as much liked, in his new regiment, as he had been by the Pioneers. The men would have done anything for him, for he was always ready to chat with them, to enter into their little grievances, and to do many a kind action.

CHAPTER 6: UNFAIR PLAY.

Five or six of the officers were married men, and had their wives with them. These, when they learned that the young subaltern had disguised himself, and enlisted in the Pioneers in order to go up with them to the front, took a lively interest in him, and made quite a pet of him. Two other regiments were at the station at the time and, consequently, there was a good deal of gaiety in the way of lawn tennis and croquet parties, small dinners and dances and, after mess, billiards and whist. Lisle soon became an expert in the former games, but he never touched either a billiard cue or a card, though he was an interested spectator when others were playing.

Baccarat was very popular with the faster set. At this game play sometimes ran high, and there was a captain in one of the other regiments who scarcely ever sat down without winning. At the beginning of the evening, when play was low, he generally lost; but was certain to get back his losings, and sometimes a considerable sum over, as the stakes rose higher. One of the lieutenants who was a chum of Lisle's was particularly unlucky. He was of an excitable disposition, and played high as the evening went on. Lisle noticed that he often paid in chits, instead of money. This was not an unusual custom, as officers are often short of cash, and settle up when they receive their month's pay. Lisle frequently remonstrated with his friend on the folly of his proceedings, and the young fellow declared that he would retire from the table, if luck went against him. But the mania was too strong for him.

"It is extraordinary what bad luck I have," he said, one day. "I almost always win at the beginning of the evening; and then, when I get thoroughly set, my winnings are swept away."

"Why don't you get up when you are a winner?"

"That would be very bad form, Bullen; a fellow who did that would be considered a cad."

"I should strongly advise you to give it up, altogether."

Lisle observed with regret that his friend's spirits fell, and that he became moody and irritable. One day, when he went into his quarters, he found him sitting with a look of misery upon his face.

"What is it, Gordon?" he asked. "I hope I am not in the way?"

"Well, it has come to this," the young officer said. "I am at the end of my tether. I shall have to leave the regiment."

"Nonsense!" Lisle replied.

"It is true. I owe a lot of money to that fellow Sanders. He has bought up all my chits, and this is a note from him, saying that he has waited two or three months, but must now request me to pay up without further delay. Besides my pay, I have only eighteen hundred pounds, that was left me by an old aunt; but that will barely cover what I owe. Of course I can hold on on my pay; but the loss of so much money will make a lot of difference, and I fear I shall have to transfer. It is hard lines, because I am now pretty high on the list of lieutenants; and shall, of course, have to go to the bottom of the list.

"The only alternative would be to enlist in some white regiment that has lately come out. There are plenty of gentlemen in the ranks. I certainly see no other way."

"I had no idea it was so bad as that, Gordon. Surely there must be some other way out of the difficulty. I could lend you a couple of hundred pounds."

"Thank you, old fellow! But I am so deeply in debt that that would make no difference."

"I am not sure that there is not something else to be done," said Lisle. "While I sit watching the play, I can see more than the players can; and since I have noticed that Sanders persistently wins, directly the stakes get high, I have watched him very closely, and am convinced that he does not play fair. It has struck me that he withdraws the money on his cards when he sees that the dealer has a strong hand, and adds to his stake when he considers that the dealer is weak.

"Now my testimony as a youngster would go a very little way, if unsupported against his; but if you will give me a solemn promise that you will never play baccarat again, I will get two or three fellows to watch him. Then, if we can prove that he plays unfairly, of course you will be able to repudiate payment of the money he has won of you."

"Good heaven! It would be the saving of me, and I will willingly give you the promise you want. But you must surely be mistaken! Sanders certainly has had wonderful luck, but I have never heard a suggestion that he does not play fair. I only know that there is a good deal of shyness about playing with him. You see, it is a frightful thing to accuse a man of cheating."

"I admit that it is not pleasant; but if a man cheats, and is found out, it is the duty of every honest man to denounce him, if they detect him.

"Well, if you don't mind, I will take Lindsay, Holmes, and Tritton into my confidence. They all play occasionally, and you must let me mention that you are altogether in his power; and that, unless he is detected, you will have to leave the regiment. Mind, don't you watch him yourself. Play even more recklessly than usual; that will make him a bit careless."

"Well, there is a possibility that you are right, Bullen, and if you can but detect him, you will save me from frightful disgrace."

"I will try, anyhow."

Bullen sent a note to the officers he had mentioned, asking them to come to his quarters, as he particularly wished to speak to them. In a quarter of an hour they joined him.

"Well, what is up, Bullen?" Tritton said. "What do you want with us?"

"It is a serious business, Tritton. That fellow Sanders owns chits of Gordon's to the amount of fifteen hundred pounds."

An exclamation of dismay broke from his hearers.

"Good heavens!" Tritton exclaimed, "how could he possibly have lost so much as that? I know that the play has been high; but still, even with the worst luck, a man could hardly lose so much as that."

"I fancy that, after the party in the mess room has broken up, several of them used to adjourn to Sanders' quarters; and it was there that the great bulk of the money was lost."

"What a fool Gordon has been!" Lindsay said. "What a madman! Such a good fellow, too!

"Well, of course, nothing can be done. If it were only a hundred or two, the money would be subscribed at once; but fifteen hundred is utterly beyond us. What is he thinking of doing?"

"Well, he has eighteen hundred pounds, and he talked of drawing out the amount and paying up, and then exchanging into some other regiment. The question, however, is, whether he ought to pay."

The others looked up at him in surprise.

"Why, of course he must pay," Tritton said; "at least he must pay, or quit the service, a disgraced man."

"I think there is an alternative," Lisle said, "and that is why I have sent for you."

"What alternative can there be?"

"Well, you know I don't play; but I like sitting watching the game, and I am quite convinced that Sanders doesn't play fair."

"You don't say so!" Tritton said. "That is a very serious accusation to make, you know, Bullen!"

"I am perfectly aware of that, and I feel that it would be mad for me to make an unsupported accusation against Sanders. But I want you three fellows to join me in watching Sanders play. My word, unsupported, would be of no avail; but if four of us swore that we saw him cheating, there could be no doubt about the result.

"For one thing, Sanders would have to leave the army. That would be no loss to the service, for he is an overbearing brute; to say nothing of the fact that several young officers have had to leave the service, owing to their losses at play with him."

"I know of two cases," Lindsay said. "There was a very strong feeling against him, but no one suspected him of unfair play. It was he who introduced baccarat here, when his regiment first came up. It had never been played here before, and you may notice that very few of his fellow officers ever take a hand.

"Well, there will be no harm in our watching. It is a thing that one doesn't like doing but, when it comes to a fellow officer being swindled, it is clearly our duty to expose the man who is doing it."

"Very well, then, this evening two of us will take our stand behind Gordon, and the other two behind Sanders."

"But how did he cheat? It seems a fair game enough."

"He does it in this way. He puts five sovereigns under his hand. That is the limit, you know. Then he looks at his card, and pushes it out. With his hand still touching it, he watches the dealer and, if he can see by his face that his card is a good one--and you can generally tell that--he withdraws his hand with four of the sovereigns, leaving only one on the card. If, on the other hand, he thinks it is a bad one, he leaves the whole five there. He does the trick cleverly enough; but I am certain that I have, four or five times, seen him do it.

"Keep your eyes on his hand. You will see that he takes up five sovereigns from the heap before him, and that he has them in his hand when he pushes the card out. You will notice how he fixes his eye upon the dealer, and that he leaves either one or five, as I have said. He does it, at times, all through the evening, especially when Gordon is dealing; for I can tell, myself, by Gordon's face whether he has a good or a bad card. Of course, he can see it, too.

"I want you all to nod to me, when you see it done. We shall let him do it two or three times, so that we can all swear to it."

All agreed to do so, and Lisle then went to Gordon's quarter's.

"Tritton, Lindsay, and Holmes are going to watch with me tonight. I think the best thing will be for you to answer Sanders' note, and tell him that you will require time to draw your money from England to pay him; but that you will play again tonight, to see if luck turns."

That evening the four young officers took their places, as arranged. Now that their attention had been directed to it, they saw that several times Sanders, although he took up five pounds, only left one on the card; and that he kept his hand upon it, up to the last moment. Each in turn nodded to Lisle.

All noticed how intently Sanders watched the dealer. Generally he left two sovereigns on the card, apparently when the dealer had a moderate card; but when he had a very low or a very high one, the trick was played. After fully satisfying himself that he had good proofs, just as Sanders was again withdrawing his hand with four sovereigns in it, Lisle threw himself forward, jerked the hand upwards, and showed the four sovereigns lying under it.

"I accuse Captain Sanders of cheating. I have seen him do this trick half a dozen times."

Sanders shook himself free, and aimed a heavy blow at Lisle; who, however, stepped aside and, before he could repeat it, he was seized by the officers standing round. A tremendous hubbub arose, in the midst of which the colonel entered the room.

"What is all this about?" he enquired.

The din subsided at once, and two or three officers said:

"Bullen accused Captain Sanders of cheating."

"This is a very serious accusation, Bullen," the colonel said sternly, "and unless you can substantiate it, may be of very serious consequences to yourself. Will you tell me what you saw?"

Lisle related the circumstances, and how the fraud was accomplished.

"You mean to say that, by watching the dealer's eye, Captain Sanders leaves one pound or five on his card?"

"That is what I said, sir. I have seen him do it on several nights. Tonight I determined to expose him, and Tritton, Lindsay, and Holmes have been watching him with me. I was induced to do so by the fact that the man has rooked Lieutenant Gordon of something like fifteen hundred pounds, for which he holds his chits."

"Mr. Tritton, you hear what Mr. Bullen says. Have you also observed the act of cheating of which he accuses Captain Sanders?"

"Yes, sir; I have seen him do it several times this evening. I believe he has done it more, but I am prepared to swear to seven times."

The colonel looked at Lindsay, who said:

"I have seen suspicious movements eleven times, but I should not like to swear to more than four."

"And you, Mr. Holmes?"

"I can swear to five times, but I believe he did it much oftener than that."

"What have you to say, Captain Sanders?"

"I say it is a conspiracy on the part of these four young officers to ruin me. It is a lie from beginning to end."

"I am afraid, Captain Sanders, that you will find it very difficult to persuade anyone that four officers, who as far as I know have no ill feeling against you, should conspire to bring such a charge. However, I shall report the matter to your colonel, tomorrow, with a written statement from these four officers of what they saw. He will, of course, take such steps in the matter as he thinks fit."

Without a word, Sanders turned on his heel and left the room, followed by the angry glances of all who were present.

"Mr. Bullen, you have behaved with great discretion," the colonel said, "in not making a charge on your first impression, but getting three other officers to watch that man's behaviour. Tomorrow I shall hold a court of enquiry, at which the major, the adjutant, and two other officers will sit with me. You will all, of course, be called, and will have to repeat your story in full.

"Lieutenant Gordon, I am shocked to hear that an officer of my regiment should gamble to such an extent as you have done. You will, of course, be called tomorrow. I think that, at the best, you will be advised to change into another regiment. I need not say that, after this exposure, the chits that you have given to Captain Sanders become null and void.

"This room will be closed for the rest of the evening."

The officers, however, gathered in the room below, and talked the matter over. There was not a whisper of regret at the disgrace that had fallen upon Sanders. His reputation was a bad one. Since his regiment had been in India one young officer had shot himself, and three had been obliged to leave the army, and in all cases it was known that these had lost large sums to him; but the matter had been hushed up, as such scandals generally are in the army. Still, the truth had been whispered about, and it was because none of the officers in his regiment would play with him that he had come habitually to the mess of the Pioneers; by which, his own regiment having been quartered in southern India until six months previously, nothing was known of his antecedents.

"We shall all have to be very careful, when you are looking on at our play, Bullen," one said, laughing. "I hadn't given you credit for having such sharp eyes; and certainly Sanders did not, either, or he would never have tried his games on, while you were standing watching him."

"I was not playing, you see," Lisle said, "and the players do not trouble about onlookers, but keep their attention directed to the dealer. Standing there evening after evening, it was really easy to see what he was doing; for he, too, kept his attention fixed on the dealer, and paid no heed to us who were looking on. He occasionally did look up at us, but evidently he concluded that we were only innocent spectators. When my suspicions were aroused, there was really no difficulty in detecting him."

"How was it that you did not interfere before?"

"Because it was only my word against that of Sanders, and it was only after Gordon told me how much he was in debt to the man; and that the latter had, that morning, written to him calling upon him to pay up, that I saw that something must be done. So I asked Tritton, Lindsay, and Holmes to watch him closely this evening, along with me."

"Well, I hope Gordon won't have to go," the other said. "He is an awfully good fellow, though he has made an abject ass of himself."

"Don't you think, Prosser, that if we were all to sign a petition to the colonel, to ask him to overlook the matter, as Gordon has received a lesson that will certainly last his lifetime, he might do so."

"It depends upon how much the matter becomes public. Of course, there must be a court of enquiry in the other regiment; and if, as is certain, a report is sent to the commander-in-chief, Sanders will be cashiered; and I should fancy that Gordon would be called upon to resign. Of course, you four and Gordon will have to give evidence before the commission. It depends, of course, how his colonel takes it; but it is certain that Sanders will have to go, and I fear Gordon will, too. I expect our colonel will get a wigging for allowing high play; though, as you say, the greater part of the money was lost in private play, in Sanders' room.

"Anyhow, it will be a somewhat ugly thing for the regiment in general, and we shall get the nickname of 'the gamblers' throughout the army."

The next morning, at eight o'clock, the little committee met. The four young officers gave their evidence, which was put on paper in duplicate and signed by them, a copy being sent to the colonel of Sanders' regiment. In a short time that officer was seen to go into the colonel's tent and, half an hour later, he came out again and went away. A few minutes after he had left, the four officers were summoned.

"I hope," the colonel said, "that we have heard the last of this most unpleasant business. His colonel tells me that this morning, as soon as he turned out, Sanders called upon him and said that he had to go to England, on urgent family business; and that, on his arrival there, he should send in his papers and retire. He gave him leave to go at once, and Sanders disposed of his horse and traps, and started by the eight o'clock train for Calcutta. In these circumstances we have decided, for the credit of both regiments, that the matter shall be held over. If, as is morally certain, he leaves the army, nothing more need be said about it. Of course, if he should return, it will be brought up.

"I should say, however, that there is no chance whatever of that. I beg of you to impress upon the officers of the regiment; which, indeed, I shall myself do at mess, to make no allusion whatever, outside the regiment, to what has occurred. The less said about it, the better. If it were at all known, and got to the ears of the commander-in-chief--and you know how gossip of this kind spreads--both his colonel and myself would get a severe wigging, for not sending in a report of it. In that case a committee would be appointed to go into the whole matter and, as a result, the regiment would probably be sent to the worst possible cantonment they could find for us, and Gordon would be called upon to retire. I will therefore ask you to give me your word that the matter shall not be alluded to, outside the regiment. There is no fear of any of Sanders' regiment hearing anything about it, as none of them were present last night.

"Upon further consideration, I think that it would be better to summon all the officers of the regiment, at once, and to impress upon them the necessity for keeping silence on the matter."

Five minutes later the officers' call sounded and, when all were assembled in the anteroom, the colonel repeated to them what he had said to Lisle and his companions; and obtained an undertaking from them, individually, that they would maintain an absolute silence on the matter.

The affair greatly added to the estimation in which Lisle was held in the regiment. His quickness in detecting the swindle, and the steps he had taken to obtain proof of his suspicions, showed that he possessed other qualities besides pluck and determination.

It is to be feared that some, at least, of the married officers either did not regard the promise of silence as affecting their wives, or had told them what had taken place before they were requested to abstain from alluding to it; for three or four of the ladies made sly allusions, when talking to Lisle, which showed that they were cognizant of what had taken place.

"Well, Mr. Bullen," one of them said, "I have up till now regarded you as little more than a boy, in spite of your pluck in going up as a native soldier to Chitral. Now I shall hold you in much higher respect, and shall regard you as a young man with an exceptionally sharp eye, and exceptionally keen discernment."

"I don't think I quite understand you, Mrs. Merritt," Lisle said innocently.

"It is all very well for you to put on that air of ignorance. You don't suppose that married men can keep matters like this from their wives? I can tell you we all admire, very much, the manner in which you saved Lieutenant Gordon from having to leave the service. He is a favourite with us all and, though he seems to have made a great fool of himself, we should all be sorry if he had had to leave us."

"Well, you see, Mrs. Merritt, I am not a married man--"

"I should think not," the lady laughed.

"And do not know how much married men feel themselves bound to keep secrets from their wives; and I can therefore neither confess nor deny that I took any part in the incident to which you are referring."

"You silly boy! Don't you see that I know all about it, and that it is ridiculous for you to pretend to misunderstand me?"

"I do not pretend, Mrs. Merritt. I only know that I have given my promise that I will keep absolute silence on the matter, and that no exception was made as to the ladies of the regiment. That, of course, lies between them and their husbands."

"Well, whether that is so or not, Mr. Bullen, I can tell you that the affair has very greatly raised you in our esteem. We all liked you before; but we really did regard you only as a young officer who had proved that he possessed an uncommon amount of pluck and determination. In future, we shall regard you as a gentleman who was ready to take no inconsiderable risk on behalf of a fellow officer."

"Thank you, Mrs. Merritt! I can assure you that I do not feel a bit more of a man than I did before; but I feel happy in having gained the good opinion of the ladies of the regiment."

After this, Lisle came to be regarded as the special pet of the ladies of the regiment. Among the officers he became a very general favourite, and his popularity was increased by the fact that he was not only one of the best shots, but one of their best cricketers; and several times did efficient service, by his bowling, in the matches between the regiment and the others cantoned with them.

Then came the news that the tribes had risen, that the Malakand had been attacked, that Chakdara, the fortified post on the Swat river, was invested, and that the tribes on this side of the Panjkora were in revolt. This, however, was soon followed by a report that the post had been relieved, that heavy losses had been inflicted upon the tribesmen, and that the trouble was over.

For some time the frontier had been in a state of tension. The Mullahs, or priests, had been inciting the tribesmen to insurrection; and one especially, who was called the Mad Mullah, had gone about from tribe to tribe, stirring the people up. He professed to be a successor of the great Akhund of Swat, and to have inherited his powers. He claimed to be able to work miracles. The Heavenly host were, he said, on his side.

His excited appeals, to the fanaticism which exists in every Pathan, were responded to in a marvellous manner. The villagers flew to arms. Still, it was thought and hoped that, when the first excitement caused by his appeals had died away, matters would calm down again. The hope, however, was short lived for, before long, the startling news came that the Mohmunds, a tribe whose territory lay near Peshawar, were in revolt; and that Shabkadr, a village within our frontier, had been raided and destroyed.

Within the next few days the Samana was invested, and the Khyber Pass was in the hands of the Afridis. The Peshawar movable column, of four guns, two squadrons of native horse, and the 20th Punjabi regiment, with a few companies of the Somersets, were sent out to Shabkadr. On arriving there they found that the bazaar had been burnt, and that the enemy had taken up a position facing the fort, about a mile and a half distant.

The cavalry skirted the cultivated ground between the force and the plateau, and pushed the enemy backward, with severe loss, into the low hills that skirt the border. Next morning the enemy were seen in possession of the lower hill, and the force moved out to attack them. They were found to be in great strength, numbering nearly seven thousand. Leaving a strong force to face the column, flanking parties came down concealed by the low hills.

"THEY CHARGED THE ATTACKING FORCE FROM END TO END"

The infantry retired in two sections, but the artillery came into action. The cavalry made their way up one of the ravines and, when they got within charging distance, they went at the enemy at a gallop. Taking the entire length of the plateau, about a mile and a half, they charged the attacking force from end to end; and drove them, demoralized, into the hills. The severity of the morning's fighting may be judged from the fact that sixty percent of the force engaged suffered casualties.

From that time, until it was determined to send an expedition into the Mohmund country, the force remained as a corps of observation. A force drawn chiefly from the Peshawar garrison was speedily got together and, on 11th September, had concentrated at or about Shabkadr fort; a general advance having been arranged for, on the 15th of the month.

In the meantime, more serious troubles had arisen with the Zakka-Khels. This tribe was the most powerful of the Pathans. They were at all times troublesome, and frequently made raids across the frontier, carrying off large quantities of cattle; and living, indeed, entirely upon plunder. The Zakhels and the Kukukbels had joined them, as well as several other smaller tribes. They believed that they could do this with impunity, for no Englishman had ever visited their wild country, with its tremendous gorges and passes. A large proportion of them were furnished with Martini and Lee-Metford rifles, and many of the others carried Sniders.

To operate against such formidable enemies, possessing almost impregnable positions, a large force was needed; and time was required to collect the troops. Still more, an enormous train of baggage animals would be required, and a vast amount of stores of all kinds.

It was clear that the time that would be occupied in the preparations of the campaign would be very considerable; but, while these were being made, it was determined that the expedition from Peshawar should move, at once, into the Mohmund country, and finish with that tribe before the main operation began; and that the Malakand division, and the Mohmund field force should carry out the work of punishment, in the stretch of country lying between Lalpura and the Swat River.

It was known that Chakdara was holding out, but that it was hardly pressed, and the first step was to relieve the garrison. Colonel Meiklejohn pushed forward, with a comparatively small force, and arrived at the Malakand on the 1st of August. The reinforcement that had reached that garrison had enabled them to take the offensive, and orders were issued for a strong cavalry reconnaissance to the Amandara valley, five miles away. They found the enemy in such force that the cavalry were obliged to retire, and they effected their retreat with great difficulty, under a very heavy fire. As the path was narrow, cavalry could only proceed in single file, exposed the while to the fire of the enemy.

Sir Bindon Blood arrived, that evening, to take the command. The main body were to move down the road; while a force under Colonel Goldney advanced up the hill to the right, and turned the enemy's flank. Colonel Goldney's attack was perfectly successful. The enemy were taken completely unawares, and entirely routed. The march of the main column, therefore, met with no opposition for some distance; then the enemy opened fire, from among the rocks on the hills.

A party of the Guides and the 45th Sikhs were ordered to take the position, at the point of the bayonet. The enemy, however, stuck to their position until they were bayoneted, or driven over the rocks. The 34th and 55th Sikhs stormed some sangars on the left and, pushing their way pluckily up the steep slopes, slowly gained the heights, step by step and, in spite of the hot fire and the showers of rocks and stones, drove the enemy out of their strongholds. On this the tribesmen lost heart and fled, hotly pursued by the cavalry, who cut them up in great numbers.

During the fighting at the Malakand, previous to the arrival of the relief, our casualties were one hundred and seventy-three killed and wounded, including thirteen British officers and seven natives. The siege of the small fort of Chakdara had been a severe one. The garrison consisted of two companies of the 45th Sikhs, with cavalry. On the evening of the 26th they were attacked, but repulsed their assailants with loss. Next morning Captain Wright, with a company of forty troopers, arrived from the Malakand, having run the gauntlet of large parties of the enemy. The whole of the day was spent in repelling rushes of the enemy and, for the next few days, Wright's garrison were unable to leave their posts.

On the 29th the enemy attacked the tower and endeavoured to burn it down; but were again repulsed, with heavy loss.

CHAPTER 7: TALES OF WAR.

As soon as it became evident that the Afridis were up, and that there would be stern fighting, the conversation in the mess room naturally turned on past expeditions against the wild tribesmen. Two or three of the officers had exchanged into the regiment, when their own went home. Having been two or three years on the frontier, they had many tales of hill fighting to tell; and these were eagerly listened to by all the younger officers, as they felt certain that they too would, ere long, be taking part in such struggles.

"A fine instance of defence," one of the junior captains said, "was that of Thobal in 1891. As you all know, I am a ranker, and I received my commission for that business. I was with a mere handful of men, thirty Ghoorkhas and fifty rifles of the 12th Burmah Infantry. We were commanded by Lieutenant Grant. I was with him as quartermaster sergeant, and general assistant. The Ghoorkhas had sixty rounds per man for their Martini rifles, the Burmah men one hundred and sixty rounds per man for their Sniders. They were a pretty rough lot, only twenty of them being old soldiers, the rest recruits.

"One morning we received news that Mr. Quintin with four civil officers, and an escort of seven British officers and four hundred and fifty-four Ghoorkhas, who had gone up to Manipur, had been massacred. Happily the news was exaggerated, but a treacherous attack was made upon the party, and Mr. Quintin and many others killed. Grant thought that this was probably the case, and determined to push on with his little force, in the hope of rescuing some survivors.

"The distance from Tamu to Manipur is about fifty-five miles. We started at half-past five, on the morning of the 28th. The difficulties were so great that we only moved at the rate of a mile an hour. At two in the morning we started again, and marched about ten miles; in the course of which we were occasionally fired at by the enemy. The moon rose at eleven, and the advance was continued.

"The resistance now became severe. The telegraph wires had been cut, taken down from the poles, and twisted about the road; and trees had also been felled across it. While we were endeavouring to clear away the obstacles, a heavy fire was poured into us. Small parties were therefore sent out to disperse the enemy, and this they did most successfully, capturing three guns and a good deal of ammunition.

"Pushing on, we issued, at six in the morning, on the hills. Before us was the village of Palel, which was garrisoned by two hundred Manipur soldiers. You must remember that Manipur had been a sort of subsidiary state, and had a regular army, drilled by Europeans. However, Grant attacked them at once, and drove them out with loss.

"After halting at Palel for some hours a start was made, at eleven o'clock at night; and at daybreak we came upon some villages, each house in which was standing alone in a large enclosure, surrounded by a wall, ditch, and hedge. We went at them and carried them, one by one, without any great loss to ourselves. Issuing on the other side, we came upon a plain about a thousand yards across. Beyond this was a bridge, on fire. The enemy were strongly posted in trenches and behind hedges.

"Grant decided to attack, and to try and save the bridge. He advanced across the plain with two sections of ten men each, supported by another section of the same strength. The rest of his force, consisting of forty men, he kept in reserve.

"I own that it seemed to me a desperately risky thing; for, from what we could see, we judged that the enemy were about a thousand strong. Grant himself led the party, and he put me in charge of the reserve. A very heavy fire was opened by the enemy; but Grant and his men steadily advanced, and succeeded in getting within a hundred yards of the enemy. Here I came up with him; and we dashed into the river, carried the enemy's trenches at the point of the bayonet, and hunted them out, from enclosure to enclosure, till they all drew off.

"By the side of the bridge was the village of Thobal; and as, with so small a force, it was impossible to advance against the overwhelming numbers that would meet us before we got to Manipur, fifteen miles away, Grant determined to hold Thobal; where he could, he thought, defend himself, and afford refuge to any who had escaped the massacre. As soon as the enemy had retired, we all set to work to prepare a defensive position; by setting fire to the crops, so as to prevent the enemy from creeping up unseen, and by making an abattis.

"The night passed off quietly. At six in the morning the enemy were seen advancing in force, but Lieutenant Grant sent out thirty men to the farthest wall of the village, some four hundred yards in advance of the enclosure; and their fire checked the enemy, and forced them to retire. At three in the afternoon the enemy advanced in great force, their line being over a mile long. Grant again occupied the front wall, and held his fire till the enemy reached a point which had been carefully marked as being six hundred yards away. Fire was then opened, the muskets being sighted for this known range. The tribesmen fell in great numbers, and drew back under the protection of their artillery, who now opened fire at a range of about a thousand yards. In half an hour they were completely silenced.

"They then withdrew to another hill, five hundred yards farther off but, even at this range, we got at them with our Martinis, and they soon began firing wildly. The infantry advanced several times, but were always driven back as soon as they reached the six-hundred-yards limit.

"It was now becoming dark, and the enemy were working round on our flank. We therefore fell back on the entrenched position and, though the enemy kept up a heavy fire till two in the morning, ammunition was too scanty to allow us to waste a cartridge, and no reply was made. At three we set to work to strengthen the defences, using baskets filled with earth and sacks filled with sand, as well as adding to the abattis.

"In the course of the day the enemy sent in a flag of truce, offering to allow us to retreat. This Grant refused to do, till all prisoners still in the hands of the Manipuris were delivered over to him. In order to deceive the enemy as to his strength, Grant put on a colonel's badge and uniform and, in his communications with the enemy, spoke and behaved as if he had the whole regiment under his command in the village. The enemy were undoubtedly misled, and wasted three days in negotiations.

"Then fighting recommenced and, at daybreak, the enemy made a determined attack upon the advance, with artillery. By eight o'clock they had pushed the attack home, and passed the line of walls and hedges a hundred yards from our position. The situation was growing serious when, leaving me in command, Grant went out with ten Ghoorkhas, crept along unobserved to the end of one of the walls and, turning this, made a sudden attack upon the enemy from behind. Taken wholly by surprise they fled, leaving six or seven dead behind them.

"At eleven o'clock they were again pressing hotly and, encouraged by the success of his first sortie, Grant determined to make another. This time he took me with him. With six Ghoorkhas he had driven the enemy from one hedge, when he discovered a party of about sixty men behind a wall, twenty yards distant.

"'Now, my lads,' he said, 'we have got to run the gauntlet, but you need not be afraid of their fire. Seeing us so close to them, it is sure to be wild.'

"Then, with a cheer, we dashed across the open. The enemy blazed at us, but their fire was wild and confused; and we were among them before they could reload, killing a dozen, and sending the rest to the right about, many of them wounded.

"On returning to the camp, we found that there were only fifty rounds left for the Snider rifles, and thirty rounds each for the Martinis. Strict orders were therefore given that no one was to fire till the enemy were within close range. However, there was no doubt that the fight was all taken out of them, by the spirit with which those two little sorties had been made. They kept up a steady fire till nightfall, but took good care not to show themselves; and they retired, as soon as they could do so, in the darkness.

"That was really the end of the fighting. Three days passed, and then a letter arrived from the officer in command of the expedition, ordering him to fall back to Tamu, whence a detachment had been despatched to meet him. This order had fallen into the hands of the enemy. They no doubt informed themselves of its contents, and were so utterly glad to get rid of us, without further loss, that they gladly sent it in to us. That night there was a heavy thunderstorm, with a tremendous downpour of rain, and under cover of it we withdrew quietly, and before long were met by the relieving force."

"That was a splendid resistance."

"Magnificent! You certainly earned your commission well, Towers.

"Now, Major, let us hear the story of the battle of Ahmed Kheyl, where you met the fanatics in force. I doubt whether the Afridis will fight in the same way; but they may and, at any rate, the story will be instructive."

"Well, it is seventeen years ago, now," the major said, "and I was a junior lieutenant. I was, as you all know, marching from Kandahar to Kabul under Sir Donald Stewart; and at Ahmed Kheyl, twenty-three miles south of Ghuzni, we met the Afghans in force, estimated at fifteen thousand foot and a thousand horse. For several days we had known that they were in the neighbourhood. Their cavalry scouts could be seen marching parallel to us, about eight miles away, on the right flank.

"On the 19th of April we marched at daybreak. The advance guard consisted of seven hundred rifles, seven hundred and fifty cavalry, and six guns; the main body of somewhat over a thousand rifles, three hundred and forty-nine sabres, and ten guns; then came the trains and hospitals, guarded by strong detachments on each flank; while the rear guard was fourteen hundred infantry, three hundred and sixteen cavalry, and six mountain guns. The length of the column was about six miles.

"Its head had marched about seven miles, when the cavalry in advance caught sight of the enemy, in position, three miles ahead. Preparations were made for receiving an attack and, at eight o'clock, the march was resumed. Half a squadron of Bengal Lancers were sent to cover the left front of the infantry brigade, which was now close to a range of low hills that ran parallel to the line of march for some distance, then made a bend to the east. The enemy were seen in position, covering the point of passage through the hills, and also upon the hills flanking the road by which the division would advance.

"When within a mile and a half of the enemy, two batteries moved out and took up positions to shell them in front; while the infantry deployed, the line on the left facing the enemy on the hills. The 2nd Punjab Cavalry were on the right of the guns, whose escort consisted of a squadron of 19th Bengal Lancers, and a company of Punjab Infantry.

"It was the general's intention to advance to the attack but, at nine o'clock, before his dispositions were completed, the whole crest of the hills held by the enemy seemed to be swarming with men. Scarcely had the guns opened fire, when the enemy swept down from the hills, in successive lines of swordsmen, stretching out far beyond either flank of our force. At the same time a large body of horse rode along the hills, threatening the left flank.

"As the swordsmen swept down on the infantry and guns, the Afghan horse came out of two ravines, and charged the Bengal Lancers before they could acquire sufficient speed to meet them fairly. The Lancers were forced back, disorganizing the 3rd Ghoorkhas, who composed the left battalion of the line. The colonel of the Ghoorkhas threw his men into company squares, and they stood their ground; but the Lancers could not be rallied until they had swept along almost the whole rear of the infantry.

"In the meantime the swordsmen on foot swept down with fanatical fury, and it became necessary to bring up the whole reserve into the fighting line. The two batteries of artillery on the right were now firing grape shot, at close range, into the mass of Afghans; but neither this, nor the fire of the infantry supporting them, could check the advance of the enemy. The batteries, having used up all their case shot, were compelled to retire two hundred yards; and the right of the infantry line was also forced back.

"The situation at this moment was horribly critical: both our flanks were turned, and the troops were a good deal shaken by the suddenness and fierceness of the attack. The enemy's horsemen, however, pushing round to the left flank, were checked by the firmness of the 3rd Ghoorkhas--who stood their ground bravely--and by the fire of the batteries on that flank. On the right the 2nd Punjab Cavalry charged and drove back the enemy, thus giving time for the two batteries to take up their fresh position, and again come into action.

"The infantry on the right also recovered from the confusion into which they had been temporarily thrown, and poured a withering fire into the Afghans. In the centre the 2nd Sikhs maintained, through out the fight, a steady and unyielding front. The steady and well-directed fire of the whole line, aided by the batteries, was creating terrible havoc among the enemy and, after an hour's gallant and strenuous exertion on both our flanks, their efforts began to slacken and, before long, the whole of them were in flight, leaving a thousand dead and wounded on the ground.

"It was calculated that they had at least two thousand casualties, while our own loss amounted to only one hundred and forty-one. They were not pursued, as the cavalry were required to guard the baggage."

"It was a grand fight, Major," the colonel said; "but you were at Maiwand also, were you not?"

"Yes; and it would be hard to find a greater contrast to the fight I have just described. The two British forces were attacked under almost precisely similar circumstances. One was splendidly commanded; and the other, it must be confessed, was badly led.

"There was a good deal against us. The day was in July, and terribly hot and, at every step the troops took, they found the power of the sun increasing, until the heat became intense. A solitary traveller, in such circumstances, would make but poor travelling; and of course it was vastly worse for troops, advancing heavily laden and formed in column. The 66th Foot had had tea, and a light breakfast before starting; but the native troops had had nothing to eat since the night before. One regiment, indeed, had no water; but the others had managed to fill their canteens during the halt at half-past nine.

"The brigade, at the end of the march, were again ordered to change front. The Grenadiers, which was a pivot regiment, did not slacken their pace and, consequently, the centre were greatly exhausted in trying to keep up with it, and were certainly in no condition to take part in the battle at midday.

"The whole thing was a hideous mistake. General Burrows had brought his line into such a position that behind him lay a great nullah and, during the course of the battle, the enemy were enabled to bring guns up to within five hundred yards on front and flank. It was a ghastly day. Both flanks were driven back, and the line became bent into the form of a horseshoe.

The two cavalry regiments, whose support should have been invaluable, behaved badly and, early in the fight, left the field.

"After the first line gave way, everything went badly. Some of the troops stood and died on the ground they held, others soon became a mob of fugitives. The loss, as long as they held their positions, was comparatively slight; but the grand total mounted up, during the retreat.

"It was a hideous business, and one that I do not like to recall. Men staggered along, overpowered by heat and thirst; falling, in many cases without resistance, under the sabre of the pursuing enemy. Had these fought properly, it is probable that not a single man, except the cowardly cavalry, would have reached Kandahar to tell the tale."

"Thank you, Major. You were also, I believe, in two or three dashing affairs before Maiwand?"

"Yes, Colonel. Certainly one of the most successful was that which Cavagnari, who was afterwards murdered at Kabul, made. It was not much of an affair, but it shows what can be done with dash.

"In 1877 we were making a canal, to tap the Swat river at a point where it enters British territory. Naturally, the Swat villagers on the other side of the frontier considered that the operation was a deep-laid plot for injuring them; and it was at the village of Sappri that the chief went down, with a number of desperate men, and murdered all the coolies engaged in the work. Cavagnari issued orders that the chief must pay a heavy fine, in money and cattle; and that the actual murderers must be tried for their crime. The Khan, however, took no notice of the demand.

"Forty miles southeast of Sappri was the British cantonment of Murdan, where the corps of Guides is permanently quartered. The greater portion of these were, however, absent on another expedition; and there remained available a few squadrons of cavalry, and eleven companies of infantry.

"Cavagnari kept his plans a profound secret. He did not even give the slightest hint of his intentions to their commanding officer, Captain Wigram Battye. So well, indeed, was the secret kept, that the officers were playing a game at racket when they were called upon to start. The first intimation that the men had of the movement was the serving out of ball cartridge, when the gates of the fort were closed in the evening. The old soldiers were well aware that this meant that fighting was at hand; and they gave a great shout, which was the first intimation to the officers that something was on foot. We were as glad as the men.

"Mules had been got in readiness, and the small detachment set off on its long night march. The mules were picked animals and in good condition, and were able to keep up with the men. After covering thirty-two miles in seven hours, we halted at the frontier fort of Abazai, seven miles south of Sappri.

"Beyond this point the country was impracticable for cavalry; and the force, now consisting of two hundred and twelve men, dismounted and marched forward on foot. After seven miles of severe toil, they arrived in the vicinity of the hostile village; and Captain Battye placed his men on the surrounding high ground, so as to completely command the place, and cut off all retreat. His disposition had been completed without arousing the enemy and, in a short time, day broke.

"Cavagnari immediately sent in a demand, to the Khan, to surrender the outlaws and pay the fine. The Khan refused to comply with the terms. There was a short but desperate fight, in which the Guides were victorious, the Khan and many of his leading men were killed, and the village captured. The fine was then exacted, and the troops marched back to Fort Abazai.

"This was a fine example of a punitive expedition thoroughly well managed. The movements were made with secrecy and rapidity. Horses, men, and mules were all in readiness. The cavalry were, on an emergency, prepared to perform the role of infantry; while the little party of infantry were ready to ride thirty miles, on mules, with the cavalry. In this raid the Guides covered forty-eight miles, without a halt; but the perfect success that attended the expedition is not often attained, especially when, as in this case, the force is unprovided with guns. Two or three little mountain guns make all the difference in expeditions of this kind for, though the Afridis will stand musketry fire pluckily enough, they begin to flinch as soon as guns, however small, open upon them.

"There is no more awkward business than an attack upon hill forts that are well held, for some of them are really formidable. I was present at the storming of Nilt fort, and the fight near Chillas--both of them awkward affairs--and in the fight at Malandrai. There had, for some time, been a state of hostilities between Malandrai, two miles across the border, and Rustam on our side of it. Information was received that several of the most important of the enemy's raiders, and a considerable number of cattle would, on a certain night, be at Malandrai; and it was arranged that two companies of Guides should start in the afternoon for Rustam, twenty-five miles distant, which they would reach after dark. At this place they were to take a short rest, and were then to follow the difficult tracks through the hills, and appear on a commanding spur in the rear of the village, at dawn. The frontal attack was to be made by six companies, who were to arrive before the bridge in the small hours of the morning. A squadron of Bengal cavalry were to move independently, and to cut off any of the enemy who might escape from the frontal attack.

"The turning party arrived after a march of eighteen hours, through a terribly rough country. The main body, unfortunately, miscalculated their distance and, instead of halting in the gorge leading to the village, in which it was known that pickets had been placed, they came suddenly upon the enemy's outposts. These fired a volley, killing the colonel and some of the men. The surprise, therefore, as a surprise failed; but an attack was made in the morning, the village taken, and the turning party extricated from its dangerous position. That is a good example of the difficulty of attacking a hill fort.

"Another instance is the attack upon Nilt fort. The place was one of great natural strength; the fort, which was a large one, faced the junction of three precipitous cliffs, several hundred feet high, where a great ravine runs into the Hunza river. Owing to the nature of the ground, the fort could not be seen till the force was within three hundred yards of it; and fire could not be properly opened upon it until within two hundred and fifty yards.

"The walls of the fort were of solid stone, cemented by mud, and strengthened by strong timbers. They were fourteen feet in height, and eight feet in thickness; and were surmounted by flanking towers and battlements, which afforded the defenders a perfect cover. In front of the main gate was a loopholed wall, completely hiding the gateway; and in front of this again was a very deep ditch, filled with abattis; while a broad band of abattis filled the space between the ditch, and a precipitous spur from the adjacent mountain. This spur was, unfortunately, inaccessible for guns and, though our infantry mounted it, their fire had no effect upon the enemy, sheltered as they were behind their battlements.

"It was therefore necessary to make a direct attack, and storm the fort on a front of only sixty yards. After a vain attempt to make some impression on the forts with mountain guns, the order was given to advance; and the Ghoorkhas, two hundred strong, and a company of sappers dashed forward into the ravine facing the west wall. A few of them managed to force their way into a weak point of the abattis, under a heavy fire from the fort; and worked round to a gateway. This was soon hacked down, and then they burst into the courtyard.

"Captain Aylmer, R.E., set to work to place a charge of gun cotton against the main entrenchment of the fort. After repeated failures, the fuse was lighted and the gate blown in. Captain Aylmer was severely wounded, in three places; and several of the men killed.

"So far the attack had been so astonishingly bold and quick that the main body were unaware of the success; and Colonel Duran, thinking the explosion was caused by the bursting of one of the enemy's guns, continued steadily firing at the fort. The position of the twenty men and three officers was precarious, indeed, as they were thus exposed to a heavy fire from behind, as well as in front. With splendid heroism, however, they held on to the advantage they had gained till some reinforcements came up; and then, pressing on through the shattered gate, they captured the fort.

"For a fortnight after this the force remained inactive, for no way of ascending the great ravine was known. At last, however, an enterprising sepoy discovered a way, and on the 19th of December a hundred men, under two lieutenants, were ordered to leave Nilt fort under cover of darkness, drop silently down into the bed of the ravine, and there await daylight.

"The portion of the enemy's position that had been selected for attack was on the extreme left, on the crest of a cliff which rose, without a break, fifteen hundred feet from the bed of the ravine. Another force, a hundred and thirty-five men and six British officers, with two guns, was to cover the advance of the storming party. At eight o'clock in the morning, fire was opened upon the enemy, as it was anticipated that the storming party were well up the cliff by this time; but unfortunately, after ascending the precipice halfway, they reached a point where the cliff was absolutely impracticable, and were obliged to descend again into the ravine.

"At two o'clock, having discovered a more practicable way, they ascended again, foot by foot; their commander working his way up with admirable judgment, moving from point to point, as opportunity offered, between the showers of stones. The enemy were now fully aware that the precipice was being scaled, and it was only the well-directed fire of the covering party that prevented them from issuing from their defences, and annihilating the party with rocks and boulders.

"The summit was reached at half-past eleven, and the first of the enemy's works captured. They rushed sangar after sangar, taking them in rear and driving out the enemy pell mell, killing many and capturing a large number of prisoners. At last the passage of the great ravine was gained, and the British force enabled to move forward again.

"The greatest credit was due to Lieutenant Manners-Smith; whose conduct, in storming the height in broad daylight, was simply magnificent; and the result showed the manner in which even young officers can distinguish themselves, and how the native troops will follow them, unhesitatingly, through dangers which would well appal even the bravest.

"It is possible, however, to demand too much from our troops; as was shown in the defence of Chillas. The post was held, in '93, by three hundred men of the Kashmir Maharajah's bodyguard, under the command of two British officers, Major Daniels and Lieutenant Moberley. For some time, Daniels had been warned that he might be attacked on the night of a Mohammedan feast. It was understood that this was on the 3rd of March and, when the night passed quietly, it was considered that the alarm had been a false one. During the next night, however, a determined attack was made, by about a thousand men; but was repulsed by steady volleys.

"Major Daniels then determined to take the offensive and attack the enemy, who were swarming in great numbers into a neighbouring village. At half-past three Moberley, with thirty-five men, went out to attack the village. After severe fighting, and some loss, he effected a lodgment in an outer line of houses; but being himself badly wounded, and finding the village too strongly held for a small party to make any further progress, he retired with his detachment to the fort.

"The enemy continued a heavy fire until half-past eight, when Major Daniels determined to attack them again; although their numbers were now swollen to between four thousand and five thousand men. He had with him only a hundred and forty available men, a number being required to garrison the fort. Dividing his little force, however, he attacked the village on two sides. The fight went on for two hours, during which one of the two attacking parties gained a partial footing in the village; but wounded men began to struggle back to the fort, and reported that Major Daniels and many men had been killed; and the remnants of the attacking party were brought back, by a native officer, at half-past eleven. The casualties in killed and wounded were very heavy, including the two British officers, four native officers, and forty-six rank and file. Fortunately the natives; believing, no doubt, that reinforcements would arrive, scattered to their homes without further action.

"Here was a case in which the native troops were ordered to perform what verged on the impossible. The houses in these native villages are almost always fortified; and to take a hundred and fifty men, to attack a place held by five thousand, was asking more than the best British soldiers could be expected to achieve.

"At any rate, the stories I have told you will give you some idea of the work we have before us. We may quite assume that such a force as is now being collected can be trusted to defeat the Afridis, if they venture to meet us in open fight; but if they resort solely to harassing tactics, we shall have our work cut out for us. It must be remembered, too, that the Afridis are far better fighters, more warlike, and of far better physique than the men engaged in the fights that I have been speaking of. They are splendid shots, and are almost all armed with breech-loading rifles, Sniders and Martinis. Their country is tremendously hilly and, although it is wholly unknown to us, we do know that there are ravines to be passed where a handful of men could keep an army at bay."

"I was with the Sikhim expedition, in '88," one of the captains said. "At that time I was in the Derbyshires. In this case it was the wildness of the country, rather than the stoutness of the defence of the Thibetans, that caused our difficulty. The force consisted of a mountain battery of four guns, two hundred men of our regiment, four hundred of the Bengal Infantry, and seven hundred men of the 32nd Pioneers. The men were all picked and of good physique, as it was known that the campaign would be a most arduous one. In addition to the usual entrenching tools, a hundred and twenty short swords were issued to each regiment, and fifty per cent of the followers were also supplied. These swords were to be used for clearing away jungle. The country was very rugged, and the work had to be done at the altitude of twelve thousand feet, where the mountains are mostly covered with forest trees and undergrowth.

"The base from which we started was thirty miles northeast of Darjeeling, and the first objective of the expedition was the fort of Lingtu, forty miles distant. The advance was made in two columns; the first consisting of two mountain guns, a hundred men of the Derbyshires, and three hundred of the 32nd Pioneers, which were to make for Lingtu; while the rest were to operate towards Intchi, where the Rajah of Sikhim resided, and thus prevent reinforcements from being sent to Lingtu.

"The latter column met with no opposition and, after accomplishing their work, retired. The first column came across the enemy at Jeluk, five miles short of Lingtu. Here the Thibetans had erected a strong stockade, at the top of a very steep ascent; and had barricaded the road with stone breastworks.

"The position was attacked, at seven in the morning, by a hundred men of the 32nd Pioneers; supported by seventy-eight men of my regiment. The guns had had to be left behind. The advance was slow and, owing to the dense bamboo jungle through which we had to pass, and the steepness of the road, great caution was necessary.

"When we had reached a spot within a few hundred yards of the stockade, fire was suddenly opened on the Pioneers. These, however, moved on steadily, without replying till, having worked their way close up to the stockade, they fired a volley; and then, with a loud cheer, charged with bayonets fixed. The Derbyshire detachment moved up into support, and the position was captured after a sharp struggle.

"A small turning party, under Captain Lumsden, had been detached to the left but, after proceeding a short distance, they found that the road had been cleared to where it passed round a precipice; and that it was defended by a party of the enemy, behind a stone breastwork, at ten yards' range. Captain Lumsden and several of his men were knocked over, and the party were brought to a complete stand. So thick was the jungle that they did not know what was going on, on either side; and the first intimation they received, of the capture of the fort, was the descent of a party of Derbyshires in the rear of the breastworks.

"The stockade, when it was examined, turned out to be a most formidable one; about two hundred yards long, both flanks resting on impassable precipices. It was constructed of logs laid horizontally, with a thick abattis of twelve trees.

"Next morning the advance on Lingtu was continued, in a dense mist. Information was obtained, from a prisoner, that they would have to cross a spot where there was a stone shoot, down which an avalanche of rocks could be hurled by the defenders. They therefore advanced with great caution, while a party of the Pioneers crept along the crest of the ridge, and attacked from the rear the party gathered at the head of the stone shoot. The road was steep and broken, and the partially-melted snow lay two feet deep on it. The Pioneers captured the stone shoot without loss, and then pushed on over the hills and, without firing a shot, charged straight at the fort; and burst their way through the main gate, before the astonished Thibetans had realized what was happening.

"Of course, as it was against an enemy of such poor fighting quality as the Thibetans, this little affair affords no idea of the resistance that we can expect in the Tirah; but it does show what can be accomplished by our men, in the face of immense natural difficulties."

CHAPTER 8: THE DARGAI PASS.

There was the greatest joy among the Pioneers, when they received instructions to prepare for an advance to Khusalghar. Officers and men alike were in the highest spirits, and not the least pleased was Lisle, who had begun to tire of the monotony of camp life. The mention of the place at which they were to assemble put an end to the discussion, that had long taken place, as to route to be followed. Six days' easy march along a good road would take them to Shinawari and, in three or four days more, they would get into the heart of the Tirah.

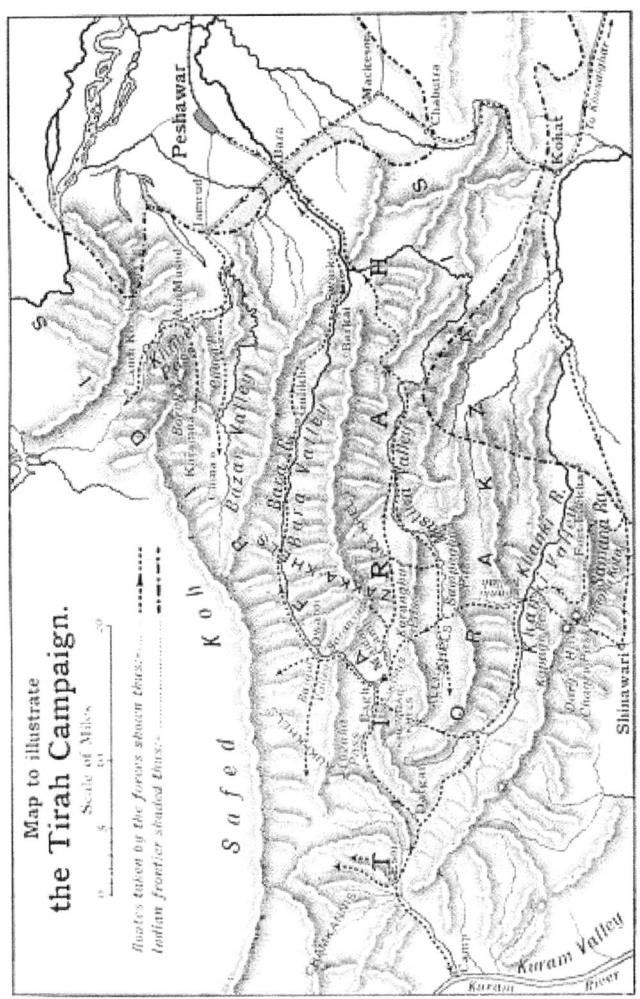

Much would depend on the conduct of the Orakzais, a powerful tribe whose country lay between Kenmora and that of the Zakka-Khels. The latter had indeed declared against us, but they were known to be very half hearted; for they felt that, lying as they did close to the British frontier, they would be sure to suffer most if we obtained the upper hand. It was hoped therefore that, after making a show of resistance, they would try to come to terms with us.

The regiment was told that it would have to provide its own carriage, and two or three days were spent in buying up all the ponies and mules in the neighbourhood. All the heavy baggage was packed up and left in store, and the regiment marched from the town in light order, with their drums and fifes playing a merry march, and the men in high spirits.

"It is worth two years in a dull cantonment, Bullen," one of the lieutenants remarked to Lisle.

"It is glorious," Lisle said, "though I expect we shall have some hard fighting; for they say that the Zakka-Khels and their allies can place fifty thousand in the fighting line and, as our column is reported to be twenty thousand strong, we shall all have our work to do. In the open they would, of course, have no chance with us but, as the fighting will be done in guerrilla fashion, from hills and precipices, our task will be no easy one. The guarding of the tremendous convoy we must take with us will, in itself, be extremely difficult."

"Yes, I expect we shall get it hot. The loss is almost sure to be heavy, but that will not prevent us from turning them out of their fastnesses."

"I wish they would let us all carry rifles, instead of swords," Lisle said. "It will be beastly having nothing to do but wave one's sword, while they are potting at us. I don't think I should mind the heaviest fire, if I could reply to it; but to be compelled to stand by idly, while the men are blazing away, would be enough to drive me mad."

"I dare say when the fighting begins, Bullen, you will soon find that there are plenty of rifles disengaged; and I don't see any reason why an officer should not pick up one of them, and take his share in firing, till he has to lead the men on to an attack."

Lisle was now nearly eighteen, of medium height, with light active figure, and likely to be able to undergo any hardships.

On their arrival at Khusalghar, they found that several regiments were already there, with an enormous amount of stores and baggage. The officers lost no time in examining the fort, that had been so nobly held by a party of Sikhs who, having for a long time held the enemy in check, had fought to the last when they burst in. One by one the noble fellows fell. One wounded man, lying on a pallet, shot three of the enemy before he was killed; and the last survivor of the little force shut himself up in a little chamber, and killed twenty of his assailants before he was overcome. Not a single man escaped, and their defence of the little fort is a splendid example of the fidelity and bravery of our Sikh soldiers.

After a few days' stay at this place, the regiment marched on to Shinawari; and here remained for some little time, until the column was made up. It was known that the Zakka-Khels and their allies had marched down and taken up their position near the Dargai hill; and that the Orakzais had, in spite of the pressure brought to bear upon them by the other tribes, determined to remain neutral. This Dargai hill must not be confused with the hill, of the same name, at which fierce fighting took place in the expedition to Chitral, two years before.

At last the welcome news came that the advance was about to take place. General Lockhart, with another column, was at Fort Lockhart, some thirty miles away; but the intermediate ground was so broken, and the force of the enemy watching him so strong, that no assistance could be obtained from him. The force assembled at Shinawari was a strong one. The King's Own Scottish Borderers, a battery of Royal Artillery, the 1st Battalion of Gordons, 1st Dorsets with a mountain battery, the Yorkshire Regiment, the Royal West Surrey, and a company of the 4th Ghoorkhas were all there. The 3rd Sikhs, with two guns, moved to the left in the Khuram Valley.

Altogether, something like fifty thousand transport animals accompanied them, with sixty thousand camp followers. The transport presented an extraordinary appearance. It included every class of bullock vehicle, lines of ill-fed camels, mules, ponies, and even tiny donkeys.

On October 17th orders were received, from General Lockhart, that the division at Shinawari was to make a reconnaissance in force towards the Khanki Valley, as the enemy had been seen moving about on the hills. A force consisting of the 3rd and 4th Brigades moved forward. The object of the reconnaissance was the summit of the hill, directly overlooking Shinawari, and over two thousand feet high. From the plain the ascent appeared to be simple but, when they started to climb, they found that it was rugged and almost impassable. There was no semblance of road, and the men had to toil up the goat paths and sheep tracks.

The Dargai ridge was from a thousand to fifteen hundred feet above the spot from which they started. On the near side it was almost a sheer precipice, and the only means of access to the top was up three steep waterways, which converged to the left of the position. It was only two hundred and fifty yards' range from the summit but, as soon as it was crossed, the steepness of the cliff afforded the assailants shelter from the enemy's fire. From this point the path zigzags up, until men in single file can reach the summit. The ridge then dips into the hollow plateau where the village lies, and then runs up two hundred feet to the cliff, making a descent of the better part of a mile. On the far side the hill slopes away to the Khanki Valley.

"We are going to begin with a sharpish climb," Lisle said to another officer. "If those fellows on the top of the cliff stick to their work, we shall have a very hot time of it."

"I expect the guns will clear them off," the other said.

"They may do that for a moment but, as we get up to the top, they will rush forward again; if they have the same pluck as the fellows I fought against, before."

As soon as the advance began, the enemy came into action; but the two batteries opened upon them, and their fire slackened somewhat. The climb was a severe one, indeed; the road became worse and worse as they advanced and, at one place, a ridge between two spurs had to be crossed with barely a foot of purchase way, and a sheer drop on both sides. When they were within two hundred yards from the summit, they had to cross an open space. The Borderers and Ghoorkhas were in front; and the latter were ordered to carry the position, while the Borderers covered their advance.

The Ghoorkhas advanced in a couple of rushes and, as they neared the summit, the enemy bolted. The Goorkhas pursued; but they did not go far, as the general, who had been with the advance guard throughout, recalled them. It was found that a village lay in the hollow of the plateau, and that sangars had been built all along the summit, and high up on the hill which covered the crest.

General Westmacott waited for two hours on the summit and, supposing that General Kempster could not make his way up, was about to withdraw his men; as large bodies of the enemy were seen, moving in a direction which threatened the left rear. As they did so, General Kempster arrived. He had experienced considerable resistance, and had lost two officers.

"That has been hard work, Lisle," his companion said, as they returned to camp.

"Yes, but the hardness consisted more in the climbing than in the fighting. I wonder we are brought back again. We shall probably have a great deal harder work, next time; for all the enemy in the Khanki Valley will no doubt be up there, waiting for us."

That evening, there was much discussion at the mess upon the expediency of evacuating the pass, when it had once been occupied. The general opinion, however, was that it was necessary.

General Lockhart was at the fort bearing his name, with a regiment of the 4th Brigade. The 2nd Battalion had remained in camp at Shinawari, and the 1st Division was still on the march to that place. It was General Lockhart's intention to divide the great force known to be in the Khanki Valley. The reconnaissance had been ordered to ascertain if a road really existed, and if it was passable for baggage. The reasons for the retirement were that a complete brigade would have been required to take the place, that the picketing of the road would have taken half a brigade, and that no commissariat arrangements had been made for the supply of a force on the plateau. Further, not a drop of water was available; and lastly, if Dargai had been held, the enemy would have massed their whole force against it; whereas, when the force withdrew, the tribesmen would be compelled to divide their force in order to watch the other road.

The conclusion arrived at, by the members of the mess, was that the retirement was probably necessary; but that the next advance would assuredly meet with much greater opposition than the first.

Three days passed; and then, at half-past four in the morning, the advance guard of General Yeatman-Biggs' column left the camp, under General Kempster, and proceeded up the Chagru Pass. It was a long, weary pull up the hill. The sappers had been working hard on the road, for the past ten days; but it was still very narrow for a whole division, and three mountain batteries. At half-past eight the force reached the summit, and the advance guard sent back news that the crest of the Dargai was held, by the enemy, in force. The enemy could be plainly made out. They had with them a black banner, which showed that they were Kambar Khels. On the far side of the opposite range could be seen great masses of tribesmen, with a dozen standards.

The 1st and 2nd Ghoorkhas, the Dorsets, and the Derbys were sent on; while the Gordons took up a position to cover the advance, with long-range volleys. As the regiments climbed up, three mountain guns massed on the Chagru Kotal; and another one, which had come in with the Northampton from Fort Lockhart, opened fire. The enemy replied, at long range, upon the advance guard of the Ghoorkhas, as they went up the centre nullah. The little Ghoorkhas came steadily on and, at six hundred yards, opened fire in volleys. This and the fire of the guns was too much for the tribesmen, who ceased to show themselves. The Dorsets had now joined the Ghoorkhas and, after a halt, again made a rush across the open to reach the cover, the Derbys firing heavily to assist them.

Until our men showed in the open, they had no knowledge in what force the position was held. Three companies of Ghoorkhas managed to reach cover beneath the cliff, but the path was strewn with the dead and dying. Captain Robinson, after getting across with his men, tried to rejoin the main body, but fell. Then the Dorsets endeavoured to join the three gallant companies of Ghoorkhas. Rush after rush was made, but the head of each melted away, as soon as the fatal spot was reached. At last, after three fruitless attempts, the helio flashed back to the general that the position was impregnable, and that further attempts would be but a useless waste of life.

Matters were looking serious. It was twelve o'clock, and the enemy still held their position. General Yeatman-Biggs realized that a check would seriously alter the course of the campaign, and he told General Kempster that the summit must be taken, at any cost. The latter started at once, taking with him the Gordons and 3rd Sikhs. It took the fresh troops the best part of an hour to climb up; and when the five regiments of infantry, the Highlanders, English, Sikhs, and Ghoorkhas, stood massed in the nullah, General Kempster helioed to the guns, asking three minutes' concentrated fire on the summit.

There were two ways to reach the cover where the company of Ghoorkhas had been lying, for three hours. The top ridge had been proved to be absolutely a death passage, but there was another path, by which General Westmacott had forced his way up, three days before, and which was shorter across the open zone of fire. A fresh regiment was to take the lead.

The colonel collected his men at the edge of the nullah, and said:

"Gordons, the general says that the position must be taken, at all costs. The Gordons are to do it!"

The signal was given, the batteries at once opened fire, and the cliff was crowned with a circle of bursting shrapnel. Then the officers of the Gordons dashed over the nullah, the pipes rolled out the charge and, with clenched teeth, the Highlanders burst into the open. The length of the exposed zone was swept with the leaden stream. The head of the upper column melted away; but a few struggled on, and others took the places of the fallen. The Sikhs, Derbys, and Ghoorkhas followed in rushes, as the firing slackened, and the cover halfway was won. A moment was allowed for breath, and then the men were up again; another terrible rush, another terrible slaughter, and the three companies of Ghoorkhas were reached.

When the enemy saw that the space was crossed, they left their sangars and streamed down the reverse slope of the hill. They could not face the men who had passed that terrible passage. Forming at the bend of the perpendicular rock, they waited till they had recovered their breath, and then proceeded up the zigzag path leading to the summit of the hill.

The fighting was over, but the loss had been great. Four officers had been killed and ten wounded, one of them mortally. The total casualties were a hundred and ninety-four killed and wounded. Of these thirty were Gordons, and the majority of the remainder were Dorsets and Ghoorkhas. Few of those who fell wounded escaped with their lives. Their comrades made desperate efforts to carry them off; but the storm of bullets, fired at so short a range, rendered it impossible; while the wounded who attempted to rise and return were riddled with bullets, as soon as they moved. When the fight was over, the whole force encamped on the Chagru Kotal.

The assailants were unable to make out why the enemy did not defend the zigzag path. Only two men could climb it abreast, and the advancing files could have been destroyed by a dozen marksmen with breech loaders. The only reasonable supposition was that, having been engaged for five hours, their ammunition was practically exhausted.

Several acts of heroism were performed in the battle. One of the pipers, Lance Corporal Milne, was shot through both legs; but still continued to play his pipes, in a sitting position. Four other pipers played right across the fatal passage, three of them being wounded. Lieutenant Tillard was the first man across. He was a fast runner, but he stopped to encourage his men, midway.

By the 25th, the whole of the two divisions were encamped on the two low hills at the mouth of the Kapagh Pass; while the stream of transport came gradually up. By that day six thousand four hundred British troops, eleven thousand two hundred and eighty native troops, seventeen thousand followers, and two thousand four hundred camels were gathered there.

In the morning a foraging party went out and, when they were returning to camp with supplies, and also with a hundred head of cattle, the enemy lined the neighbouring heights. The mountain battery came into action, and the rearmost regiment covered the retreat by volleys; but the tribesmen had all the advantage of position and, with the utmost determination, they followed. They even opened fire on the camp, causing several casualties, the total losses being over thirty.

By this time the troops were all convinced that the campaign would be a most serious one. Before them lay a country of which they were absolutely ignorant, into which no Englishman had ever penetrated; and defended by an enemy who were, for the most part, armed with first-class rifles, and were marvellous skirmishers. If the tribesmen kept to guerrilla warfare, there was no saying how long the campaign would last.

Lisle had passed through the fight unhurt. He had been almost bewildered as he crossed the fatal path, running at top speed, with men falling thickly around him. Halfway across Lieutenant Blunt, who was one of his great chums, and had joined just before him, fell. Lisle sheathed his sword and threw himself down beside him, pressing him to the ground to prevent him from moving; while he himself remained perfectly still. When the next rush of men came along, he lifted his wounded friend with great effort on to his back, and then ran on. Blunt was again twice hit; but Lisle escaped, almost by a miracle, and arrived at the foot of the precipice a minute after the last man got in. He was loudly cheered, by the men, as he did so.

He had the satisfaction of knowing that Blunt's wounds, although serious, were not considered mortal. When the regiment halted on the plateau, Lisle was warmly congratulated by the colonel and officers on the feat he had performed; but he disclaimed any particular merit.

"When Blunt fell," he said, "it was the most natural thing in the world that I should go and pick him up; and I did so almost mechanically. Luckily he was a light man but, even if he had been a heavy one, I don't think I should have felt his weight. I was scarcely conscious of the bullets whistling round me. When he fell, I knew that the tribesmen would shoot any wounded man who tried to rise, and that the only chance was to lie perfectly still, until another batch of men came along."

"You showed no end of coolness," the colonel said, "and the idea of pressing him down, and yourself lying quietly beside him showed that, in spite of confusion, your brain was clear, and that you had all your senses about you. It was a gallant action, which I shall not forget to mention when I send in my report. You deserve the V.C., but I don't suppose you will get it; so many gallant deeds were done that only a few can get the cross."

The two divisions marched on the morning of the 28th. The Northamptons and 36th Sikhs had been detached to an extremely high hill, to cover the advance. It had already been found that, although the Afridis could fight well, so long as they had the advantage of position, they were nevertheless extremely careful of their skins. After the heavy firing into camp, on the night of the return of the reconnaissance, the place had been greatly strengthened; and the positions were changed every night, a fact which so entirely surprised the enemy that, for a time, night attacks ceased altogether.

General Westmacott's brigade advanced up the Khanki nullah to the foot of the Sampagha Pass. General Gazelee's division moved along the hills, and halted at the village of Ghandaki. In the afternoon a reconnaissance pushed forward, and returned with the news that the pass appeared to be simple, and the road a good one. Tribesmen were seen upon nearly every crest. They were apparently building sangars upon the roadway.

General Gazelee was to make his attack next morning. General Westmacott, General Kempster, and General Hart, with the batteries of both divisions, were to occupy a knoll at the foot of the pass, to support the advance. The troops moved forward in the following order: the Queens, the 2nd and 4th Ghoorkhas, Yorks, and 3rd Sikhs were first; and they were followed by the 30th Sikhs, the Scottish Borderers, and the Northamptons.

In the dim light of the early morning, the distant crests were marked by the fires of the enemy. Some delay was caused by the batteries missing the tracks, but by daybreak they advanced. At half-past six the enemy fired the first shot, and then fell rapidly back. The regiments in the first line moved steadily on and, at half-past seven, the guns opened. A few shells were sufficient for the enemy's advance party, and they scuttled back. When the Ghoorkhas and Queens reached the first ridge in the pass, the enemy opened fire; but they could not stand the accurate fire of the six batteries.

A mountain battery pushed up the pass, and came into action on the enemy's first position. The pass widened out from this point, and the two leading regiments moved forward to the sloping crest of the third position. The Queens had advanced on the right, with the Ghoorkhas on their flank. The pathway was covered by the fire of the enemy, hidden behind rocks; and this was so accurate that men could hardly show themselves on the path, without being immediately shot down. The Sikhs and Borderers, however, pushed up the hill and drove the enemy out.

The defence of the pass was not so determined as had been expected, after the stand shown at Dargai. The reason, no doubt, was that though they were good skirmishers, the enemy did not care to expose themselves, either to artillery fire or close-quarter fighting. When the last crest had been gained, the force proceeded down into the Mastura Valley. The tribesmen had deserted, and set fire to, their homesteads. The villages were only a few hundred yards apart, and were well built. The valley contained many beautiful groves. There was little food in the camp, and the Ghoorkhas set to work to make chupatties, with coarse flour found in the villages.

There had been very few casualties during the day, and the men began to hope that, after the lesson taught the enemy at Dargai, no other resolute stand would be made. After a day of rest in the valley, orders were issued for the 3rd and 4th Brigades to move, at daybreak. The 2nd Brigade was to follow, the 1st being left to garrison the camp. The path was across a low ridge connecting higher ones, and offered no great facilities for resistance, and was overcome with the exchange of a few shots, only.

123

From the top of the Karanghur Pass was seen the valley of Maidan, the spot which the Afridis were wont to boast no infidel had ever gazed upon. The view was magnificent. From the foot of the slope stretched a valley, broken here and there by ravines and nullahs. Every inch of it seemed to be cultivated; and it was one wide expanse of terraced fields, sprinkled with groves and dotted with countless habitations. There was scarce an acre which had not a fortified block house, as each family built a homestead for itself, and fortified itself against all comers.

As the column entered the valley, they found that their arrival had not been expected. The livestock had been removed, but every house in the valley was stocked with supplies. Indian corn, wheat, barley, and other grain were found in abundance; and there was an ample stock of honey, potatoes, walnuts, and onions.

Bagh was the tribal centre, the Afridi parliament ground. Its mosque was situated about four miles farther up the valley. It was at this spot that orders were issued to make war upon the British. It was an insignificant building, with a mud roof supported by twenty-one pillars. The mosque was not interfered with.

It was thought that, as such little opposition was offered in the last pass, the enemy had lost all heart; but a foraging party, the next day, found the tribesmen in great force at the other end of the valley, and were compelled to retire. Another party of the enemy attempted to rush a picket of the 36th Sikhs; and a strong force pounced upon the baggage train, and killed several of the drivers; then, retiring till the main guard had passed, dashed out again and killed three of the guards, and wounded several others.

For the present, no damage was done to the homesteads; as it was hoped that the Afridis would come in and surrender. Next day a foraging party was hotly attacked and, at night, there was severe fighting round the camp. A party of elders came in, to ask what terms would be given; and were told that the tribesmen would have to deliver up their rifles, and pay a heavy fine. It was evident, from their manner, that although they would be ready to pay a fine, they would certainly not deliver up their rifles.

The troops had now settled down comfortably. They had ten days' rations in camp, and the camel convoys were coming in daily. The weather was delightful, and the nightly firing into the camp, alone, disturbed them.

A small party of foragers was, a few days later, fiercely attacked. Captain Rowcroft, who was in command, had with him only a subadar and half a dozen sepoys, when a heavy fire was opened upon him. The party could have retired, but one of the men was shot through the thigh, and it took three others to carry him. He was presently left behind, and Rowcroft went back to the body, to assure himself that the man was dead. This pause gave the enemy time to close up, and the subadar was shot, as well as the man tending him.

A mule was luckily found, and the subadar was sent to the rear. After this two men were hit, one for the second time and, as it was impossible for the four sound men to carry off their wounded, and face the enemy as well, Rowcroft chose the best spot, and determined to halt and wait for help. The Afridis could not bring themselves to rush the little party, but confined themselves to keeping up a heavy fire. Another Sikh was wounded; and the dust caused by the bullets almost blinded the others, who could scarcely see to reply. At last, just in the nick of time, a relieving party arrived and carried them off.

On the 8th General Westmacott started, with his brigade, to punish the Zakka-Khels for the continued night firing which, our commander had learned from prisoners, was kept up by that tribe. The brigade did its work thoroughly and, by evening, the whole of the eastern valley was in flames. That same evening, however, Captain Watson, a commissariat officer, was shot dead, as he stood at his own door. A curious fatality seemed to accompany this night firing. Out of the many thousands in camp, four officers only had been hit. Captain Sullivan, of the 36th Sikhs, was shot ten minutes after he had arrived in camp, having travelled post haste from England.

On the 9th a reconnaissance was ordered to Saransur, a lofty peak to the east of the Maidan valley. Across this is a pass, on one of the roads to Peshawar. General Westmacott, who was in command, took with him four regiments--two British and two Sikhs--two batteries, and a company of Madras Sappers. The foot of the hill to be scaled was less than three miles from camp, but the intervening ground was extraordinarily broken. It was, in fact, a series of hummocks from seventy to a hundred feet high; which were covered with boulders, and intersected by a river. This main nullah was also broken, on both sides, by smaller nullahs almost every hundred yards. Beyond this rugged ground there was a severe ascent. The hill had two spurs; one wooded, especially towards the summit, the other bare. The path wound up the latter, then crossed a ridge beyond, and yet another ridge behind that, with a sheer summit very like the Dargai cliff.

The force left camp at half-past seven. When they had gone about a mile, desultory shots were fired at them, from a series of well-built sangars facing the termination of the nullah. On reaching the foot of the hillside, General Westmacott was much concerned about the Dorsets on the left; who were engaged in desultory firing, and were making little progress up the nullah. Staff officer after staff officer was despatched, to direct the Dorsets to the intended line.

A little before ten the Northamptons, and Sikhs covering them in the rear, began the ascent. It was a stiff climb of a thousand feet. When the first brow was reached General Westmacott called a halt, in order that the men might get their breath and fix bayonets. Then they climbed to the next top cover, and rushed forward. The enemy evidently knew its range, and advance companies found themselves under magazine fire. Nevertheless they pushed on. An open kotal had to be passed. The men crossed it at the double and, although a heavy fire was kept up again, there was no casualty.

The advance guard was now at the foot of the sheer cliff. No news had been received of the Dorsets, who were in a very rough country, wooded almost to the summit; and the general could only hope that they were working up through this. The force pushed on and, a few minutes past eleven, the whole summit was in our possession, and the last of the visible enemy put to flight.

The intelligence officers busied themselves sketching the country. It was evident that the Saransur was the retreat of the Maidan Zakka-Khels, for all round were evidences of encampments: fire-stained walls, caves, and bags of grain. It was deserted by the tribesmen, who had been taken by surprise, and had left hurriedly. General Westmacott was anxious to be off, as it was probable that the fighting men of the enemy had merely hurried off to place their families under cover, and would return as soon as they had done so.

At two o'clock the return march began. A company of the Northamptons were placed within range of the wooded slope, which should have been covered by the Dorsets, had they come up. They were suddenly fired upon, and the men fell fast. Another company came up to help them. The enemy could not be seen, but volleys were fired into the wood. The 36th Sikhs went back to reinforce them, and the whole force were withdrawn without further casualty.

As the Northamptons were retiring across the wooded zone, the first four companies were allowed to pass unmolested; but when the fifth reached the clear ground, they were greeted with a blaze of fire. The carriage of the wounded delayed the retirement, and it was not until dusk that the foot of the hill was reached.

The enemy had taken every advantage that their knowledge of the country gave them. They had now begun to creep up the ravines, and their number increased every minute. Men were falling fast. Each man carrying a wounded comrade became a target. The Dorsets also were severely engaged. The Northamptons stuck to their work, and slowly withdrew their wounded; but the number of casualties increased alarmingly.

Then an unfortunate occurrence took place. A party of Northamptons, under Lieutenant Macintyre and Lieutenant Sergeant Luckin, turning a corner, were cut off. It appeared that they sacrificed themselves to their wounded comrades. One of the party was despatched for help, and evidently came across a small group of Dorsets. The story was, that the party were surrounded at short range when he left; for, had they left their wounded and followed him, they might have saved themselves. Next morning their bodies were found. In every case they had been wounded by bullets, before the Pathans came up and gashed them; which showed that they had fought till the last man dropped.

Lisle was not one of those who returned to camp and, in the confusion that occurred as the result of the late arrival of the troops, his absence was not discovered until the next morning. On enquiries being made, it was found that he was last seen high up in the mountains. He had been sent down, with eight men, to request the guns to direct their fire against the enemy, who were pressing the regiment during the retreat; but as he had not arrived at the guns, a strong party was at once sent out, to search for his body and those of the men with him.

Lisle had, in fact, pushed down halfway to the spot where the guns were placed, and had dismounted at the top of a nullah; when a large party of the enemy opened fire upon him. One of the sepoys at once fell dead, and another was wounded. It was impossible for him to fight his way through this force. Twilight was already falling and, owing to the rugged nature of the ground, he was by no means sure of his position.

While the men returned the enemy's fire, he looked round for some vantage ground. Fifty yards away there was a small blockhouse and, when he saw this, he at once determined to shelter in it. He and one of the men therefore lifted their wounded comrade, and Lisle shouted to the others:

"Use your magazines, and then make a rush for the hut, keeping well together."

The little party charged, meanwhile keeping up so heavy a fire, with their magazines, that the Afridis who stood between them and the house cleared off, leaving a dozen of their dead on the ground. Before they reached the block house, two more of the men were wounded but, fortunately, not severely enough to prevent them from keeping up with the others. The place was untenanted, and they rushed in and at once began to pile its contents against the door.

Lisle ordered the unwounded men to take their places at the loopholes, which served for windows in the Afridi buildings, while he himself attended to the wounds of the others. He warned the men who were firing to withdraw quickly after every shot, for the Afridis were such admirable marksmen that their bullets frequently entered the loopholes.

CHAPTER 9: CAPTURED.

When he had completed the dressing of the wounds, Lisle mounted to the upper story, which was a feature of every house in the valley. While the lower part was of stone; the upper one was built of wicker work, thickly plastered with mud, and quite useless as a protection against rifle bullets. He set to work to cut a dozen small loopholes, a few inches above the floor. From these he commanded a view all round. Then he called up the two wounded men, who were still able to use their rifles, and ordered them to lie down, one at each of the side walls; while he himself took his place over the doorway, with the rifle of the disabled man.

From here he picked off several of the enemy. His fire was returned but, as he took care to lie well back, the bullets all went over his head.

When darkness fell, he went down and directed the sepoys to man only the loopholes in the front wall. This released three men, whom he brought upstairs and posted above the door.

The Afridis continued to riddle the upper wall and the door with bullets. Several times they attempted a rush, but were unable to withstand the heavy magazine fire which met them, when within twenty yards of the house. Twice they attempted to pile faggots at the side of the door, but the defence was so strong that many of the bearers were killed, and the survivors fled.

Knowing that the Afridis were in the habit of hiding their store of grain, Lisle prodded the floor in all directions with his bayonet and, at last, found a good supply in one corner of the room. Unfortunately, however, there was only one vessel, half full of water. It would not have done to light a fire to cook the grain, as any illumination within the house would have shown the exact place of the loopholes to the enemy. Lisle therefore served out some grain to each of the soldiers, to eat raw. He gave some of the water to the three wounded men, and served out a mouthful to each of the others; telling them that they might not be relieved for some time, and that the little supply must be made to last as long as possible.

The enemy still kept up a heavy fire but, after the lessons they had received, there was but small chance that they would attempt another hand-to-hand attack. Lisle therefore told all the men to lie down and sleep, while he himself took up his place at the loophole nearest the door, and kept watch.

No attempt was made until daybreak was approaching; when, with wild yells, the Afridis again rushed forward. The men were instantly on their feet, and eight rifles flashed out.

"Magazine firing!" Lisle shouted, "but don't fire unless you see a man, and make sure of bringing him down. We must husband our ammunition."

Quietly and steadily, the men kept up their fire. This time the enemy reached the door, and Lisle was compelled to call down the two men from above. The Afridis gathered thickly round the door, tried to push it in with their heavy knives, and battered it with the butt ends of their rifles. Gradually, in spite of the fire of the defenders, they splintered it; but the barricade behind still held and, from this, the besieged poured through the broken door so galling a fire--one half emptying their magazines, and then falling back to reload while the others took their places--till at last, after suffering a loss of some thirty men, the enemy retired again, and were soon hidden in the darkness. As soon as they had gone, the garrison brought down all available material from the upper floor to strengthen the barricade.

"I don't think they will try again, lads," Lisle said.

The numbers of the besieged were, unfortunately, dwindling. One had been shot through the head, two others had been wounded, and Lisle himself had received a bullet in his shoulder. There were now but two unwounded men; but the other four were all capable of using their rifles, at a pinch. It was a relief, indeed, when day fairly broke; for then they could see their foes at a distance and, by a steady fire, force them to take to shelter. When they got into cover, the tribesmen continued to fire upon the block house; but the besieged did not reply, for they had only twenty rounds per man left.

Another mouthful of water was now served to all and, the two unwounded men having been placed in the upper story to keep watch, the others sat down under the loopholes, in readiness to leap to their feet and fire, if an alarm was given.

At length, about eleven o'clock, the fire of the enemy suddenly ceased and, a few minutes later, a relief party marched up. The men cheered lustily as the barricade was removed, and Lisle and the six men came out. The officers ran forward and warmly greeted Lisle, shaking hands with him and the men of his little party.

"Thank God we have found you alive, Bullen! We hadn't even a hope that you had survived; for we found poor Macintyre and his party, all killed and cut up. We started this morning, as soon as your absence was discovered, and have been searching ever since; but I doubt if we should ever have found you, had we not heard firing going on up here. I don't think men were ever so pleased as ours, when we heard it; for it showed that you, or some of your party, were still holding out.

"You must have had desperate fighting, for there are some forty bodies lying near the door; and we know that the enemy always carry off their dead, when they can. You must have accounted for a good many more, who have been taken away in the darkness."

"We have done our best, you may be sure," Lisle said. "We have lost two men killed, and four out of the others are wounded. I myself have got a rifle ball in my shoulder; at least, it is not there now, for it went right through. Fortunately it missed the bone, so I shall be all right again, in a day or two."

"How many were you attacked by?"

"I should say there must have been two hundred. That was about the number, when they first attacked."

"You must have been exposed to a tremendous fire. The walls are everywhere pitted with bullet marks, and the upper story seems perfectly riddled with balls; but of course none of you were up there."

"Yes, we used it as a lookout. As you see, I made four loopholes in each side and, as we lay well back, their bullets passed over our heads.

"What we want now is water. We drank the last drop, when we saw you coming. We had scarcely a mouthful each, and we have not had much more during the siege."

Flasks were instantly produced, and each man drank his fill.

"And now we had better be off," the officer in command of the relief party said. "Likely enough the Afridis will be down upon us, as soon as we move."

They were, indeed, several times fired at, as they made their way down to the camp, and at one time the resistance was formidable; but they were presently joined by another party from the camp, and the Afridis therefore drew off.

Lisle received many hearty congratulations on his return, and many officers of other regiments came in to shake his hand.

"I shall send in your name again, Mr. Bullen," his colonel said, after Lisle had made his report. "It was a most gallant action, to defend yourself so long, with only seven men, against a couple of hundred of the enemy; and the loss you inflicted upon them has been very severe, for forty fell close to the house, so that their bodies could not be carried off. I certainly should reckon that you must have killed or wounded a good many more."

"I don't think so, Colonel. No doubt we killed some more but, as it was dark for the greater part of the time, we could only fire at the flashes of their rifles. Certainly I saw twelve or fourteen fall, before it became quite dark and, as they several times tried to rush us, others might have fallen far enough from the house to be carried off by their friends."

That day General Lockhart placed, in the order of the day, the names of Lisle and his little party as having shown conspicuous gallantry, in defending themselves against a vastly superior force.

Two days later General Lockhart, himself, went out with a strong force to the top of Saransur; but met with little resistance, and the force returned at a much earlier hour than on the previous occasion, and reached camp before nightfall.

In warfare of this kind, it is the wounded who are the cause of disaster. A wounded man means six men out of the fighting line--four to carry him, and one to take charge of their rifles. A few casualties greatly reduce the fighting strength of the party. In European warfare this would not take place, as the wounded would be left behind, and would be cared for by the enemy.

The next day representatives of all the Orakzai tribes came in, and asked for terms. They were told that they must restore all stolen property, give up five hundred rifles, and pay a fine of thirty thousand rupees, and the cost of rebuilding the post they had destroyed. Representatives of three other tribes also came in, and similar terms were imposed upon them. Two of these, the Kambar-Khels and the Malikdins, were in the habit of migrating to British territory in cold weather; but the Kuki-Khels sent their families and goods, in winter quarters, to the Bara valley. The other Maidan tribes would probably have come in at the same time, but for their fear of the Zakka-Khels.

There was trouble the next day in the Mastura valley, where two officers and four men were wounded. The following night the camp was fired into, by an enemy who had crept within a hundred and fifty yards of it.

News came that General Kempster, with his detached brigade, had met with little opposition; and his search over the hills showed that the Zakka-Khels, in that direction, were severely punished.

On the 13th, the 3rd Brigade left the camp to cross the Kotal towards Saransur. Except for a few long-range shots, there was no opposition. Next day a Mullah's house was destroyed, documents found there showing that he had taken a vigorous part in the rising.

Two days later the brigade started on their return march. The 1st and 3rd Ghoorkhas were to cover the retirement, and the 15th Sikhs to hold the Kotal. The baggage train reached the Kotal by twelve o'clock, and the camp at three. The Ghoorkhas, however, had to fight hard; and were so done up that, instead of continuing to cover the retirement they passed on, leaving the Sikhs to cover.

The enemy, thinking that only a small rear guard had been left, came down in great force; but the fire was so heavy that they fell back, leaving the ground strewn with their dead. The action, however, now became general, all along the hill. Ammunition was running short, and Captain Abbott felt that, in the face of so large a force, and with fifteen or sixteen wounded, he could not retire down the ravine or valley without support. He therefore signalled for assistance; and the 46th, and two companies of the Dorsets, were detached for that purpose.

Colonel Houghton of the 36th, who was now in command, retiring steadily, found himself hampered with wounded in the rough country; while the enemy were surrounding him in increasing numbers. He was suffering heavily from the fire of the enemy posted in a small village; and he determined to seize it, and hold it for the night. Three companies of the 15th and two of the 36th therefore rushed up the hill, and were into the buildings before the Pathans were aware that they were moving against them. Those that delayed were bayoneted, the rest fled precipitately into the darkness. Their fire, however, had cost us an officer and five men killed.

Major Des Voeux on the right, having rushed a clump of buildings opposite to him, made for a second one on the far side of the nullah, in which was a small square building. The roof of the house had been burnt, and the charred beams were lying on the ground. The men rolled these, and what litter they could find into the gaps of the building; but the breastwork was barely two feet high. When the enemy returned to the attack they rushed right up to the house but, luckily, they fired high in their excitement, and the Sikhs swept them back again. The breastwork was then completed, a sentry was placed at each side of the house, and the rest lay down.

Colonel Houghton's post, which was a strong one, was not much troubled. A disaster, however, occurred to a half company, under two officers, who tried to push their way back to camp. Their bodies were found in a nullah, in the morning.

The next morning the parties were relieved by a force from camp.

On the same day General Westmacott, with the 4th Brigade, marched out. For the past three days the Malikdins and Kambar-Khels had shown a disposition to be friendly, and had made some attempt to open a grain traffic. Major Sullivan, with three other officers, pushed forward to prospect a site for a camp. Some apparently friendly and unarmed tribesmen approached them; but Major Sullivan's suspicions were excited when he saw that, instead of coming down direct, they were making a sweep that would cut off his little party. He therefore whistled for the others to join him.

When the tribesmen saw that the game was up, they poured in two volleys. Luckily the shots went high, and the four officers gained the cover of a house, and were soon joined by a Ghoorkha company. There was no doubt that the enemy had played the game of friendlies for the purpose of obtaining four officers, alive, to use as hostages.

The force then retired, bringing in the baggage animals, loaded with forage. The return was now decided upon. It was considered by the authorities that it would be less expensive to organize another expedition in the spring, when the sowing had begun; than to maintain a large force in the Tirah during the winter. The Afridis would not come down, and orders were therefore issued for destroying all the villages. These were burned, and the axe laid to the roots of the beautiful groves.

The tribal representatives of the Kambar-Khels, Alla-Khels, Malikdin-Khels, and Kuki-Khels came in. They were ordered to send in eight hundred serviceable rifles, fifty thousand rupees in cash, and all property that had been stolen.

When the force arrived at Bagh there was a sharp action, and the casualties amounted to twenty-two wounded and seven killed. The Ghoorkhas reported that they had found the enemy in great force, in the valley.

On the 22nd of November, Sir William Lockhart made a reconnaissance to Dwatoi and the Bara valley. He took with him a strong brigade, under General Westmacott. Every precaution was taken in entering this unknown country, as the road led down a defile commanded by high peaks. The Yorkshire Regiment was told off to hold the right of the advance, the 1st and 2nd Ghoorkhas were to do the same work on the left. The column was headed by the 3rd Ghoorkhas; followed by the 28th Bombay Volunteers, two companies of the Sappers and Miners, the Borderers, and the baggage; the rear guard being furnished by the 36th Sikhs.

Within a mile of camp, the Ghoorkhas were engaged with stray riflemen. A mile farther they were met by the main body, and were unable to proceed farther without support. The flanking regiments, however, presently came up, and the advance continued. The road lay in the river bed, and the men were plodding, waist deep, in water. The passage became narrower and narrower, and so rapid was the decline that the river bed became impassable, and the men made their way along by its side. The road was almost dark, so high were the cliffs and so narrow the passage between them.

Here the resistance became very formidable. The Ghoorkhas were all engaged in clearing the ridges, and the Bombay Pioneers pushed forward an advance guard, the Borderers moving up to their support. The deepest gorge was enfiladed by a party of tribesmen, with Martinis. One man fell with a broken leg. The man helping him was shot a moment later and, when a stretcher was brought back, two more of the Borderers were hit. A section of the 3rd Sikhs was detached to turn the enemy out, and then the ravine was rushed by all the rest. There was another gorge to be passed, and the enemy were pressing on both sides; but a battery was now brought into action, and soon drove them off.

Thus Dwatoi was reached, where the force encamped. It was but a small open plain, some five hundred yards across. Three miles away a gorge opened into the Rajgul valley, and it appeared that, beyond this, lay Wira valley.

All the summits were strongly picketed. Night fell, and there was no sign of the baggage. The troops were wet to the waist, there were seventeen degrees of frost, and the men had neither blankets nor food.

When morning broke there were still no signs of baggage, but at eleven it began to appear. At noon fighting began again, and the rest of the train did not arrive till about five o'clock. Fighting had been incessant the whole day. It was so severe that Sir William Lockhart determined to return to Bagh, the following day.

The arrangements were admirable. The baggage was loaded up before daybreak. The Ghoorkhas were to ascend the hills flanking the village, three companies of the Borderers were to form the advance guard, the wounded on stretchers were to follow, and the mountain battery was to take up a position to cover the retirement. By eight o'clock the last of the baggage was near the nullah. The helio then flashed to the pickets. They came in and joined the rear guard of the Sikhs, and were well in the nullah before a shot was fired.

When the Afridis fairly took the offensive they attacked with fury, and the Sikhs were obliged to signal for help. They were joined by a company of the Borderers. A party of Pathans dashed forward to seize the baggage; they had not, however, seen the few files that formed the rearmost guard, and were therefore caught between two bodies of troops, and almost annihilated. This sudden reversal of the situation seemed to paralyse the tribesmen, and the rest of the gorge was safely passed. Though the natives followed up the rear guard to within two miles of the camp, they never made another determined attack. The force lost, in all, five officers wounded, and a hundred men killed and wounded, from the 36th.

During the course of the reconnaissance Lisle had been with the rear guard, and had fallen in the torrent with a rifle ball through his leg. As every man was engaged in fighting, the fall was unnoticed and, as he could not recover his footing, he was washed helplessly down to the mouth of the defile. As he managed to reach the shore, a party of Afridis rushed down upon him with drawn tulwars; but a man who was evidently their leader stopped them, as they were about to fall upon him.

"A PARTY OF AFRIDIS RUSHED DOWN UPON HIM"

"He is an officer," he said. "We must keep him for a hostage. It will be better, so, than killing him."

137

Accordingly he was carried back to a village which the troops had left that evening. Here some women were told to attend to his wound, and the party who captured him went off to join in the attack on the British rear guard.

In the evening, the man who had saved his life returned. He was, it seemed, the headman of the village; and had been with his force in the Bara valley, where the natives of the village had retired on the approach of the British force. There Lisle lay for ten days, by which time the inflammation from the wound had begun to subside. The bullet had luckily grazed, and not broken the bone. At the end of that time, some of the principal men came to him and, by signs, directed him to write a letter to the British commander, saying that he was a prisoner, that he was held as a hostage against any further attempt to penetrate into the valley; and that, in the event of another British force approaching, he would be at once put to death.

Four of the Afridis always sat at the entrance to the house, which was one of the largest in the valley. He was served regularly with food; of which, as the valley had not been entered, there was, of course, abundance. The women in the house seldom came in to see him, except when they brought him his meals; and then it was evident, from their surly manner, that they strongly objected to his presence.

As he lay on his rough pallet, he resolved to maintain the appearance of being unable to walk, as long as possible. He knew very well that, if General Lockhart had to make another movement against the Bara valley, he could not be averted from his purpose by the fact that the Afridis held one officer prisoner, though he would assuredly revenge his murder, by destroying every house in the valley; and that he must accordingly trust only to himself to make his escape. To do this, it would be absolutely necessary to procure a disguise; and this, at present, he did not see his way to accomplish.

The guards below were relieved every few hours, and kept up their watch every day. Still, as they watched only the door, it might be possible for him to let himself down from the window at the back of the house.

On the tenth day he found himself really able to walk, without very great difficulty. Looking out of the window, one morning, he saw that the women of the house were all gathered round the guards, and talking excitedly. Evidently some messenger had come in with news from the Tirah valley. He knew, by this time, how many there were in the house, and was satisfied that they were all there.

He at once made his way down to the floor below; feeling confident that, for the moment, he would not be disturbed. Hanging against the wall were several men's dresses and clothes. He hastily took down sufficient for a disguise. They were summer clothes--for the Afridis, when leaving to act against our troops in the mountains, wear sheepskin garments. At any rate, there was little fear that their loss would be discovered until the men returned from the front.

He took the clothes up to his room, and hid them under the pallet. Then, having ascertained that the women were still engaged in talking, he took off his boots and made his way down to the lowest story, which was principally used as a storehouse. Here, among bags of corn and other stores, he saw a coil of rope. This he carried upstairs and, having hidden it, lay down again.

The rest of the day passed quietly. It was apparent that the clothes had not been missed and, with a strong feeling of hopefulness, he awaited the night. When the house was quiet he looked out. Four men were sitting, as usual, at the front of the door. Then he took off his uniform and put on his disguise, fastened one end of the rope securely, and slid down noiselessly to the ground.

Keeping the house between him and the guard, he started. Making a detour, he got free of the village, and then turned to the upper end of the valley. Half an hour's walking took him to where the force had encamped, and he soon reached the mouth of the gorge.

Here he plunged into the river. His leg hurt him a good deal, but he waded on and, after great exertions, reached the head of the gorge. His leg was now hurting him so much that he could proceed no farther so, turning off, he mounted the hills and lay down among the rocks, where there was little chance of his being discovered.

Here he dozed till morning. When he took the rope, he had thrust several handfuls of grain into his pocket; and this he had tied up in the skirt of his garment, when he started. He now munched some of it, and lay, watching the mouth of the gorge below.

Two hours after daybreak, he saw a small party of tribesmen come hurrying up through the gorge. They did not stop, but kept on their course, evidently supposing that he had pushed on to join the British camp. All day he lay hidden and, before dark, he saw the men come back again. They had evidently given up the chase and, as he had seen no searchers upon the hills, the idea that he was hiding had evidently not occurred to them.

He felt, however, that he must give his leg another day's rest before proceeding. On the following day he suffered a good deal from thirst, and dared not venture down to the river. When it was dark, however, he continued his way.

"IT WAS THE DEAD BODY OF AN AFRIDI"

Presently he saw something white, huddled up behind a rock and, climbing up, he found that it was the dead body of an Afridi, who had fallen in the fight. Beside him lay his Lee-Metford rifle. This was indeed a find. In the scanty garments that he had alone dared to take, he would be known at

140

once by anyone who happened to pass near him. He now set to work, and dressed himself in the dead warrior's garments; and took up his rifle and pouch of ammunition.

"Now," he said, "I only want something to stain my face and hands, and I shall be able to pass anywhere, if it does not come to talking."

He kept his eyes about him, and presently saw the plant which he knew Robah had used in preparing the dye for him. Pulling all the leaves off, he pounded them with the stock of his rifle, and rubbed his face with juice from the leaves. There was sufficient to stain both his face and hands.

By nightfall he entered the Maidan. Here he saw many natives gathered round the ruined houses. As he approached it, he saw that heavy firing was going on round the camp. It was greatly reduced in extent, and he guessed that a considerable proportion of the force had moved off on some punitive expedition. Between him and it, he could see many of the Afridis crouched among the rocks, ready to attack any small parties that might issue out.

He saw at once that it would be impossible to reach the camp without being questioned, and he therefore determined to fall in with the column that had gone out. For this purpose, he made a wide detour until he came upon a track where there were innumerable signs that a column had recently passed. Crushed shrubs would, in themselves, have been a sufficient guide; but there were many other tokens of the path of the army: grain dropped from a hole in a sack, scratches on the rock by the shod feet of the transport animals, an empty cartridge case, and a broken earthenware pot.

He pushed on rapidly, keeping a sharp lookout for the enemy. Some of them, passing along the hill, shouted to him to join them; but with a wave of his rifle and a gesture, showing that he intended to keep to the track, he went on.

Late in the afternoon, on mounting a high pass, he could distinctly hear firing in the distance; and his heart beat at the thought that he was near his friends. Still, between him and them the Afridis might be swarming. The risk, however, must be run.

Ascending the slope of the hill, he obtained a view of the conflict. A body of British troops was firing steadily, and another regiment was coming up to their assistance. The Afridis were swarming round in great numbers, and keeping up a continuous fire. Waiting until he saw where the Afridis were thickest, he made his way down to the firing line, and took up his position behind a rock; there being none of the natives within fifty yards of him. He now began to fire, taking pains to see that his bullets went far over the heads of the British. This he continued until nightfall, by which time the conflict had come to an end, and the British regiments, with the convoy which they were protecting, had reached camp.

CHAPTER 10: THROUGH THE MOHMUND COUNTRY.

For a time the firing ceased entirely but, soon after nightfall, a scattered fire opened round the camp. Lisle now made his way down fearlessly, until within four hundred yards of the camp. He was able to make out the white dresses of the Afridis, lying crouched behind rocks. No one paid any attention to him and, as soon as he had passed them, he dropped on his hands and knees and began crawling forward; keeping himself carefully behind cover for, at any moment, the pickets might open fire. When he approached the British lines, he stopped behind a rock and shouted:

"Don't fire! I am a friend."

"Come on, friend, and let us have a look at you," the officer in charge of the picket answered.

Rising, he ran forward.

"Who on earth are you?" the officer asked when he came up. "You look like one of the Afridis, but your tongue is English."

"I am Lieutenant Bullen," he said; and a burst of cheering rose from the men, who belonged to his own regiment.

"Why, we all thought you were killed, in that fight in the torrent!"

"No; I was hit, and my leg so disabled that I was washed down by the torrent; and the men were, I suppose, too much occupied in keeping the Afridis at bay to notice me. On getting to the other side of the pass I crawled ashore, and was made prisoner. No doubt the Afridis thought that, as I was an officer, they would hold me as a hostage, and so make better terms.

"I was put into the upper story of one of their houses but, after ten days, my wounds healed sufficiently to allow me to walk; and I have got here without any serious adventure."

"Well, I must congratulate you heartily. I will send two of the men into camp with you, for otherwise you would have a good chance of being shot down."

On arriving at the spot where the officers of the regiment were sitting round a campfire, his escort left him. As he came into the light of the fire, several of the officers jumped up, with their hands on their revolvers.

"Don't shoot! Don't shoot!" Lisle exclaimed, with a laugh. "I can assure you that I am perfectly harmless."

"It is Bullen's voice," one of them exclaimed, and all crowded round him, and wrung his hands and patted him on the back.

"This is the second time, Bullen, that you have come back to us from the dead; and this time, like Hamlet's father, you have come back with very questionable disguise. Now, sit down and take a cup of tea, which is all we have to offer you."

"I will," Lisle said, "and I shall be glad of some cold meat; for I have been living, for the past three days, on uncooked grain."

The meat was brought, and Lisle ate it ravenously, declining to answer any questions until he had finished.

"Now," he said, "I will tell you a plain, unvarnished tale;" and he gave them, in full detail, the adventure he had gone through.

"Upon my word, Lisle, you are as full of resources as an egg is full of meat. Your pluck, in going down to the lower story of that house while the women were chatting outside, was wonderful. It was, of course, sheer luck that you found that dead Pathan, and so got suitable clothes; but how you dyed your face that colour, I cannot understand."

Lisle explained how he had found a plant which was, as he knew, used for that purpose; and how he had extracted the colouring matter from it.

"You had wonderful luck in making your way through the Pathans, without being questioned; but, as we know, fortune favours the brave. Well, I shall have another yarn to tell General Lockhart, in the morning; but how we are to rig you out, I don't know."

Several of the officers, however, had managed to carry one or two spare garments in their kits. These were produced; and Lisle, with great satisfaction, threw off the dirt-stained Pathan garments, and arrayed himself in uniform.

Pleased as all the others were at his return, no one was so delighted as Robah, who fairly cried over his master, whom he had believed to be lost for ever.

"We shall not be uneasy about you again, Bullen," the colonel said, as they lay down for the night. "Whenever we miss you we shall know that, sooner or later, you will turn up, like a bad penny. If you hadn't got that wound in the leg--which, by the way, the surgeon had better dress and examine in the morning--I should have said that you were invulnerable to Afridi bullets. The next time there is some desperate service to be done, I shall certainly appoint you to undertake it; feeling convinced that, whatever it might be, and however great the risk, you will return unscathed. You don't carry a charm about with you, do you?"

"No," Lisle laughed, "I wish I did; but anything I carry would not be respected by a Pathan bullet."

Next morning the colonel reported Lisle's return, and Sir William Lockhart sent for him and obtained, from his lips, the story of the adventure.

"You managed excellently, sir," the general said, when he had finished. "Of course, I cannot report your adventure in full, but can merely say that Lieutenant Bullen, whom I had reported killed, was wounded and taken prisoner by the Pathans; and has managed, with great resource, to make his escape and rejoin the force. Your last adventure, sir, showed remarkable courage; and this time you have proved that you possess an equal amount of calmness and judgment. If you go on as you have begun, sir, you will make a very distinguished officer."

During the day Lisle had to repeat his story, again and again, to the officers of other regiments; who came in to congratulate him on making his escape, and to learn the particulars.

"I shall have," he said, laughing, "to get the printing officer to strike off a number of copies of my statement, and to issue one to each regiment. There, I think I would rather go through the adventure again, than have to keep on repeating it."

He had received a hearty cheer, from the regiment, when he appeared upon parade that morning; a reception that showed that he was a general favourite, and that sincere pleasure was felt at his return.

Lisle had been known among the men as 'the boy' when he first joined, but he was a boy no longer. He was now eighteen; and had, from the experiences he had gone through, a much older appearance. He learned, on the evening of his return, that he was now a full lieutenant; for there had been several changes in the regiment. When in cantonments other officers had joined, junior to himself; and four or five had been killed during the fighting.

"If this goes on much longer, Mr. Bullen, you will be a captain before we get back to India," one of the officers said.

"I am sure I hope not," he replied. "I don't wish to gain steps by the death of my friends. However, I hope that there is no chance of it coming to that."

After the visit of the commander to the Mohmund hill force, the troops under General Lockhart learned the history of the operations of that force, of which they had hitherto been in complete ignorance. On the 28th of August the force was concentrated. It consisted of the troops which, under Sir Bindon Blood, had just pacified the Upper Swat Valley; with a brigade, under Brigadier General Jeffreys and General Wodehouse, mobilized near Malakand. On the 6th of September orders were issued to march to Banjour, through the Mohmund country to Shabkadr, near Peshawar, and operate with a force under Major General Ellis. A force had already been despatched, under General Wodehouse, to seize the bridge over the Panjkora. This was successfully accomplished, the force arriving just in time, as a large body of the enemy came up only a few hours later.

General Meiklejohn was in command of the line of communication, and the 2nd and 3rd Brigades crossed the Panjkora without opposition. On the 13th of September the Rambuck Pass was reconnoitred, and the two brigades arrived at Nawagai. General Jeffreys encamped near the foot of the Ramjak Pass; and part of his force was detached, to prepare the road for the passage of the expedition, and to bivouac there for the night. The road was partially made, and the brigade would have passed over but, about eight o'clock in the evening, the camp at the foot of the pass was suddenly attacked. All lights were at once extinguished, and the men fell in rapidly; the trenches opening fire on the unseen enemy, who moved gradually round to the other side of the camp. It was pitch dark, for the moon had not yet risen; and the enemy poured in a murderous fire, but did not attempt to rush the camp. The troops were firing almost at random for, in spite of star shells being fired, very few of the enemy could be made out.

The fire was hottest from the side occupied by the 38th Dogras, who determined to make a sortie, for the purpose of clearing the enemy away from that flank. In spite of the fact that the ground was swept by bullets, several volunteered for the sortie. The fire, however, was too hot. Captain Tomkins and Lieutenant Bailey fell, almost the instant they rose to their feet. Lieutenant Harrington received a mortal wound, and several men were also killed and wounded, and the sortie was given up.

All night a heavy fire was kept up by the enemy, but they moved off in the morning. The camp presented a sad sight, when day broke; dead horses and mules were lying about among the tents and shelters, which had been hurriedly thrown down at the first attack. When it was learned that the assailants belonged to the Banjour tribes, living in the Mohmund Valley, a squadron of Bengal Lancers were sent off in pursuit and, overtaking them in a village at the entrance of their valley, killed many, pursuing them for four or five miles. When they returned to the village, they were joined by the Guides Infantry and a mountain battery. This was too small a force to follow the enemy into their hills, but they destroyed the fortifications of several small villages and, before night, General Jeffreys, with the rest of the brigade, arrived.

Night passed without interruption and, in the morning, the force marched in three columns; the centre keeping straight up the valley, while the other two were to destroy the villages on each side. When the centre column had advanced six miles up the valley, they saw the enemy in a village on the hill; and a detachment of the Buffs went out to dislodge them. The remainder of the column pushed on.

Two companies of the 35th Sikhs, who were in advance, went too far; and were suddenly attacked by a great number of the enemy. Fighting sturdily they fell back but, being hampered by their wounded, many of the men were unable to return the fire of the tribesmen; who formed round them, keeping up a heavy fire at close quarters. The Ghazis, seeing their opportunity, came closer and closer; their swordsmen charging in and cutting down the Sikhs in the ranks. Seventeen were thus killed or wounded. Presently, however, the Buffs arrived in support, and a squadron of the 11th Bengal Lancers charged the Ghazis, and speared many of them before they could reach the shelter of the hills; and the Buffs soon drove them away, with heavy loss.

While this was going on the third detachment, which had destroyed many of the numerous villages, was called in to join the main body. The guns had been doing good work among the flying tribesmen. A company and a half of the 35th Sikhs were told to take post, on a high hill, to cover the guns. This force, when the troops returned, diverged somewhat from the line of march which the main body were following. It was hard pressed by the tribesmen, hampered by the wounded, and was running short of ammunition; and was obliged to send for help. The general ordered the Guides to go to their assistance but, fortunately, a half company of that regiment with some ammunition had already reached them, and the party could be seen fighting their way up a steep rocky spur.

The tribesmen, confident that they could cut off the small band from the main force, rushed at them with their swords. Both the officers were severely wounded. When, however, the rest of the Guides arrived on the hill, they poured several volleys into the enemy, and so checked their advance. A Havildar then volunteered to mount the hill with ammunition. He reached the party with seventy cartridges, and carried back a wounded native officer. Other Guides followed his example, and all reached the valley as evening was closing in.

The Ghazis crept up the ravine, and maintained a hot fire upon them. It soon became pitch dark, and the difficulty of the march was increased by a heavy storm. The force lost the line of retreat and, but for the vivid lightning, would have found it impossible to make their way across the deep ravine. At ten o'clock they reached the camp.

Here they found that General Jeffreys, with part of his brigade, had not yet returned. At dawn, however, the general appeared, with his mountain battery and a small escort. They had become separated from the remainder of the brigade, and the general decided to bivouac in a village. Defences were at once formed. The trenching tools were with the main body, but the sappers used their bayonets to make a hasty shelter.

The enemy took possession of the unoccupied part of the village, and opened fire on the trenches. This grew so hot that it became absolutely necessary to clear the village. Three attempts were made, but failed; the handful of available men being altogether insufficient for the purpose.

The enemy now tried to rush the troops, and a continuous fire was poured into a small enclosure, packed with men and mules. The casualties were frequent, but the men now threw up a fresh defensive work, with mule saddles and ammunition boxes. The fury of the storm, which came on at nine o'clock, somewhat checked the ardour of the assailants; and the water was invaluable to the wounded.

At midnight four companies, who had gone out in search of the general, arrived and cleared the enemy out of the village. The casualties had been heavy, two officers and thirty-six men having been killed, and five officers and a hundred and two men wounded.

Next day the force started on their way up the valley. Their object was to attack a strongly-fortified village on the eastern side of the valley, about six miles distant from the camp. When they were within two thousand yards of the enemy's position, the tribesmen could be seen, making their disposition for the attack.

The Sikhs, Dogras, and Buffs stormed the heights on either side; but the enemy made no attempt to stand. The Guides advanced straight on the village, which was destroyed without loss. The grain found there was carried into camp. Several other villages were captured and, though the enemy were several times gathered in force, the appearance of a squadron of Bengal Lancers, in every case, put them to flight.

In the meantime, the 3rd Brigade were encamped at Nawagai. The news of the attack on General Jeffreys' column had upset the arrangements. It was of the utmost importance to hold Nawagai, which separated the country of the Hadda Mullah and the Mamunds. As the whole country was hostile, and would rise at the first opportunity, the force was not strong enough to march against the Hadda Mullah, and leave a sufficient body to guard the camp. It was therefore decided to wait, until they were joined by General Ellis' force.

Skirmishing went on daily. On the 17th, heliographic communication was opened with General Ellis. On the following day an order was flashed to them, to join General Jeffreys in the Mamund valley. This was impracticable, however, until General Ellis should arrive.

Next night a couple of hundred swordsmen crept up to a ravine, within fifty yards of the camp, and suddenly fell upon the West Surrey regiment. They were met by such a hail of bullets that most of them dropped, and of the remainder not a man reached Hallal.

On the following day a messenger arrived, from General Ellis, asking Sir Bindon Blood to meet him ten miles away. That afternoon a reconnaissance was made, as news had been received that large reinforcements had been received by Hadda Mullah. The enemy showed themselves in great force, but kept out of range of the guns though, during the return march, they followed the troops and, when darkness set in, were but two miles from camp.

At nine in the evening the enemy, who had crept silently up, attempted to rush the camp on three sides. The troops were well prepared, and maintained a steady fire; although the enemy's swordsmen hurled themselves against our entrenchments in great numbers. The star shells were fired by the mountain battery, and their reflection enabled the infantry to pour deadly volleys into the midst of the enemy, who were but a few yards distant. The tribesmen, however, completely surrounded the camp, their riflemen keeping up a heavy fire, and their swordsmen making repeated rushes.

The tents had all been struck, and the troops lay flat on the ground while the enemy's bullets swept the camp. This was kept up till two o'clock in the morning, the fire never slackening for a minute; and the monotony of the struggle was only broken by an occasional mad, fanatical rush of the Ghazis. The entrenchments were so well made that only thirty-two casualties occurred, but a hundred and fifteen horses and transport animals were killed.

The effect of this decisive repulse, of an attack which the enemy thought would certainly be successful, was shown by the complete dispersal of the enemy. Their losses had been terrible. It was ascertained that, in the surrounding villages alone, three hundred and thirty had been killed; while a great number of dead and wounded had been carried away over the passes.

On the following day General Ellis arrived. It was arranged that the 3rd Brigade should join his command. Thus reinforced, he could deal with the Hadda Mullah, and General Blood would be at liberty to join the 2nd Brigade in the Mamund Valley.

General Ellis took up a position, with the two brigades at his disposal, at the mouth of the Bedmanai Pass; and sniping went on all night. Next morning the troops moved forward to the attack. Covered by the rest of the force, the 20th Punjabis, with the 3rd Ghoorkhas in support, were ordered to make the assault, and to secure the hills commanding the pass. The enemy fought stubbornly, but were gradually driven back; their numbers being greatly reduced by deserters, after the attack on the camp. The Hadda Mullah had fled, directly the fight began; but the Suffi Mullah was seen constantly rallying his followers.

On the following morning, General Westmacott's brigade marched to a village situated at the mouth of the Jarobi gorge--a terrible defile, with precipitous cliffs on either side, the crests of which were well wooded. The resistance, however, was slight, and the force pushed through and burned the houses, towers, and forts of the Hadda Mullah. They were harassed, however, on their return to camp.

In the meantime, Sir Bindon Blood had joined General Jeffreys' brigade, which was still engaged in operations against the Mamunds. Several villages were burned, and large supplies of game and fodder carried off. The Mamunds at last sent in a party to negotiate; but it soon appeared that they had no intention of surrendering, for they had been joined by a considerable number of Afghans, and were ready for a fresh campaign. The Afghan borderers were in a good position, and were able to bring their forces to the assistance of the Mamunds with the assurance that, if they were repulsed, they could return to their homes.

General Jeffreys therefore recommenced operations, by an attack upon two fortified villages. These were situated on the lower slope of a steep and ragged hill, near enough to give support to each other, and protected by rocky spurs. The inhabitants sallied out to attack, but were checked by the appearance of our cavalry. The force then pressed forward to the high jungle.

It was evident that the spurs on either side must be captured, before the village could be stormed. The Guides were ordered to clear the spur to the left, the 31st Punjab Infantry and the Dogras the centre ridge between the two hills, while the West Kents advanced straight up the hill.

The Guides dashed up the hill with a wild yell. This so intimidated the tribesmen that, after firing a volley so wild that not a single man was wounded in the attacking column, they fled in a panic.

The Punjabis, on the other hill, were stubbornly fighting their way. The ground consisted, for the most part, of terraced fields, commanded by strongly-built sangars. Colonel O'Brien was killed, while gallantly leading his men on to the assault; but the Punjabis persisted, under the covering fire of the mountain battery, and dropped shell after shell into the Mamunds; who, however, although losing heavily, stuck manfully to their rocks and boulders, and finally were only driven out at the point of the bayonet.

The 31st were now joined by the West Kent, who came down from a spur on the west, and were able to drive the enemy out of several strong positions above the other village. On their way a half company, on reaching a sangar, were suddenly charged by a body of Ghazis. From the melee which ensued, many of the West Kents were killed and wounded, among them the officer in command.

As it was now late, it was decided to return to camp for the night. This was done steadily and deliberately, although the enemy kept up a heavy fire. The casualties of the day were sixty-one, no fewer than eight British officers being killed or wounded.

Two days' rest was given the troops, and then they marched against Badelai. The attack was almost unopposed. The tribesmen imagined that we were again going to attack their former position, and they were unable to return in time to defend the village. Their loss, however, was severe, as they came down to the open ground, and were swept by the guns of the mountain battery.

A few days afterwards the campaign was brought to an end, the enemy coming in and offering a general surrender. The expedition had been very successful, twenty-six villages having been destroyed, and all the hoards of grain having been carried off.

On the 13th of October the Mamund valley was evacuated, and the force moved into Matassa. The inhabitants here were perfectly peaceable and, beyond the blowing up of the fort of a chief, who had continued hostile, there was no fighting. The force then returned to Malakand, where it remained for two months.

Two tribes yet remained to be dealt with, namely the Bulas and Chamlas. Both refused to comply with the reasonable terms imposed upon them, by the government, for their complicity in the rebellion.

The force selected for their punishment consisted of two brigades, under General Meiklejohn and General Jeffreys. These advanced to the assault on the Tangi Pass. The Guides, 31st Punjabis, three squadrons of the Bengal Lancers, and two squadrons of the Guide cavalry were sent to Rustam, a place which threatened three passes leading into Buner. The enemy, being thus compelled to watch all three routes, were prevented from assembling in any force.

Sir Bindon Blood encamped the two brigades on Thursday, the 6th of January, at the mouth of the Tangi Pass. The detached column was to protect an entrance over the Pirsai Pass. The assault was made by the column under General Meiklejohn, and so well was the force distributed--the hills on either side being captured, while three batteries opened fire on the hill with shrapnel--that the tribesmen were unable to maintain their position. The pass was captured with only one casualty, and the troops marched triumphantly down into Buner, the first British troops who had ever entered the country.

They halted at the first village. As this place was plentifully stocked with goats and chickens, they found abundance of food.

The detached column were equally successful in their attack on the Pirsai Pass, for they met with scarcely any resistance. Our success, in capturing the two passes hitherto deemed impregnable, brought about a complete collapse of the enemy. Deputations came in from all the surrounding villages, and the tribesmen complied with the terms imposed upon them.

CHAPTER 11: AN ARDUOUS MARCH.

Lisle had heard of the operations that had been carried on by the brigade under General Gazelee, under the general supervision of Sir William Lockhart. The object was to cross by the Zolaznu Pass, to punish two of the hostile tribes on the other side; to effect a meeting with the Khuram column; and to concentrate and operate against the Chamkannis, a tribe of inveterate robbers. On the 26th General Gazelee started, and the newly-arrived wing of the Scottish Fusiliers, and two companies of the Yorkshires was to follow, on the 28th.

The approach to the pass, which was four miles to the left, was across a very rough country; and as, after advancing four and a half miles, a severe opposition was met with, most of the day was spent in dislodging the tribesmen from the villages, and turning them out of the spurs which covered the approach to the pass. Finding it impossible to make the summit that night, they encamped and, although they were fired into heavily, but little damage was done.

At dawn the expedition started again but, by accident, they ascended another pass parallel with the Lozacca. At nine o'clock the Ghoorkhas and Sikhs arrived at the top of the pass. It was very difficult and, as the baggage animals gave great trouble on the ascent, and were unable to go farther, the party camped on the top of the pass.

General Lockhart left the camp early that morning, but was also opposed so vigorously that he was obliged to encamp, three miles from the top of the pass, after having burnt all the villages from which he had been fired upon. In the morning he joined the advance party, and went ten miles down the pass. On arriving there, he found that the Queen's and the 3rd Sikhs had pushed on farther to Dargai. This was not the place previously visited of this name, which appears to be a common one in the Tirah. Plenty of hay and straw stores were found, and the troops were vastly more comfortable than on the previous night.

It was here that Lisle had overtaken the column.

Next day the whole force was encamped at Dargai, where they were received in a friendly manner by the villagers; who expressed themselves willing to pay their share of the fines imposed, and also to picket the hills. The rear guard, of two companies of Ghoorkhas and two companies of Scottish Fusiliers, arrived late in the day. They had met with great opposition. The tribesmen would, indeed, have succeeded in carrying off the guns, had not a company of the Ghoorkhas come up and, fighting stubbornly, driven them off.

Next morning the headmen of the village were summoned, to explain why they had failed to pay the number of rifles they had promised; and fire was applied to one of their houses. This had an instantaneous effect and, in a quarter of an hour, the rifles were forthcoming and the fine paid.

The force then moved on to Esor, where helio communication with the Khuram column had been effected and, that day, Sir William Lockhart and Colonel Hill--who commanded it--met. The country traversed was a beautiful one. It was admirably cultivated, and the houses were substantially built.

That day two columns went out: one under General Gazelee, to collect the fines from one of the tribes; the other commanded by Colonel Hill, to punish the Chamkannis. This was a small, but extremely warlike and hardy tribe. A short time before, they had raided a thousand head of cattle from across our border, and got clear away with them.

A portion of the force was told off, to work its way into the valley by the river gorge, while the main body ascended the path over the Kotal. They reached this at a quarter-past ten and, while they were waiting for the head of the column that had gone up the gorge to appear, fire was opened upon them. This, however, was kept down by the guns. It was an hour before the column appeared, but the whole force was not through the defile until it was too late to carry out the destruction of the villages. The column therefore retired, severely harassed, the while, by the enemy.

Next day Colonel Hill was again sent forward, with the Border Scouts, the 4th and 5th Ghoorkhas, part of the Queen's, and the Khoat Battery. They were over the Kotal at nine o'clock, and the 5th Ghoorkhas and the scouts were sent to hold the hills on the left. The Chamkannis had anticipated a sudden visit, and were in force on the left, where they had erected several sangars.

The little body of scouts, eighty men strong, fought their way up the hill; and waited there for the leading company of the 5th. Lieutenant Lucas, who commanded them, told off half his company to sweep the sangar, and then the remainder dashed at it.

The Chamkannis stood more firmly than any of the tribesmen had hitherto done. They met the charge with a volley, and then drew their knives to receive it. The fire of the covering party destroyed their composure and, when the scouts were within thirty yards, they bolted for the next sangar.

Lucas carried three of these defences, one after another, and drove the enemy off the hill. The Ghoorkhas scouts, who had been engaged thirty-six times during the campaign, had killed more than their own strength of the enemy, and had lost but one man killed and two wounded; and this without taking count of the many nights they had spent in driving off prowlers round the camp.

The work of destruction now began. Over sixty villages were destroyed in the valley and, on the following day, the expedition started to withdraw. The lesson had been so severe that no attempt was made, by the tribesmen, to harass the movement.

The column marched down to the camp in the Maidan--the Adam Khels, through whose country they passed, paying the fine, and so picketing many of the adjacent heights as to guard the camp from the attacks of hostile tribesmen. When they reached Bara they decided to rejoin the Peshawar column, without delay, as the outlook was not promising. The evacuation began on the 7th of December, but the rear guard did not leave till the 9th. It was divided into two divisions in order, as much as possible, to avoid the delay caused by the large baggage column. The 1st Division was to march down on the Mastura Valley, while General Lockhart's 2nd Division would again face the Dwatoi defile. Both the forces were due to join the Peshawar column, on or about the 14th.

General Symonds, with the 1st Division, was unmolested by the way. It was very different, however, with Lockhart.

The movement was not made a day too soon. Clouds were gathering, the wind was blowing from the north, and there was every prospect of a fall of snow, which would have rendered the passage of the Bara Pass impossible. The 3rd Ghoorkhas led the way, followed by the Borderers, with the half battalion of the Scottish Regiment and the Dorsets. Behind them came the baggage of the brigade and headquarters, the rear of the leading column being brought up by the 36th Sikhs. General Kempster's Brigade followed, in as close order as possible; having detached portions of the 1st and 2nd Ghoorkhas, and the 2nd Punjab Infantry, to flank the whole force.

The Malikdin Khels were staunch to their word, and not a single shot was fired till the force had passed through the defile. The difficulties, however, were great, for the troops, baggage, and followers had to wade through the torrent, two-thirds of the way. The flanking had used up all the Ghoorkhas, and the Borderers now became the advance guard.

Everything seemed peaceful, and the regiment was halfway across the small valley, when a heavy fire was opened on the opposite hill. General Westmacott was in command of the brigade. The Borderers were to take and hold the opposite hill, supported by a company of Dorsets and of Scottish Fusiliers. The battery opened fire, while a party turned the nearest sangars on the right flank. By three o'clock the whole of the crests were held, and the baggage streamed into camp. Fighting continued, however, on the peaks, far into the night.

No explanations were forthcoming why the enemy should have allowed the force to pass through the defile, without obstruction, when a determined body of riflemen could have kept the whole of them at bay; for the artillery could not have been brought into position, as the defile was the most difficult, of its kind, that a British division had ever crossed.

The day following the withdrawal of the rear guard, it rained in the Bara Valley, which meant snow in the Maidan. The pickets on the heights had a bad time of it that night, as some of them were constantly attacked; and it was not till three in the morning that the baggage came in, the rear guard arriving in camp about ten.

The camp presented a wonderful sight that day, crowded as it was with men and animals. The weather was bitterly cold, and the men were busy gathering wood to make fires. On the hills all round, the Sikhs could be seen engaged with the enemy, the guns aiding them with their work. The 36th Sikhs, as soon as they arrived, were sent off to occupy a peak, two miles distant, which covered the advance into the Rajgul defile. The enemy mustered strong, but were turned out of the position.

The next morning the villages were white with snow. A party was sent on into the Rajgul valley, where they destroyed a big village.

Immediately after leaving Dwatoi, the valley broadened out till it was nearly a mile wide. On the right it was commanded by steep hills; on the left it was, to some extent, cultivated. The 4th Brigade this time led the way, the 3rd bringing up the rear.

From the moment when the troops fell in on the 10th, till they reached Barkai on the 14th, there was a general action from front to rear. The advance guard marched at half-past seven. At eight o'clock flanking parties were engaged with the enemy in the hills and spurs. Serious opposition, however, did not take place until five and a half miles of the valley had been passed.

Here the river turned to the right, and the front of the advance was exposed to the fire of a strongly-fortified village, nestling on the lower slope of a hill, on a terrace plateau. The village was furnished with no fewer than ten towers, and from these a very heavy fire was kept up.

The battery shelled the spur; while the Sikhs, in open order, skirmished up the terraces to the plateau and, after a brisk fusillade, took the village and burnt it.

A mile farther, the head of the column reached the camping place, which was a strong village built into the river cleft. On the left the 36th Sikhs and part of the Ghoorkhas cleared the way; while the Bombay Pioneers, and the rest of the Ghoorkhas, became heavily engaged with the enemy in some villages on the right. All along the line a brisk engagement went on. The camp pickets took up their positions early in the afternoon, and a foraging party went out and brought in supplies, after some fighting.

Kempster's Brigade had not been able to reach the camp, and settled itself for the night three miles farther up the valley. It, too, had its share of fighting.

All night it rained heavily, and the morning of the 11th broke cold and miserable. It was freezing hard; the hilltops, a hundred feet above the camp, were wrapped in snow; and the river had swollen greatly. The advance guard waded out into the river bed, and the whole of the brigade followed, the Ghoorkhas clearing the sides of the valley. In a short time they passed into the Zakka-Khel section of the Bara Valley.

Curiously enough, the opposition ceased here. It may be that the enemy feared to show themselves on the snow on the hilltops; or that, being short of ammunition, they decided to reserve themselves for an attack upon the other brigade. Scarcely a shot was fired until the valley broadened out into the Akerkhel, where some small opposition was offered by villagers on either bank. This, however, was easily brushed aside.

The advance guard of the 3rd Brigade almost caught up the rear guard of the 4th and, by four in the afternoon, its baggage was coming along nicely, so that all would be in before nightfall. The rear guard of the brigade, consisting of the Gordons, Ghoorkhas, and 2nd Punjab Infantry, had been harassed as soon as they started and, as the day wore on, the enemy increased greatly in numbers. As the flanking parties fell back to join the rear guard, they were so pressed that it was as much as they could do to keep them at bay.

When about three miles from camp, the baggage took a wrong road. In trying a piece of level ground, they became helplessly mixed up in swampy rice fields. The enemy, seeing the opportunity they had waited for, outflanked the rear guard, and began pouring a heavy fire into the baggage. The flanking parties were weak, for the strain had been so severe that many men from the hospital escort and baggage guard had been withdrawn, to dislodge the enemy from the surrounding spurs.

The Pathans were almost among the baggage, when a panic seized the followers. As night began to fall, the officer commanding the Gordons, with two weak companies of his regiment, two companies of the Ghoorkhas, and a company of the 2nd Punjab Infantry and some Ghoorkhas, found himself in a most serious position. The guns had limbered up and pushed on, and the rear guard remained, surrounded by the enemy, hampered with its wounded, and stranded with doolies. As the native bearers had fled these doolies were, in many cases, being carried by the native officers.

The enemy grew more and more daring, and a few yards, only, divided the combatants. Captain Uniacke, retiring with a few of the Gordons, saw that there was only one course left: they must entrench for the night. He was in advance of the actual rear guard, attempting to hold a house against the fire of quite a hundred tribesmen.

Collecting four men of his regiment, and shouting wildly, he rushed at the doorway. In the dusk the enemy were uncertain of the number of their assailants and, in their horror of the bayonet, they fired one wild volley and fled. To continue the ruse, Captain Uniacke climbed to the roof, shouting words of command, as if he had a company behind him. Then he blew his whistle, to attract the rear guard as it passed, in the dark.

The whistle was heard and, in little groups, they fell back with the wounded to the house. It was a poor place, but capable of defence; and the Pathans drew off, knowing that there was loot in abundance to be gained down by the river.

As night wore on the greatest anxiety prevailed, when transport officers and small parties straggled in, and reported that tribesmen were looting and cutting up followers, within a mile of camp; and that they had no news to give of the men who composed the rear guard. So anxious were the headquarter staff that a company of the Borderers were sent out, to do what they could.

Lieutenant Macalister took them out and, going a mile up the river, was able to collect many followers and baggage animals, but could find no signs of the rear guard. Early in the morning a company of the 2nd Punjab Infantry went out, as a search party, and got into communication with the rear guard. They were safe in the house; but could not move, as they were hampered with the wounded, and were surrounded by the enemy. Two regiments and a mountain battery therefore went out and rescued them from their awkward predicament, bringing them into camp, with as much baggage as could be found.

The casualties of the day amounted to a hundred and fifty animals, and a hundred followers killed. Of the combatants two officers were wounded, and fourteen Gordons were wounded, and four killed.

Owing to the necessity of sending out part of the 4th Brigade, to support the cut-off rear of the 3rd Brigade, it was impossible to continue the march that day. Next morning, the order of the brigade was changed. The 23rd was to lead, handing over a battery of artillery to the 4th, for service in the rear guard. It was also ordered that flanking parties were to remain in position, until the baggage had passed. The advance guard consisted of the 2nd Punjab Infantry, and the 1st and 2nd Ghoorkhas. The others were told off to burn and destroy all villages on either side of the nullah. The baggage of the whole division followed the main guard.

Directly the camp was left, the sides of the nullah enlarged and, for half a mile, the road lay through a narrow ravine. The drop was rapid; for the river, swollen by the fallen snow, had become literally a torrent; and the scene with the baggage was one of extreme confusion. The recent disaster had given a frenzied impulse to the generally calm followers, and all felt anxiety to press forward, with an impetus almost impossible to control. The mass of baggage became mixed in the ravine, but at last was cleared off and, when the valley opened, they moved forward at their greatest speed, but now under perfect control.

After this the opposition became less, and the village of Gulikhel was reached by the 3rd Brigade. The village stands on the left bank of the Bara. Immediately below it a nullah becomes a narrow gorge, almost impassable in the present state of the river. It is several miles long. There was, however, a road over a neighbouring saddle. The path up from the river was narrow, but sufficient to allow two loaded mules to pass abreast. It wound for some seven miles, over a low hill, until the river bed was again reached.

The next ford was Barkhe. The advance guard was well up in the hills by midday, when it met the Oxfordshire Regiment, which had come out seven miles to meet the force; but the baggage of a division, filing out of the river bed in pairs, is a serious matter, and there was necessarily a block in the rear.

General Westmacott moved as soon as the baggage was off but, long before it was through the first defile, his pickets were engaged, and a general action followed. The enemy, fighting with extraordinary boldness, kept within a few yards of the pickets. Followers with baggage animals were constantly hit, as they came up but, at half-past ten, the rear guard regiments marched out of camp, under cover of artillery fire.

The fighting was so severe that, within an hour, the ammunition of the 3rd Ghoorkhas was expended and, shortly afterwards, the two regiments of the rear guard were forced to call up their first reserve ammunition mules. The march was continued at a rapid pace, until they reached the block caused by the narrowness of the path. Here the whole river reach became choked with animals and doolies. The wounded were coming in fast, when the Pathans, taking advantage of the block, attacked in great force, hoping to compel the retreating force to make their way down the long river defile.

General Westmacott, however, defended his right with energy; the rear-guard regiments supporting each other, while the batteries were in continual action. The Borderers, Sikhs, and Ghoorkhas stood well to their task, till the last of the baggage animals were got out of the river bed.

The country now had become a rolling plateau, intersected by ravines and thickly covered with low jungle, in which the enemy could creep up to within three or four yards of the fighting line. Progress was, consequently, very slow. To be benighted in such a country would have meant disaster, so General Westmacott selected a ridge, which he determined to hold for the night. The wearied men were just filing up, when a tremendous rush was made by the Afridis. For a moment, it seemed as if they would all be enveloped and swept away; but the officers threw themselves into the ranks, magazines were worked freely, and the very bushes seemed to melt away before the hail of shot. The tribesmen were swept back in the darkness, and they never tried a second rush. Their firing also slackened very much, and this permitted the men to form a camp, and see to the wounded.

That day the rear guard lost one officer killed and three wounded, eighteen men killed, eighty-three wounded, and six missing. The night in camp was a terrible experience. The troops had been fighting since early morning, the frost was bitter, and they had neither water, food, nor blankets. General Westmacott passed the night with the sentry line.

Early in the morning the action recommenced and, stubbornly contesting each foot, at times almost in hand-to-hand conflict with tribesmen in the bushes, the rear guard fell back. The summit of the Kotal was passed; but the enemy continued to harass their retirement down to the river, where the picket post of the 9th Ghoorkhas was reached. The retirement from the Tirah had cost a hundred and sixty-four killed and wounded. As a military achievement, this march of Lockhart's 2nd Division should have a prominent place in the history of the British army.

After a quiet day, the force marched into Swaikot. Next morning the troops in camp there gathered on each side of the road, cheering their battle-grimed comrades, and bringing down hot cakes to them. It was a depressing sight. The men were all pinched and dishevelled, and bore on their faces marks of the terrible ordeal through which they had just passed.

The advance guard were followed by the wounded. The 4th Brigade followed. They were even more marked by hardship and strife than those who had preceded them. Then the rear guard marched in, and the first phase of the Tirah expedition was at an end.

The expedition had carried out its object successfully. The Afridis had been severely punished, and had been taught what they had hitherto believed impossible, that their defiles were not impregnable, and that the long arm of the British Government could reach them in their recesses. The lesson had been a very severe one, but it had been attained at a terrible cost. It is to be hoped that it will never have to be repeated.

But while the regiment were resting quietly in their cantonment, there had been serious fighting on the road to Chitral. After some hesitation, the government had decided that this post should remain in our hands, and a strong force was therefore stationed at the Malakand. This, after clearing the country, remained quietly at the station; until news was received of the attack on our fort at Shabkadr, near Peshawar, by the Mohmunds and, two days later, news came that a large council had been held by the fanatics of various tribes, at which they decided to join the tribes in the Upper Valley of Swat.

On the 14th of August the force set out from Thana, under Sir Bindon Blood, on their march for the Upper Swat. The 11th Bengal Lancers were sent forward in order to reconnoitre the country. The enemy were found in force near Jelala, at the entrance to the Upper Swat river, their advance post being established in some Buddhist ruins on a ridge. The Royal West Kent, however, advanced and drove them off.

Then news came that several thousand of the enemy occupied a front, of some two miles, along the height; their right flank resting on the steep cliffs, and their left reaching to the top of the higher hills. The battery opened fire upon them; and the infantry, coming into action at nine o'clock in the morning, did much execution among the crowded Ghazis.

The 31st and 24th Punjab Infantry, under General Meiklejohn, had a long and arduous march on the enemy's left. The movement was successfully carried out; and the enemy, knowing that their line of retreat towards the Morah Pass was threatened, broke up, a large portion streaming away to their left. The remainder soon lost heart and, although a desperate charge by a handful of Ghazis took place, these only sacrificed their lives, without altering the course of events.

The enemy gathered on a ridge in the rear but, by eleven, the heights commanding the road were in the hands of our troops, and the Guides cavalry began to file past. When they got into the pass behind the ridge, the enemy were more than a mile away; and could be seen in great numbers, separated by several ravines.

Captain Palmer, who had pushed forward in pursuit, soon found himself ahead of his men. Near him were Lieutenant Greaves and, thirty yards behind, Colonel Adams and Lieutenant Norman. Seeing that the enemy were in considerable force, Colonel Adams directed the troop of cavalry who were coming up to hold a graveyard, through which they had passed, until the infantry could arrive. Owing, however, to the noise of the firing, Palmer and Greaves did not hear him; and charged up to the foot of the hill, hoping to cut off the tribesmen who were hurrying towards them. Palmer's horse was at once killed, and Greaves fell among the Pathans.

Adams and Fincastle, and two soldiers, galloped forward to their assistance, and were able to help Palmer back to the shelter of the graveyard. Meanwhile Fincastle, who had had his horse killed, tried to help Greaves on to Adams' horse. While doing so, Greaves was again shot through the body, and Adams' horse wounded. The two troopers came to their assistance; and Maclean, having first dismounted his squadron in the graveyard, pluckily rode out with four of his men. In this way the wounded were successfully brought in; but Maclean was shot through both thighs, and died almost instantly. The loss of the two officers, who were both extremely popular, was greatly felt by the force.

The infantry and guns now having arrived, the enemy retired to a village, two miles in the rear. Here they were attacked by a squadron of the Guides, who dispersed them and drove them up into the hills. In the meantime our camp had been attacked, but the guard repulsed the assailants, with some loss.

The enemy had lost so heavily that they scattered to the villages, and sent in to make their submission. This fight effectually cooled the courage of the natives, and the column marched through their country unopposed, and the tribesmen remained comparatively quiet during the after events.

CHAPTER 12: A TRIBAL FIGHT.

Two days after Lisle's return he was sent for by General Lockhart, who requested him to give him a full account of his capture and escape.

"This is the second time, Mr. Bullen, that your conduct has been brought before me. Your defence of that hut, when you were unable to make your retirement to the camp, with a handful of men, was a singularly gallant affair. I lost one of my aides-de-camp in the last fight, and I am pleased to offer you the vacancy. You may take possession of his horse until we return; when it will, of course, be sold. I shall be glad to have a young officer of so much courage and resource on my staff."

"Thank you, sir! I am extremely obliged to you for the offer, which I gladly accept; and feel it a very high honour, indeed, to be attached to your staff."

"Very well, Mr. Bullen, I will put you in orders, tomorrow morning."

On his return to the regiment, Lisle was warmly congratulated when they heard the honour that had been bestowed on him; but there were many expressions of regret at his leaving them.

"It will not be for long," he said, "for I suppose that, in another fortnight, we shall be across the frontier. If it had been at the beginning of the campaign, I should certainly have refused to accept the general's offer; for I should much rather have remained with the regiment. As it was, however, I could hardly refuse."

"Certainly not," said one. "It is always a pull having been on the staff, even for a short time. The staff always get their names in orders, and that gives a fellow much better chances in the future. Besides, in a campaign like this, where the division gets often broken up, there is plenty of work to do.

"Well, I hope you will soon be back with us again."

Next morning Lisle took up his new duties, and was soon fully occupied in carrying messages from and to headquarters. One day he received orders to accompany one of the senior members of the staff, to reconnoitre a pass two miles from camp. It was a level ride to the mouth of the gorge. They had scarcely entered it when, from behind a rock a hundred yards away, a heavy volley was fired. The colonel's horse was shot dead and he, himself, was shot through the leg. Lisle was unwounded, and leapt from his horse.

"Ride for your life, Bullen!" the colonel said. "I am shot through the leg."

"MY HORSE MUST CARRY TWO, SIR," LISLE REPLIED

"My horse must carry two, sir," Lisle replied, lifting the officer, who was not wholly disabled, and placing him in the saddle.

"Jump up!" the officer said.

But the tribesmen were now within twenty yards, and Lisle drew his sword and gave the animal a sharp prick. It was already frightened with the shouting of the tribesmen, and went off like an arrow. Lisle, seeing that resistance was absolutely useless, threw down his sword; and stood with his arms folded, facing the natives. An order was shouted by a man who was evidently their leader and, pausing, those who were armed with breech loaders fired after the flying horseman; totally disregarding Lisle, who had the satisfaction of finding that his sacrifice had been effectual, for the horse pursued its way without faltering.

When it was out of range, the chief turned to Lisle. The Afridis value courage above all things, and were filled with admiration at the manner in which this young officer sacrificed himself for his superior. He signalled to Lisle to accompany him and, surrounded by the tribesmen, he was taken back to the rock from which they had first fired. Then, guarded by four armed men, he was conducted to a little village standing high among the hills.

"This is just my luck," he said to himself, when he was taken to a room in the principal house. "Here I am a prisoner again, just as the troops are going to march away. It is awfully bad luck. Still, if I ever do get back, I suppose the fact that I have saved Colonel Houghton's life will count for something in my favour. It was unlucky that there was not time for me to jump up behind him, but my horse was in bad condition, and we should have been a good deal longer under fire.

"However, I ought not to grumble at my luck. I believe I am the only officer who has been taken prisoner and, as it looks as if I am to be kept as a hostage, my life would seem to be safe. I certainly expected nothing but instant death when they rushed down upon me. I have no doubt that, by this time, a messenger has reached camp saying that they have got me; and that, if there is any farther advance, they will put me to death. As I know that the general did not intend to go any farther, and that every day is of importance in getting the troops down before winter sets in in earnest, I have no doubt that he will send back a message saying that, if any harm comes to me, they will, in the spring, return and destroy every house belonging to the tribe.

"I think I may consider myself safe, and shall find plenty of employment in learning their language, which may be useful to me at some time or other. I expect that, as soon as we leave, the people here will go down into one of their valleys. The cold up here must be getting frightful and, as there is not a tree anywhere near, they would not be able even to keep up fires.

"As to escape, I fear that will be impossible. The passes will all be closed by snow, and I have no doubt that, until they are sure of that, they will keep a sharp lookout after me."

Later in the day the tribesmen returned. The chief came into the room and, by means of signs and the few words that Lisle had picked up, when he was before a prisoner, he signified to him that if he attempted to make his escape he would at once be killed; but otherwise he would be well treated. For four or five days a vigilant watch was kept over him. Then it was relaxed, and he felt sure that the army had marched away.

Then preparations for a move began. Lisle volunteered to assist, and aided to pack up the scanty belongings, and filled bags with corn. The chief was evidently pleased with his willingness and, several times, gave him a friendly nod. At last all was in readiness; and the occupants of the village, together with their animals--all heavily laden, even the women carrying heavy burdens--started on their way. It was five days' journey, and they halted at last at a small village--which was evidently private property--down in the plains at the foot of the mountains and, as Lisle judged, at no very great distance from the frontier line.

Lisle now mixed a good deal with the natives, and thus he began to pick up a good many words of their language. Now that they were down on the plains, two men with rifles were always on guard over him, but he was allowed to move freely about, as he liked.

A fortnight after they were established in their new quarters another party of natives arrived, and there was a long and angry talk. As far as Lisle could understand, these were the permanent occupants of that portion of the plain, and had been accustomed to receive a small tribute from the hill people who came down to them. It seemed that, on the present occasion, they demanded a largely increased sum in cattle and sheep; on the ground that so many of the hill tribesmen had come down that their land was eaten up by them. The amount now demanded was larger than the hill people could pay. They, therefore, flatly rejected the terms offered them; and the newcomers retired, with threats of exterminating them.

For the next few days, the tribesmen were busy in putting the village in a state of defence. A deep ditch was dug round it, and this was surmounted by an abattis of bushes. Fresh loopholes were pierced in the tower, and stones were gathered in the upper story, in readiness to throw down on any assailants.

As soon as the work was begun, Lisle signified to the chief that he was ready to take part in it, and to aid in the defence. The chief was pleased with his offer, and gladly accepted it. Lisle worked hard among them. He needed to give them no advice. Accustomed to tribal war, the men were perfectly competent to carry out the work. There were but three towers capable of defence, and in these the whole of the villagers were now gathered. Men and women alike worked at the defences. Their sheep and cattle were driven into the exterior line, and were only allowed to go out to graze under a strong guard.

A fortnight passed before there were any signs of the enemy, and then a dark mass was seen approaching. The cattle were hastily driven in, and the men gathered behind the hedge. Lisle asked the chief for a rifle, but the latter shook his head.

"We have not enough for ourselves," he said. "Here is a pistol we took from you, and a sword. You must do the best you can with them. It is probable that, before the fight goes on long, there will be rifles without masters, and you will be able to find one. Are you a good shot?"

"Yes, a very good one."

"Very well, the first that becomes free you shall have."

The assailants halted five hundred yards from the village. Then one rode forward. When he came within a hundred yards he halted, and shouted:

"Are you ready to pay the tribute fixed upon?"

"We are not," the chief said. "If you took all we have it would not be sufficient and, without our animals, we should starve when we got back to the hills; but I will pay twice the amount previously demanded."

"Then we will come and take them all," the messenger said.

"Come and take them," the chief shouted, and the messenger retired to the main body; who at once broke up, when they learned the answer, and proceeded to surround the village.

"Do you think," the chief said to Lisle, "that you could hit that man who is directing them?"

"I don't know the exact distance," Lisle said, "but I think that, if I had two or three shots, I could certainly knock him over."

"Give me your rifle," the chief said, to one of the tribesmen standing near him.

"Now, sahib, let us see what you can do."

Lisle took the rifle, and examined it to see that it was all right; and then, leaning down on a small rise of ground that permitted him to see over the hedge, he took steady aim and fired. The man he aimed at fell, at once.

"Well done, indeed!" the chief exclaimed, "you are a good shot. I will lend you my rifle. It is one of the best; but I only got it a short time since, and am not accustomed to it."

"Thank you, chief! I will do my best." Then, waving his arm round, he said, "You will do more good by looking after your men."

The chief went up to his house, and returned with an old smooth-bore gun and a bag of slugs.

"I shall do better with this," he said, "when they get close."

A heavy fire was opened on both sides; but the defenders, lying behind the hedge, had a considerable advantage; which almost neutralized the great superiority in numbers of the assailants, who were in the open. Lisle, lying down behind the bank from which he had fired, and only lifting his head above the crest to take aim, occupied himself exclusively with the men who appeared to be the leaders of the attack, and brought down several of them. The assailants presently drew off, and gathered together.

It was evident to Lisle, from his lookout, that there was a considerable difference of opinion among them; but at last they scattered again round the village and, lying down and taking advantage of every tuft of grass, they began to crawl forward on their stomachs. Although, as the line closed in, several were killed, it was evident that they would soon get near enough to make a rush.

The chief was evidently of the same opinion, for he shouted an order, and the defenders all leapt to their feet and ran to the three fortified houses. There were only three-and-twenty of them, in all. Lisle saw with satisfaction that they had evidently received orders, beforehand, from the chief; for seven were running to the chief's house, making up its garrison, altogether, to nine men; and seven were running to each of the others.

As the enemy burst through the bushes, which were but some twenty-five yards from the houses, the defenders opened fire from every loophole. At so short a distance every shot told; and the assailants recoiled, leaving more than a dozen dead behind them, while several of the others were wounded.

They now took up their places in the ditch, and fired through the hedge. Lisle at once signed to the chief to order his men to cease firing, and to withdraw from the loopholes.

"It is no good to fire now," he said. "Let them waste their ammunition."

The chief at once shouted orders to his men to cease firing, and to take their place on the lower story; the walls of which, being strongly built of stone, were impenetrable by bullets; while these passed freely through the lightly-built story above. The enemy continued to fire rapidly for some time; and then, finding that no reply was made, gradually stopped. There was a long pause.

"I think they are waiting till it is dark," Lisle said. "Tell the men to make torches, and thrust them out through the loopholes when the enemy come."

The chief nodded, after Lisle had repeated the sentence in a dozen different ways. He at once ordered the men to bring up ropes, and to soak them with oil; and then in a low voice, so that the assailants should not hear, repeated the order to the men in the other houses.

The ropes were cut up into lengths of three feet, and then there was nothing to do but to wait. The attack had begun at three in the afternoon, and by six it was quite dark. A loud yell gave the signal, and the enemy rushed through the hedge and surrounded the three houses. All had walls round them and, while the assailants battered at the doors, which had been backed up with earth and stones, the defenders lighted their torches and thrust them out, through loopholes in the upper stories, and then retired again to the ground floor.

The doors soon gave way to the attacks upon them, and the assailants rushed in, in a crowd. As they did so, the defenders poured in a terrible fire from their magazine rifles. The heads of the columns melted away, and the assailants fell back, hastily.

"I do not think they will try again," Lisle said. "If they have lost as heavily, in the other two houses, as they have here, their loss must have been heavy, indeed."

The torches were kept burning all night, but there was no repetition of the attack and, in the morning, the assailants were seen gathered half a mile away. Presently a man was observed approaching, waving a green bough. He was met at the hedge by the chief. He brought an offer that, if the Afridis were allowed to carry off their dead and wounded, they would be content that the same tribute as of old should be paid; and to take oath that it should not, in the future, be increased. The chief agreed to the terms, on condition that only twenty men should be allowed to pass the hedge, and that they should there hand over the dead to their companions.

On returning to his house, he made Lisle understand that, after the heavy loss they had inflicted on their assailants, there would forever be a blood feud between them; and that, in future, they would have to retire for the winter to some valley far away, and keep a constant watch until spring came again. When Lisle had, with great difficulty, understood what the chief said, he nodded.

"I can understand that, chief," he said, "and I think you should keep a very strong guard, every night, till we move away."

"Good man," the chief said, "you have fought by our side, and are no longer a prisoner but a friend. When spring comes, you shall go back to your own people."

It took some hours to remove the dead, of whom there were forty-three; and the badly wounded, who numbered twenty-two--but there was no doubt that many more had managed to crawl away.

Lisle now set to work to learn the language, in earnest. A boy was told off by the chief to be his companion and, at the end of two months, Lisle was able to converse without difficulty. The chief had already told him that he could leave when he liked, but that it would be very dangerous for him to endeavour to make his way to the frontier, especially as the tribe they had fought against occupied the intervening country.

"When we get among the hills, I will give you four men to act as your escort down the passes; but you will have to go in disguise for, after the fighting that has taken place, and the destruction of the villages, even if peace is made it would not be safe for a white man to travel among the mountains. He would certainly be killed."

Every precaution was taken against attack, and six men were stationed at the hedge, all night. Two or three times noises were heard, which seemed to proceed from a considerable body of men. The guard fired, but nothing more was heard. Evidently a surprise had been intended but, directly it was found that the garrison were on watch, and prepared, the idea was abandoned; for the lesson had been so severe that even the hope of revenge was not sufficient to induce them to run the risk of its repetition.

Lisle did not fret at his enforced stay. He was very popular in the little village, and was quite at home with the chief's family. The choicest bits of meat were always sent to him; and he was treated as an honoured guest, in every way.

"When you return to your people," the chief said, one day, "please tell them that, henceforth, we shall regard them as friends; and that, if they choose to march through our country, we will do all we can to aid them, by every means in our power."

"I will certainly tell them so," Lisle replied, "and the kindness you have shown me will assuredly be rewarded."

"I regret that we fought against you," the chief said, "but we were misled. They will not take away our rifles from us, I hope; for without them we should be at the mercy of the other tribes. These may give up many rifles, but they are sure to retain some and, though there are other villages of our clan, we should be an easy prey, if it were known that we were unarmed."

"I think I can promise that, after your friendly conduct to me, you will not be required to make any payment, whatever; and indeed, for so small a matter as twenty rifles, your assurances, that these would never again be used against us, would be taken into consideration."

When Lisle had been in the village about three months, one of the men came up to him and spoke in Punjabi.

"Why, how did you learn Punjabi?" he said, in surprise; "and why did you not speak to me in it, before? It would have saved me an immense deal of trouble, when I first came."

"I am sorry," the man said, "but the thought that you could speak Punjabi did not enter my mind. I thought that you were a young white officer who had just come out from England. I learnt it because I served, for fifteen years, in the 32nd Punjabis."

"You did?" Lisle said; "why, the 32nd Punjabis was my father's regiment! How long have you left it?"

"Six years ago, sahib."

"Then you must remember my father, Captain Bullen."

"Truly I remember him," the man said. "He was one of our best and kindest officers. And he was your father?"

"Yes. You might remember me too, I must have been eleven or twelve years old."

The man looked hard at him.

"I think, sir, that I remember your face; but of course you have changed a good deal, since then. I remember you well, for you often came down our lines; and you could speak the language fluently, and were fond of talking to us.

"And your father, is he well?"

"He was killed, three years ago," Lisle said, "in an attack on a hill fort."

"I am sorry, very sorry. He was a good man. And so you are an officer in his regiment?"

"No," Lisle said, "I left the regiment in the march to the relief of Chitral. They wanted to send me home, so I darkened my skin and enlisted in the regiment, by the aid of Gholam Singh; and went through the campaign without even being suspected, till just at the end."

"You went as a soldier?" the man said, in surprise; "never before have I heard of a white sahib passing as a native, and enlisting in the ranks. You lived and fought with the men, without being discovered! Truly, it is wonderful."

"I did not manage quite so well as I ought to have done; for I found, afterwards, that I had been suspected before we got to Chitral. Then Colonel Kelly took me out of the ranks and made me a temporary officer, and afterwards got a commission for me."

"It is truly wonderful," the man repeated.

From that time the native took every pains to show him respect and liking for the son of his old officer; and the account he gave, to the others, of the affection with which the young sahib's father was regarded by the regiment, much increased the cordiality with which he was generally treated. Spring came at last, and the snow line gradually rose among the distant hills and, at last, the chief announced that they could now start for their summer home.

The news was received with general satisfaction, for the night watches and the constant expectation of attack weighed heavily upon them all. The decision was announced at dawn and, three hours afterwards, the animals were packed and they set out on the march. They had started a fortnight earlier than usual for, if they had waited till the usual time, their old enemies would probably have placed an ambush.

They travelled without a halt, until they were well among the hills. Then the wearied beasts were unladen, fires were lighted, and a meal cooked. But even yet they were not altogether safe from attack; and sentries were posted, some distance down the hill, to give notice of the approach of an enemy. The night, however, passed quietly; and the next evening they were high among the hills, and camped, for the first time for three months, with a sense of security.

It was determined to rest here for a few days, for they had almost reached the snow line. This was receding fast, under the hot rays of the sun, but it was certain that the gorges would be full of fierce torrents; and that, until these abated somewhat, they would be absolutely impassable. A week was extended into a fortnight. As the snow melted the grass grew, as if by magic; and the animals rapidly regained condition and strength. Then they started again and, after encountering no little difficulty and hardship, arrived at their mountain home.

"Now, sahib," the chief said the next morning, "I will keep my promise to you, and will send four of my men with you to Peshawar. The sun and the glare from the snow have browned you almost to our colour, so there will be no occasion for you to stain your face and, in Afghan costume, you could pass anywhere. Besides, you speak our language so well that, even if you were questioned, no one would suspect that you are not one of ourselves."

"How many days will it take, chief?"

"In five days you will be at Peshawar. I know not whether you will find an army assembled there, to march again into our country; but I hope that peace has been settled. It will take the tribes all the year to rebuild their houses. It will be years before their flocks and herds increase to what they were before and, now they have found that British troops can force their way through their strongest passes, that they can no longer defy white men to enter their lands, they will be very careful not to draw down the anger of the white man upon themselves. They will have a hard year of it to repair, in any way, the damages they have incurred; to say nothing of the loss of life that they have suffered. They have also had to give up great numbers of their rifles; and this, alone, will render them careful, at any rate until they replace them; so I do not think that there will be any chance of fighting this year, or for some years to come. I am sure I hope not."

"I hope not, also," Lisle said. "We too have lost heavily, and the expense has been immense. We shall be as glad as your people to live at peace. I think I may safely say that, if the country is quiet, a messenger will be sent up from Peshawar with the general's thanks for the way in which I have been treated; and with assurances that, whatever may happen, your village will be respected by any force that may march into the country. Probably such an assurance will be sent by the men who go with me."

Another fortnight was spent in the village, for the rivers were still filled to the brim; but as soon as the chief thought that the passes were practicable, Lisle, in Afridi costume, started with four of the men. All the village turned out to bid him goodbye; several of the women, and many of the children, crying at his departure.

The journey down was accomplished without adventure; the men giving out, at the villages at which they stopped, that they were on their way to Peshawar, to give assurances to the British there that they were ready to submit to terms. On nearing Peshawar, Lisle abandoned his Afridi costume and resumed his khaki uniform.

When he arrived at the town, he went at once to headquarters. The sentry at the door belonged to his own regiment; and he started, and his rifle almost fell from his hand, as his eye fell upon Lisle.

"I am not a ghost," Lisle laughed, "but am very much alive."

"I am glad to see you again, Wilkins," and he passed in at the door.

"Is the general engaged?" he asked the orderly who, like the soldier at the door, stood gazing at him stupidly.

"No, sir," the man gasped.

"Then I will go in unannounced."

General Lockhart looked up from the papers he was reading, and gave a sudden start.

"I have come to report myself ready for duty, sir," Lisle said, with a smile.

"Good heavens! Mr. Bullen, you have given me quite a turn! We had all regarded your death as certain; and your name appeared in the list of casualties, five months ago.

"I am truly glad to see you again," and he heartily shook Lisle's hand. "There is another in here who will be glad to see you."

He opened the door, and said:

"Colonel Houghton, will you step in here, for a moment?"

As the colonel entered the room, and his eye fell upon Lisle, he stood as if suddenly paralysed. The blood rushed from his cheeks.

"I am glad to see that you have recovered from your wound, sir," Lisle said.

The blood surged back into the colonel's face. He strode forward and, grasping both Lisle's hands in his own, said in broken accents:

"So it is really you, alive and well! This is indeed a load off my mind. I have always blamed myself for saving my life at the expense of your own. It would have embittered my life to the end of my days.

"And you are really alive! I thank God for it. I tried in vain to check my horse, but it got the bit between its teeth and, with my wounded leg, I had no power to turn him. As I rode, I pictured to myself your last defence; how you died fighting.

"How has this all come about?" and he looked at the general, as if expecting an answer.

"I know no more than yourself, Houghton. He had but just entered when I called you in."

"Now, Mr. Bullen, let us hear how it happened."

"It was very simple, sir. The Afridis were but twenty paces away, when I started the colonel's horse. I saw that fighting would be hopeless, so threw down my sword and pistol. I should have been cut up at once, had not their chief shouted to them to leave me alone, and to fire after Colonel Houghton. This they did and, I was happy to see, without success."

"Then the chief sent me off, under the guard of four men, to his village; with the intention, as I afterwards heard, of holding me as a hostage. A week later we moved down to the plain. When we had been settled in our winter quarters for about two months, we were attacked by a neighbouring tribe.

"By this time I had begun to pick up enough of the language to make myself understood. I volunteered to aid in the defence. The chief gave me his rifle, and I picked off a few of the leading assailants, and aided in the defence of the village. The enemy were beaten off with very heavy loss, and the chief was pleased to attribute their defeat to my advice.

"He at once declared that I was to regard myself no longer as a prisoner, but as a guest. I spent the next three months in getting up their language, which I can now speak fluently enough for all purposes.

"All this time, a vigilant watch had been kept against another attack and, as soon as the snow began to melt, we returned to the mountains. There we remained until the passes were open; and then the chief sent me down, with an escort of four, and I arrived here a quarter of an hour before I reported myself.

"I believe that I owe my life, in the first place, to the Afridi's surprise at my sending off Colonel Houghton on my horse."

"No wonder he was surprised, Mr. Bullen. It was a splendid action; and in reporting your death, I spoke of it in the warmest terms; and said that, had you returned alive, I should have recommended you for the V.C.

"I shall, of course renew the recommendation, now that you have returned."

Turning to Colonel Houghton, he said:

"You no doubt wish to have a further chat with Lieutenant Bullen and, as there is no special work here today, pray consider yourself at liberty to take him down to your quarters."

"Thank you, sir! I shall certainly be glad to learn further about the affair."

"If you please, General," Lisle said, "I have a message to give you, from the chief. He says that, henceforth, he will be friends with the British; and that if you ever enter his country again, he will do all in his power to aid you. He hopes that you will allow them to retain their rifles and, as they only amount to some three or four and twenty fighting men, I was tempted to promise him that you would."

"You were quite right, Mr. Bullen. I suppose the men who accompanied you are still here?"

"Yes."

"Tell them not to go away. I will myself send a message to their chief."

"We will write him a letter, Colonel Houghton, thanking him for his kindness to his prisoner; sending him a permit to retain his arms, and a present which will enable his tribe to increase their flocks and herds."

"Thank you very much, sir! I shall myself, of course, send a present of some sort, in return for his kindness."

"You talk the Pathan language with facility?"

"Yes, sir. I was five months with them, and devoted the chief part of my time to picking it up."

"You shall be examined at the first opportunity, Mr. Bullen; and the acquisition of their language, as well as your proficiency in Punjabi will, of course, greatly add to your claim to be placed on staff appointments; and will add somewhat to your income.

"I hope you will dine with me, this evening; when you can give me a full account of your life in the village, and of that fight you spoke of. It will be highly interesting to learn the details of one of these tribal fights."

Lisle accompanied Colonel Houghton to his quarters with a little reluctance, for he was anxious to rejoin his comrades in the regiment.

"Now, Bullen, tell me all about it," the colonel said. "I know that you lifted me on to your horse. I called to you to jump up behind, as the Afridis were close upon us; and I have never been able to make out why the horse should have gone off at a mad gallop, with me; but no doubt it was scared by the yells of the Afridis."

"When I lifted you up, sir, I certainly intended to get up behind you; but the Afridis were so close that I felt that it was impossible to do so, and that we should both be shot down before we got out of range; so I gave the horse a prod with my sword and, as I saw him go off at a gallop, I threw down my arms, as I told you."

"As it has turned out," the colonel said, "there is no doubt that the tribesmen, valiant fighters themselves, admire courage. If you had resisted, no doubt you would have been cut down; but your action must have appeared so extraordinary, to them, that they spared you.

"I have often bitterly reproached myself that I was unable to share your fate. You are still young, and I am old enough to be your father. I am unmarried, with no particular ties in the world. You have given me new interest in life. It will be a great pleasure for me to watch your career.

"If you have no objection I shall formally adopt you; and shall, tomorrow, draw out a will appointing you heir to all I possess--which I may tell you is something like fifteen thousand pounds--and shall make it my business to push you forward."

"It is too much altogether, Colonel."

"Not at all, Bullen; you saved my life, when certain death seemed to be staring you in the face; and it is a small thing, when I have no longer need of it, that you should inherit what I leave behind.

"In the meantime, I shall make you an allowance of a couple of hundred a year, as my adopted son. Say no more about it; you are not stepping into anyone else's shoes, for I have no near relation, no one who has a right to expect a penny at my death; and I have hitherto not even taken the trouble to make a will. You will, I hope, consider me, in the future, as standing in the place of the brave father you lost, some years ago."

Lisle remained chatting with the officer for an hour, and then the latter said:

"I won't keep you any longer, now. I am sure you must be wanting to see your friends in the camp."

As soon as Lisle neared the lines of the regiment, he saw the soldiers waiting about in groups. These closed up as he approached. The sentry to whom he had spoken had been relieved, and had told the news of his return to his comrades and, as he came along, the whole regiment gathered round Lisle, and cheer after cheer went up. He had gone but a few paces when he was seized and placed upon the shoulders of two of the men; and carried in triumph, surrounded by the other men, still cheering, to the front of the mess room. He was so affected, by the warmth of the greeting, that the tears were running down his cheeks when he was allowed to alight.

The officers, who had, of course, received the news, gathered at the mess room when he was seen approaching. Before going up to them Lisle turned and, raising his hand for silence, said:

"I thank you with all my heart, men, for the welcome you have given me; and the proof that you have afforded me of your liking for me. I thank you again and again, and shall never forget this reception."

There was a fresh outburst of cheering, and Lisle then turned, and ascended the four steps leading up to the mess room.

CHAPTER 13: THE V.C.

The colonel was standing, surrounded by his officers.

"I welcome you back, Mr. Bullen," he said, as he shook the lad's hand heartily, "in the name of the officers of the regiment, and my own. We are proud of you, sir. How you escaped death, we know not; it is enough for us that you are back, and are safe and sound.

"Your deed, in saving Colonel Houghton's life at what seemed the sacrifice of your own, had been a sore trial and a grief to all of us. No doubt existed in our minds that you had been cut to pieces, and you seem to have almost come back from the dead."

The other officers then crowded round him, shaking his hand and congratulating him on his escape.

"Now, come in and tell us how this miracle has come about. We can understand that you have been held as a hostage, but how is it that you are here?

"Now, do you get up on a chair, and give us a true and faithful account of all that happened to you, and how it is that you effected your escape."

"I did not effect my escape at all," Lisle said, as he mounted the chair; "I was released without any terms being made and, for the past three months, have been treated as an honoured guest by the Afridi chief into whose hands I fell."

"Well, tell the story from the beginning," the colonel said; "what you have said only adds to our wonder."

Lisle modestly told the story, amid frequent cross questioning.

"Well, there is no doubt that you were lucky, Lisle," the colonel said, when he had brought his story to a conclusion. "The pluck of your action, in getting Colonel Houghton off and staying yourself, appealed strongly to the Afridis; and caused their chief to decide to retain you as a hostage, instead of killing you at once. I do not suppose that he really thought that he would gain much, by saving you; for he must have known that we are in a hurry to get down through the passes, and must consider it very doubtful whether we should ever return. Still, no doubt he would have detained you and, in the spring, sent down to say that you were in his hands; and in that way would have endeavoured to make terms for your release. But your assistance when he was attacked, and your readiness to take part with his people, entirely changed his attitude towards you.

"However, I don't suppose he will lose by it. The general is sure to send back a handsome present to him, for his conduct towards you.

"Have you seen Houghton yet?"

"Yes, sir; I have been with him for the past hour. He has been more than kind to me and, as he has no near relations, has been good enough to say that he will adopt me as his heir. So I have indeed been amply rewarded for the service I did him."

"I congratulate you most heartily," the colonel said; "you have well earned it, and I am sure that there is not a man in the army who will envy your good fortune. There is only one thing wanting to complete it, and that is the V.C.; which I have not the least doubt in the world will be awarded to you, and all my fellow officers will agree with me that never was it more nobly earned. You courted what seemed certain death.

"The greater portion of the crosses have been earned by men for carrying in wounded comrades, under a heavy fire; but that is nothing to your case. Those actions were done on the spur of the moment, and there was every probability that the men would get back unhurt. Yours was the facing of a certain death. I can assure you that it will be the occasion of rejoicings, on the part of the whole regiment, when you appear for the first time with a cross on your breast."

He rang the bell and, when one of the mess waiters appeared, told him to bring half a dozen bottles of champagne. Lisle's health was then drunk, with three hearty cheers. Lunch was on the table, and Lisle was heartily glad when the subject of his own deeds was dropped, and they started to discuss the meal.

"Now, Mr. Bullen," the colonel said, when the meal was finished, "I must carry you off to the ladies. They have all rejoined, and will be as anxious as we were to hear of your return."

"Must I go, Colonel?" Lisle asked shyly.

"Of course you must, Bullen. When a man performs brave deeds, he must be expected to be patted on the back--metaphorically, at any rate--by the ladies. So you have got to go through it all and, as I have sent word round that I shall bring you to my bungalow, you will be able to get it all over at once."

"Well, sir, I suppose I must do it, though I would much rather not. Still, as you say, it were best to get it all over at once."

Six ladies were gathered at the bungalow, as Lisle entered with the colonel. All rose as they entered, and pressed round him, shaking his hand.

"I have come to tell you how pleased we all were," the colonel's wife said, "to hear that you had returned, and how eager we have all been to learn how it has come about. We think it very unkind of you to stay so long in the mess room, when you must have known that we are all on thorns to hear about it. I can assure you that we have missed you terribly, since the regiment returned, and we are awfully glad to have you back again.

"Now, please tell us all about it. We know, of course, how you got Colonel Houghton off, and remained to die; and how proud all the regiment has been of your exploit; so you can start and tell us how it was that you escaped from being cut to mince-meat."

Lisle again went through the story.

"Why did you not return at once, when the chief who captured you said that you were his guest? Was there not some fair young Afridi, who held you in her chains?"

Lisle laughed.

"I can assure you that it was no feminine attractions that kept me. There were some fifteen or twenty girls and, like everyone else, they were very kind to me but, so far as I was able to judge, not one of them was prettier, or I should rather say less ugly, than the rest; although several of them had very good features, and were doubtless considered lovely by the men. Certainly there was none whom an Englishman would look at twice.

"Poor things, most of the work of the village is left to them. They went out to cut grass, fed the cattle, gathered firewood, and ground the corn; and I have no doubt that they are now all occupied with the work of tilling the little patches of fertile ground beyond the village.

"Besides, ladies, you must remember that I have a vivid recollection of you all; which would, alone, have guarded me against falling in love with any dusky maiden."

"I rather doubt your word, Mr. Bullen," the colonel's wife said; "you were always very ready to make yourself pleasant, and do our errands, and to make yourself generally useful and agreeable; but I do not remember that you ever ventured upon making a compliment before. You must have learnt the art somehow."

The lady laughed.

"I could hardly help comparing you with the women round me, but I really had a vivid remembrance of your kindness to me."

"In future, Mr. Bullen, we shall consider you as discharged from all duty. We have heard of other gallant deeds that you have done; and henceforth shall regard you, with a real respect, as an officer who has brought great credit upon the regiment. I am sure that, henceforth, you will lose your old nickname of 'the boy,' and be regarded as a hero."

"I hope not," Lisle said; "it has been very pleasant to be regarded as a boy, and therefore to act as a sort of general fag to you. I hope you will continue to regard me as so. I have always considered it a privilege to be able to make myself useful to you, and I should be very sorry to lose it.

"I can assure you that I still feel as a boy. I know nothing of the world; have passed my whole time, as far back as I can remember, in camp; and have thoroughly enjoyed my life. I suppose some day I shall lose the feeling that I am still a boy, but I shall certainly hold to it as long as I can."

"I suppose you had some difficulty in speaking with the natives?" the doctor's wife said.

"At first I had but, from continually talking with them, I got to know their language--I won't say as well as Punjabi, but certainly very well--and I shall pass in it at the next examination."

"I wish all subalterns were like you," the colonel's wife said. "Most of those who come out from England are puffed up with a sense of their own importance, and I often wish that I could take them by the shoulders, and shake them well. And what are you going to do now?"

"I am going off to find the four men who came down with me, see if they are comfortable, and tell them that the general will give them the message to their chief, tomorrow."

"What will be the next thing, Mr. Bullen?"

"The next thing will be to go to the bazaar, and choose some presents for the chief and his family."

"What do you mean to get?"

"I think a brace of revolvers, and a good store of ammunition for the chief. As to the women I must, I suppose, get something in the way of dress. For the other men I shall get commoner things. Everyone has been most kind to me, and I should certainly like them to have some remembrance of my stay.

"I suppose that there is five months' pay waiting for me in the paymaster's chest."

"I should doubt it extremely," the colonel said. "You will get it in time, but you will have to wait. You have been struck off the regimental pay list, ever since you were put down as dead; and I expect the paymaster will have to get a special authorization, before you can draw your back pay."

"I was only joking, Colonel. My agent at Calcutta has my money in his hands, and I have only to draw on him."

"So much the better, Bullen. It is always a nuisance getting into debt, even when you are certain that funds will be forthcoming which will enable you to repay what you owe. But have you enough to carry you on till you hear from your agent?"

"Plenty, sir; I left all the money I did not care to carry about with me in the regimental till."

"Then I expect you will find it there still. I know that nothing has been done with it. A short time since, the paymaster was speaking to me about it, and asking me if I knew the address of any of your relations, or who was your agent at Calcutta. He said to me:

"'I shall wait a bit longer. Mr. Bullen turned up quite unexpectedly, once before and, though I fear there is not a shadow of chance that he will do so again, I will hold the money for a time. It is just possible that he is held as a hostage, in which case we shall probably hear of him, when the passes are open.'"

Lisle went to the paymaster's at once and, finding that he had not parted with the money, drew fifty pounds. He had no difficulty in buying the revolvers and cartridges; but was so completely at a loss as to the female garments, and the price he ought to pay, that he went back to the cantonment and asked two of the ladies to accompany him shopping. This they at once consented to do and, with their aid, he laid in a stock of female garments: silk for the chief's wife; and simpler, but good and useful materials--for the most part of bright colour--for the other women. These were all parcelled up in various bundles, and a looking glass inserted in each parcel. For the men he bought bright waistbands and long knives; and gave, in addition, a present in money to the men who had come down with him.

It was evening before the work was finished, and he then returned to mess with the regiment.

"I suppose you don't know yet whether you are coming back to us, Bullen?" the major said.

"No, sir, the general did not say; but for myself, I would very much rather join the regiment. Staff appointment sounds tempting, but I must say that I should greatly prefer regimental work; especially as I should be very much junior to the other officers of the staff, and should feel myself out of place among them."

"I have no doubt that you are right, in that respect; but staff appointments lead to promotion."

"I have no ambition for promotion, for the present, Major. I am already five or six up among the senior lieutenants, which is quite high enough for one of my age."

"Well, perhaps you are right. It is not a good thing for a young officer to be pushed on too fast, and another two or three years of regimental work will certainly do you no harm."

"I have not yet asked, Major, whether we are going up into the Tirah again, this spring?"

"I fancy not. Already several deputations have come in from the tribesmen, some of them bringing in the fines imposed upon them; and all seem to say that there is a general desire among the Afridis for peace, and that deputations from other tribes will shortly follow them."

"I am glad to hear it, sir," Lisle said. "I think I have had quite enough of hill fighting."

"I think we are all of the same opinion, Bullen. It is no joke fighting an enemy hidden behind rocks, armed with Lee-Metford rifles, and trained to shoot as well as a British marksman.

"The marching was even worse than the fighting. Passing a night on the snow, any number of thousand feet above the sea, is worse than either of them. No, I would rather go through a campaign against the Russians, than have anything more to do with the Tirah; though I must admit that, if we were to begin at once, we should not have snow to contend with.

"I have been through several campaigns, but the last was infinitely the hardest, and I have not the least desire to repeat it. Whether all the tribes choose to send in and accept our terms, or not, makes no very great difference; they have had such a sharp lesson that it will certainly be some time before they rise again in revolt. There may be an occasional cattle-lifting raid across the frontier, but one can put up with that; and it would be infinitely cheaper for Government to compensate the victims, than for us to get an army in motion again, to punish the thieves.

"Moreover, having once taught them that we are stronger than they, it would be a pity to weaken them still further for, if a Russian army were to try and force its way into India, these fellows would make it very hot for them. They are full of fight and, although they are independent of Afghanistan, and have no particular patriotic feeling, the thirst for plunder would bring them like bees round an invading army.

"No, the thing has been well done, but the expense has been enormous and the losses serious; and I trust that, at any rate as long as we are stationed in Northern India, things will be quiet."

Next morning Lisle went, early, to headquarters. He had to wait a little time before he could see the general. When he went in, General Lockhart said:

"Now about yourself, Mr. Bullen. Your place has, of course, been filled up; but I shall be glad to appoint you as extra aide-de-camp, if you wish. Would you rather be on staff duty, or rejoin your regiment?"

"If you give me the choice, sir, I would rather rejoin the regiment. Staff duty in war time is extremely interesting; but in peace time, I would rather be at work with the regiment.

"You see, sir, I am very young, and much younger than any of the staff; and I am sure that I should feel very much out of place."

"I agree with you," the general said, with a smile. "I think that you are wise to prefer regimental duty. I have written home, giving my account of your gallant action; telling how you were not, as reported, killed; and recommending you, in the strongest possible terms, for the V.C."

"I am greatly indebted to you, sir. I do not feel that I have done anything at all out of the way, and acted only on the impulse of the moment."

"You could not have done better, had you thought of it for an hour," the general said; "but as I also reported your defence of that hut, I have little doubt that you will get the well-earned V.C."

There was great satisfaction among the officers and the regiment, when Lisle told them of his interview with the general.

It was soon evident, from the sale of the transport animals, that the war was over; and the regiment shortly afterwards returned to their old quarters, at Rawal Pindi, and fell into the old routine of drill.

In the middle of the following summer Lisle, while fielding at cricket in a match with another regiment, suddenly staggered and fell. The surgeon, running up from the pavilion, pronounced it as a case of sunstroke. It was some time before he was conscious again.

"What has happened?" he asked.

"You have had a bad sunstroke," the surgeon said, "and I am going to send you home, as soon as you are able to travel. I shall apply for at least a year's leave for you, and I hope that, by the end of that time, you will be perfectly fit for work again; but certainly a period of rest, and the return to a temperate climate, is absolutely necessary for you."

Long before this, a despatch had been received from England bestowing the Victoria Cross upon Lisle. General Lockhart himself came down from Peshawar and fixed it to his breast, in presence of the whole regiment, drawn up in parade order. The outburst of cheering from the men told unmistakably how popular he was with them, and how they approved of the honour bestowed upon him.

The general dined at mess, and was pleased to see how popular the young officer was with his men. He himself proposed Lisle's health, and the latter was obliged to return thanks.

When he sat down, the general said:

"It is clear, Mr. Bullen, that you have more presence of mind, when engaged with the enemy, than you have when surrounded with friends. It can hardly be said that eloquence is your forte."

"No, sir," Lisle said, wiping the perspiration from his face, "I would rather go through eleven battles, than have to make another speech."

The application for sick leave was granted at once and, a fortnight later, Lisle took his place in the train for Calcutta. All the officers and their wives assembled to see him off.

"I hope," said the colonel, "you will come back in the course of a year, thoroughly restored to health. It is all in your favour that you have not been a drinking man; and the surgeon told me that he is convinced that the brain has suffered no serious injury, and that you will be on your feet again, and fit for any work, after the twelve months' leave. But, moderate as you always are, I should advise you to eschew altogether alcoholic liquids. Men who have never had a touch of sunstroke can drink them with impunity but, to a man who has had sunstroke, they are worse than poison."

"All right, Colonel! Nothing stronger than lemonade shall pass my lips."

And so, with the good wishes of his friends, Lisle started for Calcutta. Here he drew from his agents a sum which, he calculated, would last him for a year at home. To his great pleasure, on entering the train he met his friend Colonel Houghton.

"I have been thinking for some time, lad," he said, "of applying for a year's leave; which I have earned by twelve years' service out here. I was with the general when your application for leave arrived, and made up my mind to go home with you. I therefore telegraphed to Simla, and got leave at once; so I shall be able to look after you, on the voyage."

"It is very kind of you," Lisle said. "It will be a comfort, indeed, having a friend on board. My brain seems to be all right now, but my memory is very shaky. However, I hope that will be all right, too, by the time we arrive in England."

The presence of the colonel was indeed a great comfort to Lisle. The latter looked after him as a father might have done, placed his chair in the coolest spot to be found and, by relating to the other passengers the service by which Lisle had won the V.C., ensured their sympathy and kindness.

By the time the voyage was over, Lisle felt himself again. His brain had gradually cleared, and he could again remember the events of his life. He stayed three or four days at the hotel in London where the colonel put up; and then went down into the country, in response to an invitation from his aunt, which had been sent off as soon as she received a letter from him, announcing his arrival in England. His uncle's place was a quiet parsonage in Somersetshire, and the rest and quiet did him an immense deal of good.

At the end of three months' stay there, he left to see something of London and England, and travelled about for some months.

When the year was nearly up, and he was making his preparations to return to India, he received a summons to attend at the War Office. Wondering greatly what its purport could be, he called upon the adjutant general.

"How are you feeling, Mr. Bullen?" the latter asked.

"Perfectly well, sir, as well as I ever felt in my life."

"We are sending a few officers to aid Colonel Willcocks in effecting the relief of the party now besieged in Coomassie. Your record is an excellent one and, if you are willing and able to go, we shall be glad to include you in the number."

"I should like it very much. There is no chance, whatever, of active service in India; and I should be glad, indeed, to be at the front again, in different circumstances."

"Very well, Mr. Bullen, then you will sail on Tuesday next, in the steamer that leaves Liverpool on that day. You will have the local rank of captain, and will be in command of a company of Hausas."

Lisle had but a few preparations to make. He ordered, at once, a khaki uniform and pith helmet, and a supply of light shirts and underclothing. Then he ran down to Somersetshire to say goodbye to his uncle and aunt, and arrived in Liverpool on the Monday evening. Sleeping at the hotel at the station, he went on board the next morning.

Here he found half a dozen other officers, also bound for the west coast of Africa, and soon got on friendly terms with them. He was, of course, obliged to tell how he had won the Victoria Cross; a recital which greatly raised him in their estimation.

They had fine weather throughout the voyage; and were glad, indeed, when the steamer anchored off Cape Coast. Although looking forward to their arrival at Cape Coast, the officers were not in their highest spirits. All of them had applied for service in South Africa, where the war was now raging but, to their disappointment, had been sent on this minor expedition. At any other time, they would have been delighted at the opportunity of taking part in it; but now, with a great war going on, it seemed to them a very petty affair, indeed.

They cheered themselves, however, by the assumption that there was sure to be hard fighting; and opportunities for distinguishing themselves at least as great as they would meet with at the Cape, where so vast a number of men were engaged that it would be difficult for one officer to distinguish himself beyond others.

Until he started, Lisle had scarcely more than heard the name of Ashanti; though he knew, of course, that two expeditions, those under Sir Garnet Wolseley and Sir Francis Scott, had reached the capital, the latter dethroning the king and carrying him away into captivity. Now, however, he gathered full details of the situation, from two officers belonging to the native troops, who had been hurriedly ordered to cut short their leave, and go back to take their places with the corps to which they were attached.

There was no doubt that the Ashantis were one of the most formidable tribes in Africa. Their territory extended from the river Prah to sixty miles north of Cape Coast. They were feared by all their neighbours, with whom they were frequently at war--not so much for the sake of extending their territory, as for the purpose of obtaining great numbers of men and women for their hideous sacrifices, at Coomassie. They were in close alliance with the tribes at Elmina, which place we had taken over from the Portuguese, some years before Sir Garnet Wolseley's expedition. This occupation was bitterly opposed by the Ashantis, who felt that it cut them off from free trade with the coast. In return, they intercepted all trade with the coast from the tribes behind them; and finally seized some white missionaries at their capital, and sent a defiant message down to Cape Coast.

The result was that Sir Garnet Wolseley was sent out to take command of an expedition and, with three white regiments, a small Naval Brigade, and the West African Regiment, completely defeated the Ashantis in two pitched battles, reached the capital, and burnt it. Unfortunately, owing to the want of carriers, and the small amount of supplies that were sent up, he was obliged to fall back again to the coast, after occupying the capital for only three days.

Had it been possible to leave a sufficient force there, the spirit of the Ashantis would have been broken. This, however, could not be done; and they gradually regained their arrogant spirit, carried out none of their obligations and, twenty-two years later, having quite forgotten their reverses, they resumed their raids across the Prah.

Sir Francis Scott's expedition was therefore organized, and marched to the capital. This time the former mistake was not committed. A small garrison was left to overawe its inhabitants, and the king was carried away a prisoner. The expedition had encountered no opposition. The reason for this was never satisfactorily ascertained, but it is probable that the Ashantis were taken by surprise, and thought it better to wait until they had obtained better arms. In this they were successful, for there are always rascally traders, ready to supply the enemies of their country with arms, on terms of immense profit.

The Ashantis were evidently kept well informed, by some of their tribesmen settled in the coast towns, of the state of affairs in Europe and, in the belief that England was fully occupied at the Cape, and that no white soldiers would be sent, they again rose in rebellion. They were ready to admit that the white soldiers were superior to themselves, but they entertained a profound contempt for our black troops, whom they were convinced they could defeat without difficulty.

Certainly, the force available at Cape Coast was altogether insufficient for the purpose; for it consisted only of a battalion of Hausa Constabulary, and two seven-pounder guns. Sierra Leone had a permanent garrison of one battalion of the West Indian Regiment, and a West African Regiment recruited on the spot; but few of these could be spared, for Sierra Leone had its own native troubles. The garrison of Lagos was similar to that of Cape Coast; but here, also, troubles were dreaded with their neighbours at Abeokuta. Southern Nigeria had their own regiment; while Northern Nigeria had the constabulary of the Royal Niger Company, and they had, at the time, just raised two battalions and three batteries. Fortunately, the recent dispute between the people and ourselves as to their respective boundaries had been temporarily arranged, and a portion of these troops could be utilized.

The two regiments were both numerically strong, each company amounting to a hundred and fifty men. They were armed with Martini-Metford carbines, and each company had a Vickers-Maxim gun. The batteries were provided with powerful guns, capable of throwing twelve-pound shells. The men were all Hausas and Yorubas, with the exception of one company of Neupas. This contingent were supplied with khaki, before starting; and the rest were in blue uniform, similar to that worn by the West Indian Regiments. There was, in addition, a small battalion of the Central African Regiment; with a detachment of Sikhs, who also supplied non-commissioned officers.

That the men would fight well, all believed; but the forces had been but recently organized, and it was questionable how they would behave without a backbone of white troops. The experiment was quite a novel one, as never before had a war been carried on, by us, with purely native troops.

The collection of the troops was a difficult matter, and cost no small time; especially from Northern Nigeria, which was to supply a much larger contingent than the others. These troops were scattered in small bodies over a large extent of country, for the most part hundreds of miles from the coast. There was a great paucity of officers, too; and of these, many were about to take their year's leave home, worn out and weakened by the unhealthy climate. By prodigious exertions, however, all were at last collected, and in readiness to proceed to the scene of operations.

Picking up troops at several points, the steamer at last arrived off Cape Coast; but not yet were they to land. A strong wind was blowing, and the surf beat with such violence, on the shore, that it was impossible even for the surf boat to come out. The officers had nothing to do but to watch the shore. Even this was only done under difficult circumstances, for the steamer was rolling rail under.

The prospect, however, was not unpleasing. From a projecting point stood the old Dutch castle, a massive-looking building. On its left was the town, on rising ground, with whitewashed buildings; and behind all, and in the town itself, rose palm trees, which made a dark fringe along the coast on either hand.

"It doesn't look such a bad sort of place," one of the officers said, "and certainly it ought to be healthy, if it were properly drained down to the sea. Yet it is a home of fever; one night ashore, in the bad season, is almost certain death for a white man. I believe that not half a dozen of the white inhabitants are hardened by repeated attacks of fever, to which at least three out of four newcomers succumb before they have been here many months. If this is the case, here, what must it be in the forest and swamps behind?"

All were greatly relieved when the wind abated, on the third day, and the surf boats were seen making their way out. The landing was exciting work. The surf was still very heavy, and it seemed well-nigh impossible that any boat could live through it. The native paddlers, however, were thoroughly used to the work. They ceased paddling when they reached the edge of the breakers, until a wave larger than usual came up behind them. Then, with a yell, they struck their paddles into the water, and worked for dear life. Higher and higher rose the wave behind them, till it seemed that they must be submerged by it. For a moment the boat stood almost upright. Then, when it rose to the crest of the wave, the boatmen paddled harder than ever, and they were swept forward with the swiftness of an arrow. Another wave overtook them and, carrying them on, dashed them high up on the beach.

The paddlers at once sprang out, and prevented the boat from being carried out by the receding wave. Then the officers, mounting the men's backs, were carried out; for the most part high and dry, although in some cases they were wet to the skin.

A few yards away was the entrance to the castle. Here everything was bustle. Troops were filing out, laden with casks and cases. Others were squatting in the paved court, ready to receive their burdens. All were laughing and chatting merrily. There were even troops of young girls, of from ten to fifteen years old, who were to carry parcels of less weight than their brothers.

Two officers were moving about, seeing that all went on regularly; and a number of men were bringing the burdens out from the storehouse, and ranging them in lines, ready for the women to take up.

The district commissioner, who was in charge of the old castle, received Lisle and his companions cordially; and invited them, when the day's work was over, to dine with him. Rooms were placed at their disposal.

As soon as this was done they went down to the beach, and superintended the landing of the men and stores, which was carried on until nightfall. Then, when the last boat load was landed, they came up to dinner.

After a hearty meal, one of them said:

"We shall be glad, sir, if you will tell us what has been happening here. All we know is that the fort of Coomassie is surrounded, and that we have come up to relieve it."

"It is difficult to give you anything like an accurate account," the officer said, "for so many lying rumours have come down, that one hardly knows what to believe. One day we hear that the place has been carried by storm, and that the garrison have been massacred. Then we are told that Sir Frederick Hodgson, with the survivors of the garrison, has burst his way through.

"It is certain that most of our forces are unable to push their way up, and that their posts are practically surrounded. Further, on the 18th of April the first news that the fort was being besieged reached Cambarga, three hundred and forty miles from Coomassie. Three days later three British officers, and a hundred and seventy men, with a Maxim and seven-pounder, marched under the command of Major Morris to the station of Kintanpo. After thirteen days' marching the force was increased to seven British officers, three hundred and thirty soldiers, and eighty-three native levies.

"Near N'Quanta they met with opposition and, two hours later, had a successful engagement, with only three casualties. On the 14th they fell into an ambush, and incurred twelve casualties. For two days after this they had more or less continuous fighting and, in charging a stockade, Major Morris was severely wounded. Captain Maguire then headed the charge, and succeeded in capturing the stockade.

"No further resistance was met with, though two more stockades were passed. This want of enterprise, on the part of the enemy, was due to a short armistice that had been arranged with the beleaguered garrison.

"Major Morris's force was the third reinforcement which had reached the garrison. The first to come up was a party of Gold Coasters from the south. This was the only contingent permitted by the Ashantis to enter Coomassie unopposed. The next was a detachment from Lagos, composed of two hundred and fifty men of that colony's Hausa force, with four British

193

officers and a doctor, under the command of Captain Alpin. The Adansis, who occupy the country between the Prah and the recognized Ashanti boundary, had revolted; so that for part of the way they were unopposed but, as soon as they reached the first village in the Ashanti country, they were heavily attacked. After a couple of hours' fighting, however, the advance guard took the village, at the point of the bayonet.

"Next day they reached the Ordah River. Here the enemy made a determined stand, entrenched behind a stockade. The fight lasted for four hours, and then the situation became critical. The Maxim had jammed, the ammunition of the seven-pounder was exhausted, and a great proportion of the small-arm ammunition had been expended. Captain Cox and thirty men went into the bush, to turn the enemy's position. When they reached a point where they took the enemy in rear, they charged the stockade. The enemy fled, and were kept at a run until Coomassie was reached, before dark.

"The list of casualties showed how hard had been the fighting. All the white officers had been wounded, and there were a hundred and thirty casualties among the two hundred and fifty British soldiers. The garrison now consisted of seven hundred rank and file, and about a dozen British officers; two hundred and fifty native levies, and nearly four thousand Fanti and Hausa refugees.

"The next force to move forward was the first contingent from Northern Nigeria, consisting of two companies under the command of Captain Hall, with one gun. In traversing the Adansi country Captain Hall drew up a treaty, and got the Adansi king to sign it. Then he marched on to Bekwai, the chief town of a friendly tribe; and took up his quarters at Esumeja, a day's march from Coomassie. The border of Bekwai lay a short distance on one side, that of Kokofu was half a mile to the east.

"These were an Ashanti tribe, very fierce and warlike; and the occupation of Esumeja both kept them in check, and inspired the loyal Bekwais with confidence. Here Captain Hall was joined by a second contingent from Lagos, a hundred strong; and fifty men of the Sierra Leone frontier police. The force has got no farther, but its position on the main line of march is of vital service; as it overawes the Kokofu, and facilitates the advance of further relief.

"That, gentlemen, is the situation, at present. So far as I know, the garrison of Coomassie is amply sufficient to defend the fort; but we know that they are short of ammunition, and also of supplies to maintain the large number of people shut up there.

"I am expecting the vessel with the main Nigerian contingent tomorrow, or next day; and I hope that this reinforcement will enable an advance to be made."

"Thank you, sir! It is evident that we are in for some tough fighting, and shall have all our work cut out for us."

"There can be no doubt of that," the commissioner said, gravely. "The difficulties have been greatly increased by the erection of these stockades, a new feature in these Ashanti wars. When the Bekwais put themselves under our protection, instructions were given them in stockading, so that they might resist any force that the Ashantis might send against them and, doubtless, the latter inspected these defences and adopted the idea. The worst of it is that they are generally so covered, by the bush, that they are not seen by our troops till they arrive in front of them."

CHAPTER 14: FOREST FIGHTING.

Early the next morning the transport with the Nigerian troops anchored off the town. The work of disembarkation began at once. Five of the newly-arrived officers were appointed to the commissariat transport service. The three others--of whom Lisle, to his great satisfaction, was one--were appointed to the command of companies in the Nigerian force. This distinction, the commissioner frankly informed him, was due to his being the possessor of the V.C.

Having nothing to do that day, Lisle strolled about the town. There were a few European houses, the property of the natives who formed the elite of the place; men for the most part possessing white blood in their veins, being the descendants of British merchants who, knowing that white women could not live in the place, had taken Negro wives. These men were distinguished by their hair, rather than by their more European features. Their colour was as dark as that of other natives. Lisle learned that such light-coloured children as were born of these mixed marriages uniformly died, but that the dark offspring generally lived.

All the small shops in the town were kept by this class. With the exception of the buildings belonging to them, the houses of the town were merely mud erections, with a door and a window or two. The roofs were flat, and composed of bamboos and other branches; overlaid by a thick mud which, Lisle learned, not unfrequently collapsed in the rainy season. Nothing could be done at that time to repair them, and their inhabitants took refuge in the houses of their friends, until the dry season permitted them to renew their own roofs.

The women were of very superior physique to the men. The latter considered that their only duty was to stroll about with a gun or a spear; and the whole work of cultivating the ground, and of carrying burdens, fell to the lot of the women. Many of these had splendid figures, which might have been the envy of an English belle. Their great defect is that their heels, instead of going straight to the leg, project an inch or more behind it. From their custom of always carrying their burdens on their heads, their carriage is as upright as a dart. Whether the load was a heavy barrel, or two or three bananas, Lisle noticed that they placed it on the head; and even tiny girls carried any small article of which they might become possessed in this manner.

Curiously enough, the men had no excuse for posing as warriors; for the Fantis were the only cowardly race on the coast, and had several times shown themselves worthless as fighters, when the Ashantis made their expeditions against them.

A narrow valley ran up from the sea, in one part of the town, and terminated in a swamp behind it. Here the refuse of the place was thrown, and the stench in itself was sufficient to account for the prevalence of fever. Here were the accumulations of centuries; for the Dutch governors, who were frequently relieved, had made no effort whatever towards draining the marsh, nor improving the sanitary condition of the place; nor had the British governors who followed them shown any more energy in that direction. Doubtless the means were wanting, for the revenue of the place was insufficient to pay for the expenses of the garrison; and so the town which, at a very moderate expenditure, might have been rendered comparatively healthy, remained a death trap.

As soon as the Nigerian troops had landed, Lisle reported himself to their commander. He was at once put in charge of a company, and began his duties. When, two days later, they marched up the country, he felt well pleased with his command; for the men were for the most part lithe, active fellows; very obedient to orders and ready for any work, and evidently very proud of their position as British soldiers. They had for the most part had very little practice in shooting; but this was of comparatively little consequence, as what fighting they would have to do would be in the forests, against a hidden enemy, where individual shooting would be next to impossible.

The Adansi had risen, three days after signing the treaty. Two Englishmen, going from Bekwai to Kwisa, on their way were fired upon, and the terror-stricken carriers fled. Their loads were lost, and they themselves just succeeded in escaping to Kwisa.

Captain Slater, who was in command there, was much surprised to hear of such hostility, so soon after the signing of the treaty; and he started with twenty-six men to investigate the cause. He was attacked at the same place-- one soldier being killed and ten wounded, while two were missing--and he was obliged to retire to Kwisa. Sixty Englishmen of the Obuasi gold mines, on the western frontier of the Adansi, sent down for arms, and were supplied without any mishap.

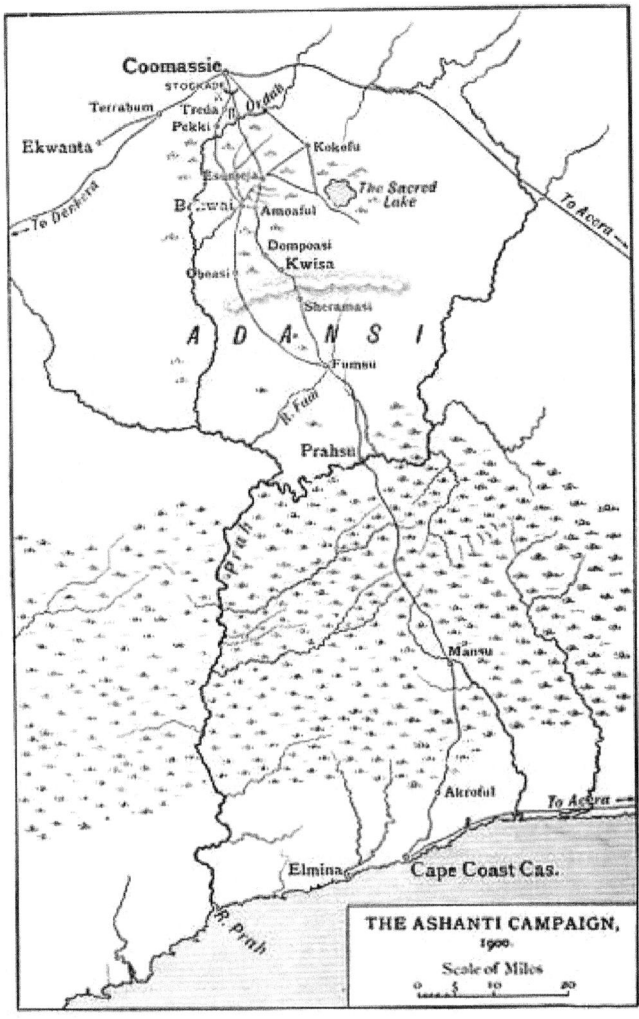

Colonel Wilkinson telegraphed orders to a force, which had started two days before, to halt at Fumsu until he joined them with the newly-arrived contingents. Colonel Willcocks now had four hundred and fifty men, under Captain Hall, at Kwisa and Bekwai; Captain Slater a handful of men at

198

Kwisa; Colonel Wilkinson a company at Fumsu; Colonel Carter the two hundred soldiers just landed on the line of march, and three hundred men from Northern Nigeria. Nine hundred reinforcements were known to be on their way. The force was scattered over a hundred and forty miles, and numerically only equal to the garrison they were going to relieve. The carriers were utterly insufficient for the transport.

The newly-arrived troops, with Colonel Willcocks and his staff in front, rode out of the town on the morning of the 5th of June. A drizzling rain was falling, but this soon ceased and the sun broke out. The road lay over low scrub-covered sand hills. It was a fair one, with the exception of bad bits, at intervals. The first day's march was a short one, as much time had been lost in getting the carriers together, and loading them up.

They halted that evening at Akroful. The place afforded but little accommodation. Five white officers slept together in one small room. There was a storm during the night, but the sky had cleared by the time the troops started in the morning.

They now entered a very different country. It was the belt of forest, three hundred miles wide, which ran across the whole country. Great as had been the heat, the day before, the gloom of the forest was more trying to the nerves. Except where the road had been cleared, the advance was impeded by the thick undergrowth of bush and small trees, through which it was impossible to pass without cutting a path with a sword. Above the bush towered the giants of the forest--great cotton trees, thirty or forty feet in circumference, and rising to the height of from two to three hundred feet. Round the tops of these many birds were flitting, but in the underbrush there was no sign or sound of life. Thorny creepers bound the trees together.

In the small clearings, where deserted and ruined villages stood, a few flowers were to be found. Here, also, great butterflies flew about.

The moist air, tainted with decaying vegetation; the entire absence of wind, or of movement among the leaves; the profound silence, broken only by the occasional dropping of water, weighed heavily on the spirits of the troops. Under foot the soil was converted into mire by the recent rains; and glad, indeed, were all, when they reached Mansu.

From this village, as had been the case at the previous halt, numbers of the carriers deserted. In order to get on, therefore, it was necessary to send out to the surrounding villages, to gather in men to take their places; and at the same time a telegram was sent down to Cape Coast, requesting the commandant there to arrest all the men who came in, and try to punish them as deserters. It was some satisfaction to know that they would be flogged, though this did not obviate the inconvenience caused by their desertion.

Through Three Campaigns

Mansu was a pleasanter halting place than the two preceding ones. It was surrounded by a clearing of considerable size; and contained two bungalows, which served as quarters for the officers. The soldiers got abundance of firewood from the forest, and the place presented a picturesque appearance, after nightfall, with its blazing fires and their reflection on the deep circle of foliage.

The march had been a depressing one, to the officers; but the native troops did not seem to find it so, and chattered, sang, and danced by their fires. Three of the officers found it difficult to swallow their food; but Lisle and another young officer, named Hallett, with whom he had been a special chum on board ship, made a hearty meal and, after it was finished, set out together for a tour round the camp, to assure themselves that everything was going on satisfactorily.

"This must be very different from your experience in the Tirah," Hallett said.

"Yes; to begin with, it was generally so cold at night, even in the valley, that we were glad of both our blankets and cloaks; while among the passes it was bitter, indeed. Then, too, the greater portion of the troops were white and, though they were cheerful enough, their spirits were nothing to the merriment of these natives. Then the camps were crowded with animals, while here there are only these wretched carriers; and almost every night we were saluted with bullets from the heights, and lay down in readiness to oppose any sudden attack.

"I suppose we shall have to do the same, when we get into the enemy's country, here. That is really the only similarity between the two expeditions. The country, too, was mountainous and, except in the valleys, there were few trees; while here we tramp along in single file, through what is little better than a swamp, and only get an occasional glimpse of the sky through the overhanging foliage. Of course it is hot in Northern India, very hot sometimes; but it is generally dry heat, quite different from the close, muggy heat of the forest. However, they say that when we have once ascended the Adansi hills, matters will be better."

"I hope so, Bullen. I found it so close today that I would gladly have got rid of all my clothes, which were so drenched with perspiration that I could have wrung them. We shall have other things to think about, however, when we get across the river; for you don't think of minor inconveniences when, at any moment, a volley may be poured into you from the bushes."

"Yes, the idea is rather creepy; but they say that the Ashantis always shoot high--the effect of the enormous charges they put into their muskets-- so that the harm done bears no proportion, whatever, to the noise. I expect our Maxims will come in very useful for clearing out the bush; and I doubt if the Ashantis will be able to stand for a moment, against our bayonets, as they have no weapons of the sort."

"No, but a good many of them are armed with spears, which are a deal longer than our muskets and bayonets. They are not accustomed, however, to work together. Each man fights for himself, and I feel convinced that they would not stand a determined charge," Hallett said.

"It is all very well to talk about a charge; but how are you going to charge through the bush, where every step has to be cut? However, I suppose our fellows can get through as well as they can."

"It would be horrid work, Bullen, for some of these creepers are a mass of spikes, which would pretty nearly tear a man to pieces, as he was forcing his way past them in a hurry."

"Yes, that is not a pleasant idea; but I own that, if what they say about the stockades they have formed is true, they will be even more formidable than the bush; for our little guns will make no impression upon them. They say that these are constructed with two rows of timber, eight feet apart; the intervening space being filled up with earth and stones so that, if they are well defended, they ought to cost us a lot of men before we carry them."

"Well, tomorrow we shall be at Prahsu. They say it is a fine open camp, as it was completely cleared by Wolseley's expedition. Of course, bushes will have sprung up again but, fast as things grow in this climate, they can hardly have attained any great height; and we shall have no difficulty in clearing the place again. There is a good rest house at the place, I hear, and we sha'n't be pigged in, as we were at Akroful."

"Why should they build a better house there than at the other stations?"

"Because, when the river is full, there is no way of getting across; and one may have to wait there for a fortnight, before it falls."

On the afternoon of the next day Prahsu was reached, after a march of twenty miles. The greater part of the house was found to be occupied by offices and stores. Fortunately, however, two or three tents had been brought along. The troops soon ran up huts of bamboos and palm leaves and, as there was a small native village close by, all were soon able to sleep in shelter.

The Prah was found to be full of water. It was here about a hundred and fifty yards wide, and circled round three sides of the position. There was no bridge, but two old wooden pontoons were found, relics of the last expedition; and these, with the aid of two old native canoes, were the only means of crossing.

On the morning after their arrival a despatch, dated May 24, was received from Captain Hall. It gave the details of his attack on Kokofu. Some thousands of the enemy were round that place and, in his opinion, no advance could be made to Coomassie till this force was destroyed.

An hour or two later another runner came in, this time from Kwisa. The despatch he brought gave details of the fighting the force at this place had had, in trying to effect a junction with Captain Hall.

The column advanced rapidly. In any place where the bush was particularly thick, volleys were fired into the undergrowth by a few men of the advance guard; for it had been found by experience in Nigeria that, if fired upon, natives generally disclosed their presence by replying.

They went on, unmolested, until they neared the village of Dompoasi. The natives of this town had sworn a solemn oath, to prevent any reinforcements from going up to Coomassie; and they had erected a stockade, six feet high. This was built in zigzag shape, so that a flanking fire could be kept up from it. It was about four hundred yards long, with both ends doubled backwards, to prevent an enemy from turning the position. In the rear was a trench, in which they could load in perfect shelter. Seats had been prepared on the neighbouring trees, for riflemen; and the undergrowth was left untouched, so that there should be nothing to excite suspicion.

The stockade did not run across the road, but parallel to it, the distance varying from twenty to thirty yards. Thus, anybody coming along the path would notice nothing unusual, though he himself would be easily seen by the defenders. A road had been cut, at the back of the entrenchments, so as to give a line of retreat to the defenders. On the northern side of the village, a similar stockade had been constructed.

Captain Roupell--who commanded the advance--became aware, from the numerous tracks and footprints, that the enemy must be in force in the neighbourhood, and advanced cautiously. He did not observe the stockade, however, so well was it hidden among the bushes. Just as they reached the farther end of it, a tremendous fire was opened. Captain Roupell was wounded, and many of the men also killed or wounded.

For a moment the troops were paralysed by the hail of lead. Then they replied with their rifles, and two Maxims and an eleven pounder were got to work. Captain Roupell, in spite of his wound, worked one of the Maxims, Lieutenant O'Malley the other, and Lieutenant Edwardes the gun. Captain

Roupell was again dangerously wounded, and Lieutenant O'Malley so severely wounded that he was forced to discontinue fire.

Lieutenant Edwardes, although he was hit early in the action, stuck to his gun. The gun team were all lying round, either killed or wounded, and he ran home the shells with a stick. He was, shortly afterwards, shot in the left arm. This incapacitated him from serving his gun; but he went and worked a Maxim, with his right arm, till a shot in the face compelled him to have his wounds dressed.

Colonel Carter was wounded in the head, and handed over the command to Colonel Wilkinson, who was himself slightly wounded at the back of the head. The men fell fast. The seven pounder and the other Maxim were completely isolated, some distance up the path. The existence of the stockade was only discovered as the undergrowth was cut away by the rain of bullets.

The officer commanding D company--which had been the rear guard all this time and, consequently, had not suffered--was in hammock with fever, and Colour Sergeant Mackenzie was in command. At this moment Mackenzie came up, and asked leave to charge the enemy. His proposal was at once sanctioned, and when half of his company had arrived they charged the stockade, other soldiers and officers near joining them. The enemy could not stand this determined attack, evacuated their position, and took to flight.

The force now prepared to retire, and this operation they performed in an orderly manner. Seven European officers had been wounded, and there were ninety casualties. Indeed, if the enemy had not fired too high, the column might have been annihilated.

Orders were sent, to Colonel Carter, telling him to remain where he was till reinforcements should arrive. A telegram was also sent to Captain Hall, instructing him to despatch a company to increase the garrison at Kwisa. In the meantime two companies of the troops on the Prah were ordered to proceed, instantly, to the relief of Kwisa, under the command of Captain Melliss and, to Lisle's satisfaction, some of his company were to form part of the force.

They started at two in the afternoon, but it was four before they got across the Prah; and they could only march ten miles that evening, which they did through a pouring rain. An early start was made, next morning. By eight o'clock they reached Fumsu, which was held by a company of soldiers under Quartermaster Sergeant Thomas; who informed them that all the troops ahead were perilously situated, short of food and ammunition, and crippled with casualties. He tried to dissuade them from going farther, saying:

"You are simply walking into a death trap. It is not fighting, it is murder. I am sure you will never get there, with only a hundred men and all these carriers."

However, orders had to be obeyed. The carriers were so limited in number that only a few days' food could be taken to the Kwisa garrison, if all the cartridges were to go on. A hundred extra rounds were served out to each man, in addition to the hundred he already had; so that there was no risk of running short, and the carriers would be relieved of much of the weight of the reserve, and could therefore carry up a larger amount of provisions. A hasty meal was eaten, and then they stepped forward for the twenty miles' march before them.

During the halt, they found out how the natives signalled. A gun was fired from the forest, the signal was repeated farther on, and continued to the next war camp. An estimate was given of the number and composition of an enemy by the number of guns fired. The force learned, afterwards, that their departure from Prahsu had been signalled in this way to the Adansis; and only the darkness and pouring rain, which delayed the enemy's movements, had saved the column from attack.

When the march was continued, therefore, the greatest precautions were taken against an ambush. A small party of twelve men marched ahead of the advance guard, and fired occasional volleys. Where the undergrowth was unusually thick, scouts moved abreast of them, cutting a way with their sword bayonets. The difficulties were so great that the column moved only three-quarters of a mile an hour. The carriers struggled on, carrying their burdens with surprising cheerfulness, staggering over the slippery mud, and frequently falling. The gun carriers had the worst time of all, for the parts into which these weapons divide are too heavy for single loads; and have to be carried, swung on bamboo poles, by four men--but often, at the acute bends in the path, the whole burden had to be supported by two.

Nevertheless, the column managed to advance. The river Fum was rising, but was still fordable, and they crossed it, with difficulty. It was now necessary to give up scouting, and depend entirely on the volleys of the men in front to discover ambuscades. One or two deserted or thinly populated villages were passed. Then, after two hours of this trying tramp, the advance guard came upon the Fum again; but at this point its volume and width were more than doubled. The river was rising rapidly, and there were no trees that could be cut down, with the sword bayonets, long enough to throw across.

At last, by good luck, at some distance farther down a native canoe was found, caught in the branches of a fallen tree. It was a clumsy craft, but it was better than nothing. Two native hammock boys and two soldiers took their places in it, and set out for the other side. When it reached the centre of the stream, however, an eddy caught it and, in an instant, it capsized.

Captain Melliss at once plunged into the river. He was a strong swimmer, and had gained the Royal Humane Society's medal for saving life at sea. His strength, however, had been taxed by the climate, and he had to call for aid. Luckily, no one was drowned. The intense chill, caused by the sudden immersion in almost ice-cold water; and the bites of the ants that swarmed over them, as they made their way back through the undergrowth from the spot where the canoe had been washed ashore, threatened an attack of fever; but this was averted by a change of clothing, a glass of neat spirits, and a dose of quinine.

It was now agreed that nothing could be done, and the force marched back to Fumsu. They recrossed the river, by means of a rope stretched from bank to bank, and arrived long after dark.

Next day it was determined to make another trial but, for a long time, no one was able to suggest where a crossing of the swollen river might be effected. It was clearly impossible to build a bridge but, after much discussion, it was agreed to make a raft. It consisted of a platform of planks, built across empty barrels; and was lashed together by the only rope at the station. A couple of natives took their places upon it, with long poles; but their efforts to push against the strong currents were quite unavailing. Then something went wrong with the rope and the raft gradually sank, the men swimming ashore.

On examination it was found that, not only were the leaking casks gone, but the rope that tied them together. The situation now appeared more hopeless than before.

It was Lisle who suggested a possible way out of the difficulty. He was wandering about the deserted native huts, when it struck him to see what the mud walls were composed of, and how the roofs were supported. Drawing his sword, he cut a large hole in one of the walls and, to his surprise, discovered that they were strengthened by lines of bamboos, which were afterwards plastered over. It seemed to him that these bamboos, which were extremely light as well as strong, would be very useful material for a raft, and he communicated the idea to Captain Melliss.

"You have solved the difficulty, Captain Bullen; there is no doubt that these will do admirably."

In a few minutes the whole of the little force, and carriers, were occupied in pulling down the huts. The question arose, how were the stakes to be tied together? While this matter was being discussed, Lisle said:

"Surely we can use some of the creepers. The natives tie up bundles with them."

The suggestion was at once adopted. Creepers were cut in the forest, and four bundles of bamboos were tied up, with cross pieces of the same material; so that they could be carried by four men, like a hammock. Four of the loads were similarly tied up. The telegraph wire was torn down from the trees, on the bank on which they were arrested; and the nearest insulator on the opposite side was broken by a shot, so that the wire hung down to the water in a gentle curve, the next insulator being fastened to a tree at a considerable distance. One end of the raft was then attached to this wire, by a noose that worked along it; and this contrivance enabled the swiftest streams to be triumphantly crossed, the loads of rice, meanwhile, being kept dry. The success of the experiment created a general feeling of relief.

On that day, an escort of fifty soldiers and some more ammunition came in, to reinforce the little garrison at Fumsu. The full number asked for could not be spared, as a rumour had arrived that the enemy would endeavour to cut off the carriers, who were making their way up from the coast.

Next morning a start was made at an early hour. Four rivers had been crossed, and five miles of the advance had been accomplished, without an enemy being seen; and the troops began to hope that they would reach Kwisa without further molestation. However, in mounting a steep rise, after crossing a river, a heavy fire was suddenly opened on them; and they had their first experience of the nature of the ground chosen by the enemy for an ambuscade.

The path zigzagged up the hill and, while the movements of the troops could be seen by the natives on its crest, dense foliage prevented the men toiling up it from obtaining even a glimpse of the enemy. Volleys were fired both to right and left. The enemy replied by firing volley after volley, and the shower of leaves showed that the bullets were flying high. It was difficult for the officers to control the extended line, and the scattered soldiers marching among the carriers were altogether out of hand, and fired recklessly.

At last, however, this was checked. The advance guard had suffered, but their fire had quelled that of the enemy. A rush was therefore made, the ambuscade carried, and the enemy put to flight.

Captain Wilson was, unfortunately, killed in the engagement. His body was put into a hammock and taken to Fumsu, a march of thirty-three miles. The force then returned to the Prah with the wounded, leaving only a small garrison of fifty men, under a British corporal.

It was a terrible march. The river had swollen, and the crossing took hours, many of the troops and carriers not arriving until the following day.

"Well, Bullen, how does this campaign compare with that in the Tirah?"

"It is infinitely worse," Lisle said. "We were only once or twice bothered by rivers, the country was open and, when the enemy crowning the hills were turned out, we were able to go through the passes without much opposition. We certainly often went to bed supperless, but on the whole we did not fare badly. At least we were generally dry and, though the cold was severe, it was not unbearable. At any rate, it was better than marching through these forests, in single file, with the mud often up to one's knees. Above all, the air was fresh and dry, and we had not this close atmosphere and this wet to struggle against.

"These fellows fight as well as the Afridis do, but are nothing like such good shots. If they had been, we should have been annihilated. I would rather go half a dozen times, through the Tirah, than once through this country.

"I think it is the darkness in the woods that is most trying. We are all bleached almost white; my uniform hangs about me loosely. I must have lost any amount of weight."

Both of the young officers had received wounds, but these were of so slight a nature that they had been able to keep their places.

"I wonder what the next move will be. At any rate, we shall be in clover at Prahsu, and be able to get into condition again by the time we make another move. Plenty of stores are sure to be lying there, while I expect that Hall and Wilkinson will be on pretty short commons."

"Well, I suppose it is all for the best."

One day they came upon a swollen river, which was so deep as to be unfordable, and the column were brought to a halt. The Pioneers, on being questioned, were of accord that it would take at least two days to build a bridge. There was a long consultation, and it was agreed that, unless something could be done, the column must retire for, by the time the bridge was built, the supply of food would be exhausted.

"If we could get a wire across," the engineer officer said, "we certainly could build the bridge in less time than I stated."

"I will try to carry it across, sir," Lisle said. "I am a strong swimmer, and I think I could do it."

"Yes, but the Ashantis are all on the opposite bank. You would be picked off before you got halfway across."

"I would try after dark. Once I got the wire across and fixed, enough men could cross, with its assistance, to clear the other bank of the enemy."

"You would find it very hard work tugging the wire across, Bullen. The stream would catch it and, as it is as much as you can do to swim the current without any drawback, it would certainly carry you down."

"Yes, sir; but if I asked for a volunteer, I should find one without difficulty."

"Well, Mr. Bullen, if you volunteer to try, I shall, of course, be very glad to accept the offer; especially as, if you keep tight hold of the wire, the stream will only send you back to this bank."

As soon as it was known that Lisle was about to attempt to swim the river, several volunteers came forward; and from these he selected one of the Sikh soldiers, not only because he was a tall and powerful man, but because he could give him orders in Punjabi. As soon as night came on, the preparations were completed. A length of wire, that would be sufficient to cross the river, was laid out on the bank from the spot that seemed to offer most advantages for a bridge. In this way, as they swam out the line would go with them, and they would be swept across the river by its pull, until they touched the bank opposite to where the other end of the line was secured.

Lisle took off his tunic, putties, and boots; and the Sikh also stripped himself to his loincloth, in which he placed his bayonet. Lisle unloaded his revolver and put it into his waistband, at the same time placing in his pocket a packet of twenty cartridges, in a waterproof box.

"You would swim better without those things, Bullen."

"No doubt, sir; but I want to have some means of defence, when I get across the stream. Some of the enemy may be lurking there, now."

"Before you start I will get the Maxim to work, and sweep the opposite bank. When you get ashore fasten the end of the wire to a tree, and then give a shout; we will stretch it tight on this side, and I will send a half company over, without delay. That ought to be enough to enable you to retain your footing, until we join you."

When all was ready, Lisle fastened the end of the wire round his body. The Sikh was to take hold a yard or two below him, and aid him as he swam. Then they stepped into the water, and struck out.

They had swum only twenty yards, when the Sikh cried out, "I have cramp, sahib! I can swim no longer!" and he let go his hold of the wire.

Rapidly, Lisle thought over the position. It was very important to get the wire across. Now that the Sikh had gone, he felt that it would pull him under; on the other hand, the brave fellow had volunteered to go with him, and he could not see him drown before his eyes. He accordingly slipped the loop of the wire over his head, and struck out with the stream.

So rapid had been the course of his thoughts that the man was still within some fifteen yards of him. He could see him faintly struggling and, swimming with long, steady strokes, soon overtook him.

"Put your arm on my shoulder," he said; "I will soon get you ashore."

The Sikh did as he was told, and Lisle turned to make for the shore they had left. To his dismay, however, he found that the centre current was carrying him to the opposite side. As soon as he found this to be the case, he ceased his efforts and allowed himself to float down. Doubtless the Ashantis would be on the watch, and any movement in the water would catch their eyes.

He could hear their voices on the bank and, occasionally, a shot was fired over his head. He felt sure, however, that he was still unseen; and determined to float quietly, till the course of the current changed, and brought him back to the side from which he started. He felt the Sikh's grasp relaxing, and threw his arms round the man's neck.

A quarter of an hour passed and then, to his dismay, he saw that he was close to the bush, on the wrong side of the river. He himself was getting rapidly weaker, and he felt that he could not support the weight of the soldier much farther. Accordingly he grasped a branch that overhung the river, pulled himself in to the shore, and there lay at the edge of the mud.

When he recovered his breath, he began to calculate his chances. The bush overhead seemed very thick, and he resolved to shelter there for a time. Occasionally he could hear the sound of voices close by, and was sure that the Ashantis were in force there.

His companions would, he was sure, regard him as dead when, on pulling on the wire, they found that it was loose; and after the failure of this attempt to establish a bridge, would probably start on their return march, without delay. He had, therefore, only himself to rely upon, beyond what assistance he could get from the Sikh, when the latter regained consciousness.

Through Three Campaigns

He poured a little spirits into the man's mouth, and presently had the satisfaction of seeing him move. Waiting until the movement became more decided, he said:

"You must lie still; we are across on the Ashanti side. They don't know we are here and, when you are able to move, we will crawl down some little distance and hide in the bushes. We must hide in the morning, for I am sure that I could not swim back to the other side, and certainly you could not do so. We are in a tight place, but I trust that we shall be able to get out of it."

"Do not encumber yourself with me," the Sikh said. "I know you have risked your life to save me, but you must not do so again. What is the life of a soldier to that of an officer?"

"I could not get across, even if I were alone. At any rate, I am not going to desert you, now. Let us keep quiet for an hour, then we shall be able to move on."

An hour passed silently, and then Lisle asked:

"How are you feeling, now?"

"I feel strong again, sahib."

"Very well then, let us crawl on."

CHAPTER 15: A NARROW ESCAPE.

Keeping in the mud close to the bank, and feeling their way in the dense growth produced by the overhanging bushes, they crawled forward. Sometimes the water came up to the bank, and they had to swim; but as a rule they were able to keep on the mud, which was so deep that they sank far into it, their heads alone showing above it. In two hours they had gone a mile, and both were thoroughly exhausted.

"We will lie here till day breaks," Lisle said; "as soon as it is dawn, we will choose some spot where the bushes are thickest, and shelter there. I am in hopes, now, that we are beyond the Ashantis. I dare say that we shall be able to get a peep through the bushes and, if we find the coast clear, we will make our way into the forest. There we may be able to gather something to eat, which we shall want, tomorrow; and it will certainly be more comfortable than this bed of mud. We must get rid of some of that before we leave."

"It would be better to allow it to dry on you, sahib. Our white undergarments would betray us at once, if any Ashantis came upon us. For my part, my colour is not so very different from theirs."

"Yes, perhaps that would be better. I must rub some over my face, as well."

"I do not care, for myself, sahib; we Sikhs are not afraid to die; but after your goodness to me, I would do anything to save you."

"What is your name?"

"Pertab, sahib."

"Well, Pertab, I think that as we have proceeded so far, we shall pull through, somehow. You have your bayonet, and I have my revolver, which I will wash and load before we get out of this. We shall be a match, then, for any three or four men we may come across. At any rate, I shall shoot myself if I see that there is no other way of escape. It would be a thousand times better to die, than be taken captive and tortured to death."

"Good, sahib! I will use my bayonet, myself; but I don't think there will be any occasion for that."

"I shall certainly die fighting. I would rather not be taken alive, Pertab; and shall certainly fight till I am killed, or can take my own life."

"Do you think that the troops will be marched away, sahib?"

"I feel sure that they will. They have only got provisions enough to take them back to camp; and as, when they pull the wire in, they will find that we have gone, they will feel quite sure that we have been drowned.

"No; we must quite make up our minds that we have got to look after ourselves. Fortunately, the Ashantis will not be able to cross the river to harass them in their retreat; unless, indeed, they know of some ford by which they can get over."

As soon as daylight began, the Sikh went down into the water and washed the mud from himself, and Lisle cleaned and loaded his pistol. Then they waited until it was broad daylight and, as they heard no sounds to indicate that any Ashantis were near, Lisle climbed up as noiselessly as he could to the bushes, and looked cautiously round. There were none of the enemy in sight. He therefore called to the Sikh to join him and, together, they made their way into the forest behind.

"The first thing to ascertain," Lisle said, "is whether the enemy are still here, and to find out for certain whether our friends have left. If they stay where they were, we can swim the river and join them; if they have retreated, and the Ashantis are still here, we shall know that there is no ford. If, however, we find that the Ashantis have gone, we shall be sure that they crossed at some ford, and will be swarming round our men; in which case it will be impossible for us to join them, and we must make our way as best we can."

They kept close to the edge of the forest, the soldier occasionally using his bayonet to cut away the thorny creepers that blocked their course. After an hour's walking, Lisle said:

"That is the spot where the troops were, last night. I can see no signs of them now.

"Now for the Ashantis."

They took the greatest pains to avoid making a noise, until they stepped out opposite the point from which they had started, the evening before. They saw no signs of the enemy.

"This is bad," Lisle said. "I can have no doubt that they have crossed the river, somewhere, and are swarming in the forest opposite. However, now that we know that they have gone, we can look out for something to eat."

For three hours they wandered about, and were fortunate enough to find a deserted village, where they gathered some bananas and pineapples. Of these they made a hearty meal; and then, each carrying a few bananas, they returned to the river and swam across, finding no difficulty in doing so now that they were unencumbered by the wire. They had not been long across before they heard the sound of heavy firing, some two or three miles away.

"It is as I thought," Lisle said. "The Ashantis have crossed the river, somewhere, and are now attacking the convoy. They will not, of course, overpower it; but they will continue to follow it up till they get near camp, and there is little chance of our being able to rejoin them before that."

Travelling on, they more than once heard the sound of parties of the enemy, running forward at the top of their speed. Evidently news had been sent round, and the inhabitants of many villages now poured in, to share in the attack upon the white men.

"It is useless for us to think of going farther, at present," Lisle said. "They will be mustering thickly all round our force, and I expect we shall have some stiff fighting to do, before we get back to camp--I mean the column, of course; as for ourselves, the matter is quite uncertain. We may be sure, however, that they won't be making any search in the bush and, as even in the Ashanti country you cannot go through the bush, unless you cut a path, it will be sheer accident if they come across us. At any rate, we may as well move slowly on, doing a little cutting only when the path seems deserted. If we keep some forty or fifty yards from it, so as to be able to hear any parties going along, and to make sure that they are moving in our direction, that is all we can do.

"Of course, everything will depend upon the result of the fight with the column. There is no doubt that they are going to be attacked in great force; which, as far as it goes, is all the better for us. If it were only a question of sniping by a small body of men, the colonel would no doubt push steadily on, contenting himself with firing occasional volleys into the bush; but if he is attacked by so strong a body as there appears to be round him, he will halt and give them battle. If so, we may be pretty sure that he will send them flying into the bush; and they won't stop running till they get back to the river. In that case, when we have allowed them all to pass we can go boldly on, and overtake the column at their halting place, this evening.

"If, on the other hand, our fellows make a running fight of it, the enemy will follow them till they get near Coomassie, and we shall have to make a big detour to get in. That we shall be able to do so I have no doubt, but the serious part of the business is the question of food. However, we know that the natives can find food, and it is hard if we do not manage to get some.

"Making the necessary detour, and cutting our way a good deal through the bush, we can calculate upon getting there in less than four days' march. We have food enough for today, and a very little will enable us to hold on for the next four days."

They moved slowly on. The firing increased in violence, and it was evident that a very heavy engagement was going on. Two hours later they heard a sound of hurrying feet in the path and, peering through the bush, saw a crowd of the Ashantis running along, in single file, at the top of their speed.

"Hooray! It is evident that they have got a thorough licking," Lisle said. "They will soon be all past. Our greatest fear will then be that a few of the most plucky of them will rally in the bush, when they see that none of our troops come along. Our troops are not likely to follow them up, as they will be well content with the victory they have evidently gained, and resume their march."

They waited for an hour and, when they were on the point of getting up and making for the path, the Sikh said:

"Someone is coming in the bush."

In another minute, four natives came suddenly upon them; whether they came from the force that had been routed, or were newly arriving from some village behind, the two fugitives knew not; nor, indeed, had they any time to consider. They threw themselves, at once, into one of the divisions at the base of a giant cotton tree.

These divisions, of which there may be five or six round the tree, form solid buttresses four or five inches thick, projecting twenty or thirty feet from the front, and rising as many feet high; thus affording the tree an immense support, when assailed by tropical storms.

"TWO OF THEM FELL BEFORE LISLE'S REVOLVER"

The natives, seeing that the two men were apparently unarmed, rushed forward, firing their guns as they did so. Two of them fell before Lisle's revolver. One of the natives rushed with clubbed musket at him but, as he delivered the blow, the butt end of the musket struck a bough overhead and

215

flew out of the man's hand; and Lisle, putting his revolver to his head, shot him. The other man ran off.

Lisle had now time to look round and, to his dismay, the Sikh was leaning against the branch of a tree.

"Are you hit?" he asked.

"Yes, sahib, a ball has broken my right leg."

"That is a bad business, indeed," Lisle said, kneeling beside him.

"It cannot be helped, sahib. Our fate is meted out to us all, and it has come to me now. You could not drag me from here, or carry me; it would be impossible, for I weigh far more than you do."

Lisle was silent for a moment.

"I see," he said, "that the only thing I can do is to push on to camp, and bring out assistance. I will leave you my pistol, when I have recharged it; so that if the native who has run away should bring others down, you will be able to defend yourself. As, however, you remained on your feet, he will not know that you were wounded; and will probably suppose that we would at once push on to join our companions. Still, it will be well for you to have the weapon.

"Now, let me lower you down to the ground, and seat you as comfortably as I can. I will leave these bananas by you, and my flask of water. It is lucky, now, that I did not drink it all when I started to cross the river.

"I suppose they will have halted at the same camp as before. It was a long march, and we must still be ten or twelve miles away from it, so I fear it will be dark long before I get there."

"You are very good, sahib, but I think it will be of no use."

"Oh, I hope it will! So now, give me your turban. I will wrap it tightly round your leg, for the bleeding must be stopped. I see you have lost a great deal of blood, already."

He bandaged the wound as well as he could, and then he said:

"I will take your sword bayonet with me. It can be of no use to you and, if I do happen to meet a native upon the road, it may come in very handy."

"The blessing of the Great One be upon you, sahib, and take you safely to camp. As for myself, I think that my race is run."

"You must not think that," Lisle said, cheerily; "you must lie very quiet, and make up your mind that, as soon as it is possible, we shall be back here for you;" and then, without any more talk, he made his way to the edge of the path.

There he made a long gash on the bark of a tree and, fifty yards farther, he made two similar gashes. Then, certain that he could find the place on his return, he went off at a trot along the path.

It was eight o'clock in the evening before he reached camp. On the way, he had met with nothing that betokened danger; there had been no voices in the woods. When about halfway to camp, he came across a number of dead bodies on the path and, looking into the bush, found many more scattered about. It was evident that the little British force had turned upon their assailants, and had effected a crushing defeat upon them.

He was hailed by a sentry as he approached the camp but, upon his reply, was allowed to pass. As he came to the light of a fire, round which the white officers were sitting, there was a general shout of surprise and pleasure.

"Is it you or your ghost, Bullen?" the commanding officer exclaimed, as all leapt to their feet.

"I am a very solid person, Colonel; as you will see, if you offer me anything to eat or drink. I am pretty well exhausted now and, as I have got another twenty-mile tramp before I sleep, you may guess that I shall be glad of solid and liquid refreshment."

"You shall have both, my dear boy. We had all given you up for dead. When we saw you washed down, we were afraid that you were lost. The only hope was that the current might bring you over to our side again, and we went two or three miles down the stream to look for you. We hunted again still more carefully the next morning, and it was not until the afternoon that we moved.

"We encamped only three miles from the river, hoping still that you might come up before the morning. We started at daybreak this morning. We were harassed from the first, but the affair became so serious that we halted and faced about, left a handful of men to protect the coolies and carriers; and then sent two companies out into the bush on each side, and went at them. Fortunately they fought pluckily, and when at last they gave way they left, I should say, at least a third of their number behind them.

"We did not stop to count. I sent a small party at full speed along the path, so as to keep them on the run, and then marched on here without further molestation.

"And now, about yourself; how on earth have you managed to get in?"

"Well, sir, I can tell it in a few words. The current took us to the opposite shore. We lay concealed under the bushes overhanging the bank, and could hear the enemy talking behind the screen. On the following day the voices ceased, and we made our way up to the camp; and found, as we expected, that you had gone and, as we guessed, the Ashantis had set off in pursuit. We went on through the forest and, of course, heard the firing in the distance; and saw the enemy coming along the path, terror stricken. We were waiting for a bit, and felt sure that they had all passed; when a party of four men came from behind upon us. I don't think they belonged to the force you defeated. They were within twenty yards when they saw us.

"We jumped into one of the hollows at the foot of a cotton tree. The whole four fired at us and then, as they supposed that we were unarmed, made a rush. I shot two of them as they came on. One of the others aimed a blow at me, with the butt end of his gun. Fortunately the weapon caught one of the creepers, and flew out of his hand. My revolver had in some way stuck, but it all came right just at the moment, and I shot him. The fourth man bolted.

"When I looked round to see what the Sikh was doing, he was leaning against the tree, with the blood streaming from his leg; the bone having been broken by one of their balls. Well, sir, I bandaged it up as well as I could, and left him my revolver; so that he might shoot himself, if there was a likelihood of his being captured. I then set off, as hard as I could go, to fetch assistance for him."

"The troops have had a very heavy day, Bullen," the colonel said, gravely. "How far away is it that you left the man?"

"About ten miles, I should say."

"Well, they are all willing fellows, but it is a serious thing to ask them to start on another twenty miles' journey, within an hour or two of getting into camp."

"I think, sir, if you will allow me to go down to where the Sikhs are bivouacked, and I ask for volunteers to bring in their comrade, they will stand up, to a man."

Lisle's confidence in the Sikhs was not misplaced. As soon as they heard that a comrade, who they believed had been drowned while trying to get the wire across the river, was lying alone and wounded in the forest, all declared their willingness to start, at once.

"I will take twenty," Lisle said; "that will be ample. I have just come down the path myself, and I saw no signs, whatever, of the enemy; still, some of them may be making their way down, to carry off their dead. If they are, however, their astonishment at seeing us will be so great that they will bolt at the first volley."

"Are you going back with us, sahib?"

"Yes, I must do so, or you would never find the place where he is lying."

"We will take two stretchers," the sergeant--a splendid man; standing, like most of his companions, well over six feet--said, "and you shall walk as far as you are able, and then we will carry you. When will you march, sahib?"

"I am going to get something to eat and drink first and, if you will fall in, in half an hour I will be with you again."

"Where is Pertab wounded, sahib?"

"He is shot through the leg, three or four inches above the knee, and the bone is broken."

"Did the man get off, sahib?"

"I can't say for certain," Lisle said, with a smile. "Four men attacked us. They all four fired. I shot three of them with my revolver, and the fourth bolted. Whether he was the man who really shot your comrade, or not, I cannot say; but you see, the chances are that he was not."

The grim faces of the Sikhs lit up with a smile.

"You paid them out, anyhow," the sergeant said. "I don't think we are very deeply in their debt."

Lisle went back to the campfire. The best that could be found in camp was given to him, and the colonel handed him his own whisky flask. While he ate, he related the story in full.

"Well, it is a fine thing for you to have done," said the colonel; "a most creditable affair. I know that you are a pretty good marcher; but I hardly think that, after a long day's work, you can set out for a march of nearly double the length."

"I have no fear of the march, Colonel. The Sikhs have volunteered to carry a stretcher for me. I shall, of course, not get into it, unless I feel that I cannot go another foot farther; but the mere fact that it is there, and in readiness for me, will help me to keep on. The Sikhs have done just as long a march as I have, and I hope that I shall be able to hold on as long as they can. I should hate to be beaten by a native."

"Ah! But these Sikhs are wonderful fellows; they seem to be made of iron, and march along as erect and freely as they start, when even the Hausas and Yorubas are showing signs that they are almost at the end of their powers. I must say that I consider the Sikhs to be, all round, the best soldiers in the world. They cannot beat Tommy Atkins, when it comes to a charge; but in the matter of marching, and endurance, Tommy has to take a back seat. He will hold on till he fairly breaks down, rather than give in; but he himself, if he has ever campaigned with the Sikhs, would be the first to allow that they can march him off his feet."

"Have you got a spare pair of shoes in your kit, Bullen?"

"Yes."

"Then I should advise you to take those you have on, off; and put on a fresh pair."

"I will take your advice, sir; but I really think that it would be best to follow the custom of the native troops, and march barefooted."

"It would not do," the colonel said, decidedly. "The soles of their feet are like leather. You would get half a dozen thorns in your foot, before you had gone half a mile; and would stub your toes against every root that projected across the path. No, no; stick to your shoes."

Lisle changed his boots, and then went across to the Sikhs; who fell in as they saw him coming.

"You have got everything, sergeant?" he asked.

"Yes; a hundred and thirty rounds of ball cartridge, the two stretchers, and some food and drink for our comrade."

"You have got a good supply of torches, I hope. There may be some small risk in carrying them, but I am convinced that the Ashantis will not venture to return, tonight, whatever they may do tomorrow. With three torches--one at the head, one in the middle of the line, and one in the rear-- we should be able to travel through the paths better than if we had to grope our way in the dark."

The little party at once moved off, many of the officers and men gathering round, to wish them good luck and a safe return. Four hours took them to the spot where Lisle had turned into the path. For the last mile he had had three torches burning in front, so that he should not overlook the signs he had made on the trees.

"There it is, sergeant," he said, at last, "two slashes; the other one is on the left, fifty yards on."

They turned off when they came to this.

"Here we are, all right, Pertab!" Lisle said, as they came to the tree.

"Allah be praised!" the man said, faintly. "I seem to have been hearing noises in the wood, for a long time; and when I heard you coming, I was by no means sure that it was not an illusion, like the others."

"Here are twenty of your comrades with me, Pertab, and we shall soon get you into camp."

"I didn't expect you till morning," the wounded man said. "I thought that you would be far too tired to come out and, without you, they could not have found me."

"They would have carried me, had it been necessary; but I managed to hold on pretty well.

"Now, my men, get him upon the stretcher, and let us be off. Pour the contents of that bottle down his throat; that will keep him up, till we get back."

For another four or five miles, Lisle kept along but, to his mortification, he was obliged at last to take to the stretcher. The four Sikhs who carried it made light of his weight. Once or twice, on the way, some dropping shots were fired at the party; but these were speedily silenced by a volley or two from the rifles.

It was four o'clock in the morning when they re-entered camp. The fires were already lighted and, as the party entered, the troops received them with loud cheering; which called all the white officers out from their shelters.

"You have done well, my fine fellows," the colonel said to the Sikhs. "Now, get some food at once, and then lie down for three or four hours' sleep. I shall leave two companies with you; I don't think that, after the thrashing we gave them yesterday, the enemy are likely to trouble us--at any rate, not before the afternoon, and by that time you will have rejoined us."

"We can march on now, sahib."

"No, no," the colonel said; "a thirty-six-mile march, through this bush, is a great deal more than a fair day's march for anyone; and I am not going to see such good men knocked up, by asking too much of them. So just go, and do as I order you. You may be sure that I shall put the deed you have accomplished in my orders of today.

"Well, Mr. Bullen," he said, as he came to the spot where Lisle was sitting, with his shoes and stockings off, rubbing his aching feet, "so you could not outmarch the Sikhs?"

"No, sir, and I did not expect to do so. I went at their head all the way there, and four or five miles back; but should have had to give up, even if I had been told that a big fortune awaited me, if I got in on foot. I should have had to say:

"'Well, then, somebody else may have it; I can go no farther.'"

"Well, you have done uncommonly well, anyhow; uncommonly well. I don't suppose there are five white men in camp who could have done so much. After this you may be sure that, if you have need of an expedition, the Sikhs would follow you through fire and water, if they were allowed to volunteer for the service.

"I should have been glad to recommend you for the Victoria Cross, for your conduct right through the affair; but you have got it. But I fear that, although you would get every credit for your doings, the authorities would consider that it did not come under the head of deeds for which the Victoria Cross is given."

"I am sure I have no desire for another V.C., even if two could be given."

No attack was made on the following day, and it was evident that the Ashantis had taken to heart the lesson that had been given them. Two days later the column marched into the fort, and Colonel Willcocks went out to meet it.

The colonel's reports had been sent in by a runner. As the Sikhs came along, the colonel ordered them to halt and, as Lisle marched up at the head of his company, he made a sign to him to come up.

"Captain Bullen," he said, "I have much pleasure in congratulating you on the manner in which you saved the life of the Sikh soldier, who volunteered to swim that river in flood in order to carry a wire across; and still more for the manner in which you made what I should say was a record march, in this country, to bring in a man who had been wounded, in a fight with a small party of the enemy."

Then he turned to the Sikhs.

"Soldiers," he said, "I cannot praise you too heartily for having volunteered, at the end of a long and exhausting march, to undertake another still longer and more fatiguing, in order to bring in a wounded comrade. It is an act of which you may be proud; but not altogether a surprising one, for we know well that we can depend upon the Sikhs, on all and every occasion."

Lisle had been carried into the fort. His feet were so tender and swollen that he could not possibly walk farther, and he was consequently taken down by the carriers, during the last two days' march. Hallett sauntered up, as soon as he was put into a hospital hut.

"Hillo, Bullen, so you have broken down! A nice example to set to your Hausas, isn't it?"

"I suppose it is," Lisle laughed; "but the Hausas did not march as far as I did."

"No? What were you doing? Scouting half a mile ahead of them, on your own account?"

"Not exactly; I only went the width of a river, and yet, the result of that was that I had to do an extra march of some twenty miles."

"Now you are speaking in riddles, Lisle; and if there is one thing I hate, it is riddles. When a fellow begins to talk in that way, I always change the subject. Why a man should try to puzzle his brain, with such rigmarole things, is more than I can imagine."

"Well, Hallett, I really feel too tired to tell you about the matter. I can assure you that it is no joke, being carried down fifteen miles on a stretcher; so please go and ask somebody else, that's a good fellow."

In a quarter of an hour Hallett returned again, put his eyeglass in his eye, and stood for a couple of minutes without speaking, regarding Lisle furtively.

"Oh, don't be a duffer," the latter said, "and drop that eyeglass. You know perfectly well that you see better, without it, than with it."

"Well, you are a rum chap, Bullen. You are always doing something unexpected. I have been hearing how you and a Sikh started to swim the

Ordah, when it was in flood, with a wire; how you were washed away; how you were given up for lost; how, two days later, you returned to camp and went straight out again, with a party of twenty Sikhs, took a little stroll for ten miles into the bush--and of course, as much back--to carry in the Sikh soldier you had had with you, but who had been wounded, and was unable to come with you. I don't know why such luck as this is always falling to your lot, while not a bit of it comes to me."

"It is pure accident, Hallett. You will get a chance, some day. I don't know that you would be good for a thirty-mile tramp, but it must be a consolation to you that, for the last five miles, I had to be carried."

"It is a mercy it is so," Hallett said, in an expression of deep thankfulness, "for there would have been no holding you, if you had come in on your feet."

CHAPTER 16: THE RELIEF OF COOMASSIE.

"I certainly should not have volunteered for this work, Bullen, if I had known what it was like. I was mad at not being able to go out to the Cape, and as my regiment was, like yours, stationed in India, there was no chance of getting away from there, if I had once returned. Of course, I knew all about the expeditions of Wolseley and Scott; but I forgot that these were carried on in the dry season, and that we should have to campaign in the wet season, which makes all the difference in the world. We are wet through, from morning till night--and all night, too--and at our camping places there is no shelter. The low-lying land is turned into deep swamps, the little streams become great unfordable torrents, and the ground under our feet turns into liquid mud. It is really horrible work, especially as we get very little food and less drink. It is not work for dogs."

"It is all very well for you to grumble, Hallett, but you know just as well as I do that, if the offer were made to you to go home, at once, you would treat it with scorn."

"Oh, of course I should! Still, one may be allowed to have one's grumble and, after all, I think we are pretty sure of some stiff fighting, which makes up for everything. I am not afraid of the enemy a bit, but I do funk fever."

"I don't think we are likely to get fever, so long as we are on the move; though I dare say a good many of us will go down with it, after the work is done. We have only to think of the starving soldiers and people, in Coomassie, to make us feel that, whatever the difficulties and dangers may be, we must get there in time. The great nuisance is, that we can get no news of what is doing there. We constantly hear that the governor, with a portion if not all of the force, has broken out, some days since; and we begin to look out for them; and then, after a time, comes the news that there has been no sortie whatever. It is really most annoying, and I am often kept awake at night, even after a day's fight, thinking of the position of the garrison."

"I don't think, if there were a hundred garrisons in danger," Hallett laughed, "it would affect my sleep in the slightest. I lie down as soon as I have eaten what there is to eat, which certainly is not likely to affect my digestion; and however rough the ground, I am dead asleep as soon as my head touches it, and I do not open an eye until the bugle sounds in the morning. Even then I have not had enough sleep, and I always indulge in bad language as I put on my belts, at the unearthly hour at which we are always called. I don't begin to feel half awake till we have gone some miles."

"You would wake up sharp enough, Hallett, at the sound of the first gun."

"Yes, that is all right enough; but unless that comes, there is nothing to wake one. The close air of the forest takes out what little starch you have in you, and I verily believe that I am very often asleep, as we march."

"It is monotonous, Hallett, but there is always something to see to; to keep the men from straggling, to give a little help, sometimes, to the wretched carriers."

"You are such a desperate enthusiast, Bullen. I cannot make out how you keep it up so well. I really envy you your good spirits."

"They are indeed a great blessing; I had plenty of occasion to make the most of them, when I was marching in the ranks of the 32nd Pioneers, on the way up to Chitral. Still, they came naturally enough, there; and I am bound to acknowledge that it is hard work, sometimes, to keep them up here."

"I think that it would really be a mercy, Bullen, if you were to pour a bucket of water over my head, when the bugle sounds. I have no doubt I should be furious with you, and should use the strongest of strong language; but still, that would not hurt you."

"Except when the carriers bring up our bundles of dry clothes, we lie down so soaked that you would scarcely feel the water poured over you. At any rate, if you really think that it would do you good, you had better order your servant to do it; that is to say, if you don't think you would slay him, the first morning."

"No, I suppose I must put up with it, as best I can; but really, sometimes I do envy the colonel's little terrier, which frisks along all day, making excursions occasionally into the bush, to look for rats or mongooses. He seems to be absolutely tireless, and always ready for anything.

"Well, I shall turn in, now, and try to dream that I am on a feather bed, and have had supper of all sorts of dainties."

"I would not do that, if I were you. It would be such a disappointment, when you woke up."

"Well, perhaps it might be," Hallett said, despondently. "I will try to dream that I am with you on that Chitral expedition, and am nearly frozen to death; then possibly, on waking, I might feel grateful that things are not so bad as I thought they were."

They spent a few pleasant days at Prahsu and, while there, received the news that a column had started, from Tientsin, for the relief of the Europeans collected in the various legations at Pekin, news which created general satisfaction.

"I have no doubt they will have some stiff fighting," Hallett said, as he and Lisle sat down to breakfast, after hearing the news. "One thing, however, is in their favour. As they will keep by the river all the way, they will never be short of water. The last news was that they were collecting a large flotilla of junks, for carrying up their provisions. Lucky beggars! Wouldn't I like to change places with one of them! I hope all the different troops will pull well together for, with a force of half a dozen nationalities, it is almost certain that there will be some squabbling."

"I should hardly think that there would be any trouble, Hallett. Of course, it was reported in the last mail that the Russians, French, and Germans were all behaving somewhat nastily; but as the Japs have the strongest force of all, and the Americans stick to us, I should think that things will go on well. It would be a disgraceful thing, indeed, if troops marching to the relief of their countrymen could not keep the peace among themselves. Of course, there may be fighting; but it is morally certain that the Chinese cannot stand against us, and I imagine that, in proportion to the numbers, their casualties will enormously exceed ours.

"Britain has her hands pretty full, at present, what with the big war in the Transvaal, and the little one here, and another in China. It is a good thing we thrashed the Afridis, two years ago. If we had not, you may be sure that there would be an even more formidable rising on our northern frontier than that we quelled. News travels marvellously fast, in India; the Afridis always seem to know what is going on elsewhere, and I am pretty sure that they would be up, all over the country, if they had not had to give up the greater portion of their rifles, and had not more than enough to do to rebuild their houses. So we have something to be thankful for."

"I am glad that Marchand business did not come off just at the present time," Hallett said. "You may be sure that we should have had a war with France; it was a mighty near thing, as it was."

"Yes; I think they would not have backed down, if we had been busy with Boers, Chinese, and black men. They were at fever heat as it was; and we could have done nothing, if we had had two hundred and fifty thousand men engaged at the Cape."

"It would have made no difference," Lisle said, scornfully, "we have plenty of soldiers at home. Every barrack was crowded with men, as we came away; and there were a great number of the militia and volunteers, to back them up. Above all there was our fleet which, however much the Frenchmen value their warships, would have knocked them into a cocked hat in no time.

"Well, I suppose it is time to go out and inspect our men."

"I suppose it is, Bullen," Hallett said despondently, as he stretched himself. "If there were no inspections and no parade, an officer's life would be really a pleasant one."

Lisle laughed.

"And if there were no inspections and parades there would be no soldiers, and if there were no soldiers there would be no need for officers."

"Well, I suppose that is so," Hallett said, as he buckled on his sword. "Now, just look at me; do I look like an officer and a gentleman? Nobody could tell what was the original colour of my khaki; it is simply one mass of mud stains."

"Well, I do think you hardly look like an officer and a gentleman--that is to say, you would hardly be taken for one at Aldershot. Fortunately, however, there are no English ladies here to look at you and, as the blacks don't know what an officer and a gentleman should be, it doesn't matter in the slightest."

While at Prahsu, there was nothing to do but to speculate as to what would be the next move. Colonel Willcocks kept his plan to himself, for information as to our movements reached the enemy in a most extraordinary manner.

It was a busy camp. Bamboo grass-covered sheds, for stores, were in course of construction. The engineers were employed in making a road, to take the stores and troops across the Prah.

Three of the wounded officers--Captain Roupell, Lieutenants Edwardes and O'Malley--were invalided, and left for home in a convoy with over a hundred wounded. This was necessary, owing to the fact that there was no

Roentgen apparatus in the colony, and it was found impossible to discover and extract the slugs with which the great proportion were wounded.

It was unknown that four hundred men of the West African Regiment, with nearly twenty officers, and a company from Jebba were on their way to reinforce them. Three officers were away to raise native levies in Denkera and Akim, and there were rumours about more troops from other parts of the world. But the one thing certain was that some more troops were coming down from Northern Nigeria.

Colonel Burroughs arrived with a strong party, and Lisle and Hallett prepared to go up again. No resistance was met with, as far as Fumsu; but it was found that a foot bridge that had been thrown across the river was washed away, and communication with the other bank was thus cut off. To the disgust of the officers and men, they were called out to a false alarm and, when dismissed, went back to bed grumbling. When they rose again, the men cleaned their arms and received their pay and rations. The latter amounted to but a pound of rice a day, but this was subsequently increased. The officers were little better off, for there was, of course, nothing to buy.

Two companies had gone on in advance to open the main road, find out the ambushes and stockades, and to join Colonel Wilkinson at Bekwai. Those who remained in camp had little to do, and were therefore glad to spend their time on fatigue duty; the officers building shelters for themselves, while the men erected conical huts, until the station was covered with them.

A day or two after their arrival a letter, written in French on a scrap of paper, was brought down. It stated that the garrison could hold out until the 20th, a date that was already past. Supplies were urgently wanted. It also warned the relief column that there was a big stockade within an hour of the fort. Colonel Willcocks sent out a messenger at once, asking that every available man should join him; but the man never reached the coast, and no help came from there.

Sir Frederick Hodgson had then been out of Coomassie four days, and was making his way down to the coast through a friendly country; with an escort of six hundred soldiers, and all his officers but one, who had remained in the fort with a hundred men.

On the morning of the 27th Colonel Burroughs, with five hundred men, started on his journey north. Scouts flanked the advance guard, thereby preventing the chance of an ambuscade; but greatly delaying the column, as they had to cut their way through the bushes. They halted that night at Sheramasi. A detachment was left at a village at the foot of the hills. Just as the head of the troops arrived at the top, they were fired into from behind a fallen tree. A sharp fight took place for nearly an hour, until the enemy were turned out of their position, and pursued through the bush, by a company which had moved round their flank. Kwisa was reached after dark, when it was found that the place had been entirely destroyed by the enemy.

Next morning they moved forward with the greatest caution, fully expecting that there would be another terrific fight at Dompoasi. This place, though only four miles from Kwisa, was not reached till nightfall. Darkness set in with heavy rain, and the officers commanding the two leading companies held a council of war, and decided to call in the scouts--who were useless in the dusk--to make a dash for the village, and try to rush it before preparations could be made for its defence.

The terrible downpour of rain was all in their favour. The enemy's scouts, who had reported the advance upon Kwisa, had given up the idea of watching, that night; and they and the whole war camp were at their evening meal. The noise of the rain drowned the sounds of feet, and the troops were in the village before the enemy entertained a suspicion of their approach.

A scene of wild confusion then ensued. The enemy rushed wildly to and fro, while our men poured volley after volley into them. Savages have no idea of rallying, when thus taken by surprise. Many fell; some fled into the forest; others ran down the prepared pathway and manned the big stockade, but the troops rushed forward, and soon compelled them to quit it.

Half a company were sent into the bush, to follow up the flying foe. They remained out all night, and did much execution among the Adansis. This was the first real success gained over them.

Pickets and sentries were thrown out in a circle round the village. At midnight, the troops got a scratch meal under the protection of the huts. Many guns were captured, some Sniders, many cakes of powder, and much food which was cooking over the fires when the troops entered the village. Some of the rifles that had belonged to the men who had fallen in the unsuccessful attack were found, together with three thousand rounds of ammunition to fit them. All this was accomplished without any casualties to our troops.

The next day was spent in destroying the two great stockades, cutting down the bush round them, and blowing up the fetish tree; as well as burying the enemy's dead, thirty in number. On the evening of the next day, Bekwai was gained.

Colonel Burroughs determined, after this success, to get rid of the next danger by making another attack on the entrenchments and war camp at Kokofu and, with five hundred men and four Maxims, he started out for that place. But the task was too heavy for him, and the enemy were quite ready to receive our troops. They were in great force, and fought bravely for some hours. The turning movement which was attempted failed; and the colonel decided, at last, to retire to Bekwai. This the troops accomplished safely, although the enemy followed them till they reached the town. Lieutenant Brumlie was killed, six other officers were hit slightly; and one British non-commissioned officer and three soldiers were killed, and seventy-two men wounded.

After this, no fighting took place until Colonel Willcocks arrived to carry out the main object of the expedition. Convoys of stores, however, kept pouring in incessantly and, to Lisle's delight, a large box of provisions, which he had bought before starting from Cape Coast, arrived.

Then Colonel Neal arrived, with the Sappers. He and his men built a bridge across the Fum. It was twelve feet above the water, but within thirty-six hours it was swept away.

While the troops were waiting, a runner came in and reported that heavy firing had been heard round Coomassie. On the evening of the 30th of June, news came that Colonel Willcocks would start the next morning. He would have but a small escort of fighting men, but a very large number of carriers, to bring in the stores intended for Coomassie.

Colonel Willcocks reached Fum on the night after leaving the Prah. As the supplies were failing at Kwisa, and another post, Captain Melliss took down a convoy to them, with twenty days' rations, and succeeded in doing so without opposition.

Colonel Willcocks pressed on, leaving all baggage behind. The defeat of the Dompoasis had its effect, and the little column joined Colonel Burroughs's men unopposed. The combined force then pushed on, until they arrived at a town under the sway of the King of Bekwai.

Next morning they marched to Bekwai. Here it was decided to evacuate Kwisa, for a time, and bring up the garrison that had been left there.

The next march was laborious, and wet, as usual. The troops marched into the little village of Amoaful, where Sir Garnet Wolseley had fought the decisive battle of his campaign, and saw many relics of the fight. Signal guns were heard, at various times, acquainting the enemy of our advance. The column stayed here for three days, which both soldiers and carriers enjoyed greatly, for the fatigues of the march had fairly worn out even the sturdy and long-enduring British troops.

Colonel Willcocks went forward with his staff to Esumeja, where the three companies, of which the garrison was composed, had already suffered sixty casualties. The Pioneers, some carriers with hatchets, and some of the Esumeja were sent out, a hundred yards down the road to Kokofu, to cut the bush on each side and build two stockades. This was done to deceive the garrison, there, into the belief that we were about to advance on the place by that road.

The ruse succeeded admirably. The general there sent information to the commander-in-chief of the Ashanti army, and the latter at once despatched a considerable number of men to reinforce the garrison. Thus the resistance along the main road was greatly reduced; and the Kokofu, standing on the defensive, did not harass the force upon its march.

On the evening of the 11th, a starving soldier made his way down from the fort with this message:

"Governor broke out, seventeen days ago. Garrison rapidly diminishing by disease, can only last a few more days, on very reduced rations."

Six star shells were fired, that night, to let the garrison know that help was coming, but they never saw them.

At midnight, the last contingent from Northern Nigeria, the Kwisa garrison, and an escort of two companies of the West African contingent arrived. This brought the force up to the regulation strength of one battalion, on its war footing. At sunset the officers were called, and orders were given for the next day's work.

The direction of the march was, even at that moment, a profound secret. The column was to be kept as short as possible, and only two carriers allowed to each officer. Only half rations were to be issued.

At daybreak the advance sounded, and the force moved out. It consisted of a thousand rank and file, sixty white men, seventeen hundred carriers, six guns, and six Maxims. The rain fell in ceaseless torrents. The road was practically an unbroken swamp, and the fatigue and discomfort of the journey were consequently terrible. The Ordah river was in flood, and had to be crossed on a felled tree.

The distance to Pekki, the last Bekwai village, was fifteen miles. It did not lie upon the main road, but that route had been chosen because a shorter extent of hostile country would have to be traversed, and the march thence to Coomassie would be only eleven miles; but it took the relief force nineteen and a half hours to get in, and the rear guard some two hours longer. Darkness fell some hours before they reached their destination and, thence forward, the force struggled on, each holding a man in front of him.

Nothing broke the silence save the trickling of water from the trees overhead, and the squelch of the mud churned up by marching columns. At times they had to wade waist deep in water. The exhausted carriers fell out by dozens, but their loads were picked up and shouldered by soldiers, and not a single one was lost.

The men got what shelter they could in the huts of the village and, in spite of wet and sleeplessness, all turned out cheerfully in the morning. The start was made at eight o'clock, in order that the men might recover a little from the previous day's fatigue.

The enemy's scouts were encountered almost on the outskirts of the village and, in a short time, the advance guard neared the village of Treda. It was a large place, with a very holy fetish tree. It stood on the top of a slope and, long before the rear guard had fallen out at Pekki, it was carried by a brilliant bayonet charge, by the Yorubas and the Sierra Leone frontier police. The enemy fought stubbornly, in the village; but were driven out with only some half-dozen casualties on our part.

Thirty sheep were found in the village, and they were a Godsend, indeed, to the troops. As in every other place, too, numbers of Lee-Metfords, Martinis, and Sniders were found.

Treda was burnt by the rear guard. The Ju-ju house, which was the scene of the native incantations, was pulled down, and the sacred trees felled. The enemy, however, were not discouraged; but hung upon the rear, keeping up a constant fire. Some of them proceeded to attack the Pekki people.

Fighting went on at intervals throughout the day, and it was decided to spend the night in a village that had been taken, after some resistance. This place was less than halfway on the road from Pekki to Coomassie. During the night a tropical deluge fell, and the troops and carriers were, all the time, without shelter.

Late that evening Colonel Willcocks called the white officers together and, for the first time, told them of the plan formed for the advance. He said that, after marching for an hour and a half, they would reach a strong fetish stronghold, where a fierce resistance might be looked for; but the final battle would be fought at the stockades, two hundred yards from the fort. He intended to attack these without encumbrance. A halt would therefore be called, at a spot some distance from the stockades; which would be hastily fortified, with a zereba and a portion of the troops. Here all the carriers and stores would be placed. Then the fighting force would take the stockades, return for the transport, and enter Coomassie. By this means there would be no risk of losing the precious stores and ammunition.

So determined was Colonel Willcocks to reach the forts, at all costs, that he gave orders that, if necessary, all soldiers killed should be left where they fell.

At four o'clock next morning the bugle sounded and, at the first streak of dawn, the column moved off. The march was maintained under a heavy skirmishing fire but, to the general surprise, the fetish town of which Colonel Willcocks had spoken was found deserted. Night was approaching, so that the plan proposed overnight could not be carried out. The troops, therefore, went forward hampered by the whole of the carriers and baggage of the column.

At four o'clock action began, at the point where the Cape Coast and Pekki roads converged towards Coomassie. The Ashantis had taken up a position on slightly rising ground--a position which was favourable to the assailants, as it tended to increase the enemy's inclination to fire high. Each of the roads was barred with massive entrenchments, which stretched across them into the bush, and flanked with breastworks of timber. These obstacles had been originally intended to envelop the garrison. Consequently, the war camps were on the British side of the stockades.

The battle began by a heavy fire, from the bush, upon both flanks of the rear guard. The attack on the left was soon successfully repulsed. On the other side, however, the roar of musketry never ceased, the enemy moving along abreast of the column, protected by a stockade expressly prepared; until they approached the main stockade, where they joined their companions. About fifty yards from the stockades, which were still invisible, a fresh path diverged towards the left; and the officers commanding the scouts were discussing what had best be done, when the enemy poured in a terrific volley from their fortified position in front, slightly wounding one officer and four soldiers. The rest immediately took shelter behind a fallen tree, which was lying across the path.

Colonel Wilkinson, commanding the advance guard, ordered up the guns. These were massed in a semicircle behind the fallen trees, and opened fire on the unseen foe; while the Maxims poured their bullets into the adjacent bush. The reply of the enemy was unceasing and, for an hour and a half, the battle raged, the distance between the combatants being only forty yards. Then Colonel Willcocks gave the order to cease firing and, in a minute, a strange silence succeeded the terrible din. The Ashantis, too, stopped firing, in sheer surprise at the cessation of attack; but soon redoubled their fusillade.

The leading companies moved up and formed in line, to the front and rear flank. Then came the inspiring notes of the charge and, with a cheer, the whole of the advance guard sprang forward into the bush. The dense undergrowth checked the impetus, as the soldiers had to cut their way with their knives but, as they did so, they maintained their deep-toned war song. As they got more into the open, they rushed round and clambered over the stockade; and the enemy, unable to stand the fury of their charge, fled in panic.

As a prolonged pursuit was impossible in the bush, and as daylight was fading, the troops were recalled at once. The first thing to be done was to pull down the stockade along the fetish road, to enable the transport to pass. When this was done, Colonel Willcocks collected the troops nearest to him and moved forward, at their head, along the broad road.

Their delight, when they emerged into the open and saw Coomassie ahead of them, was unbounded. Keeping regular step, though each man was yearning to press forward, they advanced steadily. The silence weighed upon them; and a dread, lest they had arrived too late, chilled the sense of triumph with which they had marched off. At last, the faint notes of a distant bugle sounded the general salute, and a wild burst of cheering greeted the sound. The bugles returned the call with joyous notes. Then the gate opened, and Captain Bishop, Mr. Ralph, and Dr. Hay came out, followed by such few of the brave little garrison as still had strength to walk.

Just at this moment, a great glow was seen in the distance. The flying enemy had fired the Basel Mission. A company therefore started at once, at the double, to drive them off.

The relieving force had, indeed, arrived only just in time. The means of resistance had all been exhausted, and another day would have seen the end. The garrison had held out desperately, in the hope that Colonel Willcocks would be able to fulfil the promise he had sent in, that he would arrive to relieve them on the 15th of July; and he had nobly kept his word to an hour, at the cost of an amount of hard work, privation, hardship, and suffering such as has fallen to the lot of but few expeditions of the kind.

The Ashanti rising was the result of long premeditation and preparation. On the 13th of March, the governor of the Gold Coast, accompanied by Lady Hodgson, left Accra to make a tour of inspection. On his way up country he was received with great friendliness at all the villages and, when he arrived at Coomassie on the 25th, he found a large number of Ashanti kings, who turned out in state to meet him. A triumphal arch had been erected, and a gorgeous procession of kings and chiefs marched past. There was no sign of a cloud in the horizon.

Several days passed quietly, and Sir Frederick Hodgson had several meetings with the chiefs about state matters. Gradually the eyes of the governor's followers, accustomed as they were to savage ways, saw that all was not right; and a wire was despatched, asking for reinforcements of two hundred men. These arrived on the 18th of April.

Captains Armitage and Leggatt, with a small party of soldiers, went out to the neighbouring village to bring in the golden stool. This was regarded by the natives with considerable veneration, and was always used as the throne of the king, as the sign of supreme authority. When they reached the village the party were fired upon, the two officers being wounded; and had to retire without having accomplished their purpose.

It was clear now that rebellion was intended. The native kings were all sounded, and several of them decided to side with us, among them five important leaders. On the 25th the Basel Mission servants were set upon, and several of them killed. The Ashantis then attacked and captured the villages in which the friendly natives and traders lived, and set fire to these and to the cantonment. The refugees, to the number of three thousand five hundred, with two hundred children, crowded round the fort, imploring the mission to allow them to enter.

It was wholly beyond the capacity of the fort to accommodate a tenth of their number. Troops were therefore ordered down from the barracks, and formed a cordon round the fugitives. The fort gate was closed, and a rope ladder led down one of the bastions. In this way, only one individual could enter at a time, and the danger of a rush was obviated.

Close round the walls, huts were erected to shelter the fugitives, who were exposed to all the inclemency of the weather. Thus passed some wretched days and worse nights, sleep being constantly interrupted by alarms, due to the fact that the rebels were in possession of all the buildings in the place, except the fort, many of which they loopholed.

On the 29th a determined attack was made, the enemy advancing boldly across the open, and fighting long and obstinately. Captain Marshall, however, with his two hundred and fifty native troops and friendly levies, taught them such a lesson that they never again tried fighting in the open. A hundred and thirty corpses were found and buried, and many more were carried off, while the fighting was going on.

That evening Captain Apling came in with his little column, but without food and with little ammunition. Aided by these troops, the outlying official buildings were occupied; and the friendly natives lodged in huts a little farther from the fort.

Through Three Campaigns

Things remained quiet until the 15th of May, when Major Morris arrived with his force. He too was short of food and ammunition, and famine already began to stare the beleaguered garrison in the face. Meanwhile the enemy had been busy erecting stockades, to bar every outlet from Coomassie. Many attempts were made to take these entrenchments; but they always failed, as they could not be pushed home, owing to want of ammunition; and the troops became, to some extent, demoralized by want of success.

Although the food had been carefully husbanded, it was running perilously low. Rations consisted of one and a half biscuits, and five ounces of preserved meat, per day. Five ponies, brought up by Major Morris, and a few cows kept at the Residency were killed and eaten. A few luxuries could still be bought from the native traders, but at prodigious prices. A spoonful of whisky cost 2 shillings, a seven-pound tin of flour 6 shillings, a box of matches 2 shillings, and a small tin of beef 2 pounds, 16 shillings.

The refugees fared much worse. They had no reserve of food, and foraging was next to impossible. As a result, they died at the rate of thirty and forty a day.

When only three and a half days' rations were left, it was decided that something must be done, and a council of war was called. It was then agreed that those who could walk should make a dash for it; and that a garrison of three Europeans, and a hundred rank and file, should be left behind. For these twenty-three days' rations could be left.

Major Morris, as senior officer, was to command the sortie. The direct road down to the Cape was barred by a great force of the rebels, and he therefore chose the road that would lead to the Denkera country. If that could be reached, they would be in a friendly country. The line to be taken was kept a profound secret, and was not revealed until ten o'clock on the evening before starting. The force consisted of six hundred soldiers, with a hundred and fifty rounds of ammunition a man, seven hundred carriers, and about a thousand refugees.

There was a mist in the morning, and the garrison who were to remain made a feint, to direct the enemy's attention to the main road. The column was not engaged until it reached a strong breastwork, at Potasi. This was taken after a severe fight; and Captain Leggatt, who commanded the vanguard, was mortally wounded. Four men were also killed, and there were nine other casualties.

A part of the stockade was pulled away, and the force moved forward. It was constantly attacked on the way and, on one occasion, Captain Marshall was seriously wounded in the head. Numbers of soldiers, refugees, and carriers fell out from exhaustion, and had to be left behind. Nearly all the carriers threw away their loads, and the men who carried the hammocks of the two ladies found themselves unable to support the weight.

The night was spent at Terrabum, eighteen miles from Coomassie; some two thousand human beings being crowded into the village, in a deluge. The soldiers were posted round the camp, in the form of a square.

The second day was a repetition of the first--heavy rain, muddy roads; dying soldiers, carriers, and refugees; attacks by the enemy. Twelve miles farther were made that day.

Thus seven days were passed. Captains Marshall and Leggatt both died. The ladies bore their trials wonderfully, as they had to tramp with the rest, along the miry track. At last Ekwanter, in the friendly Denkera country, was reached, and the force rested for two days. They then set out again and, after a terrible march, in the course of which they had to cross many swollen rivers, they arrived, two weeks after they had left Coomassie, half starved and worn out, on the coast.

In the meantime the three white officers, Captain Bishop of the Gold Coast Constabulary, Assistant Inspector Ralph, Lagos Constabulary, and Doctor Hay, medical officer, remained behind, with a hundred and fifteen Hausas, few of whom were fit for the task of holding the fort. After the departure of the column, the Ashantis swarmed down on the fort, thinking that it was entirely evacuated. They were met, however, with a heavy fire from the Maxims, and soon withdrew.

The first duty of Captain Bishop was to tell off the men to their posts. The soldiers who were to man the guns were ordered to sleep beside them. The ammunition was examined, and found to amount to a hundred and seventy rounds a man. The rations were calculated, and divided up for the twenty-three days that they were intended to last.

Attempts were then made to burn the native shanties, for sanitary reasons. They were so soaked, however, with water, that all attempts to burn them failed; till June 27th, when a short break in the rain enabled them to be fired. When they were all burned down, the Residency windows on the windward side were opened, for the first time.

Sickness, unfortunately, broke out very soon; and three of the little band died on the first day. This rate mounted higher and higher, and at last smallpox broke out. So dismal was the prospect that the men sank into a dull despair.

A few women traders hawked their wares outside the fort. A little cocoa, worth a farthing, cost 15 shillings; plantains were 1 pound, 6 shillings each; and a small pineapple fetched 15 shillings. The men received 3 shillings daily, in place of half a biscuit, when biscuits ran short; and this ready cash was willingly bartered for anything eatable.

Three heart-breaking weeks passed thus. Two-thirds of the troops had been buried outside the fort, the remainder were almost too weak to stand. When the food was all gone, it was arranged that they should go out to forage in the darkness, each man for himself. The three white men, each with a dose of poison, always stuck together and, come what might, agreed not to fall alive into the hands of the enemy.

However, on 14th July reports were brought in that firing had been heard. The news seemed too good to be true, but an old native officer declared that he had heard distant volleys. It was not until four o'clock on the next day, however, that a continuous and tremendous roar of guns convinced them that a relief column was at hand. The three imprisoned officers opened their last comfort, a half bottle of champagne, and drank success to their comrades. Several of the troops died while the fighting was going on, the excitement being too much for their weakened frames.

At last the Ashantis were seen flying in terror. Then the two buglers blew out the general salute, time after time till, at six o'clock, the head of the relief column came in view. The gate was thrown open, and those of the little garrison who were able to stand went out, to welcome their rescuers.

Five star shells were fired, to tell those left behind at Ekwanter that the relief was accomplished. Then the outlying quarters were occupied, and all slept with the satisfaction that their struggles and efforts had not been in vain, and that they had succeeded in relieving Coomassie.

CHAPTER 17: STOCKADES AND WAR CAMPS.

"Well, Hallett, here we are," Lisle said the next morning, "and thank God neither of us is touched, except perhaps by a few slugs. Of these, however, I dare say the surgeon will rid us this morning. It has been a big affair and, if we live to a hundred years, we are not likely to go through such another."

"I wish you would not be so confoundedly cheerful," Hallett said, gloomily; "we have got to go down again, and the Kokofu are to be dealt with. We shall probably have half a dozen more battles. The rain, too, shows no signs of giving up, and we shall have to tramp through swamps innumerable, ford countless rivers and, I dare say, be short of food again before we have done. As to going through such work again, my papers will be sent in at the first hint that I am likely to have to take part in it."

"All of which means, Hallett, that just at the present moment a reaction has set in; and I will guarantee that, if you had a thoroughly good breakfast, and finished it off with a pint of champagne, you would see matters in a different light, altogether."

"Don't talk of such things," Hallett said, feebly; "it is a dream, a mere fantasy. It doesn't seem to me, at present, a possibility that such a meal could fall to my lot.

"Look at me, look at my wasted figure! I weighed nearly fourteen stone, when we started; I doubt whether I weigh ten, now."

"All the better, Hallett. When I first saw you, on shore at Liverpool, I said to myself that you were as fat as a pig.

"'He would be a fine-looking young fellow,' I said, 'if he could get some of it off. I suppose it is good living and idleness that has done it.'"

Hallett laughed.

"Well, perhaps I need not grumble at that; but the worst of it is that I have always heard that, when a fellow loses on active service, he is sure to make it up again, and perhaps a stone more, after it is over."

240

"Yes, it is clear that you will have to diet, when you get home. No more savoury dishes, no more champagne suppers; just a cut of a joint, a few vegetables, and a ten-mile walk after."

"Don't talk of such things," Hallett said, impatiently; "rather than live as you say, I would put up with carrying sixteen stone about with me. What is the use of living, if you are to have no satisfaction out of life?"

"Well, Hallett, my advice to you in that case is, make love to some young lady, directly you reach England; and marry her in a month, before you have begun to assume elephantine proportions. Once hooked, you know, she cannot sue for divorce, on the ground that you have taken her in; and she will have to put up with you, whatever size you may attain."

"Look here, Bullen," Hallett said seriously, "I know you mean well, but the subject is a very sore one with me. However, seriously, I will try to keep my fat down. If I fail I fail, and shall of course send in my papers; for I don't care to be made a butt of, by young subalterns like yourself. The subaltern has no sense of what is decent and what is not, and he spares no one with his attempts at wit."

"Why, you are a subaltern yourself, Hallett!"

"I am within two of the top of the list, please to remember, and you have still four above you, and I am therefore your superior officer. I have put aside youthful folly, and have prepared myself for the position of captain of a company. I make great allowances for you. You will please to remember that you are five years my junior, and owe me a certain share of respect."

"Which I am afraid you will never get," Lisle said, laughingly. "I should as soon think of acting respectfully towards a Buddhist image, simply because it is two thousand years old. However, since the subject is so painful to you, I will try not to allude to it again."

"Is there anything you would wish me to do, sir? I have no doubt I shall have plenty of work to do, but I dare say I shall be able to find time to do anything my senior officer may require."

"Get out, you young scamp," Hallett growled, "or I shall throw--" and he looked round "--I don't see what there is to throw."

"Hallett, I am afraid that this rest is going to do you harm. I have found you a very companionable fellow, up to now; but it is clear that a night's rest and high living have done you more harm than good."

So saying, with a laugh, Lisle put on his helmet and went out.

There was, as he said, much to do. Everywhere there were proofs of the rigidness of the siege. Even in the houses in which they were quartered, which had been occupied by the enemy, the walls were pitted with bullets.

At eight o'clock a party of men went out, to destroy the stockades and burn the enemy's camps. In the one in which the Ashanti commander in chief had his headquarters were found over a thousand huts and bamboo camp beds.

The troops now saw the method of investment for the first time. It consisted in making large entrenchments, to barricade all the roads and tracks. In the bush between these were similar stockades, to complete the circle of fortifications and afford flank defences. All these were joined by a wide path; so that, as soon as one position was attacked, it was reinforced by those to right and left.

The remainder of the troops and carriers were engaged in trying to remedy the shockingly insanitary condition of the place. The staff were employed in examining the matter of stores and provisions, ammunition, and medical comforts; which were to be left behind for the relieving garrison. The labourers worked in relays, as did the rest of the soldiers.

High grass had grown almost up to the fort walls, and had to be cut down. While this was being done, skeletons and corpses in all states of decomposition were met with. Almost all had died of starvation. At first the bodies of those who died had been buried, but latterly their friends had become too weak to perform this office; and the poor wretches had crawled a few yards into the jungle, to die quietly. Such numbers of bodies were found that they had, at last, to be burned in heaps. Few, indeed, of the four thousand fugitives who had gathered round the fort, reached the coast with the force that had fought their way out.

The doctors were busy all day with the refugees, the old garrison, the thirty casualties from the fight of the day before, and several white men down with fever.

The Ashantis had burnt all the cantonments of friendly natives, but had left the old palace of Prempeh uninjured. This structure was burnt during the day.

The order for officers to assemble was sounded in the evening, and it was arranged that the return march was to start at four on the following morning. The coveted post of leading the column was given to a company of the West African Frontier Force.

They were a little sorry that they were so soon to leave the place. The fort itself was a handsome, square stone building, with towers at the four corners. The resident's quarters had a balcony, and excellent rooms. There was also, of course, barrack accommodation, store rooms, and a well. Quick-firing guns were mounted on the circular bastions. The surrounding buildings were bungalows, with broad verandahs; and the force would have been well pleased to remain for a few days, and enjoy the comforts provided for them.

The force to be left was under the command of Major Eden; and consisted of three officers, one doctor, three British non-commissioned officers, a hundred and fifty men of the West African Frontier Force, and a few Gold Coast Constabulary gunners; with fifty-four days' rations, and a plentiful supply of ammunition.

The column was a terribly long one, owing to the enormous number of invalids, wounded, women, and children. They halted for the night at the village halfway to Pekki. The villages on the road were all burnt down, to prevent opposition next time we passed; and all crops were destroyed. This work the soldiers quite enjoyed. Continued explosions occurred during the burning of the huts, showing how large an amount of ammunition the natives possessed.

Next night they arrived at Pekki. The king had prepared a market, so that the starving force got a more substantial supper than usual. Here the column was to divide. Colonel Willcocks was to go straight through to Bekwai; while the second portion, with the wounded and cripples, was to take two days.

They halted at Bekwai for two or three days, to give rest to the soldiers; a large proportion of whom were suffering from coughs, sore throats, and fever, the result of their hardships. Two thousand carriers were sent to fetch up more stores.

Preparations were then made for an attack on Kokofu, which was a serious menace to the troops going up or down. The column for this purpose, which was under General Moreland, consisted of six companies, which were to be brought up to eight. With three of the larger guns and two seven-pounders, they started for Esumeja on the 22nd. The force was a compact one, the only carriers allowed being one to each white man, to take up some food and a blanket. Major Melliss commanded the advance.

They marched rapidly, as it was all important to take the enemy by surprise. Some distance short of Kokofu, they stopped for breakfast. Then the officers were assembled and, when the plan of attack had been formed, the column moved cautiously on.

The place was only a mile away, so that an attack was momentarily expected. The troops entered a deserted village, and there halted. A few sentries were thrown out, and the colonel held a short council of war with Major Melliss and two of his other officers. After some discussion, it was decided that a Hausa company should go on, and rush the stockade with the bayonet, without firing. If they carried it, they were to proceed along the river bank beyond, and so place themselves as to cover the advance of the guns.

The scouts were called in; and the Hausa company set off, in fours, along the path. When they had marched a hundred yards, the little band that formed the advance signalled that they made out something ahead and, when they rounded the next sharp turn of the road they saw, not thirty yards away, a great six-foot stockade, extending far into the bush on either side. It lay halfway down a gentle slope, a situation which favoured the assailants for, naturally, the hill would increase the impetus of the charge.

The order was sent down in a whisper, "Stockade ahead, prepare to charge."

The men kept together as closely as possible. The buglers rang out the charge and, with a shout, the Hausas rushed at the stockade. In an instant the white leaders scaled the timbers, and the men followed at their heels.

To their astonishment, the place was empty. The surprise was complete. It was clear that the enemy had no information, whatever, of their approach; and the guard from the stockade had gone to feed, with their companions, in the war camp.

The bugle had told them what was coming and, with a roar, thousands of black figures dashed up towards the stockade. There was nothing for it but to charge and, with fixed bayonets, the Hausas dashed forward, regardless of the heavy fire with which they were met.

Enormously as they outnumbered their assailants, the sight of the glittering bayonets and the cheers of the Hausas were too much for the enemy. Those in front, after a few more shots, turned and fled; the Hausas following in hot pursuit. The river turned out to be of no depth; and it had not, as reported, a parapet for defending the passage. Hard as the Hausas tried to overtake the enemy, the Ashantis, being fleeter of foot, kept ahead but, though the shouting and running were beginning to tell on the pursuers, still they held on.

The path gradually became firmer; and suddenly, when they turned a corner, there was Kokofu in front of them. From almost every house, running for their lives, were naked Ashantis. The sight restored the men's strength; and they redoubled their efforts, with the result that they killed some thirty of the enemy.

The pursuit was maintained until they reached the other end of the town. Then the company was halted. The officers had difficulty in restraining their men, who implored them to press on in pursuit; but a general permission to do so could not be given. No one knew whether the main column had followed them; and it was possible, too, that the Ashantis might rally and return. Half the company, however, were permitted to continue the pursuit, and to keep the Ashantis on the run.

With shouts of delight, the men darted off in the darkness. In a short time they were recalled, and the company then marched back to the centre of the town. Here they found that the main body had come in. Two companies had been sent out, right and left into the bush, to keep down sniping fire, and hurry the enemy's retreat. Pickets and sentries had been thrown out round the town. Soldiers were eating the food that the enemy had cooked. Piles of loot were being dragged out of the houses; among which were quantities of loaded guns, rifles, and powder barrels. The native soldiers were almost mad with delight; and were dancing, singing, and carrying each other shoulder high, shouting songs of triumph.

But short time could be allowed for rejoicing. The various company calls were sounded and, when the men were gathered, the town was methodically razed, and a collection of over two hundred guns were burnt.

The troops, however, had reason for their joy. The Kokofu army of some six thousand men, who had repulsed two previous attacks, were a mass of fugitives. In the course of one week, the Ashantis had suffered two crushing defeats in their strongest positions.

As soon as the work was done, the force set out on their return march. Their appearance differed widely from that of the men who had silently, and in good order, advanced. Scarcely a man, white or black, was not loaded with some token of the victory. All were laughing, or talking, or singing victorious songs.

A halt was made, to destroy the stockade and the war camp. The former was found to be extremely strong and, had it been manned by the enemy, the work of capturing it would have been very serious, indeed.

When they arrived at Esumeja, the garrison there could scarcely believe that the success had been so complete, and so sudden. Bekwai was reached as twilight was beginning, and here the whole of the garrison, with Colonel Willcocks at its head, was drawn up to receive them. The men were heartily cheered; and the Hausa company, which had done such splendid service, were halted and congratulated by Colonel Willcocks. Then after three cheers the force, which had been on foot for sixteen hours, was dismissed, and returned to its quarters.

"Well, Hallett, how do you feel?"

"Better," Hallett said. "I felt tired enough, after the march there but, somehow, I forgot all about it directly the fight began. Everyone was so delighted and cheery that, really, I came in quite fresh."

"I knew it would be so," Lisle said. "It has been a glorious day and, if you had come in moping, I should have given you up as hopeless."

"And I give you up as hopeless, the other way," Hallett replied. "You always seem brimming over with fun; even when, as far as I can see, there is nothing to be funny about."

"Well, it really has been a glorious victory; and I only wish we had both been with the Hausa company who first attacked. They really won the game off their own bat, for we had nothing to do but to pick up the spoil.

"There was not much worth carrying away, but I am glad of some little memento of the fight. I got the chief's stool. I don't quite know what I am going to do with it, yet; but I shall try to get my servant to carry it along; and it will come in handy, to sit down upon, when we encamp in a swamp.

"What did you manage to get?"

"I picked up a small rifle, a very pretty weapon. Do you know, I quite approve of the regulation, in South Africa, that officers should carry rifles instead of swords. I have never been able to understand why we should drag about swords, which are of no use whatever while, with rifles, we could at least pot some of the enemy; instead of standing, looking like fools, while the men are doing all the work."

"I agree with you, there. In the Tirah campaign I, several times, got hold of the rifles of fallen men, and did a little shooting on my own account. Officers would all make themselves good shots, if they knew that shooting would be of some value; and even three officers, with a weak company, could do really valuable service. I certainly found it so, when I was with the Punjabis. Of course, I was not an officer; but I was a really good shot with a rifle, and succeeded in potting several Pathan chiefs."

"I suppose," Hallett said, mournfully, "that about the time when I leave the army as a general, common sense will prevail; and the sword will be done away with, except on state occasions."

"It is very good of you to look so far ahead, Hallett. It shows that you have abandoned the idea of leaving the army, even if you again put on flesh.

"I rather wonder that you should modestly confine yourself to retiring as a general. Why not strive for the position of a field marshal, who has the possibility of becoming commander in chief? It may be, old fellow that, if you shake yourself together, you may yet attain these dignities. You were always very jovial, on board ship; and I trust that, when we get out of this horrible country, you will regain your normal spirits."

"I am not so sure that I shall get out of the country; for I often feel disposed to brain you, when you won't let me alone; and I fear that, one of these days, I may give way to the impulse."

"You would have to catch me, first," Lisle laughed; "and as I believe that I could run three feet to your one, your chance of carrying out so diabolical an impulse would be very small.

"But here is the boy with our supper, which we have fairly earned, and to which I shall certainly do justice.

"What have you got, boy?"

"Half a tin of preserved meat, sah, done up with curry."

"Let us eat, with thankfulness.

"How much more curry have we got, boy?"

"Three bottles, sah."

"Thank goodness!" said Hallett, "that will last for some time; for really, tinned beef by itself, when a man is exhausted, is difficult to get down. I really think that we should address a round robin to the P.M.O., begging him to order additional medical comforts, every night."

"You are belying yourself, Hallett. You have taken things very well as they came, whatever they might be; save for a little grumbling, which does no harm to anyone and, I acknowledge, amuses me very much."

"I have no expectation or design," Hallett grumbled, "but it seems to amuse you. However, I suppose I must put up with it, till the end."

"I am afraid you will have to do so, Hallett. It is good for you, and stirs you up; and I shall risk that onslaught you spoke of, as we go down to the coast again."

"When will that be, Lisle?"

"I have not the smallest idea. I should imagine that we shall stay, and give these fellows thrashing after thrashing, until we have completely knocked the fight out of them. That won't be done in a day or two. Probably those we have defeated will gather again, in the course of a day or two; and we shall have to give them several lickings, before we dispose of them altogether."

The news of the victory at Kokofu spread fast, and the Denkeras poured in to join the native levies. There was now a pause, while preparations were made for a systematic punitive campaign. Captain Wright was sent down to Euarsi, where three thousand Denkera levies had been collected; and superintended the cutting down of the crops in the Adansi country, to the south and west. The Akim levies were to act similarly, in flank, under the command of Captains Willcocks and Benson; while a third body of levies, under Major Cramer, guarded the upper district. A company was sent to Kwisa to guard the main road, which was now reopened for traffic.

Convoys went up and down along the entire route, bringing up supplies of all sorts; but those going north of Fumsu still required strong escorts. Large parties went out foraging, almost daily, to villages and farms for miles round. These bodies were compact fighting forces, and took out considerable numbers of unladen carriers.

When a village was found the troops surrounded it, while the carriers searched it for hidden stores. Then they would march away to other villages, until every carrier had a load; when the force would return, and store the results of the raid.

The remnants of the reconcentrating Ashanti army were reported to be somewhere in the bush, east of Dompoasi. It was necessary to clear them out before the Adansi country could be subdued, and the line of communication be at all safe. Consequently a flying column--of four hundred of the West African Field Force, one large and one small gun of the West Indian Rifles, to be joined by the Kwisa company--was despatched, under the command of Major Beddoes, against the enemy. They had to strike out into the bush by almost unknown roads, and great difficulties were encountered. Fortunately, however, they captured a prisoner, who consented to lead them to the enemy's camp, on condition that his life would be spared.

Three days later, an advance was made on the camp. The column had hardly started when they were attacked. The enemy held a strong series of fortified positions; but these were captured, one after another.

A couple of miles farther, they again met with opposition. The enemy, this time, occupied the bank of a stream. The Maxims at once opened fire on them, and did such great execution that the Ashantis rapidly became demoralized, and fled. Close to the rear of this spot was found a newly-constructed stockade, some three hundred yards in length; but the fugitives continued their flight without stopping to man it.

When they advanced a little farther, the force was severely attacked on all sides. The enemy pushed up to within a few yards of our men. Once they even attempted to rush the seven pounder; but were repulsed by the heavy volleys of the West Indian Rifles, who were serving it. Lieutenant Phillips and Lieutenant Swabey were severely wounded, and two other officers slightly so. The Adansis made another desperate attempt to cover their camp, and they were not finally driven back until nearly dusk.

It was found that the rebels had discovered the advance of Major Cramer's levies while they were still a day's journey away. They were, therefore, not only anxious to repulse our force, so that they could fall upon the other one; but were fighting a splendid rear action, so as to cover the retreat of their women, children, and property, which had been gathered there under the belief that the existence of the camp was unknown to us.

Meanwhile, at Bekwai, the list of sick and invalids steadily increased; and every convoy that went down to the coast was accompanied by a number of white and black victims to the climate. The kits of the men who died realized enormous prices. A box that contained three cakes of soap fetched 27 shillings, and a box of twenty-five cheroots 2 pounds, 2 shillings.

On the 31st of July a runner arrived, from Pekki, stating that the town was going to be attacked in force, the next evening, as a punishment for the assistance it had rendered the white men. Major Melliss was accordingly ordered to proceed thither the following morning with two guns, a Hausa company with a Maxim, and a column of carriers. They were to remain there a day, and put the place in a state of defence; and then they would be joined by a force under Colonel Burroughs, which was to complete the relief of Coomassie, by doubling its garrison and supply of stores.

The little party started, and tramped along the intervening fifteen miles much more comfortably than usual; as the rains had temporarily ceased, and the track had been greatly improved by the kings of Bekwai and Pekki. There was great difficulty in crossing the bridge over the Ordah river, but the guns were at last taken over safely, and they arrived at Pekki at half-past four in the afternoon.

They were received with delight by the villagers, who had been in a state of terrible fear. The war chief put his house at the disposal of the officers. Fortunately, no attack was made by the Ashantis. Hasty fortifications were erected, and a rough bamboo barracks built for the force. Here, for the first time since the beginning of the campaign, the Hausas received a small issue of meat, and their delight was unbounded.

Some scouts, who had been sent out in the neighbourhood of the town, brought in a wounded Hausa who had been left behind in the governor's retreat and, for six weeks, had managed to hide himself in the bush, and live upon roots that he found at night.

On the afternoon of the 4th of August, Colonel Burroughs and his force arrived; bringing with him a fresh half battalion of the Central African Regiment, with two large guns and two seven-pounders. This raised the total strength to seven hundred and fifty. It was decided that it would be necessary to proceed without delay to Coomassie; for no signals had been received from the fort, for two successive Sundays, and there was a rumour that the Ashantis had again attacked it. The column therefore moved forward, next day.

The garrison, when they arrived, was to be brought up to three hundred soldiers and ten white men; the stockades round Coomassie were to be destroyed; and then the relief column were to fight their way down the main road, which had been hitherto closed for all traffic.

At first the column met with no opposition but, when they reached Treda, the people of that place fired heavily upon them. After driving these off the force proceeded, but were soon met by an Ashanti force. They attacked only the transport and hospital, and their tactics were clever. They had formed a series of ambushes, connected by a broad path. The head of the column was allowed to pass, unattacked; then the carriers were fired into heavily and, when the tail of the column passed, they ran along the path to the next ambush and renewed their tactics.

Their plan, however, was soon discovered and, in order to checkmate it, a gun was placed in the path, crammed with case shot, the infantry were got ready to fire in volleys, and a Maxim ranged for rapid fire. Presently the enemy were seen, hurrying along to occupy the next ambush; and the big gun poured its contents into their midst, while the troops fired well-directed volleys at them and, when they fled in confusion down the path, the Maxim swept numbers of them away. The attacks immediately ceased, and the column proceeded on its way; rejoicing that, for once, they had beaten the Ashantis at their own game.

They arrived at the fort at six o'clock in the evening; and found that, although the garrison had been harassed by sniping, no serious attack had been made upon them. It was known that there were still four stockades occupied by the Ashantis; and it was decided that two columns, each three hundred strong, should sally out the next morning, and each carry two of the fortifications. The companies under Lisle and Hallett formed part of the force under Major Melliss, which was to destroy the stockade on the Bantama road; while the other, under Major Cobbe, was to attack that near the Kimtampo road. After this had been done, arrangements were to be made for the attack on the other two stockades.

The start was made at ten o'clock. At first everything went well. The Basel Mission House was passed and, as they marched on without seeing any signs of life, it was believed that no opposition would be met with. They advanced, however, with great caution. Suddenly, news was sent back from the advance guard that the village of Bantama had been sighted, just ahead; and that the enemy were running out from it. The force advanced, and found the fires in the village still burning. At the other end the track through it divided; but the defiance signal, a large vulture lying spread-eagle fashion, showed the line the fugitives had pursued. This was followed and, in a short time, a stockade was seen at the foot of a slope, some eighty yards away.

How far it extended into the bush on either side, there was no means of knowing; nor could it be ascertained whether it was defended, for no signs of life were visible. The carriers were ordered to bring up the Maxim but, before they could get the parts of the gun off their heads, a deafening volley flashed out from the stockade. Several of the carriers fell, wounded by the slugs, and the rest fled.

The little weapon, however, was soon put together, and opened fire. But rifle bullets were useless against a six-foot tree trunk. The enemy, moreover, were firing on our flank, and it was thought that they might be working round to attack the rear. An effort was therefore made to cut a path through the bush, under the impression that it was not so thick inside. The jungle grass, however, prevented this from being carried out, and the heavy gun was therefore ordered up.

When it began to play upon the fort, as far as could be determined, the enemy's fire grew momentarily heavier. Then it was seen that a number of men were firing from a high tree, in the rear of the stockade. Colour Sergeant Foster turned a Maxim upon it. He was severely wounded on the left shoulder, but he said nothing about it, and poured such a shower of lead into the tree that it was, at once, deserted by the enemy.

The din was deafening. Every white man belonging to the leading company had been hit, and the ground near the gun and Maxim was strewn with the dead and dying.

Major Melliss gave the word:

"Mass the buglers, form up left company, and both charge!"

The buglers stood up, waiting for the word to blow. One of them was instantly wounded but, though the blood was streaming down his face, he stuck to his work. The word "Sound the way!" was given, and the Hausas sprang wildly forward and dashed down the slope, Major Melliss at their head.

Contrary to custom, the Ashantis were not terrified at the sight of the bayonets and, through their loopholes, kept up a heavy fire. The assailants, however, soon reached the stockade. Two white men scrambled up the timbers, which were slippery with blood; and jumped down, eight feet, on the other side, where they were soon joined by numbers of their men. The enemy, however, stood their ground bravely, and there was a fierce hand-to-hand fight. But the bayonet did its work; and the enemy, who were getting more and more outnumbered, at last turned and fled, hotly pursued by the victors.

A turn in the path revealed the war camp. It was an enormous one, but already the last of its garrison were disappearing in the forest, taking any path that afforded a chance of safety. The assembly sounded, and the pursuit was abandoned; as another company came forward, at a steady double, with orders to proceed up the road to the next village. This they were to burn, and then return to the war camp.

The work of destroying the war camp at once began. The troops lined its outskirts, while the carriers cut down and burnt the huts. Then a party set to work to pull down the stockades, which turned out to be nearly three hundred yards long, and crescent shaped--a fact that explained why we had suffered so severely from crossfire.

At last, sheets of flame showed that the work was accomplished, and the company that had gone on in advance returned, and reported the destruction of the village behind. The little force then gathered, and proceeded to Bantama, a sacred village at which human sacrifices had been perpetrated, for centuries. This place was razed to the ground.

On the left, the sound of continuous firing told that Major Cobbe was still heavily engaged. There was, however, no means of moving through the bush to his assistance. The force therefore returned to the fort.

It was late before the firing ceased, and Major Cobbe's column came in, with the wounded on hammocks and stretchers. The first two signal shots had slightly wounded Major Cobbe and a white colour sergeant. After a prolonged fight, the former had finally turned the right of the enemy's position, with two companies of the Central African Regiment; but lost heavily, owing to the thick grass and slow progress.

Meanwhile the West African company had engaged a stockade similar to the one we had rushed, but horseshoe in form. Thus our men had been almost completely surrounded by a circle of fire. When, however, the flanking movement had at last been completed, the enemy were charged simultaneously from the front and flank, whereupon they broke and fled. The large war camp behind had been looted and burnt, and the stockade pulled down. The guns had failed to penetrate this, and the defenders were only driven out at the point of the bayonet, after a fight of two hours' duration.

The loss had been heavy. Half a dozen white officers were wounded, and seventeen Sikhs had been killed or wounded, out of a total of fifty who had gone into action. The total casualties mounted up to seventy.

CHAPTER 18: A NIGHT SURPRISE.

With the exception of replenishing the supplies of ammunition, cleaning rifles, and burying the dead, nothing further was done that afternoon. In the evening a consultation was held, in the fort, among the principal officers. The situation was a difficult one. An immense amount of ammunition had been expended, and it was decided that it was out of the question to draw upon the supplies that had been sent up for the garrison. There were still two strongly-entrenched positions, and strong opposition was anticipated to the clearing of the main road. Every round would, therefore, be required for this work. This seemed to preclude the idea of taking the other two stockades.

The choice therefore remained of making the assault upon these, and then returning through Pekki; or of leaving them and going back by the main road, the route laid down in their instructions. Neither of these plans was satisfactory, for each left half the programme undone.

It was suggested that a night attack might be attempted. In that case, not a shot must be fired, and the attack must be made by the bayonet alone. The moon rose early, and it was almost high at eight o'clock.

Of course, it was extremely risky to venture upon such a plan, with superstitious black troops. The object of assault, however, could be located the next day, and the danger of losing their way would thereby be reduced to a minimum. Further, it was decided that no dependence, whatever, be placed on any native guide. Finally, it would be eminently undesirable to leave Coomassie again in a state of siege.

It was clear that only one of the stockades could be carried in this manner, as the other would be placed on its guard. It was therefore decided that the one on the Accra-Coomassie road was the most suitable; first because it joined the main road to Cape Coast, and secondly because the capture of the stockade would isolate the remaining one on the Ejesu road, which the Ashantis would probably abandon, as both the adjacent camps had fallen into our hands.

Through Three Campaigns

As the result of this decision Captain Loch was sent out, at twelve o'clock on the following day, to reconnoitre the position. His men, by creeping through the tall grass and clambering among the tall trees, succeeded in reaching a large cotton tree within seventy yards of the enemy's entrenchment. Climbing this, they obtained a good view of the enemy's stockade and camp behind it.

At that moment a roar of voices was heard, and hostile scouts poured out from the camp. The object of the expedition, however, had been attained; and the soldiers retired rapidly, without casualties.

At five in the afternoon the officers assembled at Colonel Burroughs's quarters. Here the details of the work were explained to them. They were to fall in at eight o'clock, and deliver the attack between nine and ten. The Maxims were to follow in rear of the infantry, and no other guns were to be taken.

Only five hundred men were selected to go. Captain Loch's company were to take the lead, as a reward for the scouting they had done in the morning. Major Melliss' company was to follow. The companies in the rear were to move to the flanks, when the stockade had been taken, so as to guard against an attack from the other war camp.

An early meal was taken, and then the officers sallied out for a last inspection of the company; which was, by this time, assembling outside the fort gate. Silently the troops fell into their allotted position. Then the word was passed down the line that all was ready. The officers gave their final orders to the men--no smoking, no talking, no noise, no firing, bayonet only. As if nothing unusual was occurring, the bugle from the fort sounded the last post.

At the start the pace was for some time good but, after passing Prempeh's palace, the road became a tortuous track and, at every yard, the tall grass became thicker and, here and there, a fallen tree lay across the path. The dead silence that prevailed rendered every one nervous. At last they came in sight of the great cotton tree. Here all halted, and crouched down.

Two leading companies formed up and were awaiting orders when, suddenly, two signal guns were fired and, instantly, the line of timbers was lit up by a glare of fire, and a crashing volley of slugs was poured in. Lieutenant Greer, who was in front of the column, fell, seriously wounded. Then, with a shout of rage that almost drowned the order, "Charge!" they leapt to their feet and dashed forward.

Nothing could stop the impetuous charge and, when they reached the stockade, they scaled it and poured headlong over it. In front of them was the war camp, through which ran a road, now crowded with the panic-stricken defenders. As the enemy ran from their huts, they were cut down in numbers with swords and bayonets. The din was tremendous; yells, shouts, and groans rent the air. The path was strewn with corpses.

The headlong race continued. Three villages had been passed, but there was a fort behind. This also was carried. Then there was a halt, on account of the exhaustion caused by the speed with which all had run. There was no fear that the panic-stricken foe would rally; but there was the possibility of a counter attack, by the Ashantis from the war camp to the left; for it was not known that the panic had spread to these, also, and that they too had fled in disorder, never to return.

The four camps were burnt, one after another; the stockades pulled down; and the force, still half mad with the excitement of the fight, marched back to the fort. The number of casualties was very small. Hardly one, indeed, had taken place, except those caused by the first volley of the enemy.

In one of the houses they entered, a child was found asleep. It had been left behind, and had not been aroused by the noise. Terrified as it awoke, it clung to a white man for protection, and was taken by him to a place of safety.

The force reached camp at eleven o'clock, having accomplished their work with a success altogether beyond expectation. At eight o'clock next morning, the column paraded for its march down. All the wounded who were unfit for duty were left in the fort.

Not long after the start, the scouts sighted another stockade. The troops formed up for the attack; but they found, to their surprise, that it was deserted. Both the stockade and the war camp behind were destroyed, without opposition.

Pressing forward they passed entrenchment after entrenchment, but all were deserted. River after river was forded, breast high, but no enemy was met with; although some of the entrenchments were exceedingly formidable, and could not have been carried without very heavy loss.

The scouts captured a young girl, from whom valuable information was obtained. She had been sent out, like many of the other women, to get supplies for the army at Ejesu, where the queen mother was. It appeared that the queen had been greatly upset by the night attack, and the capture of all the entrenchments; and had collected all her chiefs to decide what had best be done, now that the siege of Coomassie had been raised. Then it was understood why the advance had not been opposed. But for this council, we should have found every stockade occupied in force.

The expedition pushed on, and arrived at Bekwai without having to fire a shot. The garrison there was formed up to receive and cheer them and, what was still more appreciated, a ration of fresh meat and another round of medical comforts were served out.

"Well, Bullen," Hallett said, the next morning, "here we are again. I wonder how long we shall get to rest our wearied bodies."

"For my part," said Lisle, "I sha'n't be sorry when we are afoot again. It has been hard work, and there has been some tough fighting; but anything is better than being stuck in one of these dreary towns. Fortunately we have both escaped bullets, and have merely had a slight peppering of slugs and, as we have both been put down in the reports as slightly wounded, on three occasions, we may feel grateful, as it always does a fellow good to be mentioned in the casualty list; and it should help you to attain that position we spoke of, the other day, of commander-in-chief."

"I renounce that dream utterly, and aspire to nothing higher than colonel. It must really be an awful bore to be commander-in-chief. Fancy having to go down to your office every morning, and go into all sorts of questions, and settle all sorts of business. No, I think that, when I get to be a colonel, my aspirations will be satisfied."

"I don't know that I should care even about being a colonel, Hallett. Long before I get to that rank, I am sure that I should have had quite enough of fighting to last for a lifetime, and would be quite content to settle down in some little place at home."

"And marry, of course. A fellow like you would be sure to be able to pick up a wife with money. My thoughts don't incline that way. I look forward to the Rag as the conclusion of my career. There you meet fellows you know, lie against each other about past campaigns, eat capital dinners, and have your rub of whist, regularly, of an evening."

"But, my dear Hallett, think how you would fatten out under such a regime!"

"Oh, hang the fat, Bullen; it would not matter one way or another, when you haven't got to do yourself up in uniform, and make tremendous marches, and so on. I should not want to walk, at all; I should have chambers somewhere close to the club, and could always charter a hansom, when I wanted to go anywhere. Besides, fat is eminently respectable, in an elderly man."

Lisle laughed merrily.

"My dear Hallett, it is useless to look forward so far into the future. Let us content ourselves with the evils of today. In spite of your grumbling, you know that you like the life and, if the bullets do but spare you, I have no doubt that you will be just as energetic a soldier as you have shown yourself in this campaign; although I must admit that you have sometimes taken it out in grumbling."

"Well, it is very difficult to be energetic in this country. I think I could be enthusiastic, in anything like a decent climate, but this takes all the spirit out of one.

"I think I could have struggled over the snow in the Tirah, as you did. I can conceive myself wearing the D.S.O. in European war. But how can a man keep his pecker up when he is wet through all day, continually fording rivers, and exposed all the time to a pelting rain and, worse than all, seeing his friends going down one after another with this beastly fever, and feeling sure that his own turn will come next?

"I should not mind so much if we always had a dry hut to sleep in, but as often as not we have to sleep on the drenched ground in the open and, consequently, get up in the morning more tired than when we lie down. I have no doubt that, after all this is over, I shall become a cripple from rheumatism, or be laid up with some other disorder."

"I don't suppose you will do anything of the sort, Hallett. Of course this fever is very trying but, although men are being constantly sent down to the coast, the number who die from it is not great. Only some six or seven have succumbed. I expect myself that we shall both return to our regiments in the pink of condition, with our medals on our breasts, and proud of the fact that we have gone through one of the most perilous expeditions ever achieved by British troops; and the more wonderful that, except for a handful of English officers and non-commissioned officers, it has been carried through successfully by a purely native army.

"I don't think we quite recognize, at present, what a big affair it has been. We have marched through almost impenetrable bush; we have suppressed a rebellion over a great extent of country, admirably adapted for the mode of warfare of our enemies; and we have smashed up an army of well-armed natives, in numbers ranging from six, to ten to one against us."

"Yes, yes, I know all that; and I don't say that it has not been a well-managed business; and I dare say I shall look back on it with pleasure, some day, when I have forgotten all the miseries we have suffered. Besides, though I do grumble, I hope we are not going to stick here long. I could do with a week of eating and drinking--that would be the outside. It is wretched enough tramping through swamps, but I think I should prefer that to a prolonged stay in this hole."

"For once I agree with you thoroughly, Hallett. It is bad enough to march in West Africa, but it is worse to sit still. It is only when you try to do that, that you find how much you are pulled down; and the longer you sit still, the less disposed you are to get up; whereas, on the march, you are so full of the idea that you may be ambushed, at any moment, that you have no time to think of your fatigues."

"Yes, there is no doubt of that, Bullen; so I mean to spend all the time I have to spare here on my back; and sleep, if I can, continuously."

"Don't flatter yourself that you will be allowed to do that. You may be sure that they will find ample work for lazy hands to do. Now it is time to buckle on our swords, and go out and inspect our fellows. I can see that they are mustering already."

"I wish those white non-commissioned officers would not be so disgustingly punctual," Hallett grumbled. "They are splendid when it comes to fighting, but they never seem to know that there is a time for work and a time for play--or, at any rate, they never let others play."

"They are splendid fellows," Lisle said. "I really do not know what we should have done without them. There would be no talking of lying down and going to sleep, if they were not there to look after the men."

"I don't think it would make any difference to you," Hallett said, "for it seems to me that you are always looking after your men."

"So are you, Hallett. You are just as keen about getting your company into order as I am, only you always try to look bored over it. It is a stupid plan, old man, for I don't think that you get the kudos that you deserve."

"My dear Bullen, you may argue forever, but if you think that you can transform me into a bustling, hustling fellow like yourself, I can tell you that you are mistaken. I know that I do what I have to do, and perhaps may not do it badly, but I don't go beyond that.

"When they say 'Do this,' I do it; when they don't say so, I don't do it; and I fancy it comes to about the same thing, in the end."

"I suppose it does," Lisle laughed, as they issued from their hut.

"These poor fellows look as if they wanted a rest more than we do, don't they?"

"They look horribly thin," Hallett said.

"Yes, it is well that the blacks have such good spirits, and are always ready to chatter and laugh when the day's work is over--that is, if it has not been an exceptionally hard one.

"Well, though I don't care about staying long here, myself, I do hope they will give the poor fellows time to get into condition again, before starting. I fear, however, that there is very little chance of that."

This, indeed, turned out to be the case. Two days later, reinforcements arrived from the coast, to increase the total strength available for punitive expeditions. Two strong parties then started, under Colonel Haverstock and Colonel Wilkinson. They were to travel by different routes, and to join hands in the neighbourhood of the sacred fetish lake, where large numbers of Ashantis and Kokofu were reported to have assembled. The Hausa companies did not accompany them, the columns being largely composed of the newly-arrived troops--who were, of course, eager to take their share of the fighting.

Lisle and Hallett did a little grumbling, but they really felt that they required a longer period of rest, and they could not help congratulating themselves when the columns returned, ten days after, without having exchanged more than a shot or two with the enemy.

They found that the country round the lake was thickly inhabited. Many of the villages had been burnt and, in all cases, the sacred trees had been cut down. It was quite clear that the spirit of the enemy was greatly broken, and that the end was approaching.

"We must certainly congratulate ourselves upon having a comfortable time of it, here," Lisle said, "instead of a ten days' tramp, without any great result. We can manage to keep ourselves dry in this hut, now that our men have covered it thickly with palm leaves; whereas they have had to sleep in the open, pretty nearly every night."

"It was good for them," Hallett said; "the fellows looked altogether too spick and span, when they marched in. It is just as well that they should get a little experience of the work we have been doing, for months. I saw them, as they marched in, look with astonishment at the state of our men's garments--or rather, I may say, their rags. They would have grown haughty, if they had not had a sample of the work; and their uniforms looked very different, when they came back, from what they were when they marched away. There is nothing like a fortnight's roughing it in the bush to take a man, whether white or black, a peg or two down in his own estimation.

"I was amused, the first day they arrived, when I saw their faces at the sight of their rations. It was quite a picture. Thank goodness we have had nothing to grumble about, in that way, since we got our box from the coast. Chocolate for breakfast, brandy and water at dinner, preserved meat, are quite a different thing from the stuff they manage to give us--two or three ounces of meat, about once a week. Those boxes of biscuits, too, have been invaluable. The ration biscuits were for the most part wet through, and there wasn't a wholesome crunch in a dozen of them. We have certainly improved a lot in appearance, during the last fortnight; and I believe that it is due to the feeding, more than the rest."

"It is due, no doubt, to both," Lisle said; "but certainly the feeding has had a good deal to do with it."

"Those tins of soup," said Hallett, "have been really splendid. I believe I have gained seven or eight pounds in weight, in spite of this sweltering heat."

"You have certainly filled out a bit. I was rather thinking of asking you to hand over all the soups to me, so that you should not gain weight so fast."

"That would have been a modest request, indeed, Bullen!"

"It was a case of true friendship," Lisle laughed. "I know how you have appreciated your loss of flesh."

"You be blowed!" Hallett said. "If they would run to half a dozen tins a day, I can tell you I would take them, whatever the consequences."

"Well, really, I do think, Hallett, those few cases have saved us from fever. I felt so utterly washed out, when we arrived here, that I began to think I was in for a bad attack."

"Same here, Bullen. I fought against the feeling because I dreaded that hospital tent and, still more, being carried down country."

"Yes; we certainly did a clever thing, when we bought up everything we could, that day we were in Cape Coast. Our servants, too, have turned out most satisfactory. Poor beggars! though the weather has been so bad, there has scarcely been a night when they have not managed to make a little fire, and boil water either to mix with our tot of rum, or to make a cup of tea."

"Yes, they have turned out uncommonly well. We must certainly make them a handsome present, when this is all over. It was awfully lucky we brought up a good supply of tea with us, and condensed milk. I am certain that the hot drink, at night, did wonders in the way of keeping off fevers."

"That is so, Lisle; there is nothing that will keep the wet out, or at least prevent it from doing harm, like a cup of hot tea with the allowance of rum in it. I am sure I don't know what we should have done, without it. That tea and milk were all that we could bring, especially as our carriers were cut down to one man, each."

"That was your idea, Lisle, and I agree that it has been the saving of us. I was rather in favour of bringing spirits, myself; but I quite admit, now, that it would have been a great mistake. Besides, half a dozen pounds of tea does not weigh more than a couple of bottles of spirits; which would have been gone in four or five days, while the tea has held out for months. I never was much of a tea drinker before. It is all very well to take a cup at an afternoon tea fight, but that was about the extent of my indulgence in the beverage. In future I shall become what is called a votary, and shall cut down my spirits to the narrowest limit."

"That would be running to the opposite extreme, Hallett. Too much tea is just as bad as too much spirits."

"Ah! Well, I can breakfast with coffee or cocoa. The next time I go on the march, I shall take two or three pounds of cocoa in my box. Many a time I have longed for a cup, when we have started at three o'clock in the morning, and have felt that it would be well worth a guinea a cup. Now I shall have the satisfaction of always starting with a good warm drink, which is as good for hunger as thirst. I have often wondered how I could have been fool enough not to bring a supply with me."

"Yes, it would have been very comforting," Lisle agreed; "we shall know better, another time."

"I trust that there will never be another time like this for me. I shall be ready to volunteer for service in any part of the world, bar Western Africa. They say that the troops at the Cape are going through a hard time, but I am convinced that it is child's play in comparison with our work here. Why, they have hours, and indeed days, sometimes, without rain. Just think of that, my dear fellow! Just think of it! And when the rain does fall, it soon sinks into the sandy soil and, if they lie down at night, they only get wet on one side, and have waterproof sheets to lie on. Just think of that! And yet, they actually consider that they are going through hardships!"

"They say, too, that the commissariat arrangements are splendid. They get meat rations every day--every day, mind you--and I hear they even get jam. It is enough to fill one with envy. I remember I was always fond of jam, as a boy. I can tell you that, when I get back to civilization, one of my first cries will be for jam. Fancy jam spread thickly on new bread!

"And men who have all these luxuries think that they are roughing it! Certainly human ingratitude is appalling!"

Lisle laughed.

"But you must remember that there are compensations. We get a fight every two or three days, while they have often to tramp two or three hundred miles, without catching sight of an enemy at all."

"There is certainly something in that," Hallett said. "I must admit that that is a great consolation; and it is satisfactory, too, that when we do fight we are fired at principally with slugs; which we both know from experience are not pleasant customers, but at any rate are a great improvement upon rifle bullets, pom poms, and shells of all sizes.

"Yes, I don't even grudge them the jam, when I think how awful it must be to be kept, for months, at some miserable little station on the railway, guarding the roads. We get restless here at the end of three or four days, but fancy spending months at it!"

"Besides, Hallett, in such places they get their rations regularly, and have nothing to do but to eat and get fat. If you were living under such conditions, you would be something awful at the end of six months of it."

"There is a great deal in that," Hallett said, thoughtfully. "Yes; I don't know that, after all, the gains and advantages are not with us; and indeed, if we had our time to go over again, we could make ourselves fairly comfortable.

"In the first place, I should purchase a large ground sheet, which I might use as a tent. I would have a smaller one to lie upon, and the biggest mackintosh that money could buy. Then, as you say, with a good supply of tea and chocolate, I could make myself extremely happy.

"I cannot think why the authorities did not point out the necessity for these things, before we started. They must have known it was going to rain like old boots, all the time. I don't mean, of course, the authorities at Cape Coast, because I don't suppose any of these things could have been picked up there; but we should have been told, when we got our orders, that such things were essential. Really, the stupidity and thoughtlessness of the War Office are beyond belief."

"I should advise you to draw up a memorial to them, pointing out their want of thought and care; and suggesting that, in every room, there should be a printed reminder that mackintoshes and ground sheets are essential, in a campaign in Western Africa in the wet season."

"Yes, and cocoa and tea," Hallett said, with a laugh. "I should like to hear the remarks of the War Office, when my communication was read. It would flutter the dove cot, and the very next steamer would bring out an intimation that Lieutenant John Hallett's services were no longer required."

"No doubt that would be the case, Hallett; but think what an inestimable service you would have done, in campaigning out here!"

"That is all very well, Bullen, but I should recommend you to try your eloquence upon someone else. Perhaps you might find someone of a more self-sacrificing nature who would take the matter in hand."

"Perhaps I might, but I rather fancy that I should not. The only man who could do it is Willcocks. After the victories he has won, even the War Office could hardly have the face to retire him from the service for making such a suggestion. Besides, the public would never stand it; and he is just the sort of fellow to carry out the idea, if he took to it."

"I agree with you, Bullen, as in the end I almost always do, and should suggest most strongly that you lay the matter before him. No doubt, if he applied, the War Office would send out a hundred waterproofs and two hundred ground sheets, for the use of the officers, by the next ship sailing from England."

"I might do it," Lisle laughed, "if it were not that the rainy season will be at an end before the things arrive here."

"That is a very good excuse, Bullen; but I hope that, at any rate, you will carry out your idea before the next wet season begins--that is, if we are kept on here, as a punishment for our sins."

At this moment one of the non-commissioned officers came in with a letter, and Hallett opened it.

"Oh dear," he said, in a tone of deepest disgust, "we are off again!"

"Thank goodness!" Lisle said. "You know we were just agreeing that we have had enough of this place."

"I often say foolish things," Hallett said, "and must not be taken too literally. Here is an end to our meat rations, and to all our other little luxuries. Besides, I have been getting my tunic washed, and it will certainly take three or four days to dry in this steaming atmosphere."

"Well, my dear fellow, you can put it on wet, for it is certain to be wet before we have gone a quarter of an hour. My tunic has gone, too, but at any rate they will both look more respectable for the washing.

"Well, I suppose we had better go across to headquarters and find out what the route is, and who are going."

As they went out, they saw the return of the Central African Regiment. They had been more fortunate than the other regiments, having captured and razed Djarchi. They had taken the enemy by surprise, and run them right through the town, with only a single casualty. They had ascertained that the enemy had been commanded by the brother of the Ashanti commander-in-chief, and that he had been killed in the fight.

A very large amount of spoil had been captured, the first haul of any importance that had been made during the campaign. Among the loot were the king of the Kokofu's iron boxes, containing much official correspondence; union jacks, elephant tails, and other symbols of royalty, together with gold ornaments, gold dust, and two hundred pounds of English money; numbers of brass-nailed, vellum-backed chairs, part of the Ashanti chief's regalia; robes, guns, ammunition, drums, and horns, and also sheep and poultry.

A company was at once despatched to the Sacred Lake, to join Major Cramer's levies, which had been told off to act as locusts and eat up the country. Colonel Wilson was ordered to go to Accra, to reorganize and recruit the remnant of the Gold Coast Force; so that, when the campaign was over, they could again take over the military control of the colony. It was also decided that Bekwai could no longer be occupied, and that all the stores there should be removed to Esumeja, as the whole main road up to Coomassie would shortly be open.

At last all was in readiness for the general and final advance. All the Adansi country to the south, and Kokofu to the east had been conquered, and the roads cleared. The next step was to clear Northern Ashanti; neglecting altogether, for the present, the parties of the enemy between the southern boundaries of Ashanti territory and their capital.

It was therefore decided to move the whole of the headquarters staff and the advance base to Coomassie, Esumeja being selected as the point, between it and Kwisa, to be held in force. The general plan was to send up all the stores, carriers, and troops via Pekki, as had been done on both previous occasions. This would reduce the chance of attack and loss to a minimum while, simultaneously, a fighting column with the smallest possible transport would follow the road through Kokofu and take Ejesu, which was the residence of the queen mother, and the headquarters of the remnant of the Ashanti army.

The general opinion was that it would be the last fight of the year. Colonel Brake, who was the last arrival, having had no chance of a fight hitherto, was selected for the command. The whole force was to advance, and five thousand carriers were required to effect the movement.

There was general joy when it was known that Bekwai was to be evacuated. It was a dull, dirty place, surrounded by dense, dark forests, and was in a terribly insanitary state. Europeans were rapidly losing their strength, and an epidemic of smallpox was raging among the natives, of whom a dozen or more died daily.

On the 28th of August Colonel Burroughs left Bekwai, with seven hundred and fifty men, and three thousand carriers taking ammunition and baggage. The column was fully two miles long. They had an extremely heavy march, and did not arrive at their destination till night. The carriers returned to Bekwai the next day, so as to be ready to march out at daylight, on the 30th, with the second column.

The troops at Pekki being in enforced idleness, half of them marched out to attack the enemy's war camp, which had for so long threatened Pekki. The place was found to be evacuated, and it and the bush camps on the way were all burnt.

The second column had now well started. The downfall of rain continued without intermission, and the roads became worse than ever. The day after the first column left Pekki, Colonel Brake started with eight hundred men and two guns.

The news came in that the king of Akim had been asked, by a number of the Kokofu, to intercede on their behalf for peace; and a messenger with a flag of truce came in from the Djarchi district. The appearance of the messenger was singular. He was completely clad in white, even his skin being painted that colour, and he carried an enormous white flag. He was well received, but was sent back with a message that the chiefs must come in themselves.

On the 30th Colonel Willcocks arrived and, the next day, the whole force started in fighting formation for Coomassie, where they arrived after twelve hours' march. The distance was only twelve miles, so the condition of the roads may be well imagined by the time the column took to traverse them.

CHAPTER 19: LOST IN THE FOREST.

On the way up, Lisle met with a very unpleasant adventure. He and Hallett had been sent out, with a small party of men, to enter the bush and drive out any of the enemy who might be lurking, for the purpose of attacking the carriers and rear guard. They went some distance into the bush but, though they came upon tracks that had recently been cut, they saw none of the enemy. Some men were planted on each of these paths; and the two officers, who had followed one a little distance farther into the bush, were on the point of turning, when they heard men cutting their way through the undergrowth behind them.

"Hide, Hallett!" Lisle exclaimed, "they must be enemies."

"THEY SAW A STRONG PARTY OF THE ENEMY CROSSING THE ROAD"

As noiselessly as they could they took refuge in the thick bush and, a minute later, saw a strong party of the enemy crossing the road that they had just passed along. There were several hundred of them. Some thirty or forty halted on the path. The others continued to cut a track through and, in five minutes, a scattered fire was opened, showing that they had come in contact with the troops. The fire was kept up for some time, and then died away; whether because the troops had retired, or because the natives had turned off and taken some other line, they could not be sure. Later they heard very heavy firing abreast of them, and guessed that the Ashantis had followed some other path, and come down on the convoy.

Peering through the bushes, from time to time, they found that those who had halted on the path were still there, probably in waiting for some chief or other who was to take command of them.

"We are in a nice mess, Bullen," said Hallett. "By the sound the convoy is still moving on, so how we are to rejoin them, I don't know."

"Yes, we are certainly in a hole and, if these fellows stop here till night, I see no chance of our being able to move. The slightest rustle in the bushes would bring them down upon us, in no time. The firing is getting more and more distant every moment and, no doubt, a big body of the enemy have engaged our fellows.

"I have been in a good many tight places, but I think this is the worst of them. Our only course, so far as I can see, is to wait till nightfall; and then, if these fellows still stick here, get into the path again, and follow it up till we come to some path going the other way. Then it will be a pure question of luck whether we hit upon the enemy, or not. If we do, of course we must fight till the last, keeping the last shot in our revolvers for ourselves. I have no intention of falling into their hands alive, and going through terrible tortures before I am put to death."

"That really seems to be the only thing to be done, Bullen. However, we must hope for the best."

When night fell, a fire was lit by the party on the path.

"The beggars evidently mean to stay here," Lisle said, "and even if they moved away we should be no better off for, as the column will be ten miles away by now, we should really have no chance of regaining it."

When night fell they crept out of the bush, taking the greatest care not to make any noise, for the natives were but thirty yards away. They crawled along for forty or fifty yards and then, a turn in the path hiding them from sight, they rose to their feet and pushed on.

They found, however, that it was no easy matter to make headway. It was pitch dark, owing to the canopy of leaves, and they had to feel their way at every step. The path, moreover, was constantly turning and twisting. After travelling for upwards of two hours, they came to a point where two paths met and, without knowing, they took the one that led off to the left. This they followed for some hours, and then lay down to rest. They awoke at daybreak.

"I wonder where we have got to," Hallett said.

"I am afraid somehow we have gone wrong," Lisle exclaimed, after looking round, "and the light seems to be coming from the wrong quarter, altogether. We must have turned off from the main path without knowing it, and tramped a long distance in the wrong direction."

"I believe you are right, Bullen. What on earth are we to do now? Retrace our steps, or push on and chance it?"

"We have the choice of two evils, Hallett, but I think it would be better to go on than to turn back. In the first place, however, we must search for something to eat. We crossed several little streams on our way, so I don't think we are likely to be hard up for water; but food we must have. The natives are always able to find food in the forest and, if we cannot do that, we may come upon some deserted village, and get some bananas. We might even steal some, at night, from a village that is not deserted. At any rate, it is useless to stay here."

They set out at once, moving cautiously, and stopping frequently to listen for the soft trail of naked feet. They came at last to the spot where they had left the other track. Here they held another council, and decided that there was too much risk in turning on to the main path again; as that was sure to be occupied by the enemy, who would be burying their dead, or examining any loot that they had captured from the carriers. After proceeding two or three miles, they came upon another path on the right.

"This path," said Lisle, "will take us in the proper direction."

"I doubt if we shall ever get there," Hallett said. "I am feeling as hungry as a rat, already; and we have seen nothing to put between our lips since we started out, yesterday morning."

"It is a little rough," Lisle said cheerfully, "but we must hit upon a village, presently."

"I should not mind, if the path went on straight," Hallett said, "but it zigzags so much that we can never feel certain that we are going in the right direction."

"Well, you see," said Lisle, "we have passed two tracks to the left, since we struck into this road. I cannot help thinking that these must lead to villages, and that the one we are following is a sort of connecting link between them. I vote that we stop at the next one we come to."

"All right, old man! It seems to me that it will make no great difference which way we go. Indeed, so far as I can make out, by the glimpses we get of the sun, the path has turned a great deal, and is now going right back to that from which it started."

"I am afraid you are right, Hallett. However, there is one thing certain. The Ashantis don't cut paths through their forests without some reason, and I should not be surprised if we come to some large village, not far ahead."

After walking for another half hour, they found the bush getting thinner, and they could soon see light ahead. They went very cautiously now and, at last, stood at the end of a large clearing, in which stood an Ashanti village.

"Thank God there is something to eat ahead!" said Hallett. "There are lots of bananas growing round the village and, when it gets dark, we will get two big bunches. That should last us some time."

Utterly exhausted, they both lay down just inside the bush. Many villagers were moving about and, twice, native runners came in. The afternoon passed very slowly; but at length the sun set, and darkness fell quickly. They waited a couple of hours, to allow the village to get comparatively quiet; then they crept forward, and cut two great bunches of bananas from the first tree they came to and, returning to the forest, sat down and ate a hearty meal.

"I feel very much better," Hallett said, when he had finished. "Now, let us talk over what we had better do next."

"I should say we had better keep along by the edge of the bush, and see if we can strike some other path. It would be useless to go back by this one, as it would simply take us to the place we started from."

Hallett readily agreed to this suggestion, and the two officers started and gradually worked round the village. Presently they struck another path. Turning up this they again pushed forward, each carrying his bunch of bananas. After walking two hours, they lay down. The darkness was so dense that their rate of progress was extremely slow.

In the morning they went on again but, after walking for some hours, they came suddenly upon four of the enemy. As soon as these saw them, they rushed on them with a yell, firing their guns as they did so. Both were struck with slugs; and Lisle was knocked down, but quickly jumped to his feet again, revolver in hand. The Ashantis charged with their spears, but the revolver bullets were too much for them and, one by one, they dropped, the last man being shot just as he reached them. Two were only wounded, but Lisle shot them both.

"It would never do," he said, "for any of them to get to a village, and bring all its occupants upon us. We are neither of us fit to do much running, and the beggars would be sure to overtake us."

"It is horrid," Hallett said, "though I admit that it is necessary."

For four days they wandered on. The path never seemed to run straight. Though they found a plentiful supply of bananas, their strength was gradually failing.

On the fourth day they came upon a sheet, doubtless a portion of some officer's baggage that had been looted. Hallett, who was walking fast, passed it contemptuously. Lisle, however, picked it up and wound it round his body.

"We can lay it over us, Hallett, at night. It will at least help to keep the damp off us."

"We sha'n't want it long," Hallett said; "I think the game is almost up."

"Not a bit of it," Lisle said, cheerfully. "In spite of the turns and twistings we have made, I think we cannot be far from Coomassie, now. I thought I heard the sound of guns this morning, and it could have been from nowhere else."

Late that afternoon they came suddenly upon a great war camp and, at once, sat down in the bushes.

"What is to be done now?" Hallett said. "We cannot go back again. We are neither of us fit to walk a couple of miles."

Lisle sat for some minutes without answering him, and then said suddenly:

"I have an idea. I will cut down a sapling, seven or eight feet long; and fasten the sheet to it, so as to make a flag of truce. Then we will walk boldly into the village, and summon it to surrender. It is a bold stroke, but it may succeed. We know that most of them are getting tired of the war. We can give out that we have lost our way in the bush and, if the fellows take it kindly, well and good; but if not, we shall have our revolvers, and shall, of course, use them on ourselves."

"I am game to carry it out, Bullen. Your idea is a splendid one. Anyhow, it is our last chance. I really don't think I could go a mile farther. We know enough of their language to make ourselves understood."

"Yes. What with our servants, the Hausas, and the carriers, we have both picked up a good deal of the language."

With renewed spirits they cut down a sapling, stripped it of all its leaves and branches and, fastening the sheet to it, walked straight down towards the camp. There was an immediate stir in the camp. Many of the Ashantis ran for their arms but, when they saw that the two officers were alone, they calmed down. Presently two chiefs advanced, followed by some twenty warriors.

"Now, Bullen, muster up your knowledge of the language, and address them. Lay it on pretty thick."

"Chiefs," Lisle said, "we are come to you from the governor of Coomassie. He says that it must be clear to you, now, that you cannot stand against the white man; and that you will only bring ruin upon yourselves, and your country, by further resistance. They have therefore sent us to say that, if you will surrender, a small fine only shall be imposed upon you; and that your soldiers may retire to their villages, after having laid down their arms. While you are talking about this, we shall be glad if you will give us some provisions; for we have lost our way in the bush, coming here, and need food."

"If you follow me into the village," one of the chiefs said, "provisions shall be served to you, while we talk over what you say. We shall be glad of peace; for we see that, however strongly we make our stockades, your soldiers always take them. Our men are beginning to long to return to their people, for they have fought many times, and already have begun to complain. Do you guarantee our safety, if we return with you to your fort?"

"I can promise that," Lisle said. "We respect brave men, and are anxious that there should be an end to this fighting. When it is over, you will again live under the protection of our government, and the past will be forgotten. You attacked us without reason, and have suffered heavily for it. This is the third time that we have had to come up, and we hope that it will never be necessary to do so, again. We recognize each other's valour; we have each made sacrifices; and we hope that, when this war is over, we shall live together in peace. Had we only been armed as you are, the fortunes of war might have gone differently; but we have rifles and guns, and these must always give us victory, in the long run."

"We will talk it over," the chief said. "While we do so, you shall have food."

So saying, he turned and led the way to a house in the village, where food and native spirit were set before them.

"Your dodge has succeeded admirably," Hallett said, as they were waiting for the meal. "I think they will surrender."

"I hope they will," Lisle said; "but at any rate, I think they will treat us as coming in under a flag of truce; and will perhaps send an escort with us back to the camp. However, they are preparing a meal for us and, if the worst comes to the worst, it is much better to die full than fasting."

In a quarter of an hour two women entered; one carrying a bowl with four chickens, and a quantity of rice; the other a large jug of water, and a smaller one of native spirit. Not a word was spoken, while the meal was being eaten. At the end, nothing but bones remained of the four chickens.

"Thank God for a good dinner!" Hallett said, after the meal was over. "I feel, at present, at peace with all men; and I can safely recommend the chiefs, when they arrive at Coomassie, as being first-rate fellows; while I am sure that the chief will be greatly pleased that we have secured the submission of their tribe. It will be a big feather in our caps. When I came in here, I thought I could not go another mile to save my life; now I feel perfectly game for a seven or eight mile march to Coomassie."

At this moment, they noticed that there was a great hubbub in the camp. Half an hour later, the chiefs entered.

"We accept the terms you bring," one of them said, "and will go with you on condition that, if the terms are not as you say, we shall be allowed to return here, unmolested."

"That I can promise you," Lisle said. "We have not come here without reason, and the terms we offer are those that you can accept without dishonour. I can assure you of as good treatment as you have given us; and permission to leave the fort, and return to your people, if you are dissatisfied with the terms."

A quarter of an hour later the party--consisting of the two chiefs, ten armed followers, and the two officers--set out. The camp was, they learned, about six miles from Coomassie. After a march of three hours, they emerged from the forest into the cleared space round the fort. When they reached the outlying sentries they were challenged, but a word from Lisle sufficed to pass them on.

As they approached the fort a number of soldiers gathered round them and, when they neared the entrance, Colonel Willcocks himself came out.

"You remain here with the chiefs, Bullen. I will go on, and explain matters to the chief."

Lisle nodded, and Hallett hurried forward, while the others halted.

"Why, Mr. Hallett," Colonel Willcocks said, "we had given you up for dead; you and Mr. Bullen, whom I see over there. Whatever have you been doing now?"

Hallett gave a brief account of their adventure.

"You will probably be annoyed at us for acting as your messengers but, as we have induced the two leaders of the large war camp to come in, I trust that we shall be forgiven. We have promised them permission for their force to return, unmolested, to their villages; and I may say, from the formidable stockades they have made there, this result could not have been achieved, otherwise, without very heavy loss.

"I wish to say that the idea was entirely Bullen's. It seemed to be the only chance of getting through; for we were both utterly exhausted, when we reached the village."

"I think you have done extremely well, Hallett. I was about to send a force to capture that camp; and I am glad, indeed, of being relieved of the necessity of doing so. It means, perhaps, the saving of a couple of hundred lives. Besides, we should probably not have caught quarter of them; and the rest would have taken to the bush, and continued to give us trouble.

"Tell me exactly what the terms are, upon which they are willing to surrender."

"Simply the lives and freedom of the chiefs; and permission to their men to retire, unmolested, to their villages."

"Those are exactly the terms I have offered to some of their chiefs, who had sent in to ask for terms. Now, I will speak to them myself."

He accordingly walked forward, with Hallett, to where the chiefs were standing.

"I am glad, indeed, chiefs," he said, "that you have decided to take no further part in the war. You will stay here with us, until I hear that your camp is broken up; and you will then be at liberty to return to your own grounds. I thank you for receiving my messengers so kindly; as a reward for which I shall, when you leave, present you each with five hundred dollars. Henceforth, I trust that you will always remain on good terms with us, do all you can to aid us by sending in carriers, and will accept our rule frankly and truly.

"Now, I will ask you to come into the fort; where you will be treated as guests, until I hear of the dispersal of your camps."

The chiefs were much gratified by their reception; and sent off the escort, at once, to order the camp to be abandoned and burnt, and the stockades to be pulled down. Then they followed Colonel Willcocks into the fort, where a room was assigned to them, and everything done for their comfort.

As soon as the governor had retired with them, the other officers flocked down round Hallett and Lisle, to learn their adventures. Both were warmly congratulated upon their safe return; and Lisle came in for a large share of their congratulations when, in spite of his protestations, Hallett insisted on giving him the largest share of credit for the manner in which he had suggested the scheme, and had unquestionably been the means of saving their lives.

"Hallett had everything to do with it, except that," he said; "and that was only an accidental idea. We mutually helped each other, during those long days of tramping; and it was most fortunate for me that he was with me for, had I been alone, I don't think I should have had the strength of mind or body to hold on, when the prospect seemed altogether hopeless."

As they went down to the lines of their company, they were surrounded by the delighted blacks; who continued to cheer so heartily that it was some time before they could get an opportunity to tell what had taken place. Cheers again broke out, when the stories were finished. The men insisted on shaking their hands, and then started a war dance to show their satisfaction.

Then both retired to a shelter erected for them and, lying down, slept for some hours. When they awoke they ate a hearty meal; after which they agreed that, in a day or two, they would be fit for duty again.

"I shall mention your conduct in my despatches," the colonel said, next day. "You have not only saved your own lives; but have rendered very important service, in inducing those two chiefs and their followers to submit. From the information that we have been able to get, their camp was very strongly fortified, and could only have been taken after hard fighting; and even then, as has happened on all previous occasions, the main body would have escaped, rallied again a short distance away, and given us all the trouble of dispersing them, once more. As it is, I have no doubt that the influence of their chiefs will keep them quiet and, indeed, scattered as they will be among their villages, it will be difficult to persuade them to take up arms again.

"On second thoughts, I allowed them to leave this morning, with a column that was starting to collect the arms of the garrison. They seemed quite in earnest; and will, I have no doubt, succeed in inducing their men to part with their arms, without a squabble."

The detachment, indeed, returned in the evening. The success of their mission had been complete; and the natives had handed over their arms, and started off with their chiefs into the forests, after burning the camp and razing the stockades. They all seemed highly pleased that they should not be called upon for more fighting, and had individually taken an oath that they would never again fight the white men.

Several other flags of truce came in, and many chiefs surrendered. The Queen Mother, the most important of the leaders, tendered her submission. Colonel Willcocks gave her four days in which to prove the truth of her submission by coming in, in person. Shortly, however, before the truce expired, she sent in an impudent message that she would fight till the end.

Some of the chiefs who had been foremost in their opposition, and who had personally taken part in the torture and death of those who fell into their hands, were tried by court martial; and either shot or hanged, it being necessary to prove to the natives that even their greatest chiefs were not spared, and that certain punishment would be dealt out to those who had taken part in the murder of soldiers, or carriers, who had fallen into their hands.

The greatest tragedy of this campaign became known, on the 8th of September, through a letter from a native clerk who was with the Akim levies, which were commanded by Captains Willcox and Benson. These levies had worked up on our right flank, as we advanced from the south, in the same way as the Denkeras had done on the west. They were as cowardly, and as terrified of the Ashantis, as all the other neighbouring races. In fact, the only work they were fit for was living in deserted villages, or cutting crops and eating up the produce.

Three thousand of these levies were ordered to cooperate with Colonel Brake's column. They were met by the Ashantis, and bolted as soon as the latter opened fire; and Captain Benson, deserted by his cowardly followers, fell. In a letter he had sent home, a few days before his death, he expressed in the strongest terms his opinion of the men under his command, saying:

"If it comes to a real show, after all, Heaven help us! Three-quarters of my protective army are arrant cowards, all undisciplined, and quite impossible to hold."

The native levies cannot be compared with the disciplined troops. They were simply a motley mob, armed with stray guns, arms, and powder, and their pay is what they can loot; whereas the African private's drill and duties are identical with those of the British private. His orders are given to him in English, and his knowledge of our language is probably superior to that of most Indian or Egyptian soldiers; while the British soldiers in West Africa are rarely able to understand the language of their men.

A column had started, at once, to Captain Willcox's assistance. They returned, however, in ten days, having been unable to come up to him, as he had retired fifty miles farther to the east. They had no fighting, the enemy having gone north; but they ascertained that all the country immediately to the south was free from rebels and desirous of peace. The spot where Captain Benson's action had been fought was strewn with dead bodies, baggage, and rifles; evidence of the disordered flight. It seemed that the levies bolted, as soon as they were fired on. Then, with a few trained volunteers, the white men hastily entrenched themselves; and held out till late in the afternoon when, their ammunition having run short, they were compelled to retire, which they did fighting. It was during the retreat that Captain Benson was shot.

Another column came in on the following day, after five days' reconnaissance. It had gone by the same road by which the governor had broken out, on the 23rd of June. The road was entirely deserted, the villages destroyed, and the crops burnt. They made no attempt to search the bush but, on the path, they found ninety-eight headless skeletons; a painful testimony of the number of soldiers and carriers who had died of privation, and hardship, during the retreat.

Information now came in that, to the north, the most reckless of the Ashantis had again concentrated, and were determined to make another stand. On the 16th there was a big review of the seventeen hundred troops and the nine guns of the garrison. The heavy guns were exercised on a stockade, similar to those of the enemy. Hitherto they had not been altogether successful; as it was found that, owing to the large bursting charge, the range had to be estimated at double its real distance. Six shots smashed a barricade which was six feet high by six feet thick.

Friendly chiefs, who were invited to witness the experiment, were profoundly impressed; and there can be no doubt that the feat was reported to the enemy in the field, for they raised no stockade in the future, and reverted to their old plan of bush fighting.

The heavy and continuous rains were now rapidly bringing on sickness, and the officers were attacked in forms that were quite novel to them.

"I don't know what is the matter with me," Lisle said, one morning, "but I am swollen all round the neck. I once had mumps, when I was a little boy and, if it were not so ridiculous, I should declare that I had got them again."

Hallett burst into a fit of laughter.

"I expect you are going to have all your old illnesses again--scarlet fever, measles, whooping cough, and the rest. We must see that the hut is fitted up for you, with something as much like a bed as possible, and a fire for making a posset, or whatever they give you."

"It is all very well for you to laugh, Hallett, but look at my neck."

"Well, it is swollen," Hallett agreed; "and I expect that you have caught a cold, when we were wandering about in the bush. Seriously, I should advise you to put a piece of warm flannel round your neck, or else go across and consult the doctor."

"I think I will do so, Hallett. It hurts a good deal, I can tell you and, as you see, I can hardly drink my tea."

After breakfast was over, he went to the tent of the principal doctor.

"I have come, sir," he said, "to ask you about my neck."

"You don't say so, Bullen! Why, yours is the third case I have seen this morning! Let me look at it.

"Yes, the symptoms are just the same as in the others. If this were England, I should say that an epidemic of mumps has broken out; but of course it cannot be that.

"Well, I have sent the other two into hospital, and you had better go there, too. Is it painful?"

"It is rather painful, and I can hardly swallow at all."

"Well, when I come across to the hospital, I will put you in with the others. I certainly cannot make out what it is, nor why it came on so suddenly. The only thing I can put it down to is the constant rains that we have been having, though I really don't see why wet weather should have that effect. I should advise you to keep on hot poultices."

In the evening another patient came in, and Lisle burst out laughing, when he saw that it was Hallett.

"Oh, you have come to the nursery, have you? I hope you have made up your mind to go through scarlet fever, or measles, Hallett?"

"Don't chaff. It is no laughing matter."

"No? I thought you took it quite in that light, this morning. Well, you see we have all got poultices on; and the orderly will make one for you, at once. My face is bigger than it was this morning, and what it is going to come to, I cannot imagine. Although the doctor said, frankly, that he did not understand it; he seemed to think that there was nothing very serious about it."

The next day the swelling had abated and, two days later, both of them were discharged from the hospital; to their great delight, for they heard that a column was just going to start, and that their companies were included in it.

On the following day the column started. It was nearly a thousand strong, with guns, and rations for twenty-eight days. This force was to penetrate into the northwestern country. The enemy here had sent an impudent message that they would not surrender; and that, if they were attacked, they intended to revert to their former tactics, and direct all their efforts to shooting down the officers and, when these were disposed of, they would have little difficulty in dealing with the native troops.

On the second day, when twenty-five miles from Coomassie, the enemy were met with in force; and it was found that the message they had sent was true, for there was no stockade, and the enemy resorted entirely to sniping. They were commanded by Kofia, one of the most turbulent and determined of their chiefs. The attack did not come as a surprise for, the day before, a number of Ashantis had been found in a village which was rushed. The active allies now searched the woods thoroughly, and succeeded in ascertaining the spot where the enemy had their war camp. They had been careful that the Ashantis had no notion of our approach, and a number of them were shot down by the Maxims and rifles.

The enemy, who held a strong position on the hilltop, rushed down and attacked our front and flank. Their number was estimated at four thousand. Three companies on each side entered the bush, and soon succeeded in pressing the enemy into a path; where they were fiercely charged by the West African Field Force, under Major Melliss. That officer was wounded; and Captain Stevenson, who was close to him, was shot in the chest.

For a moment the soldiers wavered but, almost immediately, dashed on again to avenge the loss of their officers. The charge was very effective. Those of the enemy who gradually assembled were bayoneted, and the rest fled.

Captain Stevenson's death was greatly regretted. He and Captain Wright, of another company, had asked for leave to accompany the force. As the one had no better claim than the other, Colonel Willcocks suggested that they should toss for it. They did so, and Captain Stevenson won; but what he deemed his good fortune cost him his life.

After the fight was over, there was a short pause to reorganize the force; and an advance was made to a village, three miles ahead, the intention being to attack the next morning. That evening, however, a flag came in, with an offer to surrender. Word was sent back that the offer would be accepted, if made unconditionally; and at seven o'clock in the evening a chief, a large number of men, four hundred guns, and some sheep arrived. They said that Kofia was holding a village, farther on; and would again give fight there. The force returned with them to Coomassie.

The next day, some scouts brought in the news that the enemy had again concentrated, and their numbers had been raised to four thousand by their junction with another fighting tribe. Kofia was in command, and a big war camp had been established some twelve miles away on the Berekum road. Berekum itself, which was a hundred and forty miles to the north, was reported to be invested, and had asked for help but, as so large an Ashanti force was near at hand, no men could be spared for the purpose.

A column twelve hundred strong, with five guns, and every available man in the garrison who could carry a gun, moved out early on the 29th, to give battle. It was followed by a supply column, and the bulk of the carriers.

Nine miles were accomplished without any opposition. Then a small Adansi outpost retired on their approach. The commandant decided to halt, for the night, at a deserted village. It was a miserable place. The huts had all been burnt by the rebels; so that the troops had to sleep in the open, in a steady downpour of rain. The Europeans tried to get rest in some hastily-constructed shelters, but a perfect tornado of wind was blowing, and swept the ground on which they were built.

Next day the troops marched, in their drenched clothes, through a heavy rain. Between seven and eight, however, this ceased and, almost at the same moment, a tremendous fire burst out upon them. The advance guard and support at once became engaged, but the enemy clung with such determination to their position, and contested every foot of the ground so stoutly, that two companies of reinforcements had to be called up.

Two companies were sent out into the bush, and eventually succeeded in getting partly behind the enemy, and forcing them to retreat. More troops were sent out on the left; and a company was instructed to move through the bush, on an extended line. In this way the enemy were driven out of the jungle, and forced to retire slowly up the hill.

Then the main column started, led by Major Melliss and headed by the Sikhs. The enemy, however, did not fly; and Major Melliss dashed into the thick of them, with the few men he could collect. An Ashanti fired at him, at close quarters; but a native soldier ran the man through. As they struggled on the ground, another Ashanti fired at Major Melliss, hitting him in the foot. He was practically unarmed, as he could use neither his sword nor his revolver; and would have been killed, had not another officer come up and shot the wounded Ashanti.

As the head of the column reached the spot, a heavy fire was directed upon the enemy, who were soon in headlong flight. The village in the rear of the position was taken, at the point of the bayonet. One hundred and fifty of their dead were found, lying on the battlefield; and it was learned, from prisoners, that over five hundred had been wounded.

The defeat was a crushing one. Several of their most determined chiefs were found among the dead. So hopelessly demoralized were the enemy that they never rallied again.

The victory had been achieved with very small loss, owing to the excellence of Colonel Willcocks' force. The casualties consisted only of two officers severely, and two slightly wounded; and twenty-six rank and file killed and wounded.

When the wounded had been dressed, and the scattered units collected, an advance was made to the next village; where the wearied troops slept, as it was still doubtful whether the rebels might not rally. Major Cobbe was sent on, next morning, with eight hundred men. He was to go as far as he could, but to return the next evening.

The march was a very trying one, the weather terrible. After going four miles they reached the bank of an unfordable river, some forty yards wide. The Pioneers, although they had no technical equipment, succeeded in making a rough bridge by the afternoon; and Major Cobbe decided to push on to Kofia. At ten o'clock they reached this place and, to the general relief, it was found to be deserted. The troops, therefore, marched in and turned into the huts, amid a howling tornado.

The return journey, next day, was even worse. The tracks, in many parts, were now covered with between two and three feet of water. The bridge, though submerged, had fortunately not been carried away; and the troops were able to cross, and march into camp the same evening, having carried out their orders without encountering the smallest opposition.

CHAPTER 20: AT HOME.

It was now found necessary to give the worn-out troops a long rest. They had been on constant service, for months; the stream of invalids that had been sent down to the coast daily increased, and the sick list had already reached an appalling length. The want of fresh rations was very much felt, and any large combination of troops not only caused great discomfort, but engendered various diseases, smallpox among them. In addition to this, as the black soldiers always go barefooted, their feet had got into a deplorable state.

The halt, however, had a good effect; and there was general satisfaction that it was unlikely that they would be called upon to make further efforts, as no news came of fresh gatherings of the enemy.

Colonel Willcocks now saw that the time was come to issue a proclamation promising, henceforward, to spare the lives of all rebels that surrendered. This was done, with the result that large numbers of the enemy came in. Almost all of them declared that they would have surrendered, long ago, had they not feared to do so.

On October 6th, the Commandant and British Resident held a state levee. It was attended by all the friendly and submitted kings. These vied with each other in their pomp; they were dressed in gorgeous robes and carried their state umbrellas, while their attendants danced round them, beating drums and blowing horns. After the palaver was over, target practice took place, with the guns. Canvas dummies were riddled with bullets by the Maxims; and stockades, specially constructed for the purpose, were demolished by the big guns. The natives retired, greatly impressed.

Two days later, Colonel Willcocks got up a rifle meeting for a cup; and he himself took his place among the competitors.

Five days later, news came that a fresh force of the enemy had gathered. Two columns were sent out--one of seven hundred and the other of five hundred men--but, though they traversed a wide stretch of country, they had no fighting. They received, however, the submission of a number of chiefs and villages.

The new commander of the Ashanti force was captured, tried, and hanged. The queen also was caught and, on the 24th of April, a telegram was sent home with the words:

"The campaign is at an end."

There can be no doubt that this expedition will lead to great results. The natives of Ashanti and the surrounding tribes have received a lesson that will not be forgotten for a great number of years and, long before that time, it may be hoped that civilization will have made such strides there that there will be no more chance of trouble. They have been taught that they are absolutely unable to stand against the white man; that neither distance, the thickness of their forests, stockades, nor weather can check the progress of British troops; and that resistance can only draw down upon them terrible loss, and the destruction of their villages and crops.

They had received no such lessons in the previous expeditions. That of Governor Sir Charles M'Carthy had been entirely defeated, and the governor himself killed. Another expedition, in 1867, met with a total failure. Sir Garnet Wolseley, in 1873, marched to Coomassie but, though he burnt the place, he had at once to fall back to the coast. In 1895 Sir Francis Scott led an expedition which, for some reason or other, met with no resistance.

Now Ashanti had been swept from end to end, and fire and sword had destroyed the major part of the villages. Garrisons were to be left, at Coomassie, strong enough to put down any local risings; and the natives had been taught that, small as our army might be in their country, it could at any time be largely augmented, at very short notice. Most of all, they had learned that, even without the assistance of white soldiers, the native troops--whom they had hitherto despised--were their superiors in every respect.

The completion of the railway to Coomassie has enabled troops to be sent up from the coast, in a few hours, to the heart of the country; and the numerous companies formed to work the gold mines will, in themselves, prove a great check to trouble as, no doubt, the miners will, in future, be well armed.

Colonel Willcocks left the headquarters staff a few days after the despatch of his telegram. He rode through a two-mile avenue of troops and friendly natives and, on arriving at Cape Coast, had a magnificent reception. Major C. Burroughs remained in command of Coomassie, with a strong garrison.

A few days later, the rest of the force moved down to the coast. Lisle and Hallett were carried down in hammocks, for both were completely worn out by the hardships of the campaign and, as there was no limit to the numbers of carriers that could be obtained, they gladly acquiesced in the decision of the medical officer that they ought to be carried. Both, indeed, had the seeds of fever in their system and, when they arrived at Cape Coast, were laid up with a sharp attack. As a result they were, like the great portion of the officers who had gone through the campaign, invalided home.

A day after his arrival in London, Lisle was visited by his friend Colonel Houghton, at whose house he had spent most of his leave when he was last in England.

"I saw your name in the paper, yesterday, as among the returned invalids; and thought that I should find you in the hotel where you stayed before."

"I wrote yesterday afternoon to you, sir."

"Ah! Of course, I have not got that letter. And now, how are you?"

"I am a little shaky, sir, but the voyage has done wonders for me. I have no doubt that I shall soon be myself, again."

"You have not seen the last gazette, I suppose?"

"No, sir."

"Well, there was a list of promotions, and I am happy to say that you have got the D.S.O. for your services. I dare say you know that you succeeded to your company, just six months ago?"

"No, I did not know that. I knew that I stood high among the lieutenants, and expected to get it before long; but I am proud, indeed, of the D.S.O."

"To have won the V.C. and the D.S.O. is to attain the two greatest distinctions a soldier can wear.

"Now, you had better come down with me to my place in the country; the air of London is not the best, for a man who has been suffering from African fever."

"I certainly want bracing air, and I shall be only too glad to go home with you; for I feel it is more my home than any other in England."

As soon as Lisle began to recover a little, Colonel Houghton introduced him to his neighbours, who made a good deal of the young soldier. Five years had elapsed, since he had started with the Pioneers for Chitral, and he was twenty-one.

Soon after he went to the colonel's, he was speaking to him of his friend and constant companion in the late campaign; and the colonel at once invited Hallett down. Hallett accepted the invitation, and soon joined them. He had pretty well recovered, and the campaign had knocked all his little laziness and selfishness out of him. He also had received the D.S.O.

"I am sure, Colonel Houghton," he said one day, "that I owe a tremendous lot to Lisle. He was always cheerful, and his unmerciful chaffing kept me alive. I am quite sure I should never have got through that time, when we were lost in the forest, if it hadn't been for him. I was a confirmed grumbler, too; but he never let me indulge my discontent. Altogether you have no idea, Colonel Houghton, how much he did for me."

"Well, you know, Captain Hallett, how much he did for me."

"No, sir," Hallett said, in surprise; "he has often spoken to me of you, and of your kindness to him; but he did not tell me about anything he had done for you."

"Well, he saved my life at the risk of his own. If he has not told you the story, I will."

And he related the manner in which Lisle had won his V.C.

"Why did you not tell me about it, Bullen? It was a splendid thing to do. You did tell me, I remember, how you got the V.C. by helping to get an officer out of the grasp of the Afridis, but you gave no details."

"There was nothing to tell about it, Hallett. I only did what I am sure you would have done, in my case."

"I am by no means sure of that," Hallett said. "I am always slow in making up my mind about anything; and should never have thought of putting a wounded officer on my horse, and sending him off, while I remained to be cut to pieces. I hope I should have stood by him, and been cut down with him; but I am certain that I should not have thought of the other thing, with the Afridis rushing down upon me, only thirty yards away.

"You ought to have let me know about it. You did bully me a great deal, you know; and though it was all for my good, still I think I should have put up with it better, if I had known that you had done such a thing as that."

"I think you put up with it very well, Hallett. Chaffing you, and getting you sometimes into a rage--which was pretended, rather than real--did me a lot of good. I am sure I should have given in, several times, had you not acted as a sort of tonic; and had I not been sure that it did you as much good as it did me."

A month after Hallett's arrival, the colonel said, one morning:

"Good morning, Lisle! I am going out with the hounds, tomorrow. They meet near here. As you are not great riders, I won't press you to go with me but, at least, you will ride with me to the meet. It is sure to be a good gathering, and you will probably meet some nice girls; who will, no doubt, have much greater attractions, for young fellows like you, than a gallop round the country."

"They have no particular attraction for me, sir," Lisle laughed. "It will be time enough for that, in another eight or ten years. It is more in Hallett's line."

"But we shall be chaffed, if we don't ride after the hounds, Colonel," Hallett said.

"Not at all," the colonel replied, "you have a first-rate excuse. You are only just recovering from fever. That would get you no end of commiseration and pity."

"In that case," Lisle said, "I think I should prefer staying at home. I don't feel that I need the least pity, and don't want to get it on false pretences."

"It won't be false pretences," the colonel said. "I have taken care that all the ladies I shall introduce you to should know what you did for me, and how you did it."

"I am sorry to hear it, Colonel. It is really hateful, being regarded as a man who has done something, especially at my age. However, I shall leave Hallett to bear the brunt of it. I know that he is on the lookout for a wife."

"I don't think you know anything of the sort, Lisle. It will be time for that when I get my majority."

"Ah! That is all very well, Hallett; I know you took a good half-hour dressing your hair, previous to that dinner party last week."

"It has to be brushed. It was nearly all cut off, when we were in Cape Coast, and one doesn't want to go out looking like a fretful porcupine."

So, laughing and joking, they started the next morning. There was, as the colonel had predicted, a large meet. Many ladies came on horseback, and others in carriages. The two young officers were soon engaged, chatting and laughing, with the latter.

"Do you mean to say that you are not going to ride, Captain Bullen?" one of the ladies on horseback said.

"In the first place, Miss Merton, I am an infantry officer and, except for a few weeks when I was on the staff of Colonel Lockhart, I have never done any riding. In the second place, I am forbidden to take horse exercise, at present. Moreover, although no doubt you will despise me for the confession, I dislike altogether the idea of a hundred men on horseback, and forty or fifty dogs, all chasing one unfortunate animal."

"But the unfortunate animal is a poacher of the worst kind."

"Very well, then, I should shoot him, as a poacher. Why should a hundred horsemen engage in hunting the poor brute down? Bad horseman as I am, I should not mind taking part in a cavalry charge; but hunting is not at all to my taste."

"You like shooting, Captain Bullen?"

"I like shooting, when there is something to be shot; in the first place, a dangerous animal, and in the second, an animal that is able to show fight. I have several times taken part in tiger hunts, and felt myself justified in doing so, because the animals had made themselves a scourge to unarmed villagers."

"I am afraid that you are a sort of Don Quixote," the girl laughed.

"Not quite that, Miss Merton; though I own I admire the good knight, greatly. We are going to move off, now, to the covert that has to be drawn; and I know I shall shock you, when I say that I sincerely hope that nothing will be found there."

The whole party then moved off, and the hounds were put into a covert. Five minutes later, a whimper was heard. It soon spread into a chorus, and then a fox dashed out from the opposite side; followed, in a couple of minutes, by the whole pack.

"Well, that is fun, is it not, Captain Bullen?" said a girl, to whom he was talking, in one of the carriages.

"It is a pretty sight," he said, "and if the fox always got away, I should like it. As it is, I say honestly that I don't."

The meet now broke up, and the carriages dispersed. Hallett and Lisle accepted an invitation to lunch with the ladies to whom they were talking. Two hours later, Lisle was on the point of leaving, when a groom rode up at full speed.

"Is Captain Bullen here?" he asked.

With a presentiment of evil, Lisle went out.

"The colonel has had a bad accident, sir. He was brought in, half an hour ago, by the servants. I understand that he asked for you; and three of us at once rode off, in different directions, to find you."

Lisle called Hallett and, in five minutes, they were mounted and dashed off. As they entered the house, they were met by the surgeon.

"Is he badly hurt'?" Lisle asked, anxiously.

"I fear that he is hurt to death, Captain Bullen. His horse slipped as it was taking a fence, and fell on the top of him. He has suffered severe internal injuries, and I greatly fear that there is not the least hope for him."

"Is he conscious?" Lisle asked, with deep emotion.

"Yes, he is conscious, and I believe he understands that his case is hopeless. He has asked for you, several times, since he was brought in; so you had better go to him, at once."

With a sinking heart, Lisle went upstairs. The colonel was lying on his bed.

"I am glad you have come in time, my dear boy," he said faintly, as Lisle entered. "I am afraid that I am done for, and it is a consolation for me to know that I have no near relatives who will regret my loss. I have had a good time of it, altogether; and would rather that, as I was not to die on the battlefield, death should come as it has. It is far better than if it came gradually.

"Sit by me, lad, till the end comes. I am sure it will not be long. I am suffering terribly, and the sooner it comes, the better."

The ashy gray of the colonel's face sufficed to tell Lisle that the end was, indeed, near at hand. The colonel only spoke two or three times and, at ten o'clock at night, passed away painlessly.

Upon Lisle devolved the sad work of arranging his funeral. He wrote to the colonel's lawyer, asking him to come down. Hallett had left the house at once, though Lisle earnestly begged him to stay till the funeral was over. The lawyer arrived on the morning of the funeral.

"I have taken upon myself, sir," Lisle said, "to make all the arrangements for the funeral, seeing that there was no one else to do it."

"You were the most proper person to do so," the lawyer said, gravely, "as you will see when the will is read, on our return from the grave."

When all was over, Lisle asked two or three of the colonel's most intimate friends to be present at the reading of the will. It was a very short one. The colonel made bequests to several military charities; and then appointed his adopted son, Lisle Bullen, Lieutenant in His Majesty's Rutlandshire regiment, the sole heir to all his property.

This came almost as a surprise to Lisle. The colonel had indeed told him that he had adopted him, and he was prepared to learn that he had left him a legacy; but he had no idea that he would be left sole heir.

"I congratulate you, sir," the lawyer said, when he folded up the paper. "Colonel Houghton stated to me, fully, his reasons for making such a disposition of his property and, as he had no near relations, I was able to approve of it heartily. I may say that he has left nearly sixteen thousand pounds. The other small legacies will take about a thousand, and you will therefore have some fifteen thousand pounds, which is all invested in first-rate securities."

"I feel my good fortune, sir," Lisle said quietly, "but I would that it had not come to me for many years, and not in such a manner."

The meeting soon after broke up, and Lisle went up to town and joined Hallett at the hotel they both used.

"Well, I congratulate you heartily," Hallett said, when he heard the contents of the will. "It is a good windfall, but not a bit more than you deserve."

"I would rather not have had it," Lisle said, sorrowfully. "I owe much to the colonel, who has for the past three years given me an allowance of two hundred pounds a year; and I would far rather have gone on with that, than come into a fortune in this manner."

"I can understand that," Hallett said; "the colonel was a first-rate old fellow, and his death will be an immense loss to you. Still, but for you it would have come three years ago and, after all, it is better to be killed hunting than to be shot to pieces by savages.

"Well, it will bring you in six or seven hundred pounds a year, a sum not to be despised. It will enable you to leave the army, if you like; though I should advise you to stick to it. Here are you a captain at twenty-one, a V. C. and D. S. O. man, with a big career before you and, no doubt, you will get a brevet majority before long."

"I have certainly not the least idea of leaving the army. I was born in it, and hope to remain in it as long as I can do good work."

"What are you going to do now?"

"I shall go down there again, in a fortnight or so."

"Would you be disposed to take me with you?"

"Certainly I shall, if you will go. I had not thought of asking you, because everything must go on quietly there, for a time; but really I should prize your company very much."

"Well, the fact is," Hallett said, rather shamefacedly, "I am rather smitten with Miss Merton, and I have some hopes that she is a little taken with me. I heard that she has money but, although that is satisfactory, I would take her, if she would have me, without a penny. You know I have three hundred pounds a year of my own; which is quite enough, with my pay, to enable us to get on comfortably. Still, I won't say that, if she has as much more, we could not do things better."

Lisle laughed.

"I thought you were not a marrying man, Hallett! In fact, you have more than once told me so."

"Well, I didn't think I was," Hallett admitted, "but you see, circumstances alter cases."

"They do, Hallett, and your case seems to be a bad one. However, old man, I wish you luck. She is an exceedingly nice girl and, if I were ten years older, I might have been smitten myself; and then, you know, your chance would have been nowhere."

"I quite feel that," Hallett said; "a V.C. is a thing no girl can stand against.

"If you will take me, I will go down with you and stay a little time, and then try my luck."

"That you certainly shall do. I can hardly do anything in the way of festivities, at present; but there is no reason why you should not enter into anything that is going on."

So they went down together. Ten days later, all the families round came to pay visits of condolence; and to each Lisle said that, although he himself could not think of going out, at present, his friend Hallett, who had come to stay with him for a month, would be glad to join in any quiet festivity. So Hallett was frequently invited out, Lisle accompanying him only to the very quietest of dinners.

One evening Hallett returned in the highest glee.

"Congratulate me, my dear fellow," he said. "Miss Merton has accepted me and, after she had done so, I had the inevitable talk with her father. He told me, frankly, that he had hoped that his daughter would make a better match. I of course agreed with him, heartily; but he went on to say that, after all, our happiness was the first consideration, and that he felt sure that it would be secured by her marriage with me. He said that he should allow her four hundred pounds a year, during his and her mother's lifetime. At their death there would be a small addition to her allowance, but naturally the bulk of his property would go to her brother. Of course, I expressed myself as infinitely grateful. I said that he had not enquired about my income, but that I had three hundred pounds a year, in addition to my pay; and should probably, some day, come into more. He expressed himself as content and, as I had expected, asked me whether I intended to leave the army. I said that that was a matter for his daughter to decide; but that, for my part, I should certainly prefer to remain in the service, for I really did not see what I should do with myself, if I left it. I said that I had been very fortunate in having, to some small extent, distinguished myself; but that if, after some experience of India, she did not care for the life, I would promise to retire."

"'I think you are right,' he said. 'It is a bad thing for a young man of seven or eight and twenty to be without employment. Your income would be insufficient to enable you to live, with comfort, as a country gentleman; and you would naturally find time lie heavy upon your hands, if you had nothing to do.'

"He was good enough to say that he thought his daughter's happiness would be safe in my hands and, as she would be able to have every luxury in India, he thought that the arrangement would be a very satisfactory one. It is awfully good of him, of course, for she could have made an infinitely better match."

"You have, of course, not settled anything about the date, Hallett?"

"No; I expect we shall settle about that when I see her, tomorrow. Of course, it must be pretty early, as we had letters, yesterday, to go up to town to be examined by the board; and we have both picked up so much that, I fancy, we shall be ordered back to our regiments pretty sharply. You see, every man is wanted at present and, as we both had a year's leave before we went out to West Africa, it is not unnatural that they should send us off again, as soon as they can. I dare say, however, they will give us a couple of months; and I suppose we shall want a month for our honeymoon, in which case we ought to be spliced in a month's time; if she can get ready in that time, which of course she can do, if she hurries up the milliners and other people."

"I have no doubt she could, in the circumstances," Lisle laughed. "Well, old man, I do congratulate you most heartily. She certainly is a very charming young woman. I expect I shall not get leave again, till the regiment comes back; which will be another five years yet, and perhaps two or three years longer, if there is any action going on anywhere. I can tell you I am not so hot about fighting as I used to be. The Tirah was sharp, but it was nothing to West Africa, which was enough to cure one of any desire to take part in fighting.

"If we are going to have a fight with Russia, I certainly should like to take part in that. That would be a tremendous affair, and I fancy that our Indian soldiers will give a good account of themselves. If it is to be, I do hope it will come before I leave the army. I am certainly in no hurry to do so."

"You would be a fool, if you were," Hallett said. "Thanks to your luck in getting a commission at sixteen, and to the loss of so many officers in the Tirah, you are now a captain at twenty-one, certainly the youngest captain in the service. Of course, if there is no war, you can't expect to continue going up at that pace; but you certainly ought to be a major at thirty, if not before. You may command a regiment within five or six years later, and be a brigadier soon after that, for you will have that by seniority. Of course, if you marry you will have to consider your wife's wishes; but she is not likely to object to your staying on, if you get to be a major, for a major's wife is by no means an unimportant item in a regiment."

"Ah! Well, we needn't think about that," Lisle laughed, "especially as, if there is war with Russia before we come home, a good many of us will certainly stay out permanently. Well, old man, I do congratulate you, most heartily."

Miss Merton, after some demur, agreed that it would be just possible for her to be ready at the end of a month. Three days later the two friends went up to town and, after undergoing a medical examination, were told that they must rejoin their regiments in a couple of months. As both regiments were in India, they decided to return in the same ship.

"I am not sorry that we are off," Lisle said, when they met on the deck of the P. and O. steamer. "I was getting desperately tired of doing nothing and, after you had gone off with your wife, on the afternoon of the marriage, I began to feel desperately lonely. Of course, I have always been accustomed to have a lot of friends round me; and I began to feel a longing to be with the regiment again and, if we had not agreed to go out together, I think I should have taken the next steamer."

Six weeks later Lisle rejoined his regiment, where he was heartily welcomed.

"Now you are a brevet major, Mr. Bullen, I am afraid that you will cease to be useful to us all; for of course we cannot be sending an officer of that exalted rank about to do our messages. However, several nice boys have joined, while you have been away."

"I shall always be happy to be employed," Lisle laughed, "and I dare say I am no older than many of the subalterns."

"I suppose you have had hard times?"

"Very hard. I thought that the Tirah business was about as hard as one would have to go through, in the course of one's soldiering; but I was greatly deceived. When I say that for six months I hardly ever had dry clothes on, and that I waded something like a hundred rivers, you may guess what it was like.

"And we had our full share of fighting, too. I was very fortunate in only getting hit three or four times, with slugs; but as we were for the most part fighting against men hidden in the bush, it was unsatisfactory work, though we always did lick them in the end. I can assure you that I do not wish for any more service of that kind.

"Have the tribes been quiet since I went away?"

"Quiet, as far as we were concerned. Of course, there have been a few trifling risings along the frontier but, as a whole, even the Zakka-Khels have been quiet. I don't think there will be any trouble, on a large scale, for some time to come."

"Then there is a prospect of a quiet time; that is to say, if the Russians will keep quiet."

"That is a very strong 'if,' Major Bullen; but I think that, if there is trouble, it will be in China."

"In that case, no doubt a good many regiments will be sent from here. I hope that it will be our good fortune to be among them."

"Well, in that case," the colonel said, with a laugh, "you will have to restrain your ardour, and give a chance to other men. You have got the V.C. and the D.S.O., which ought to satisfy you; to say nothing of having got your company, and brevet majority, at the age of twenty-one. You must be content with that, otherwise the regiment will rise against you."

"That would be very unpleasant," Lisle said, with a laugh. "I will try to suppress my zeal. I can assure you that I am perfectly conscious of the incongruity of being in such a position, at my age."

At present Lisle is with his regiment, and the prospect of a war with Russia is no nearer than it was.

The End

Printed in Great Britain
by Amazon

62553307R00170